SOLDIER OF ROME:
THE SACROVIR REVOLT

Soldier of Rome: The Sacrovir Revolt

A Novel of the Twentieth Legion During the Rebellion of Sacrovir and Florus

James Mace

Author of *Soldier of Rome: The Legionary*

iUniverse, Inc.

New York Lincoln Shanghai

Soldier of Rome: The Sacrovir Revolt
A Novel of the Twentieth Legion During the Rebellion of Sacrovir and
Florus

Copyright © 2008 by James M. Mace

iUniverse books may be ordered through booksellers or by contacting:

iUniverse
2021 Pine Lake Road, Suite 100
Lincoln, NE 68512
www.iuniverse.com
1-800-Authors (1-800-288-4677)

Because of the dynamic nature of the Internet, any Web addresses
or links contained in this book may have changed
since publication and may no longer be valid.

Certain characters in this work are historical figures, and certain events portrayed did take
place. However, this is a work of fiction. All of the other characters, names, and events as
well as all places, incidents, organizations, and dialogue in this novel are either the products
of the author's imagination or are used fictitiously.

ISBN: 978-0-595-48331-0 (pbk)
ISBN: 978-0-595-60420-3 (ebk)

Printed in the United States of America

Historical Notes

Every novel within the *Soldier of Rome* series is historically based, at least as much as I have been able to make possible. While I have to take considerable literary license whenever there is a gap in historical records, at no time have I deliberately altered recorded history. Given that historical sources often-times conflict with each other, there is still room for interpretation and dispute. This is very much the case in *The Legionary*, where accounts of the Battle of Idistaviso are disputed by Germanic and Latin sources. In these cases, I have had to decide either which text was most believable, or at least which would best go with my story. Germanic sources do not even mention the assault on the Angrivarii stronghold, though it is detailed by the Roman historian, Tacitus.

Certain historical characters, in particular the Emperor Tiberius and his mother Livia, I have taken a more sympathetic role towards. Many things written about them were born out of gossip rather than fact, in which case I discarded that which I found not to be believable. This is particularly true regarding the death of Germanicus. While historians such as Tacitus and Suetonius have speculated much into their roles in Germanicus' demise, none can actually say for certain whether either was involved or not. Since it is all speculation, I felt alright with giving my own version of what I think actually happened. This however is strictly my own interpretation and by no means absolute.

To answer the often-asked question, yes the Pontius Pilate depicted in *Soldier of Rome* is the same man made famous in The Bible. Since so little is known about Pilate's career before his governorship of Judea I was able to rather effortlessly insert him into the story. Some apocryphal accounts have Pilate stating that he was in fact at the Battle of Idistaviso. Ironically, I had completely fabricated his participation in the battle, only discovering this information after I had already published *The Legionary*. And while Pilate's wife, Claudia Procula, was a real person, her relation to Centurion Valerius Proculus is fictitious. Her sister Diana is also a fictitious character.

While I have worked to keep this series as historically accurate as possible, I have had to take a lot more literary license with *The Sacrovir Revolt*, particularly because it is not as well documented in any histories that I have read. While I have done everything possible to write a rich and intriguing story, at no time have I deliberately changed known historical facts. Be that as it may, any inaccuracies that may exist in the *Soldier of Rome* series, and that I have not already cited, are errors on my part and completely unintentional.

Bibliographical Note

All superscripted texts are drawn from the Annals of Tacitus, Book III.

Courage which goes against military expediency is stupidity; if it is insisted upon by a commander, irresponsibility.

Don't fight a battle if you don't gain anything by winning.

—Erwin Rommel

The entire Soldier of Rome series is dedicated to the men of Company C, 2nd Battalion, 116th Cavalry

"Cobra Strike!"

Acknowledgements

While my intent has always been to make *Soldier of Rome* into a series, I am still in a sense of disbelief that I am now finished with the second book. While it may have taken longer than I would have liked, if not for those who continued to support me, it may not have happened at all. I could just as easily have sat back and been happy with having a single book in print; however this was not to be Artorius' destiny! The following deserve my undying gratitude for their support through this endeavor.

To God I give the ultimate thanks. I am grateful not just for the gift of storytelling, but also the will and tenacity to see this through to fruition.

My sister Angela; for your tireless editing that made what was a complete train wreck into something readable. *And yes, it was me who put my hand in the cake!* To Mum and Dad for your continuous love and support.

Justin "Vitruvius" Cole for taking the time to do the cover art. Pure testosterone, Brother! In addition to Justin, I must also thank Clint Hanson and Gunnar Klaudt for taking the time to read the initial drafts of this book. I promise not to take so long getting the third book out!

Special thanks to Mike Daniels and Rusty Myers of Legio VI, Ferrata; and Michael Knowles of the Ermine Street Guard. You are each a credit to Roman historians everywhere; your technical advice, as well as validation from a historical perspective, have been invaluable.

To my closest friends, who not only motivated me to keep this story going, but who also inspired many of the characters found in the series; Don "Praxus" LaMott, Mike Lower, Nic Fischer, Ryan "Decimus" Small, Chris "Camillus" Irizarry, David Gehrig, James Philpott, and Christopher Harvey. And finally, to my brother "legionaries" that I've had the continuing privilege of serving with since the Iraq war.

Preface

It has been three years since the Germanic wars against Arminius and the Cherusci. Gaius Silius, Legate of the Twentieth Legion, is concerned that the barbarians-though shattered by the war-may be stirring once again. He also seeks to confirm the rumors regarding Arminius' death. What Silius does not realize is that there is a new threat to the Empire, but it does not come from beyond the frontier; it is coming from within, where a disenchanted nobleman looks to sow the seeds of rebellion in Gaul.

Legionary Artorius has greatly matured during his five years in the legions. He has become stronger in mind; his body growing even more powerful. Like the rest of the Legion, he is unaware of the shadow growing well within the Empire's borders, where a disaffected nobleman seeks to betray the Emperor Tiberius. A shadow looms; one that looks to envelope the province of Gaul as well as the Rhine legions. The year is A.D. 20.

Cast of Characters

Soldiers:

Titus Artorius Justus—A young legionary serving with the Twentieth Legion

Magnus Flavianus—Artorius' best friend and fellow legionary, he is of Nordic descent

Statorius—A Decanus (Sergeant) of legionaries and Artorius' section leader

Flaccus—Tesserarius of the Second Century

Camillus—Signifier of the Second Century

Marcus Vitruvius—Optio of the Second Century and Chief Weapons Instructor, he is Artorius' mentor

Platorius Macro—Centurion of the Third Cohort's Second Century

Valerius Proculus—Commander of the Third Cohort

Calvinus—Commander of the Fifth Cohort

Flavius Quietus—Centurion Primus Pilus of the Twentieth Legion

Pontius Pilate—A Military Tribune of the Twentieth Legion

Gaius Silius—Senatorial Legate and Commanding General of the Twentieth Legion

Felix Spurius—Legionary Recruit

Praxus, Decimus, Valens, Carbo, Gavius—Legionaries

Noble Romans:

Tiberius Caesar—Emperor of Rome

Livia Augusta—Mother of Tiberius and widow of Emperor Augustus Caesar

Vipsania Agrippina—Former wife of Tiberius and mother of Drusus

Germanicus Caesar—Adopted son and heir of Tiberius/defeated the Germanic tribes under Arminius four years previously

Drusus Julius Caesar—Son of Tiberius and his first wife, Vipsania Agrippina

Claudius—Brother of Germanicus/suffers from lameness and speech impediment

Livilla—Sister of Germanicus and Claudius/wife of Drusus

Antonia—Mother of Germanicus, Livilla and Claudius/daughter of Marc Antony and widow of Tiberius' brother Drusus Nero

Agrippina—Wife of Germanicus and half-sister of Vipsania, she mistrusts and despises the Emperor

Lucius Aelius Sejanus—Commanding Prefect of the Praetorian Guard, he is Tiberius' most trusted advisor

Claudia Procula—Betrothed to Pontius Pilate, she is also a distant cousin of Centurion Proculus

Diana Procula—Claudia's older sister and domina of the Proculus family's Gallic estate

Gauls

Julius Sacrovir—A Gallic nobleman, seeking to incite rebellion in the province

Julius Florus—Sacrovir's deputy, he is deeply in debt to Rome and sees rebellion as a means of salvaging his fortunes

Heracles—A mysterious Greek who offers his services to Sacrovir and Florus

Taranis—Chief of the Sequani tribe

Belenus, Broehain, Lennox, Kavan—Gallic Nobles

Farquhar—Son of Lennox, he is a student at the Augustodunum University

Kiana—Daughter of a Gallic noble, she is the love of Farquhar's life

Alasdair—Son of Kavan and best friend to Farquhar

Radek, Ellard, Torin—Escaped slaves who join Sacrovir's rebellion

Roman Military Ranks

Legionary—Every citizen of the plebian class who enlisted in the legions started off as a legionary. Duration of service during the early empire was twenty years. Barring any promotions that would dictate otherwise, this normally consisted of sixteen years in the ranks, with another four either on lighter duties, or as part of the First Cohort. Legionaries served not only as the heart of the legion's fighting force, they were also used for many building and construction projects.

Decanus—Also referred to interchangeably as a *Sergeant* in the series, Decanus was the first rank of authority that a legionary could be promoted to. Much like a modern-day Sergeant, the Decanus was the first-line leader of legionaries. He supervised training, as well as enforced personal hygiene and maintenance of equipment. On campaign he was in charge of getting the section's tent erected, along with the fortifications of the camp.

Tesserarius—The first of the *Principal* ranks, the Tesserarius primarily oversaw the fatigue and guard duties for the Century. He maintained the duty roster and was also keeper of the watch word. On a normal day he could be found supervising work details or checking on the guard posts.

Signifier—The Signifier was a man much-loved on pay days. He was the treasurer for the Century and was in charge of all pay issues. On campaign he carried the Century's standard (Signum) into battle. This was used not only as a rallying point, but also as a visual means of communication. Traditionally he wore a bear's hide over his helmet, draped around the shoulders of his armor. Because of his high level of responsibility, the Signifier is third-in-command of the Century.

Optio—The term *Optio* literally means *'chosen one'* for he was personally chosen by the Centurion to serve as his deputy. He would oversee all training within the Century, to include that of new recruits. In battle the Optio would either stand behind the formation, keeping troops on line and in formation, or else he would stand on the extreme left, able to coordinate with adjacent units.

Centurion—In addition to being its commander, the Centurion was known to be the bravest and most tactically sound man within the Century. While a stern disciplinarian, and at times brutally harsh, it is borne out of a genuine compassion for his men. The Centurion knew that only through hard discipline and sound training could his men survive in battle. He was always on the extreme right of the front rank in battle; thereby placing himself in the most precarious position on the line. Mortality rates were high amongst Centurions because they would sacrifice their own safety for that of their men.

Centurion Pilus Prior—Commander of a cohort of six centuries, the Centurion Pilus Prior was a man of considerable influence and responsibility. He not only had to be able to command a century on a line of battle, but he had to be able to maneuver his cohort as a single unit. Such men were often given independent commands over small garrisons or on low-level conflicts. A Centurion Pilus Prior could also be tasked with diplomatic duties; such was the respect foreign princes held for them. At this level, a soldier had to focus not just on his abilities as a leader of fighting men, but on his skills at diplomacy and politics.

Centurion Primus Ordo—The elite First Cohort's centuries were commanded by the Centurions Primus Ordo. Though the number of soldiers under their direct command was fewer, these men were senior in rank to the Centurions Pilus Prior. Men were often selected for these positions based on vast experience and for being the best tacticians in the legion. As such part of the duty of a Centurion Primus Ordo was acting as a strategic and tactical advisor to the commanding general. Generals such as Caesar, Marius, Tiberius, and Agrippa were successful in part because they had a strong circle of First Cohort Centurions advising them.

Centurion Primus Pilus—Also referred to as the *Chief* or *Master* Centurion, this is the pinnacle of the career of a Roman soldier. Though socially subordinate to the Tribunes, the Centurion Primus Pilus possessed more power and influence than any, and was in fact third-in-command of the entire legion. He was also the commander of the elite First Cohort in battle. Upon retirement, a Centurion Primus Pilus (and possibly Centurions of lesser ranks as well) was elevated into the Patrician Class of society. He could then stand for public office, and his sons would be eligible for appointments as Tribunes. Even while still serving in the ranks, a Centurion Primus Pilus was allowed to wear the narrow purple stripe of a Patrician on his toga; such was the respect Roman society held for them.

Tribune—Tribunes came from the Patrician class, often serving only six month tours with the legions. Though there were exceptions, many Tribunes stayed on the line only long enough to get their "ticket punched" to a better assignment. Primarily serving as staff officers for the commanding Legate, a Tribune would sometimes be given command of auxiliary troops if he proved himself a capable leader. Most were looking for a career in politics, though they knew they had to get as much experience as they could out of their time in the legions. In *Soldier of Rome*, Pontius Pilate is an example of a Tribune who elects to stay with the legions for as long as he is able; preferring the hard life of a soldier to the soft comforts of a political magistrate.

Laticlavian Tribune—Most commonly referred to as the *Chief* Tribune, he was a young man of the Senatorial class starting off his career. Second-in-command of the legion, his responsibility was incredible, though he was often aided by the Master Centurion, who would act as a mentor. A soldier's performance as Chief Tribune would determine whether or not he would be fit to command a legion of his own someday. Given the importance of military success to the future senator's career, he would no doubt make every effort to prove himself competent and valiant in battle.

Legate—The Legate was a senator who had already spent time in the legions as a Laticlavian Tribune and had proven himself worthy of command. Of all the possible offices that a nobleman could hold, none was dearer to a Roman than command of her armies.

Legion Infantry Strength (estimated)

Legionaries—3,780

First Cohort Legionaries—700

Decanii—610

Tesserarii—59

Signifiers—59

Options—59

Centurions—45

Centurions Pilus Prior—9

Centurions Primus Ordo—4

Centurion Primus Pilus—1

Tribunes—6

Chief Tribune—1

Legate—1

The Julio-Claudians

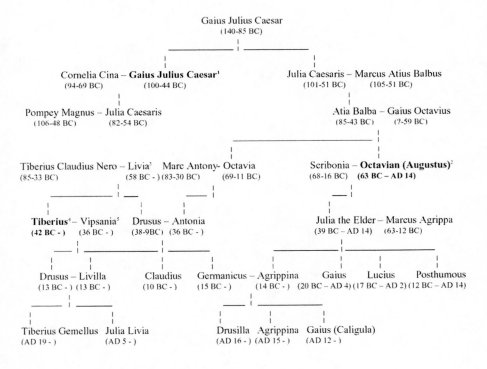

1—Dictator of Rome 49-44 BC
2—Emperor of Rome 27 BC—AD 14
3— Third wife of Augustus from 38 BC to AD 14
4—Emperor of Rome AD 14—Present
5—Daughter of Marcus Agrippa through his marriage to Caecilia Attica

Note: This is not an all-inclusive family tree, but shows the Julio-Claudians that appear or are referenced in the Soldier of Rome story. For example, Germanicus and

Agrippina had nine children altogether, three of whom died young. Augustus was also married a total of three times, with Livia being his last wife.

The Families of Artorius and Magnus

Primus Artorius Maximus – Persephone (1st Wife) – Juliana (2nd Wife)
(31 BC -)   (28 BC - AD 9)   (34 BC -)

Metellus[1] – Rowana[2]   **Artorius**[3]
(10 BC - AD 9) (10 BC - ?)   (2 BC -)

1—Killed in Action, Teutoburger Wald, Germania
2—Disappeared soon after the Teutoburger Wald disaster. Current whereabouts are unknown.
3—Full name: Titus Artorius Justus

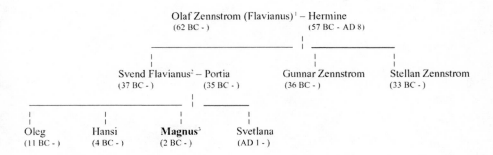

Olaf Zennstrom (Flavianus)[1] – Hermine
(62 BC -)   (57 BC - AD 8)

Svend Flavianus[2] – Portia   Gunnar Zennstrom   Stellan Zennstrom
(37 BC -)   (35 BC -)   (36 BC -)   (33 BC -)

Oleg   Hansi   **Magnus**[3]   Svetlana
(11 BC -) (4 BC -) (2 BC -)   (AD 1 -)

1—A minor overlord in the Nordic realms, he served twenty-five years as a Roman Auxiliary, earning his family Roman Citizenship, before returning to his homeland. Was given the Roman name Flavianus.

2—The only son of Olaf to remain within the Roman Empire after his father's retirement. Kept the Roman name Flavianus, though as a family tradition he still gives his children Nordic surnames.

3—Full name: Magnus Flavianus

▼

CHAPTER 1

CHANGES IN THE RANKS

Fortress of Legio XX Valeria, Cologne, Germania
February, A.D. 20

It was a brisk winter morning; the sun cast its light on the semi-frozen ground. Snow crunched underfoot as the two legionaries eyed each other. Artorius and Vitruvius had faced each other on the sparring field on the first Thursday of every month for several years now. Originally they had sparred once a week, but Vitruvius' duties as the Century's Optio, combined with the sheer beating Artorius' body was suffering, had caused the men to cut back their bouts. Artorius was baffled that in five years he had not once defeated his adversary and mentor. He swore that Vitruvius was not even human. Both men wore a standard-issue legionary helmet, while wielding a practice gladius and wicker shield. The weight of these was twice that of service weapons, though both men hardly noticed.

Artorius was a strong young man of twenty-two years and had been in the army for five. He was of average height, though his frame was massive, wrought with powerful muscle; his biceps threatening to tear through the sleeves of his tunic. His brutal physical strength and skill in battle were becoming legendary. He had learned his lessons so well from his mentor that he had made a name for himself not just within his Century and Cohort, but within the entire Legion. Many had challenged him to similar sparring sessions, only to be dispatched like amateurs. Even soldiers from the elite First Cohort held a large amount of respect for the young legionary. Only one man potentially stood between him and the title of *Legion Champion*. Optio Vitruvius had held that title for so long that it had fallen into disuse; there was no one in the entire Twentieth who could come close to defeating him.

Vitruvius was of similar build to Artorius; though he was slightly taller, he looked to be as muscular. He possessed the quickness and agility of a cat, and was able to wield his gladius with terrifying speed and skill. Unlike most veterans, his body was devoid of any noticeable scars from battle. Secretly he hoped that Artorius would best him someday. That would show that his young protégé had learned his lessons, and that there was nothing left to teach him.

More than three years before, during the triumphal games in Rome that followed the defeat of Arminius and the Germanic tribes, Vitruvius had killed a gladiator that many considered to be invincible. He had dispatched the man with such contemptuous ease that it was still the talk of the Legion to that day; to say nothing of the enormous wagers won by the friends and associates of Vitruvius. Indeed, Artorius had been brave enough to wager an entire stipend of seventy-five denarii-a third of his yearly wages-and had walked away with a considerable sum following Vitruvius' victory. The gladiator's owner, a weasel of a Gaul named Julius Sacrovir, had lost a large quantity of his fortune that day. He had left Rome screaming curses towards Vitruvius, as well as the entire Roman army.

"By the gods, but it is cold!" Artorius muttered as he blew hard into his hands; he despised being cold. Even five years on the Rhine frontier had failed to thicken his blood. He wished they could have used the Cohort's indoor drill hall; however it was being used that day to train recruits.

"That's alright, a little exertion and you won't even notice," Vitruvius replied as he waved his gladius about, warming up his joints and muscles. "You ready?"

Artorius nodded as both men settled into their fighting stances. As if on cue, both soldiers lunged forward, punching with their shields, looking for openings with which to strike. They had faced one another so many times; that they each knew the other's fighting style by heart. Theirs was truly a test of pure skill, seeing as how their physical power was so close that neither could claim it as an advantage.

Artorius brought his shield down in an attempt to smash the Optio's foot. Vitruvius pulled his foot back and stabbed at Artorius' exposed face. Quickly the young legionary dodged his head to the side. As he did so, he brought his shield back up and caught Vitruvius in the face. Vitruvius stumbled, though Artorius knew better than to attack recklessly. Too often he had tried to follow up on such an advantage, only to have victory snatched from him by the crafty and skilled

Optio. Instead he settled back into his fighting stance once more. Vitruvius lunged in, allowing their shields to collide. Immediately he swung his shield to the left in order to block the stab he knew was coming. Instead Artorius stepped to his own left and worked his arm past Vitruvius' shield. With an elbow to the wrist, he knocked the shield away. As the Optio dropped his shield, he swung his left hand up and caught Artorius on his helmet cheek guard with a roundhouse punch. The young legionary fell to the ground, dazed, while Vitruvius wrenched his shield from his hand. Artorius instinctively rolled to his side and sprung to his feet, lunging. Vitruvius countered. Both men stopped in mid-attack, catching their breath. Vitruvius' gladius point was resting against Artorius' throat, while the legionary had his poised to thrust underneath the Optio's ribcage. In a real battle each man would have slain the other. Vitruvius stood breathing hard for a second while Artorius took a step back and threw his gladius straight down into the snow.

"Damn it!" he cursed, removing his helmet. "Five years and this is the best I can do?" He was certain that he would finally best Vitruvius. The Optio started laughing.

"Hey, a draw is better than another thrashing. Besides, I think I've finally found someone to succeed me as Chief Weapons Instructor for the Century."

"Who is it?" Artorius asked. Vitruvius raised an eyebrow.

"Artorius, did I hit you so hard that you've gone completely dense?" he asked, looking down at his hand, which was bleeding. Artorius dropped his head and chuckled to himself.

"I guess you did ring my bell a little bit," he replied as he rubbed the sore spot on his cheek. Vitruvius clapped him on the shoulder.

"Come on. I've got a meeting with the Centurion. Do you mind putting my practice weapons away?"

"Not at all," Artorius replied as he took both shields and swords over to the armory. As he walked he thought about his fight with Vitruvius. Something in his mind told him that it would probably be their last. He regretted not getting the much desired victory over the man who had taught him so much. He then considered the significance of becoming the Century's Chief Weapons Instructor. It was a position usually occupied by a Decanus or above, or failing that at least someone already on immune status. Artorius met none of these conditions.

Centurion Macro was slowly pacing back and forth behind his desk, both hands clasped behind his back. Vitruvius walked in to see that Flaccus the Tesserarius and Sergeant Statorius were in the office as well.

Macro was fairly young for a Centurion, being that he was only in his early thirties. War and the life of the legions had done much to age him. What ravaged him the most was that he was one of the few survivors of the Teutoburger Wald disaster; something he never fully recovered from. The traumatic shock of the massacre had caused his jet black hair to gray on the sides and back almost overnight. He was a ruggedly handsome man, though his hands and face bore visible scars from countless adversaries.

Flaccus was perhaps the oldest soldier in the Century. His face was gnarled by the affects of age perhaps a little too much wine. A few wisps of grey hair adorned the sides of his head. Vitruvius was bald himself and was quick to chastise the Tesserarius for refusing to accept the loss of his hair. Flaccus was a good soldier, although a bit one-dimensional for Vitruvius' liking. He knew drill and regulations by heart, but he lacked imagination.

"I found someone to succeed me as Chief Weapons Instructor," Vitruvius announced as he walked in.

Macro grunted as he continued to pace back and forth. Vitruvius looked over at Flaccus, puzzled and decided it was best to wait. With that, he stood next to the other two men, with his hands clasped behind his back. At length Macro finally spoke.

"The reason why I have called you in here is because this affects you all. To start with, Vitruvius I must first congratulate you. Centurion Justinian of the Third Century has elected to retire after twenty-eight years in the army. The entire chain-of-command was unanimous in its recommendations that you be selected to succeed him." He paused to let the words sink in. Vitruvius stood rigid, though in his eyes Macro could see the sense of disbelief. He turned his gaze towards Flaccus and Statorius.

"Flaccus, I have decided that you will replace Vitruvius as Optio. I know you only have a handful of years left before your own discharge and retirement, and I feel this is the best way for you to serve out your final years in the army.

"Sergeant Statorius, you will be promoted to Tesserarius. I need you to recommend a successor to take over your section." Statorius did not hesitate before announcing his recommendation.

"Praxus is senior to the other legionaries in my section. He is also the most experienced and one they all look up to."

"Not Praxus," Macro replied immediately. Statorius looked crestfallen. Praxus had committed a grievous error by falling asleep on sentry duty once, and had been caught by Centurion Macro. Macro had burned his orders which at that time would have promoted him to Sergeant. He also stripped him of his immune status, which he later reinstated. That had been six years before, and Statorius was hoping that Macro would finally let Praxus advance up the career ladder that he was certain he was meant to take. Macro saw the concern on the Decanus' face.

"Praxus will be moving to take over for Sergeant Sextus, who has also elected to retire from the Legions." Vitruvius smiled when he thought about Praxus commanding the section that he had led before Sextus.

"What about Artorius?" Vitruvius asked. All eyes fell on him. "I also recommend that he replace me as Chief Weapons Instructor. I feel that he is ready to take charge of his own section." Macro looked over at Statorius.

"Sergeant?" he asked. Statorius thought for a second and then nodded.

"He's young, but he is well educated, and has demonstrated sound leadership potential. Hell, he and Praxus practically run the section as it is."

"It's settled then," Macro said, slamming his hands down on his desk. *"Camillus!"* The Century's Signifier strolled in.

"No need to shout," he said in his usual good-natured manner, "I was listening at the door the entire time." Macro ignored him.

"Get me Praxus and Artorius," he directed. Camillus nodded, and exited. Vitruvius walked out as Camillus dispatched an orderly to summon the two legionaries. He felt bad in a way. Camillus had been on the promotion fast-track early on in his career, though everything seemed to have stagnated once he made Signifier. Technically he was third in command of the Century, and should have been the next Optio. Vitruvius had passed over both him and Flaccus, having been promoted directly from Decanus to Optio. And now Flaccus would pass up the Signifier as well.

It was impossible to gauge Camillus' age. He possessed a boyish, almost cherub face that perpetually made him look like he was still a young boy; though he was certainly much older. Vitruvius figured that the Signifier had never shaved a day in his life. Camillus' face was always more filled out during the winter months, making him look even younger. It was an odd thing, the way his weight would drastically fluctuate throughout the year. During the campaign season's warm months he would be lean and fit from the countless miles of marching while carrying the Century's Signum. During the winter he put on what he referred to as his 'protective coat' of fat from inactivity and too many hearty meals.

"So, *Centurion* Vitruvius, is it?" Camillus asked with a sincere smile.

"Not yet," Vitruvius replied. "Though I have to say I feel kind of bad for you. This is the second time you've been passed over for Optio." Camillus waived his hand dismissively.

"Vitruvius you've got to remember, I'm a lot younger than you and Flaccus. The only reason I made Signifier as fast as I did was because at the time the Century was in a crunch, and it seemed like none of you jackals knew basic mathematics. I got my rank because they needed somebody to do the payroll, that's all. Besides, I have a pretty comfortable billet here! An Optio's pay is only marginally higher than mine, and the duties and responsibilities are nightmarishly more complex. If I can tell you a secret, I'm the one who told Macro to put Flaccus in your spot. I'm holding out for a Cohort standard bearer position, or perhaps even Aquilifer someday." The position he referred to was that of the man who carried the Legion's eagle standard into battle. He was also the senior secretary and treasurer of the Legion, whose rank and pay was equal to that of a Centurion Primus Ordo.

"Still, you shouldn't sell short your own leadership abilities," Vitruvius countered. "The younger guys look up to you. They respect you because your demeanor is so relaxed, and yet you still have a sense of valor and command presence that I don't think you realize." Camillus shrugged at that.

"I only let it come out when I'm in a bad spot. You know they gave me the *Silver Torque for Valor* at Idistaviso for protecting the standard." Vitruvius gave a slight chuckle at the memory.

"I remember. You stabbed a barbarian with the Signum and then planted it in his chest!"

"Yeah, and I couldn't get the damn thing unstuck! I had to fight off a swarm of those bastards to keep them from getting their hands on it. I was scared to death because I knew if I let them carry off the standard, Macro would have had my balls!"

The rest of the section watched as Statorius and Praxus packed all of their personal belongings and gear, and as Artorius moved to Statorius' bunk. The Decanus had a slightly larger living space than the legionaries and Artorius intended to take full advantage of this. Praxus would move to a similar bunk in Sergeant Sextus' section one block of rooms over, the former Decanus having already moved to a billet in the First Cohort while waiting for his retirement papers to come through. Sergeant Statorius would get his own quarters at the end of the barracks, next to those of the Signifier and the Optio.

As Statorius walked out with the last of his belongings he stuck his hand out, which Artorius readily accepted.

"Take care of these men," the Sergeant said. "They served me well, and I know they'll do the same for you." Artorius nodded and clasped his former section leader's hand even harder.

"I won't let you down," he replied as Statorius made his way down the long hallway to his new quarters. After he had gone, Artorius turned and appraised what was left of the section, *his* section now.

There was Decimus, the most experienced legionary in the section. Three times he had been awarded the Rampart Crown for having been the first soldier over the wall of an enemy stronghold; a feat which had never been replicated within the Legion. Decimus' hair was a lighter color, giving off a slightly reddish tint. He was taller than most of the men with a lean build. He reminded Artorius of a monkey the way he could climb the most difficult obstacles with ease.

Valens was the resident letch, who had quite the notorious reputation for his exploits with women of ill repute, though his standards were practically nonexistent. This perplexed many, because he was rarely drunk and could not blame his debaucheries on being inebriated. Still he was a rock solid soldier, and extremely competent in battle. He bore a perpetually deviant grin and constantly twitching left eye.

Carbo, the lover of wine and spirits, did not look like the typical legionary. Slightly overweight with a florid complexion that made him look perpetually out of breath, his appearance was very much deceiving. He was reliable in a crisis, and had been decorated for valor on numerous occasions. Besides wine, his other weakness was a local tavern wench that he swore repeatedly had a twin sister.

Then there was Gavius, who had come through recruit training with Artorius five years before. Orphaned at a young age, his family name alone had allowed him to join the legions. At first thought by many to be meek and unassuming, he had proven his mettle time and again during the campaigns against Arminius. He was also one of the most skilled javelin throwers that Artorius had ever seen.

And finally there was Magnus, the Norseman. He had also gone through recruit training with Artorius and was his best friend. He was of similar height and build as Artorius, though the mop of blonde hair on his head and piercing blue eyes betrayed his less than purely Latin origins. Along with Decimus, he was one of the better educated legionaries, and Artorius hoped to see him rise through the ranks as well some day. Magnus was a natural leader, one who did not need rank to command respect. There were two vacancies within the section, though Artorius knew it was rare for sections to ever be at full strength. While having additional legionaries to share the workload would be welcome, the section agreed that they did like having the extra space. Indeed, one of the vacant bunks had been converted into a type of shrine where relics and trophies won on campaign by the legionaries were displayed.

"So does this mean you'll be buying the wine later?" Magnus asked.

"Not tonight," Artorius replied as he lay down on his bunk. "Besides, they won't do the ceremony until tomorrow, so it's not even official yet."

"Yeah, best not screw things up the night before," Decimus added. "Don't want to end up like Praxus and have to wait another six years for promotion to roll around!" Artorius snorted at that. Indeed, Praxus should have been promoted years before, yet it took a long time for the scourge of his mistake to erase itself.

That night as Artorius sat writing at his small desk there was a knock at the door.

"Come!" he shouted and Praxus stuck his head in. Artorius was by himself, the rest of the section enjoying a night off. He looked up from the letter he was writing to his father under the soft glow of an oil lamp. He smiled when he saw his friend and peer, and waived him in.

"So how are the boys assimilating?" Praxus asked as he grabbed a stool and sat across from Artorius.

Gaius Praxus had been a peer mentor to Artorius; the most experienced and quick-thinking legionary he had met. He was fairly tall-about the same height as Decimus-his hair shorn on the sides and back and very short on top. Artorius frequently accused him of keeping his hair so short in order to hide the gray.

"They seem to be adapting alright. Of course we haven't been officially promoted yet, so maybe it just hasn't sunk in. Carbo and Valens seem to be perfectly happy where they are, and besides I don't think either of them can read or write, so any hopes of promotion are out for them. I was a bit concerned that there might be some resentment from Decimus, though."

"I wouldn't worry too much about him," Praxus answered. "Decimus is educated and a good soldier, but he has little aspirations when it comes to having to lead other legionaries. I think his ambition is to keep getting himself decorated on campaign so that he can get moved over to the First Cohort and enjoy Veteran status as soon as possible. Usually that doesn't happen until one has been in sixteen years; however I have seen legionaries transferred to the First based on merit. What about Gavius and Magnus? I remember when you all came through recruit training together." Artorius shrugged.

"I think they're happy for me, Magnus especially. He has a lot of potential, and I hope that I don't overshadow him. Given the right kind of mentoring, I think he should get his own section some day, sooner rather than later I hope.

Funny thing is you know both of them are older than me? Only a few months in Magnus' case, mind you, but it does seem a bit odd that I am not only the section leader, I'm also the youngest."

"It is experience and what one does with it that makes a leader, not his age," Praxus reached across the desk and gave Artorius a friendly slap on the shoulder.

"So how do you like your new section?" Artorius asked. Praxus shrugged.

"They seem like a decent lot," he answered. "I've known most of them for some time. Four of the lads were there back when Vitruvius was the Decanus. Two are brand new recruits, in the middle of training. I think you'll be getting a chance to work with them soon enough."

Artorius nodded. He had almost forgotten about the additional responsibilities laid on him. He was going to be appointed the Chief Weapons Instructor as well. It was an additional duty, and one that meant extra incentive pay, which he liked. He just had to learn quickly how to go about organizing the training schedules for sections and assessing individual soldiers, particularly recruits. Plus he knew there were numerous duties that as a Decanus he would have to oversee as well. It all seemed overwhelming. Praxus saw his concern.

"Don't worry too much about it. They don't start individual weapons training for a couple of weeks. That will give you time to go over the lesson plan that Vitruvius left."

"I just have to make sure my own section is in order before then," Artorius replied.

"Hey, just be glad you have all veterans and no recruits to worry about," Praxus smiled. "Your boys are pretty much self-sufficient and can take care of themselves. They'll help pick up the slack if they see you getting overwhelmed. Remember we used to do the same for Statorius." Artorius furrowed his brow in contemplation at that.

"Yeah, he did seem to come to you and me a lot. I never really gave it much thought."

"He came to me because I had the most experience, and he came to you because he was grooming you to replace him. I know he had brought your name up to Vitruvius and Macro on more than one occasion. Vitruvius especially commended your talents and leadership potential. Truth be told Artorius, I think that all three of them see you going places within the Legion. Once you get assimilated into your new duties you should start learning the duties of the senior officers in the Century. Camillus and Flaccus would be glad to help you, and you already know Statorius is looking out for you."

"I won't lie to you, Praxus," Artorius said after a moment's contemplation, "I've oftentimes watched Macro, Dominus, Proculus, and even Master Centurion Flavius. And I've thought to myself, 'I'll be there someday.' Pretty presumptuous, I know." Praxus shook his head at that.

"Not really," he replied. "I remember how young Macro was when he was promoted to Centurion. I think he was only twenty-nine or thirty. If I were to place a wager on it, I would bet that you seen the Centurionate at an even younger age than he did. Normally one has to be at least thirty to even be considered for the promotion; however we all know there are exceptions to every rule. Augustus set quite the precedent when he was given the Consul's chair at nineteen; sixteen years shy of the minimum age requirement." Artorius started laughing, and then sobered when he saw Praxus' face showed that he was serious.

"Are you kidding me?" he asked, perplexed. "I don't think the rules the senatorial class chooses to apply to itself are relevant to mere plebs like us. You've got to remember, Macro got accelerated to Centurion after that corruption scandal that came to light after Tiberius was recalled to Rome. If I remember right, more than twenty Centurions in the Legion were discharged in disgrace."

"Twenty-seven actually," Praxus replied. "And no you wouldn't remember, because you weren't even in the army yet!"

"All the same," Artorius continued, "the point I'm making is that I would have to go from a junior section leader to Centurion within six years, and I don't see a mass number of vacancies coming open like that. It would also mean having to probably bypass the Principal ranks of Tesserarius and Signifer."

"Vitruvius did it," Praxus replied with a shrug. "He was selected for Optio when he was still a Decanus, and he only held the Optionate for three years."

"Yes, but he had plenty of years as a section leader before that," Artorius replied. "Don't get me wrong, I appreciate your vote of confidence. It took me five years to become a section leader, which I admit is no small feat. However, unless there's another big shake-up of some sort, I imagine I'll be at least the same age Macro was, if not older, before I rise to Centurion."

"You make your own destiny, Artorius," Praxus clapped him again on his shoulder. "Take care of your men, prove yourself to be the leader that Macro, Vitruvius, and Statorius know you are, and your path will show itself to you."

*　　　*　　　*　　　*

Julius Sacrovir sat at a small table in a dark corner of the nearly empty tavern, brooding. He was middle-aged noble, who only wore the Roman toga out of reluctance. He was a Gaul first, though he did keep his graying hair short and his face clean-shaven; after all he never wished to be mistaken for mere peasant stock. His family had long ago inherited the franchise of Roman citizenship during Julius Caesar's dictatorship, despite their Gallic ancestry. His was a noble family of great wealth and status in the province who had adopted the name Julius, as did many of the other noble Gallic families, much to his distaste. It was sickening to him that they should take the name of a man who had brought so much suffering and hardship to Gaul. Hundreds of thousands had been murdered during Caesar's nine year campaign. His wars of conquest had never carried the endorsement of the Senate, and had been entirely of his own making.

It had been almost seventy-two years since Alesia fell, ending the Gallic wars. Caesar's nemesis, Vercingetorix, had surrendered in hopes of saving his people. Instead, those that weren't butchered were sold into slavery. As a way of showing his admiration for his worthy adversary, Caesar had Vercingetorix imprisoned for six years, all the while treating him as a royal guest. At the end of that time, he was paraded in Caesar's long-awaited Triumph and then ritualistically strangled for the amusement of the mob.

Sacrovir's grandfather had fought at Alesia, and had vehemently protested Vercingetorix's surrender. The Averni and Aedui, to which Sacrovir's family belonged, were spared by Caesar in order to secure alliances with those two tribes. With so many of the noble families decimated, they and other pardoned nobles were able to exponentially increase their land, wealth, and power. Greed drove them, and greed made them sell out completely to Caesar and to Rome.

In secret, Sacrovir celebrated the Ides of March, the date when Caesar was murdered. He loathed the Julio-Claudians that had spawned out of Caesar's heirs. His successor, Octavian, had married into the powerful Claudian family, and created a dynastic monarchy as Emperor Caesar Augustus. The current occupant of the Imperial Throne was about as un-Caesar as a man could be. While Julius Caesar had died because he had wanted to become Emperor, and Augustus had realized that dream through politics and civil war, Tiberius was the most reluctant ruler Sacrovir had ever heard of. In tactics and war he had been one of the most feared commanders Rome had ever unleashed. His service record was impeccable; never tasting defeat in battle and every campaign won. Even the great Julius Caesar had been beaten on occasion; his army repelled by the Gauls at Gergovia.

Tiberius' weakness lay in his reluctance to assume ultimate power, and the Senate had goaded him into accepting the mantle of Augustus. Although all had wished for a return to the Republic, they were terrified of Tiberius, afraid that he was not genuine in his reluctance. Sacrovir smiled at the thought. Tiberius was the reluctant Emperor who oversaw a Senate that was weak and impotent. Sacrovir knew he need not worry about Tiberius' skill in battle, for he would be unable to take to the field in the event of a rebellion. His best field commanders were now of no concern. Caecina Severus had started to succumb to the effects of age and decades of campaign. And Germanicus ... Germanicus was of no concern anymore. The timing was perfect.

Anger and disgrace sowed the seeds of rebellion in Sacrovir, for in spite of his nobility he was prohibited from membership in the Roman Senate, as were all non-Latins, regardless of birth or social status. The ignominy was hard to swallow. He was granted all the other privileges of the Roman nobility, and had to pay the same taxes as well. The Emperor was said to be sympathetic to the cause of nobles from around the Empire trying to stand for senatorial membership, however the so-called *pure* Roman nobility had created such outcry that Tiberius had let the issue drop. They were meek like mice anytime he asked them to make a decision regarding rule and administration of the Empire, and yet they became like a pack of rabid dogs when their social order was threatened. This grievous insult was one of Sacrovir's prime reasons for wishing to lead an uprising of the Gallic nobles. His personal reasons though, were much darker. His soul seethed with a lust for revenge against the Roman legionaries who had humiliated and cost him so much.

Across from Sacrovir sat Julius Florus. Florus was another Gallic nobleman, whose family had attained Roman citizenship years before and had also adopted the name of the hated dictator. He was a few years younger than Sacrovir and had allowed himself to decline physically due to his love of the extravagant lifestyle. His face was round and his complexion florid; a noticeable belly protruding.

Though he enjoyed a very rich and pampered life, Florus too felt aggrieved that he was prohibited from standing for senatorial membership. Since this rejection, he had become disaffected by Roman rule in Gaul. He was also heavily in debt from the demands of his lifestyle, as well as some bad investments, and was now facing poverty. When Sacrovir had first come to him with the possibility of raising a rebellion, he was immediately aroused by the possibility. In his youth he had dreamed of martial glory, and in his most private thoughts he knew that this ambition involved defeating the seemingly invincible legions of Rome. His Roman citizenship was meaningless to him and he would rather have lived as a lord of Gaul than a pseudo-noble of Rome. If he could put a sword through the moneylenders at the same time, then so much the better!

"I hoped you would have chosen a place a little less public," Florus seemed uncomfortable, looking around at the few patrons in the tavern. Most were local farmers and shop owners, though there was the occasional well-dressed merchant from Rome. Sacrovir waived a hand dismissively.

"When we have rallied more to our cause, I will concern myself with secrecy. But for right now I assure you we are in friendly territory. You see that man behind the bar?" He pointed to where a surely-looking fellow stood wiping down the bar top with a greasy rag. He was older, bald, with just a trace of gray stubble on his face, and a belly that protruded and rubbed against the wood.

"What of him?" Florus asked, looking over his shoulder.

"This place is all he has. He makes a decent living off the drunkenness of locals and merchants. He is also nearly impoverished, owing to the enormous debts acquired at the hands of the Roman moneylenders. If he does not do something drastic soon, he will be reduced to begging on the streets."

"A perfect candidate," Florus observed. Sacrovir nodded.

"Yes, and there are many more like him, *thousands* more! Your own people, the Treveri have been equally manhandled and oppressed. The *Pax Romana* of Augustus has only led to the indebtedness of our nobles, and the enslavement of our people. Gaul is slowly but surely losing her identity. Gauls now dress like Romans, they talk like Romans, they build their cities like Romans, and they even bear Roman names. Just look at *our* names! Both our families adopted the name 'Julius' in honor of the man who committed the wholesale murder of our people, and for what? So that we could see our culture and heritage vanish before our eyes?" He took a long quaff of ale before continuing.

"I need you to rally as many sympathetic nobles as you can from amongst your people. There are many who feel the same strain of taxation and debt that we do, combined with the insult of being denied the right to stand for what is supposed to be attainable for all noble citizens! If we wait too long, the entire nobility of Gaul will be bankrupt and enslaved, our influence with the people lost. Now is the time to strike, while we can still rally popular support. Start spreading the seeds of dissention, rally the most trustworthy of your peers, and meet me in Augustodunum in thirty days."

Florus nodded then stopped. "But what of the army? Surely you do not think the Emperor will just allow us to throw off the yoke of Roman oppression and secede from the Empire do you? The Rhine army is but a few weeks march from here." At this Sacrovir smiled; an evil glint in his eye.

"I do not believe the Roman army will be much of a problem," he asserted. Florus raised his eyebrows, his face showing skepticism.

"Do tell."

"All in good time my friend. Very soon all shall be revealed. But I will reveal this: grave and scandalous news should be reaching the army on the Rhine shortly which will benefit our cause."

Florus grunted. "I can't wait to hear this 'grave and scandalous news.'"

"I just need to verify a few facts before I speak of it," Sacrovir affirmed. "Now let us drink to the days when Gaul was free!"

✱   ✱   ✱   ✱

The Second Century stood in parade formation in front of their billets. Vitruvius was conspicuous by his absence, being sworn into the office of Centurion by Valerius Proculus, the Cohort Commander, as well as Gaius Silius, the Legate of the Twentieth Legion. Caecina Severus, who had commanded the Twentieth during the campaigns against Arminius, had finally been allowed to retire. Silius had been brought in to replace the Commander of the Fifth Legion just prior to the last campaign of the war against Arminius. His leadership qualities had so impressed the Emperor that when his tenure was over Tiberius did not hesitate in granting his request for another command.

From top to bottom, the soldiers being promoted were brought before the Century. First was Flaccus, as he accepted the staff that signified his promotion to Optio. Next, Sergeant Statorius was handed the scroll with his appointment to the position of Tesserarius. Artorius held his breath as he waited for the next set of orders to be read. The Century was in a column formation, and he stood at the extreme right of his section. Praxus stood directly in front of him, at the right of his own section. Artorius' heart raced as Praxus was called forward to receive his promotion orders, his palms sweating as the newly promoted Decanus returned to his place in formation.

"*Legionary Artorius, post!*" Artorius stepped off and marched to the front of the formation, facing the Centurion. Flaccus handed Macro two scrolls, each bearing a set of orders.

"Legionary Artorius, as a testament of your sound leadership, demonstrated valor, and fidelity to the Twentieth Legion, you are promoted to the rank of *Decanus*, Sergeant of Legionaries. Sergeant Artorius, you are hereby appointed as Chief Weapons Instructor for the Second Century. The individual fighting abilities of the men of the Second Century now rest in your capable hands." With his left hand, he handed him both sets of orders, clasping his right hand with his own. "Congratulations, Sergeant," he said in a low voice. The Century erupted into an ovation as Artorius took his place with his section, poorly concealing a grin.

Artorius sat at his small desk that evening, reviewing the lessons that Vitruvius had drawn up years before. He found it ironic when the former Chief Weapons Instructor himself came walking into the section's room. He still wore the standard lorica segmentata body armor, though now it bore a harness of leather straps over the top, bearing his medals and decorations. It was tradition for Centurions to display all of their awards for valor, even during day-to-day garrison operations. Vitruvius would also soon trade in his segmentata and buy a suit of either lorica hamata mail, or else squamata scale armor. In addition to displaying their decorations, Centurions were expected to purchase their own distinctive armor as well.

Artorius marveled at the number of awards Vitruvius had received over the years. There were numerous campaign medals and silver torques for valor displayed. Rumor spoke of him being decorated for valor eleven times over the course of his career, though this could never be verified. He did know that Vitruvius had been awarded the Civic Crown, Rome's highest award for valor. He and Statorius saved the life of their former Optio during the battle at the Ahenobarbi Bridges several years before. Statorius had also been awarded the Civic Crown, though both men would only be required to wear it during formal functions. The newly appointed Centurion also wore the transverse crest, signifying his rank, atop his helmet, and he carried the traditional vine stick.

"That helmet looks good on you," Artorius said, rising to his feet in respect. Vitruvius motioned for him to take a seat as he removed his helmet and grabbed a stool.

"I see you found my old notes for conducting weapons drill," he remarked, pointing to the parchments on Artorius' desk. "They were mainly just notes I made to myself when I was learning the job. I had been thrown into the position, and pretty much had to teach myself the job. Eventually it all became second nature."

"I only hope I can do the same," Artorius replied.

"You will," Vitruvius answered, "because if you don't, you and I *will* start up our little sparring sessions again!"

"Yes Sir," Artorius replied with a nod. Vitruvius looked down and shook his head.

"*That* is a term of address that is going to take some getting used to! How about we let it go when it's just you and I, okay?"

"Sure thing Sir," Artorius replied with a smirk.

"We've known each other long enough to drop the formalities when the men aren't around. You're about the last person I need calling me 'sir,' as if I need to be reminded that I am now a Centurion!" He and Artorius both laughed at that as Vitruvius continued.

"You know they're talking about reviving the *Legion Champion* tournament. Flavius has tasked one of the Cohorts to renovate the old arena outside the fortress; it hasn't been used in years. There's also been a lot more individual sparring in the drill hall."

"When will the tournament take place, if it does happen?" Artorius asked.

"Springtime, probably," Vitruvius answered. "With no campaigns pending, I think it will be a welcome distraction for the men." Artorius sat back in his chair and placed his hands behind his head.

"It will be welcome" he agreed. "But why bother? No one can best you!" The Centurion shook his head.

"No, I'm done. It's time I stepped aside. *You* had better be entering, though. You are a marked man. A number of the lads, especially those in the Third Cohort, think you are the one to beat." Artorius folded his hands on his desk and contemplated this.

"Really, Vitruvius?" he asked. The Centurion was shocked at the sincerity in his young protégé's voice.

"Are you kidding me? There's a reason why you're a Chief Weapons Instructor. Second," he snorted. "And probably most important, you fought me to a draw. That's never been done before. If you compete in this tournament-and I know you will-and lose, I will *have* to enter. If someone can best you, then he is the man that I've been looking for all these years; the one who is better than I am."

"That is quite an obsession you have," Artorius replied. "It is almost as if you want to find someone that is better than you."

"I'm not a god, Artorius," Vitruvius replied soberly. "No matter how good a man is, he is still just a man. And no man is invulnerable. I am beatable; you've proven that. It is time the name 'Artorius' was venerated as the master of close combat." The Centurion then rose to his feet, Artorius did the same.

"Anyway, just wanted to see how you're assimilating. I know you have some new recruits that you will be working with soon. With your permission, I would like to observe their training with you. Oh, I know Macro will be there, but I want to see my former pupil as the master." With that, they clasped hands hard.

"It is a daunting responsibility that I leave you with," Vitruvius continued, "however I know that our boys are in capable hands." With that he left the room. No sooner had Centurion Vitruvius walked out, when Magnus rushed in, winded as if having ran a great distance.

"Artorius, Macro is calling for all section leaders immediately! There's been a terrible tragedy."

"What is it?" Artorius asked as he rushed for the door. Magnus' face was grim. He took a deep breath and fought to keep his voice from shaking.

"Germanicus is dead."

CHAPTER 2

▼

A SON OF ROME MOURNED

Macro stood behind his desk. Flaccus, Camillus, and Statorius stood behind him, all looking grim. Even Camillus had lost his perpetually cheerful nature. The Signifier then sat down in a chair, his head lowered, and hands in his hair. Germanicus was greatly revered by the legionaries even after he left the Rhine army for the east. Even though many of the men had never met him personally, they still bore the same honor and affection that they would for their own fathers. Those who met him remembered the occasions fondly.

Indeed, Germanicus had looked after his men as a father would his sons. His tactical savvy was unparalleled, and his personal valor in battle had been an inspiration. Like Tiberius before him, Germanicus never led from behind the army. To him, his life was no more important than that of his lowest legionaries, and if they were in danger, so was he. His concern for their welfare had been genuine, and he had always made it a point to meet with individual soldiers. When he spoke to his legionaries, he spoke to them as men, with dignity and respect. His loss would shake the Rhine Legions to their very foundations.

Artorius was among the last of the section leaders to arrive. Many were talking excitedly. Germanicus' death could very easily cause a serious disruption within the Legion, which would in turn lead to civil unrest within the province.

"*At ease!*" Optio Flaccus shouted. Immediately there was silence. Centurion Macro then spoke.

"Before we start letting rumor and emotions run rampant throughout the ranks, we need to make certain that we deal strictly with the facts of the matter. We have just learned that our former commander, Germanicus Caesar, is now dead." His voice was cold and distant, his emotions blunted by the tragedy.

"Given his age and the fact that he was in prime health, rumors of murder are spreading like wildfire. The gossips have even conspired to implicate the Emperor in this affair. Let it be known that we will not tolerate such talk from amongst our men! Tiberius has many enemies in Rome, enemies that will do anything to slander his name. Yet we must not forget the real man who led us on this very frontier before becoming Emperor of the Roman Empire; a task I may add that he never wanted." Macro was an impassioned supporter of the Emperor, especially since he had been one of the soldiers welcomed back into the army by Tiberius himself after the Teutoburger Wald disaster.

"As for the talk of murder," he continued, "there is already a suspect in custody at this time. Some of you may have heard of Gnaius Calpurnius Piso, the former Governor in the east. He is the primary suspect, along with his wife, Plancina. Let our men know that while we all mourn the loss of a Son-of-Rome, we do not seek to meet out our own form of justice. Let the courts in Rome decide Piso's fate!

"More importantly, if there are dissidents amongst the provinces, they will see the death of Germanicus, along with the Emperor's implications, to be a sign of weakness. We dishonor Germanicus if we allow ourselves to fall into disarray, to forget ourselves as Romans and as legionaries. To allow calamity to fall upon the province will undo everything he fought for. Make certain your men understand this. That is all." With that, the host of men who led the Century dispersed.

Artorius returned to his section's barrack to see that all of his men were gathered around, talking very fast. They stopped when they saw him enter.

"What's happened?" Decimus asked.

"We've heard awful rumors, rumors that we cannot believe to be true," Gavius added.

"I know," Artorius replied and took a deep breath. "Sit down, men." Here was his first challenge as a leader of legionaries. Very carefully he explained everything that Macro had said, emphasizing the need to remain focused on their own section of the Empire, and not to be distracted by events in Rome which they could not control.

"Piso," Carbo muttered. "I wish I could gut the bastard myself!"

"Well you can't," Magnus retorted. "Artorius is right; the only way we can do right by Germanicus is to continue as he would have wanted us to." He looked to Artorius who nodded his assent, thankful for the support from his friend.

"Still, can you even believe the talk of the Emperor himself being involved?" Valens added in disgust. "It makes no sense." Decimus leaned back onto his elbows on his bunk and shook his head.

"Absolutely not," he replied. "If Tiberius ever saw Germanicus as a threat, he would have realized otherwise after the mutiny on the Rhine when there were those who tried to make him Emperor. He was loyal, and Tiberius knew it."

"Just doesn't make any sense," Valens repeated, "I can't believe that so many in Rome would see Tiberius as having ordered Germanicus' demise."

"And yet that is probably what history will remember," Carbo added. "Historians are fickle, and they like a good story of murder and deceit. They will leach off the rumors and gossip about Tiberius like fucking locusts." His voice rose as he spoke.

"Easy Carbo," Artorius said. "We cannot be putting faith in the gossips and slanderers back home. If we did, there would be anarchy and chaos at every change in the winds. *We are better than that.* If historians choose to condemn Tiberius, posterity will be betrayed." Artorius stood and looked each man in the eye. "But know that I will not tolerate any mention of the Emperor's name as a suspect in this affair!" It was the first time he asserted his authority over his men. Magnus leaned forward, resting his forearms on his legs and interlocking his fingers.

"You don't have to worry about that from us, Artorius," he said quietly, his Nordic blue eyes taking in the slightly nervous glances from the others. "We know our job, and we know where our loyalties lie. Ultimately they lie with the State and with the Emperor. And at the end of the line, they lie with you." The rest of the section nodded in agreement.

"You can count on us," Decimus added. Artorius gave a tight-lipped smile and nodded in acknowledgement. When he was at last alone he sighed in relief; he had his men's trust and loyalty. The first test was over.

*   *   *   *

Livia sat in the dark, resting the side of her head on her hand. A true stoic, she betrayed no public emotions when the news of Germanicus' death broke. But alone in the dark, she allowed the tears to fall and privately mourned the loss of her grandson. What wounded her most were the slanders that implicated her and the Emperor as accomplices to his murder. Though Livia was a hard-hearted woman, she was not so callous as to have wished for the death of her own blood. And yet, because she had not allowed herself to become a weeping, wailing spectacle in public, she was scorned and looked upon with suspicious eyes.

She was taken back to years before when Germanicus' father, Drusus died while on campaign in Germania. She had also been inconsolable then, yet never did she betray her emotions publicly. Tiberius had even then scorned her for her lack of grief; as if he knew what it was like to bury a child! At least then she had had Augustus to turn to, she thought with a sigh. Long into the nights he would hold her close as she sobbed uncontrollably, her heart torn asunder. But Augustus was gone as well, taken to the halls of the gods six years before. Livia Augusta was alone in her grief.

Her remaining son, Tiberius Caesar, Emperor of Rome, would be of little to no comfort to her. She knew that he too mourned the loss of an able commander and loyal son. In addition to being his nephew by blood, Germanicus had been adopted by the Emperor. Many would say he had Germanicus removed to clear the way for his own son to succeed him to the Imperial Throne. For that had been a condition set by Augustus, that Tiberius would adopt Germanicus as his own son and give him precedence in the succession. Germanicus had been related to Augustus by blood, whereas Drusus the younger was not.

The notion of altering the imperial succession through murder was preposterous to Tiberius, for he was free to choose whomever he wished to follow him. With Augustus gone the Senate dared not oppose him at anything he set his mind to anymore. A stroke of the pen would have placed Drusus over Germanicus as heir to the Empire, and yet he had left the succession intact.

Tiberius' focus through his grief would now be on clearing of his own name, an impossible task in Livia's mind. As much as he tried, Tiberius had none of his brother's charm or political sense. His callous demeanor was always making him enemies. She sensed that no matter what happened, even after Piso was tried and executed, Tiberius would forever be slandered by the ignominy of Germanicus' murder, and she with him.

Livia saw the death of Germanicus as further proof that the Julio-Claudians were a cursed family, one that the Fates took distinct pleasure in tormenting. Of her sons, Drusus, though infatuated with that archaic Republic, was the one universally adored by the people; and he had died before his thirtieth birthday. Tiberius may have once been loved by the legions, but even that was questionable now; to say nothing for the spite he garnered from the Senate. Of Drusus' sons, Germanicus had been the strong one who bore all of his father's most desirable traits; military skill, political savvy, and a love of the plebs. He had succumbed at the young age of thirty-four. That only left Claudius, the stuttering, half-crippled imbecile who should have never seen his first birthday. Livia could never fathom how Drusus could have sired such a wretch! She blamed it on Drusus' insistence that his wife Antonia accompany him on every campaign, even when pregnant. Surely the rough life had stunted the lad's development from the womb!

Livia sighed once more. Drusus the younger was the only hope left for the Julio-Claudians. He was Tiberius' only son, and the only grandchild of Livia worthy of his heritage. He was also all that stood between the Emperor and his scheming Praetorian Prefect, Sejanus. As part of the prosecution against Piso, Drusus could be the key to helping Tiberius separate himself from the accused murderer of Germanicus.

Unfortunately for Tiberius, his name was too closely attached to Piso's. It was conveniently forgotten that Piso had first been appointed by, and been a close friend of, Augustus himself. And while Piso had been a friend to Tiberius, there was no doubt as to his guilt. He had even gone so far as to try and reassert his authority as soon as Germanicus was dead, inciting a rebellion against the newly appointed Legate who had replaced him. Roman soldiers had died as a result, and Piso would be condemned in their deaths as well. In order to save himself, Tiberius would have to allow Piso to be sacrificed. If not, the stain on his name and character would be irreparable.

The Emperor listened to the howling mob outside the palace. Two Cohorts of Praetorian Guards had been dispatched to secure the grounds, lest the crowd become violent. The Emperor was most disturbed by the events of late. It seemed as if the gods were mocking him, forcing him to become so stern and alienating towards his own people, not even allowing him to properly mourn the loss of his nephew and adopted son. What was worse was that it was members of his family who exacerbated the situation. Germanicus' widow, Agrippina was especially maddening to deal with. She was the source of many of the rumors regarding his involvement in Germanicus' murder. Tiberius scoffed at the notion. If Germanicus had been a threat, he would have crushed him years before, and without having to resort to petty murder.

Sejanus stood patiently with his hands behind his back. The Praetorian Prefect was becoming more and more useful to the Emperor. It seemed like he had the solution to everything that vexed him. If only his son, Drusus, were half as helpful! Drusus was steadfast friends with Agrippina, something the Emperor had never fully come to accept.

"You'll have to give him up," Sejanus said coolly, referring to Piso. Tiberius turned and faced him.

"I know. Piso has been a loyal friend for many years, both to me, as well as the Divine Augustus. What vexes me is that he has had the audacity to implicate me in his scheme to overthrow Germanicus, as if I had in fact endorsed his plans of sedition and murder. I would have settled for banishing him, had he not tried to save his own skin by bringing me down with him." The Emperor's voice drifted off and the mob outside could be heard growing louder.

"If you simply banish Piso, Agrippina and her followers will come at you personally in full-force. The trial will be starting soon, and there is only one real way in which it can end." Tiberius' face hardened.

"I have no issue with dispensing justice upon the guilty, even if they are old friends. What I will not tolerate is some spoiled bitch telling *me* how to run this Empire simply because she is the granddaughter of Augustus! Why could she have not been like her sister?" Tiberius was referring to his former wife, Vipsania, who he still adored, even after being divorced from her for many years. Tiberius turned back to the window.

"From the sounds of the mob, you would think they already had the butcher's hooks under his chin," Sejanus replied, coolly. He was referring to the barbaric practice of handing the executed bodies of condemned criminals over to the mob. In the case of those who had committed treason or other heinous crimes, the mob would drag the corpse through the streets by butcher's meat hooks. The body would then be desecrated and thrown into the Tiber River. No burial would be allowed, and families of the condemned scarcely ever tried to retrieve the bodies, out of fear of being beaten and savaged by the mob. Tiberius had witnessed such spectacles on more than one occasion. He grimaced at the thought of such being Piso's pending fate.

"Very well," he said at last. "We will allow the trial to follow its course. In the end, Piso will pay the price for his crimes. And Agrippina had better tread lightly in my presence thereafter!"

*   *   *   *

Artorius felt the sweat bead up on his neck as he eyed the new recruits. There were eight altogether. He did not realize they were that far under strength. He wondered why none had come to his section, but then realized that Macro was in fact doing him a favor by leaving him under strength, since his men were all veterans. It gave Artorius a chance to adapt to his position before having to deal with having recruits in his own section. It was not so much the task of training recruits that made him nervous; it was the fact that his Centurion, along with Centurion Vitruvius, was watching him. At first he kept thinking to himself, *how would Vitruvius do this?* He shook his head and dismissed the notion. He came to realize that Vitruvius was no longer the Chief Weapons Instructor, he was. Slowly he walked down the line of new men, eyeing each one for potential strengths and weaknesses. Most looked average in build, though two were slightly overweight, and one was rail thin. The overweight recruits he wasn't concerned about. Physical training would strip the baby fat off of them. Getting the skinny recruit to put on enough weight would be a challenge. After a quick walk down the line, he turned and faced the men, aware of the extra sets of eyes on his back.

"Recruits," he began, "my name is Sergeant Artorius; I am the Chief Weapons Instructor for the Second Century. Today you will start to learn the basic fundamentals of close-combat drill. First off, each of you will grab a practice gladius and shield from the cart." As they retrieved their practice weapons, Artorius saw looks of surprise on most of their faces at the weight of each. One of the overweight recruits grunted as he tried to heft the gladius and shield.

"How the hell are we supposed to use these in battle?" the recruit complained. "These bloody things weigh a ton!" Before the young man could blink, Artorius was standing nose-to-nose with him.

"What in the fuck did you say, recruit?" he shouted, his relaxed demeanor gone in a flash. *"I didn't realize that I had given you permission to speak!"* The recruit trembled as he saw Artorius clench and unclench his fists, his enormous forearm muscles pulsing. Artorius possessed such sheer size and muscle mass that he outweighed even the heaviest recruits by at least thirty pounds. This only added to his intimidating presence.

"I was just pointing out how heavy these practices weapons are ..." before the recruit could finish, Artorius butted him in the face with the short brim on his helmet. He then put his face next to the man's ear.

"You listen to me real hard, *recruit*. You open your mouth and complain like a little bitch on my drill field again, and I will tear your balls off and stuff them down your throat! Are we clear?"

"Yes Sergeant," the recruit gulped. Artorius started to turn away, but then spun around and slammed the back of his fist into the recruit's stomach, just below the ribcage. The young man gasped and fell to his knees, his breath taken from him.

"Get up," Artorius growled into the recruit's ear. As the man struggled to his feet, gasping and coughing, Artorius immediately became nonchalant again, his relaxed demeanor returning. He then went about demonstrating the proper use of the gladius and shield. After having shown them the proper stance and how to punch with their shields, he had them practice with the six-foot stakes that were set into the drill field. Once satisfied, he then showed them how to properly use the gladius as a stabbing weapon.

For the next hour he had them drill on the training stakes. He remembered back to his first day on the stakes. His had been trembling badly, exhaustion overcoming him, when Centurion Macro had motivated him to keep going with a serious of blows from his vine stick. Artorius could see the recruits facing similar dilemmas as fatigue gripped them. Out of the corner of his eye he could see Centurion Macro pacing back and forth behind the recruits, waiting for one to drop his weapons or try and rest before Artorius had told them to cease. One poor recruit missed the stake completely with a stab and stumbled forward, falling face first onto the ground. As he struggled to his feet, Macro lunged at him and brought his vine stick down hard on the recruit's helmet, sending him sprawling to the ground.

"*You clumsy jackal!*" he roared. As the Centurion chastised and kicked the hapless recruit, Artorius noticed one of the others had stopped attacking his stake and was instead watching and laughing at the ordeal. Artorius walked up behind him silently and cuffed him hard across the ear. The recruit gave a yelp of surprise and pain, and was terrified when he saw the Sergeant glaring at him. He immediately went back to drilling with his shield and gladius without Artorius uttering a word.

When he felt like they had pushed themselves hard enough, Artorius gave the order for them to rest. All were drenched in sweat and leaning on their practice shields. One of the overweight recruits was dry heaving and trying to keep from vomiting.

"You throw up on my drill field and you will be cleaning it up with your tongue," Artorius asserted. The young man looked up at the Decanus, his face pale and clammy. He swallowed hard and stood upright, breathing deeply.

Artorius was surprised to see that the skinny recruit had held up well comparatively. He was soaked in sweat and completely exhausted, however he had neither stumbled nor given up at any point. Artorius then told them to take off their helmets and have a seat on the grass. He then stood facing them, his hands behind his back.

"Recruits," he began, "today you have taken the first steps towards learning how to fight as legionaries. What I did not tell you earlier is that the practice gladius and shield are in fact twice as heavy as service weapons." He saw a look of relief cross the faces of several of the young men. Artorius smirked at that. He then noticed that Optio Flaccus had arrived to take the recruits to their next phase of training for the day.

"By drilling with these practice weapons, you will be able to handle your service weapons more easily," he continued. "As you progress through your training, your bodies will become stronger, your muscles more conditioned. Remember what you learned today, and we will expound upon it tomorrow. That is all." As he turned to walk away, he heard one of the recruits address him.

"Excuse me, Sergeant?" Artorius turned to see it was the recruit he had chastised earlier for complaining about the weight of the practice weapons. The young man was standing rigid, his hands clasped behind his back.

"What is it?" Artorius asked, folding his arms across his chest.

"I ... I wanted to apologize for my behavior earlier. It was unbecoming, and I assure you it will not happen again."

"What is your name, recruit?"

"Felix Spurius, Sergeant," he replied. "I'm the bastard son of a magistrate of Ravenna. I'm here to prove my worth to my father, as well as to myself."

"You can prove yourself by becoming stronger in the mind, as well as the body," Artorius replied. "Each drives the other. A strong mind will carry the body beyond its limits, thereby making it stronger. Learn your lessons well, and you'll be alright."

"Thank you Sergeant," the recruit replied and Artorius waived for him to go join his fellow recruits, who were getting briefed by Optio Flaccus.

After he dismissed the recruit, Artorius walked over to where Centurions Macro and Vitruvius had been watching. He had completely forgotten that they were even there. Both men had their arms folded, but did not look displeased.

"Not bad," Vitruvius remarked with a smile.

"Well done," Macro added. "When you finish stowing your training gear, I need you to come to the Century office. We need to discuss your own training regime for the Legion Champion tournament."

"Yes Sir," he replied with a nod. Vitruvius winked at him as both Centurions walked away. Artorius took a deep breath and blew out hard. He was genuinely surprised that the training had gone as well as it had. The physical chastising was to be expected when recruits were raw and undeveloped. He again thought back to when he had been in their place. The extreme conditioning had been a wakeup call for him, given that his entire physical training regime up to that point had consisted of gaining size and power. Artorius still possessed an extreme amount of muscle size, and was considered by many to be the most physically powerful soldier in the entire Legion. However, he had supplemented his training with extreme amounts of conditioning as well. In truth he knew that stamina was far more important for a legionary than raw power, however he still worked hard to maintain his size and strength as a matter of personal pride.

He walked into the Centurion's office and sat down across from Macro, who was leaning back in his chair, his feet up on his desk.

"I take it you have given some thought to how you are going to prepare for the Legion Champion tournament?" Macro asked. Artorius shook his head at that.

"To tell you the truth Sir, I've been totally focused on preparing for weapons training with the recruits, not to mention the day-to-day running of my section." Macro frowned slightly and nodded.

"Well I can understand you being quite busy," he replied, "especially since you are new to both duties. You do know however that every legionary who fancies himself as a master of close combat is looking to beat you."

"So I've been told," Artorius retorted, dryly.

"The thing is," Macro continued, "these men all know your talents. They will push themselves to be at their best in order to beat you. I know that you haven't been sparring as regularly as you would like, and we need to fix that. Your duties as Chief Weapons Instructor are paramount and cannot be changed. However, you can delegate your tasks as Decanus to one of your more competent legionaries. Anyone you might have in mind?"

"Magnus would be the most logical choice," Artorius replied.

Macro cracked a partial smirk. "You're not just saying that because he is your friend, I hope." Artorius was taken aback by that.

"Sir, I hope you think better of me than that!" he said indignantly. "Believe me, our friendship is irrelevant. Magnus has the respect of the entire section; they listen to him and follow his lead without question." Macro raised a hand for Artorius to cease.

"At ease Sergeant, I understand. I wasn't accusing you of showing favoritism; I just want to make certain that it is avoided in this Century. Very well, I'm going to elevate Magnus to *immune* status. Appoint him as acting section leader until the tournament is over. When you are not conducting weapons drill with the recruits or preparing lesson plans, I want you focusing on your own preparations for the tournament. I had thought to ask Vitruvius to come back to be your sparring partner, however that would be in poor taste, given that he has his own representative to prepare. If you wish to use members of your section as sparring partners, by all means do so. I'll get Statorius to lay off hammering your guys too much on the duty roster. However, do not allow them to use that as an excuse to be lazy. If they are getting out of fatigue details, they need to be sparring with you, understood?"

"Yes Sir," Artorius replied with a nod. "I'll spar with them until they beg me to put them on shit detail!" Macro grinned, then stood and extended his hand, which Artorius clasped.

"I know you'll make this Century proud." Artorius saluted and walked out of the office. He was partially relieved that at least now he could pawn off some of his duties. At the same time he was nervous about the pressure Macro was putting on him. He figured he would go practice some drills on the training stakes and work off some of his nerves. He was shocked to find Magnus waiting for him at the stakes, equipped with a practice shield and gladius. His friend grinned at him as Artorius approached.

"What, you didn't think I was going to let you practice on your own, did you?" Magnus asked. Artorius shook his head, set down his weapons, and started to stretch and warm up his muscles.

"How did you find out?" he asked as he stretched out his chest and upper arms.

"Decimus told me," Magnus replied with a shrug. Artorius started laughing.

"Okay, I'm not even going to ask how he found out!"

"It *is* a unique talent that he has," Magnus observed. "So you want to do some stake drills and then spar?"

"Yeah, I need to work some of the rust off," Artorius replied as he donned his helmet. "Alright, shield drills first. We'll start by working on boss-punches as well as bottom-shield strikes."

"You got it," Magnus replied as he set into his fighting stance. While punching an opponent with the metal boss on the center of the shield was preferable, there were times when one could tilt the shield up and jab with the brass strip on the bottom for improved reach. This was particularly effective when an adversary was disengaging. Artorius was shocked by the sheer speed and tenacity Magnus displayed. He seemed to have a preference for using bottom-shield strikes to keep his enemy at a distance. It had been some time since they had fought side by side in actual combat, and Artorius was feeling very much out of condition.

"You like using the underside of your shield," he pointed out to Magnus as he continued to work his own strikes.

"It frustrates my enemy," Magnus replied as he lunged forward quickly to demonstrate a rapid stab with his gladius. "They become desperate in their attempts at closing the distance with me that I can bait them into falling onto my blade."

"A sound tactic," Artorius commented between deep breaths, "but don't attack too high. Someone could slip underneath your shield." His own shield arm was starting to limber up and he felt his rhythm coming back.

"I always keep that in mind, hence why I keep my gladius at waist height. You want to switch to gladius drills?"

"Yeah," Artorius replied, his heart starting to race as sweat started to form up on his brow. "High and low attacks, keeping your shield at the defensive." On order both men started to stab at the wooden stakes, not once pausing or losing their rhythm. Artorius kept Magnus in his peripheral vision, making certain that he kept pace with his friend. He realized that if given the opportunity, Magnus could give him a run for the Legion Champion title. Having his friend at his side forced him to push himself harder than he ever could on his own, and he was once again thankful for the motivation.

Time and again they assaulted the training stakes, incorporating more foot-work and movement, as well as executing combinations of blocks and strikes with both the shield and gladius.

"Switch up your combinations," Artorius ordered. "Use multiple shield attacks to set up your gladius strikes." He was starting to have trouble speaking as it took all he had to keep his breathing regular. His hips were starting to ache from using them to magnify the impact of his blows. He had no idea how long they had been drilling, though he knew it was far longer than he would have gone had Magnus not been there. At length he finally stepped away from the stakes.

"Alright, that's enough for now." His heartbeat was ringing in his ears and his face was completely flushed. He set his weapons down and rested with his hands on his knees.

"Thank the gods for that!" Magnus slurred as he dropped his weapons and fell to his back in an overtly dramatic manner. He took his helmet off and tossed it aside, his arms falling straight out at his sides. "I didn't think you were ever going to end this!"

"I was too afraid of looking weak in front of you," Artorius replied, removing his own helmet and having a seat on the grass. "Having you here has certainly pushed me beyond what I thought I was capable of."

"Just don't be asking me to spar right now," Magnus remarked, his eyes closed and his arms still stretched out at his sides. "I don't think I can even stand up just yet." The two friends stayed like that for a while, allowing their bodies to cool down and their heart rates to return to some semblance of normal. Artorius found his mind drifting as he stared off into the distance.

"Do you think he's guilty?" he asked after some contemplation.

"Do I think who's guilty?" Magnus asked in return, rolling onto his side. The color had returned to his face, though his hair was sticky and matted from the dried sweat. Both men started to stretch out their sore limbs to prevent them from stiffening up.

"Piso," Artorius replied. "I know he and Germanicus hated each other, but would he really resort to murder?"

"I don't know," Magnus said, rolling onto his back once more, placing his hands behind his head. "Someone murdered Germanicus; the evidence overwhelmingly showed signs of poisoning. I mean, who else had a motive?"

"That's what troubles me," Artorius remarked as sat down and brought his feet together to stretch out his groin. "I know we've been told to silence any implications of the Emperor; however one cannot help but wonder; did Tiberius somehow see Germanicus as a threat of some sort? I don't see how, after all Germanicus was his successor to begin with."

"Hard to tell, given that what we hear may not be all the facts," Magnus conjectured. "I honestly doubt that we will ever know for certain. What gets to us is often-times hearsay and rumor, born often out of delusional fantasy."

"That is for damn sure," Artorius observed as he rolled onto his back and pulled his knees into his chest, stretching out his back. It hurt and yet felt good at the same time. He let out a sigh of relief as he let go and extended his legs out as far as he could. "I've got to tell you Magnus, I worry about the lads sometimes. Germanicus was well-loved by everyone in the entire army. I only hope that justice, or at least the perception of justice, can be done. Otherwise I don't know how the troops will react. It is not good to allow such strong emotions that his death stirs to simmer for too long without a resolution."

"I wonder if that's not at least part of their reason for wanting to send us on a sortie back across the Rhine," Magnus pondered. "They keep us busy for a time while this mess gets sorted out in the courts back in Rome. Hopefully by the time we get back word of a resolution reaches the Rhine."

"What sortie?" Artorius asked as he stared at his friend dumbfounded.

"Oh sorry," Magnus replied with a grin. "Decimus told me."

"I do wish he would let me know these things before he goes and tells everyone else," Artorius mused.

CHAPTER 3

▼

SHADOWS OF CONSPIRACY

The apartment in Augustodunum was tucked back at the end of an old, dank alley. This was the less than civilized section of the city, infested with the dregs of society that the populace pretended did not exist. Sacrovir found it ideal for conducting business that he preferred to keep away from his estate.

He conducted many such "business" meetings over the last few months. First it was with Florus, then with a few of the more disaffected nobles that Florus brought with him. He started gathering a larger circle of conspirators. A whispered word here, an overheard conversation there and loyalists to Gaul were found. The chiefs of many ancient tribes had flocked to his calling. Through them the battle cries of freedom from Roman oppression would be heard. Sacrovir counseled his followers on patience.

"All in due time," he told them with a smile that had nothing to do with humor. "One cannot fight without good weapons."

He listened to the rain outside, rolling his plan over in his mind. He was becoming more convinced at their chances of success with every meeting. He waited impatiently for his guests of the evening; guild leaders of the Gallic metal smiths whose loyalties were not necessarily to Gaul, but lay in coin. Sacrovir knew he would require a large contingent of heavy infantry in order to have a chance against the legions. Even the few individual cohorts that manned the small garrison stations would be a formidable threat against an untrained and ill-equipped force. Roman soldiers were well armored, and more importantly ingrained with an iron discipline which made them utterly fearless in battle.

Sacrovir knew he would require sound tactical leaders to assist him in battle preparations and they might be more difficult to procure. The Romans fought in close order lines of battle, and it was standard procedure for the legions to unleash a storm of javelins before closing with their enemy. Their swords, the gladii, were simple, yet fearsome weapons. He was thankful that the cohorts he would face lacked artillery and possessed little, if any cavalry. Legionary infantry was all he had to concern himself with, as daunting as that was. Many a foe had faced the legions with overwhelming numbers of the bravest warriors, only to break once javelin and gladius had been employed. There *had* to be a way of overwhelming their forces without succumbing to the Romans' shock weapons and tactics.

Patience, he thought to himself. *Our friends will help us to conquer the Romans one step at a time.*

Sacrovir knew all of these things, and worked with his fellow conspirators to try and find ways to negate the Romans' advantages. It was Taranis, a nobleman of the Sequani, who came up with the concept of encasing some of their men completely in plate armor which would be impervious to the Roman javelins. They could be used as the vanguard, who would break up the legionary formations, allowing the lighter-armed troops behind them to dispatch the Romans piecemeal. Formation was everything to legions; fighting together as one was what allowed them to time and again defeat superior numbers. Once their formations collapsed, they could be overwhelmed. Of course breaking that formation would require a corps of men with enormous strength, not to mention the astronomical cost of outfitting them. In this, Sacrovir was not overly concerned. He had money, and money could buy anything. He intended to prove this in his meeting with the smiths.

His thoughts were interrupted by a knock at the door. With one hand on his long-sword, he peered through the small hole in the door. Three well-dressed men were standing on the landing. All looked rather irritated, as well as nervous at their surroundings. Sacrovir kept them waiting for several minutes before he opened the door.

"To be inconspicuous is not in any of your natures I see," he hissed as he impatiently waived the wet and uncomfortable men to a table in the center of the room. The men snorted as they took their seats.

"Surely you do not expect us to walk around dressed as mere peasant stock!" one of the men retorted. He was fat with a thick, well maintained mustache on his upper lip. He was slightly bald, with his long hair in the back kept in a pony tail. Several exotic rings adorned his hands, matching his equally elaborate attire.

"If you expect to have any part in this contract, you will!" Sacrovir snarled, slamming his hands on the table. Two of men were taken aback. The fat one did not jump, but took a sudden interest in his rings, which he fiddled with.

"Very well. You do realize, I expect to be recompensed for any inconvenience I have to endure in meeting here," he replied. Sacrovir waived a hand dismissively.

"You need not concern yourself with that. You will all be paid handsomely enough, I assure you. Each of you owns a large guild of metal smiths; the best in all of Gaul. This contract will require one-third of your best men. I emphasize that I want only the best; I want men who can turn out high quality arms in short order. They, along with all of their equipment, will be moved to a remote site I have acquired in the hills. There they will be put to work."

"You expect us to up and move one-third of our best smiths, *and* all of their tools?" one of the men asked indignantly, raising his bushy eyebrows.

"I told you, you will be well paid for this," Sacrovir continued smoothly. "It would not do for the Romans to start sticking their arrogant noses into our affairs. They may ask questions were they to find out that we are mass producing arms and armor."

"So you really do intend to go through with your little rebellion," the fat leader said.

"Indeed I do," Sacrovir replied. "For too long our nobles and our people have been subjected to the hypocrisy of Roman rule. You yourselves are of the Patrician class; you pay Roman taxes, and are subject to their laws. And yet you are denied the most basic rights which your so-called peers in Rome entitle themselves to! Think of this as your duty to your nation and your heritage to help us through off the yoke of Imperial oppression." He snickered inwardly, seeing the patriotic spark in their eyes. Such men were sheep; sheep lured by want of money. He was now able to lead them around by the nose; provided that the ring was made of gold.

"Gentlemen, I cannot stress enough how much secrecy is paramount in this contract, hence why I do not ever want to see any of you here dressed so ostentatiously again. Once your men are established and have their smiths moved to their appointed location, we will discuss the remainder of the contract and how much they will be required to manufacture. In the meantime, here is a down payment for the movement costs, as well as a little stipend to make the effort worth your while." With that he snapped his fingers and a servant appeared from a dark corner of the room, bearing three small scrolls. He handed them to Sacrovir, who in turn handed one to each of the men.

"What are these?" Bushy eyebrows asked. Sacrovir rolled his eyes in disgust.

"How far do you think you would get if you left here bearing gold?" he asked condescendingly. "There are thieves and brigands in this part of town who would have your gold *and* your heads before you could shit yourselves in terror. Consider yourself lucky that you were not robbed on the way here. Read them. I assume each of you knows how to read." They read their scrolls and looked at each other amazed. The quiet guild leader smiled greedily.

"These notes bear my seal, which you will each take to a separate bank to withdraw your money. I have accounts all over the province, so no one will take any notice. You have five days to get your smiths and equipment ready to move. On the fifth day, I will send messengers and escorts." He rose abruptly to feet, signaling that the meeting was over.

"Do we have an agreement, gentlemen?" Each man extended their hands to him, which he grasped firmly as he ushered them out to where it was still raining. A smug grin then spread across his face. Florus would be pleased. After all, he was helping to finance this venture, and would want to see measurable progress. The manufacturing of so many arms and armor would take time; however time was something Sacrovir felt comfortable that he had.

*   *   *   *

Statorius sat on top of the desk in the Century's main office scribbling notes onto a large parchment. Gathered around sat all the section leaders within the Century. It was the first such meeting Artorius had attended. Though Magnus would be acting in his place soon enough, he felt he should at least attend a few of the section leader meetings to make certain he knew how things operated. Around the end of each month, the Tesserarius would call together all of the Decanii in order to establish the duty and training schedules for the next month. Each section leader had a wax tablet and stylus with which to take his notes. Statorius seemed to be checking off all the applicable days of the month, his brow wrinkled in thought. Finally he spoke.

"Alright, let's get started. The first thing I need is three guys for latrine duty from the first till the fourth. Ostorius, I'll need two from you, and Praxus, I'll need one from you."

"I know just who I'm going to give you," Praxus replied. "Got somebody on my 'shit list;' no pun intended." That got a slight chuckle out of some of the men, though it was a well-used joke. He and Ostorius gave the names to Statorius, who wrote them down on his roster.

"Okay, next we've got stable duty on the third," the Tesserarius continued. "Rufio, I'll need one of your men for that. And Artorius, I'll need two men for road repair on the sixth." Artorius looked at his list of names briefly. He was short two men as it was, and with Macro's assurances he hoped that Statorius would not overtax him.

"I can give you Valens and Magnus," he answered. Statorius nodded and wrote the names down.

"Oh, and I'll need one more from you for latrines again, this time from the sixteenth to the twentieth," Statorius added.

"I'll give you Carbo." This caused the Tesserarius to chuckle.

"He'll love you for that," Statorius remarked. "He complained to me for an entire week once when I put him on latrines."

"What did you do?" Artorius asked, intrigued.

"I volunteered him for latrines for the next six months. I have to say I don't think anyone in the Legion knows the intricacies of our sewage system better than Carbo," he snickered.

After about an hour the roster was finalized for the next month. Artorius made sure to keep from offering up Decimus for any details, seeing as he was an *immune*, and therefore exempt from fatigue duties. Magnus' elevation to immune status was to take effect on the seventh, so Artorius knew he could still be used up until then. As soon as Statorius called the meeting, he made his way towards the door.

"Sergeant Artorius!" the Tesserarius called after him. Artorius closed his eyes and for a moment froze in place, thinking he was in trouble. The room emptied as he walked over to where Statorius still sat on top of the desk. He clasped his hands behind his back, waiting for his superior to speak.

"I see you are catching on," Statorius began.

"It's coming along slowly but surely, Sir," Artorius replied.

"Come off it Artorius, you don't have to act so formal around me," Statorius replied. "I heard you impressed Macro with your conducting of weapons drill with the recruits." Artorius shrugged at that.

"I spent so much time out there with Vitruvius that it all kind of came naturally. To tell you the truth, I'm a bit nervous about everything. I have the men's trust, though I feel like I'm putting up a front of false confidence most of the time. Was it that way for you?" Artorius was indeed feeling overwhelmed by his duties. Before, when not on details or mandatory drills, he had had quite a relaxing time when the Legion was in garrison. The operations tempo had slowed considerably since the wars against Arminius and the Cherusci had come to an end. Now, when most of his soldiers were enjoying leisure time, he was working on training schedules, detail rosters, and conducting lesson plans for the recruits. He truly cherished his off time, and he was finding that as a Decanus he had much less of it.

"It took some time," Statorius answered. "After a while I got used to it. I admit that I was not tasked nearly as much as you. Remember, I did not have any additional duties, like you do. Things will slow down once the recruits finish training. How much longer do they have?"

"Six weeks," Artorius replied. "They've only just started working with me."

"You need to let me know when they are ready to move past the training stakes. I need to put that time on the duty roster as well, so that we can assign sparring partners for your recruits." Artorius made a note of it on his tablet. *Just one more thing to try and remember,* he thought to himself.

"Now that you mention it, I'll have to get with Pilate and see when he can schedule a time to conduct basic artillery training," he said out loud as he made more notes. As he started towards the door, Statorius grabbed him by the shoulder.

"Hey, don't think you have to do this alone," he remarked. "You can delegate some of your duties to your more competent troops. Magnus is probably your best bet. Decimus is good too, though he lacks Magnus' ambition. And if you need anything, you know where to find me." Artorius nodded in reply.

"Funny you should mention that," he remarked. "Macro said the same thing. In fact, he directed me to have Magnus act as section leader while I train up for the Legion Champion tournament. Of course, I'm sure he will be one of my primary sparring partners, so his days will be full as well."

"He will manage," the Tesserarius replied. "I know you are new to the position, but it is never too early to start training your successor."

"So how are your new duties?" Artorius asked, wanting to shift the subject off him. Statorius shrugged.

"I spend a lot of time with Flaccus. He was Tesserarius for more than seven years, so he knows the position better than any. And speaking of which, I have to get this over to him and then time to do my patrol of the rampart sentries." With a wave he dismissed the Sergeant.

Artorius left without a word. As he walked out the door, he saw Praxus was there waiting for him.

"Statorius chew on your backside a bit?" he asked.

"No," Artorius laughed, reviewing his notes as he walked, "though I thought for certain that he was going to, for whatever reason."

"He expects a lot of you, as does everyone else." Artorius stopped reading and looked at him. Praxus was quick to explain. "Because of your extra duties, you get paid more than the rest of us section leaders. For example; Rufio has been in the army for over fourteen years, four as a Decanus, yet with your incentive pay you make about a third more than he does. Statorius' way of thinking, the highest paid Sergeant needs to be the one who sets the highest standards. And to be quite frank, I agree with him." Artorius nodded.

"Believe me; they make certain I earn that incentive pay. I'm just glad Vitruvius kept good notes, otherwise I'd be completely lost as Chief Weapons Instructor."

"Oh come on! Why do I have latrine duty next month?" Carbo complained.

"Keep whining and you will have it every day for the next six months," Artorius answered. He was mildly irritated and was in no mood to put up with any of the incessant bickering and complaining that usually followed after the duty roster was posted.

"Better yet, spend less time getting drunk and learn a skill so that you don't have to show up on the duty roster anymore," Decimus taunted. This elicited a string of colorful profanity from Carbo. Decimus' schedule for working in the leather shops, a skill which had given him his immune status as well as incentive pay, was given to Artorius at the start of each month by the Primus Ordo who supervised all of the Legion's specialists.

Artorius shook his head and left the room. He noticed that Magnus was not in the barracks. Not that it mattered. Magnus was the least likely to complain about anything, no matter how unpleasant. Artorius figured that was why he did not like the thought of giving the less desirable details to his old friend. *Old friend.* The term sat hard with him. Though Magnus was one of his closest companions, he had to make it a point to not show favoritism towards him. Everyone knew the two were best of friends, however Artorius could never allow it to show when it came to things such as assigning duties, otherwise he would lose the confidence and trust of his soldiers.

It certainly wasn't easy adapting to the change from *Legionary* to *Sergeant*, however it was something he was just going to have to get used to. He would need to talk to Magnus soon. He had yet to tell him about Macro elevating him to immune status. Artorius smiled at how ecstatic Magnus would be, particularly when it came to the extra pay.

While the Decanii of the Second Century had been at their meeting, Centurions and Optios of the entire Cohort were in a meeting of their own. There were six eighty-man Centuries within the Cohort, which fell under command of the Centurion Pilus Prior, who also commanded the First Century. Valerius Proculus was the Pilus Prior for the Third Cohort, and had been for some years. A veteran soldier in his forties, his gray hair was just starting to recede from his forehead.

"As you all are fully aware," he began, "it has been some time since we last crossed the Rhine in any force to let the barbarians know we are still here." The Centurions and Optios nodded in agreement. All had fought against Arminius, the hated war chief of the Cherusci who had orchestrated the Teutoburger Wald disaster eleven years previously. Centurion Platorius Macro, Commander of the Second Century, had survived that disaster. The campaigns against Arminius had been fierce and brutal, many thousands of barbarians paying the ultimate price for their treachery. Though Arminius himself had eluded capture, the Cherusci were completely shattered and had scattered to the winds. The Battle of Idistaviso, near the Weser River, had broken his army; the assault on the Angrivarii stronghold annihilated his people.

"The Commanding General thinks it is time for us to reconnoiter east of the Rhine," Proculus continued, "so that we may not only show our presence to the Germans, but to also see to it that they are not massing against us again."

"How large of a force are we talking about?" Centurion Vitruvius asked.

"No more than three Cohorts," Proculus answered. "Command feels that any more than that will provoke the locals into thinking we are invading again. Our cavalry assets are few, and they are constantly taxed to the limit as it is; hence why the task has fallen on us. We will move across the Rhine in ten days. From there we will split off, all Centuries moving online, each taking an assigned sector as you can see on this map."

"Sir, will that not leave us exposed to attack?" the Optio from the Fifth Century asked.

"Possibly," Proculus answered, "which is why we must make contact with the local tribal chiefs as soon as possible, and gauge from them the demeanor of their people. They also need to understand that it is their responsibility to keep the fanatics in check. We must make certain that they understand any hostile act towards us will be construed as an act of war, and will be followed by another full-scale invasion. It has only been four years since Idistaviso. While there may be some who wish for the opportunity to spill our blood, there are many more who remember all too well the consequences."

Macro sat back in his chair, arms folded, brooding over what was being proposed. While the risks were there, he completely agreed with Proculus' assessment. He was curious to see how things had or had not changed since they crossed back to the west of the Rhine four years earlier. This mission would be much different than their last; one of reconnaissance and information gathering. There would a lot fewer of them this time as well. He still detested the barbarians; the horror of Teutoburger Wald never fully left him. It was a pity that this wasn't another invasion. A part of him hoped that the Germans would become openly hostile upon Roman soldiers crossing the Rhine. An opportunity to slay a few more of the bastards would not be unwelcome.

*   *   *   *

Tiberius sat before the assembled Senate. Piso stood with his defense counsel off to one side. The defendant stared at him the entire time, though the Emperor pretended not to notice.

"Piso," Tiberius spoke, "was my father's representative and friend, and was appointed by myself, on the advice of the Senate, to assist Germanicus in the administration of the East. Whether he provoked the young prince by willful opposition and rivalry, and had rejoiced at his death or wickedly destroyed him, is for you to determine with minds unbiased. Certainly if a subordinate oversteps the bounds of duty and of obedience to his commander, and has exulted in his death and in my affliction, I shall hate him and exclude him from my house, and I shall avenge a personal quarrel without resorting to my power as Emperor. If however a crime is discovered which ought to be punished, whoever the murdered man may be, it is for you to give just reparation both to the children of Germanicus and to us, his parents.

"Consider this too, whether Piso dealt with the armies in a revolutionary and seditious spirit; whether he sought by intrigue popularity with the soldiers; whether he attempted to repossess himself of the province by arms, or whether these are falsehoods which his accusers have published with exaggeration. As for them, I am justly angry with their intemperate zeal. For to what purpose did they strip the corpse and expose it to the pollution of the vulgar gaze, and circulate a story among foreigners that he was destroyed by poison, if all this is still doubtful and requires investigation?

"For my part, I sorrow for my son and shall always sorrow for him; still I would not hinder the accused from producing all the evidence which can relieve his innocence or convict Germanicus of any unfairness, if such there was. And I implore you not to take as proven charges alleged, merely because the case is intimately bound up with my affliction. Do you, whom ties of blood or your own true-heartedness have made his advocates, help him in his peril, every one of you, as far as each man's eloquence and diligence can do so. To like exertions and like persistency I would urge the prosecutors. In this, and in this only, will we place Germanicus above the laws, by conducting the inquiry into his death in this house instead of in the forum, and before the Senate instead of before a bench of judges. In all else let the case be tried as simply as others. Let no one heed the tears of Drusus or my own sorrow, or any stories invented to our discredit."[1]

A silence fell over the hall. The Senators were even more perplexed than before. None could fully gauge the Emperor's intent. Did he wish them to convict or acquit? And what reparations would there be if they passed the wrong verdict? All were terrified of incurring Tiberius' wrath, should they displease him.

For his own part, Tiberius had been intentionally evasive. He was honest when he said that he wanted the Senate to pass sentence fairly and without bias. If they voted the way they thought he wanted them to, then there was no justice and the trial would be a complete farce.

Tiberius did in fact mourn the loss of Germanicus. He was fond of the young man who had proven himself time and again. He had vanquished the Cherusci and avenged the treachery of Teutoburger Wald. The only solace Tiberius could find in the loss of Germanicus was that at least now Agrippina would never become Empress. He wondered if that was part of her mourning. He shuddered at the thought of what it would have been like, had Germanicus attained the Imperial throne, with that bitch trying to rule through him. Livia had held tremendous influence over Augustus; however her methods were subtle and non-self serving. Agrippina, on the other hand, would seek to assert herself fully, demanding power and majesty onto her own person. Tiberius then contemplated his son's wife. Since Drusus was now his heir, would Livilla serve him well as Empress? Livilla was a spoiled little girl in Tiberius' mind, but harmless enough. She would be quite content to throw lavish banquets and entertain Senators and foreign royalty.

He then contemplated Agrippina's reaction to the new circumstances. While Drusus considered Agrippina a friend, the Emperor wondered just how genuine her feelings of friendship were. Would she look to undermine or cause harm to Drusus or Livilla as a means of hurting him? Tiberius could not be sure, but he would make note of it and warn Drusus to watch himself around that vile woman. He did not wish Drusus to cease in his friendship with Agrippina, rather he would rather he kept her close and under watch.

*   *   *   *

Plancina was frantically pacing in the atrium of the house she and her husband were being kept, when the door opened. Livia entered the foyer, her face expressionless. Plancina immediately fell to her knees and clutched at Livia's stola, weeping uncontrollably.

"Oh Livia, you've got to help me! Agrippina's friends will not stop at condemning my husband. They will kill our son and me as well! *Please,* you've got to help me!" She came to her feet, her face white and her eyes wild; fearful tears flowing freely down her cheeks. Her expression unchanged, Livia backhanded the woman sharply across the face.

"Do you *really* think I will help save anyone who played a part in my own grandson's death? To say nothing for the sedition and rebellion your wretched family has been the cause of!" she hissed. Plancina held a hand over her cheek, which was turning red, and shook her head.

"No," she replied, "it wasn't me, I swear it! I had nothing to do with Germanicus' murder. Please you must believe me!"

"Oh come off it, woman!" Livia scoffed. "Your husband was little more than your whipping dog. He never could make a decision even so simple as how to wipe his own bottom without consulting you! And don't think I don't remember the hatred that existed between you and Agrippina well before Germanicus was ever sent to the east. So don't play so innocent with me, otherwise I'll come up with the most unpleasant means of disposing of you imaginable! And believe me, my imagination runs deep." Plancina fell to her knees again, her hands folded together against her forehead. She ceased in her sobbing, but her body still trembled.

"You must believe me," she pleaded. "Yes, I did hate Agrippina, and I still do. I've never denied that. And it seemed like both of them were bent on our family's downfall. The quarrels between Piso and Germanicus started from the day they arrived. It never ceased. We had to do something, lest our family be ruined!"

"So you resorted to sedition and murder." It was a statement, not a question. Plancina shook her head frantically.

"No," she said softly. "If I bore any guilt, I would gladly share the same fate as my husband. I only told him he had to do something about Germanicus. I had no idea he was going to have him murdered, and then start an insurrection amongst the legions. I'm amazed we even walked out of that place alive. Piso was a changed man after that. I could no longer speak with him, my influence over him completely evaporated." She gazed up at Livia, eyes red and puffy, her cheeks tear stained. Again she took hold of Livia's stola.

"Livia, if you cannot save me, please allow my son to be spared. He truly is innocent in this affair. After all, could a son, even a grown one, really deny his own father? I'm so afraid for him, and I don't know what else to do."

"You will compose yourself, woman, and you will do exactly as I tell you," Livia replied, sternly. "You will tell me who committed the act of murder against my grandson. I want names, and where they can be found. Furthermore, you will separate yourself from your husband's defense." Plancina nodded and rose to her feet, a fleeting hope glimmering in her eyes.

"There was a notorious woman named Martina. She made poisoning people an art form. Her price was quite high; it nearly bankrupted my husband. She's being offered immunity from the prosecution if she will testify against Piso."

Livia raised an eyebrow. "Continue." Plancina swallowed hard.

"She is supposed to be arriving within the next few days. There is a squalid tavern that she plans to stay at. It's rather inconspicuous, and fitting for her type. Oh Livia, does this mean you intend to help us?" She clutched Livia's stola, only to have the Empress slap her across the face once again.

"I have promised you nothing! You will get no such promises of safe passage from me, vile woman. If you know what is good for you, you will distance yourself from your husband, and do exactly as I tell you." With that, Livia turned and left the room. Plancina sank into a chair, her hand again on her swollen cheek, her mind in torment. She did not know whether there was any hope for her and her son or not. Their fate lay solely in the hands of Livia, who would dispose of them as she saw fit.

*   *   *   *

Artorius walked up as the section was checking the contents of their baggage cart. Magnus and Valens were inspecting their tent, making certain that there were no holes or signs of rot in the leather. Carbo and Gavius were inventorying the stakes and poles for their tent, while Decimus checked the cart for serviceability with several other soldiers from the Century. Four sections would share a cart, with which they would load their tents, cooking utensils, as well as most of their rations. Each Legionary carried about a week's worth of hard biscuits, which would serve as a supplemental ration in the event of an emergency.

"So would you mind explaining to me just why we're crossing the Rhine again?" Carbo asked.

"We're going to have a look and see what are old enemies are up to, if anything," Artorius replied. "A simple reconnaissance mission. Shouldn't take more than a couple of weeks to find out what their intentions are."

"There have also been rumors regarding the demise of Arminius," Magnus added. "I'm pretty certain Silius is looking to see if we can verify these."

"That will break a lot of hearts if he is dead," Gavius added, the sarcasm thick in his voice. "I just think it's a pity we didn't get that bastard when we had the chance!"

"But hey, at least our fearless leader here killed that other jackal, Ingiomerus," Valens remarked. "I mean come on, Artorius; you cannot tell us that that wasn't at least somewhat satisfying!" Artorius shrugged as he helped Magnus and Valens finish rolling up their tent and hoist it onto the cart.

"I didn't really notice at the time," he replied. "We were a little bit preoccupied trying to fight our way into that stronghold, and besides I did not know who he was. I just noticed that he was a lot older than most of the other warriors."

"If I remember right, it was one of the auxiliary troopers that identified him," Magnus remarked. "Germanicus had them check all the bodies and see if we had netted anyone of importance." Carbo and Gavius had finished inventorying their stakes and poles, and had set about bundling them up and loading them onto the cart as well. Carbo gave an audible sigh.

"You know, we haven't talked much about Germanicus since we received word of his death. You guys cannot tell me you haven't been thinking about it, though." Carbo had been thoroughly devoted to his former commander, in spite of the fact that the two had never met personally.

"Do you guys remember the night before Idistaviso, when the Aquilifer came and had supper with us?" Decimus asked.

"I remember that," Artorius replied. "I thought it was rather strange, but he seemed like a decent enough fellow."

"Well I heard from Camillus that that was not the Legion's Aquilifer, but rather it was Germanicus himself. He had decided to disguise himself as such, so that he could gather what he could about our morale and disposition." Everyone smiled and nodded at Decimus' statement, though none were necessarily surprised.

"You know, that actually doesn't surprise me," Magnus thought aloud. "What I want to know is, do you just like hanging out at the Principia, or what? You always seem to be the first one to find out anything that's going on." Decimus shrugged at the assessment.

"Camillus is an old friend of the Aquilifer, so we go and see him sometimes. His position gives him a lot of access to information the rest of us will never be privy to, which makes him quite the useful source. He has been keeping us informed as to all the latest gossip from Rome regarding Piso's trial."

"And you didn't think to share any of this with the rest of us?" Valens asked.

"I know the death of Germanicus is a painful subject for us all," Decimus answered, "so I've kept most of what Camillus has told me to myself."

"So what *did* he tell you?" Artorius persisted. Decimus paused before continuing.

"Only that it is getting bad in Rome," he replied. "All the supporters of Agrippina continue in their assault against the Emperor, blaming him for Germanicus' death."

"Agrippina, she's always been a bit of a puzzle to me," Carbo replied. "You know there were times when it seemed like she had a genuine concern for the lads, and others when she was standoffish and completely self-righteous."

"I had to deal with her once," Valens mused. "She seemed to think I was coming on to her." Carbo had been taking a drink from his water bladder, and at Valens' remarks he spewed water everywhere and started to laugh and cough uncontrollably.

"For the love of … why does that not surprise me, Valens?" he asked, completely perplexed.

"I don't even remember what I said," Valens remarked. "I wasn't even checking her out; it was her maidservant that had the really cute ass … anyway, Agrippina starts screaming at me, calling me all sorts of foul names. I didn't know whether to be insulted or flattered. Then she chases me out of the room with some sort of club in her hand! Of course she stopped when one of the Tribunes came in and saw the spectacle."

"You never told us about this!" Carbo said.

"Yeah, well I was a bit embarrassed that I had almost gotten thrashed by a woman. Tribune Pilate was very understanding and promised not to say a word to anyone." Artorius just shook his head and continued to load equipment onto their cart. They had all forgotten how they had even gotten on the subject in the first place, which suited Decimus just fine. He decided he would not tell them just yet what he had learned about the fate of Martina, the notorious alchemist.

✳   ✳   ✳   ✳

Martina ate greedily from the bowl of figs Livia offered her. The journey had been long and tiring, and she was still recovering from the shock of having been found by Livia's agents. She had no sooner sat down in the inn's tavern to eat when she was apprehended by three armed men. They brought her to a private room in the back where Livia sat alone at a table.

"You were a hard one to find," Livia said wryly with a genial smile. Martina smiled back and shrugged.

"When one does not wish to be discovered …" she left the rest of her reply hanging as she continued to eat.

"Do you take much pleasure in your trade?" Livia asked. Martina only shrugged.

"It's a job. I mean somebody has to be there to do the dirty work I suppose. I've been studying medicines and poison most of my life." Livia nodded politely.

"So tell me," she said, pouring Martina a goblet of wine, "how was it that you came into the employment of the Pisos?" Her interrogation of Plancina was fresh in her mind and she earnestly wished to know the truth. There was no doubt that Martina had acted as Germanicus' executioner, there was just the question of at whose bequest.

The portly woman paused in her eating. "From what I gathered, Plancina had been hounding Piso for some time to do something about Germanicus. She was never very committal though." She added and took a long drink of wine before continuing. "Piso was beside himself as to what to do. I swear that man could never make up his own mind!" She snorted and helped herself to the bread. "Finally I guess he decided he'd had enough and sent a servant to come see me. I took the job, of course. Though the price for an Imperial Prince was quite large, I assured him!"

"I'm sure it almost *bankrupted* him," Livia replied with a small laugh. Her demeanor was very pleasant, something that confirmed Martina's belief that Livia, as well as the Emperor himself, had been plotting Germanicus' downfall for some time.

Martina cared not for the intricacies of Imperial politics. In truth, she found the entire Julio-Claudian family to be rather perverse. When not fighting the world, they were fighting each other!

"So Plancina played no part in the ordeal, then?" Livia mused, hoping Martina would take the bait.

"I wouldn't say that," she replied and paused thoughtfully. "For once she was the one who was ambiguous as to what should be done. She knew by incurring Germanicus' ill will her husband was in jeopardy, not to mention that Agrippina—she's quite the vindictive one! I almost wish they had asked me to do her as well. I probably would have done it for free." The pleasant smile on Livia's face was no longer pleasant as Martina suddenly felt a stabbing pain in her belly.

"Oh, I must have eaten too fast!" she said with a short, unconvincing laugh. She began to feel hot and sticky. Sweat beaded on her forehead. She looked at Livia in alarm. The Empress' demeanor was no longer pleasant.

"You underestimated the Julio-Claudians, you really did," Livia said almost conversationally. "You obviously believe the slander and thought I could have been so ruthless as to have had a hand in the murder of my own blood? You are an abomination!" Martina was suddenly in a panic. Her stomach was turning in knots, and she was starting to feel dizzy. She went to reach for Livia, only to find that her hand was trembling badly, and refused to function properly.

Martina might have been little more than a peasant, but she was not stupid and realized why Livia arranged their "meeting." She tried to stand, but found her body was already too weak to support her bulk and she fell ungracefully on the floor.

"What is going to happen to me?" she asked, her eyes wide with panic. Livia stood over her.

"You should know. It's what you gave Germanicus." Her voice was ice as she continued. "I know history and slanderers will forever damn me, finding some way to connect me to his death. But my own conscience is clear, knowing that in my little way I avenged my grandson." Martina could only stare in terror, her mouth gaping like a fish. Her breath came in short gasps, her chest felt like it was in a vice. The pain in her belly spread through her body. In her fading vision she saw a man standing over her. Everything around her had turned to black, but he stood out clearly. The man was dressed as a legionary Legate; eyes were full of wrath, his sword drawn. She knew his face, and it terrified her.

He's come for me! she thought as what remained of her breathing came in short rasps. No longer could she speak, and all she could see was the form of the man seeking his revenge on her.

Livia walked over to the door and gave it a short rap. A man wearing a legionary tunic, sword belt, and cloak walked in and bowed.

"My friend seems to have fallen ill," Livia said, looking at Martina's body with mock concern. "Be so kind to see to it she is taken care of." With that she swept out of the room.

"Yes Lady," he replied.

CHAPTER 4

▼

RETURN TO GERMANIA

Ietano swallowed hard when he received word that Roman soldiers were approaching. It had been four years since he had seen a Roman. He had been wounded at Idistaviso, and arrived at the Angrivarii stronghold in time to watch the Romans destroy it. He claimed Bructeri heritage even though he was a Cherusci by blood and tried to put the scourge put on the disgraced and decimated Cherusci in the past. Being one of Arminius' closest confidants brought him much in the way of glory and honor. He since became chief of a small tribe of scattered Cherusci.

"How many?" he asked the young warrior who was trying to catch his breath after running a great distance to give Ietano the news.

"It appears to be a single Cohort," he answered. *Strange*, Ietano thought. *A single Cohort moving on its own?* Either the Romans had become more confidant to the point of being almost arrogant since their victory, or they were laying a trap to provoke war once again.

Ietano took a deep breath. "Summon the village elders," he ordered. "We will see what these Romans want. Rest assured that if an entire Cohort is moving our way there are more." A small gathering of the tribe leaders and warriors made their way towards the approaching legionaries.

As they walked through the thick woods and came upon a large clearing. Ietano was still impressed with the way the soldiers moved in step with one another, their red and gold shields close together, javelins protruding forward. They wore the standard armor of segmented plates, which caught the glint of the sun. Eight men marched abreast in the columns. At the head was a soldier bearing the Cohort's standard, and another that was unmistakably the Centurion Pilus Prior. His armor was adorned with his medals and decorations that set him apart from the other soldiers as well as the transverse crest that adorned the top of his helmet.

"Cohort … halt!" Proculus shouted. Artorius' section was directly behind Proculus in the front rank. He gazed with distain at the small gathering that arrived to meet them. It was a group of ten men, mostly elderly.

Artorius' mind briefly drifted back to a time of horrendous battles. He had been decorated for valor, having personally killed the war chief Ingiomerus, the uncle of Arminius. Though openly docile, the men who came to parlay with the Romans exuded a tension-filled air of hate. Their clansmen may have died by the thousands, but those who survived lost none of their will to fight, nor their lust for glory. Artorius snorted at the notion. He had found honor in serving as a soldier of Rome, but not the elusive "glory" that supposedly accompanied it. To him glory was just a word one used to compel men to perform as one's puppet. Julius Caesar had often spoken of it, and yet what of the men who had executed the horrific tasks he had set them to? Was there glory for them? Perhaps, but it was fleeting at best.

A small number of warriors had started to gather behind their village elders. One in particular stared at Artorius. He was slightly irritated with the barbarian's blatant stare.

"Find out what you can here," Proculus told Macro. "I'll take the rest of the Cohort on ahead."

"Yes Sir," Macro replied. Ietano approached the Centurion as the rest of the Third Cohort continued its march.

"What business brings the legions of Rome to our lands?" He asked as neutrally as possible. "It has been some years since we've seen soldiers venture across the Rhine."

"Circumstances were slightly different then," Macro replied politely. "We have come to make certain that your people remain peaceful and are no threat to Roman interests."

"If you see us as a threat, why not just come and conquer our lands?" one warrior blurted out. "Is that not the Roman way?" Ietano blanched at the man's outburst. Before he could speak, Macro turned to the warrior.

"Do not try my patience, *barbarian*. If you doubt that Rome can take your lands at leisure, think back to the final days of the war four years ago." Macro strained to keep his voice as neutral as Ietano. "You are Cherusci are you not?"

Ietano hissed at the brash warrior to keep silent then said, "The Cherusci are no more," He sighed resignedly. "Your attempt to exterminate all of us may have failed, but you succeeded in wiping out the Cherusci influence from these lands."

Artorius was a little surprised to hear the bitter regret in his voice as if he were almost ashamed of his blood.

"What of Arminius?" Macro asked, seeing no need to delay looking for what he sought. "You practically revered him as a god, and yet his head was offered to the Emperor after the war."

"Arminius is dead. He was recently murdered by some of the other chiefs, hoping Rome would not return to our lands and leave us in peace." He snorted, "such a waste that was!"

"Indeed. You did not play a role in his death, then?" Macro asked bluntly. Ietano raised his head proudly.

"*I* stood by Arminius till the very end. I am proud to have fought beside such a magnificent warrior and chief!"

Macro nodded and gave a dismissive wave of the hand. Just then the warrior who had been staring at Artorius stepped forward purposefully.

"*Murderer!*" he screamed, pointing towards Artorius who raised his eyebrows.

"Who in the bloody hell …" Macro began when Ietano stepped in front of the raging warrior putting himself between the enraged warrior and Artorius.

"No, Thrax! This is not the way; we are no longer at war with Rome!"

"To hell with Rome!" Thrax spat. "My sister and her children died at his hands! They had no part in that war!"

"What in the name of Mercury is this man ranting about?" Macro sighed exasperated. He secured the information they came for and he wanted to leave. The barbarians' stink carried on the wind. Unfortunately, the Legion was downwind.

Thrax's outburst caused a stir amongst the warriors, and suddenly Macro found himself wishing that Proculus had not left them there.

"This bastard ran his sword through my sister! He murdered her children!"

"Instead of fighting, like the rest of the warriors in your tribe," Artorius replied calmly, "you hid like a scared little girl?" Then he bit his tongue. *Nice going, Artorius,* he said to himself. *That's just going to make things worse.*

Thrax screamed in rage and he tried to push his way past Ietano who stood fast in his way. The warrior was a big man, taller than Artorius by a few inches, though leaner in physique. A great two-handed sword was strapped to his otherwise bare back. The Sergeant looked over at his Centurion, who gave a curt nod. Artorius steeled himself to fight the enraged German.

"If your man is so bent on destroying me, he can have me." Artorius planted his javelin in the ground and stepped out from the formation. Ietano still did not move out of the way.

"I think it is only fair, and in the spirit of your people's warrior traditions, that these two men be allowed to settle their differences," Macro observed, his arms folded across his chest. Ietano shook his head.

"This is not the way to keep peace with Rome," he replied.

"Kill him and cut out his heart, Thrax!" a young boy shouted as he pushed his way to the front of the crowd. No older than twelve, he carried a spear and shield tailored for his size.

Artorius snorted in contempt. "Your grievance with me is about your sister and her children yet *you* also send children to their deaths?" He paused and continued, "that is not the *Roman* way."

"That will do, Sergeant." Macro said quietly, privately pleased with Artorius' daring remark.

At Ietano's command a few other warriors surrounded Thrax and half pushed, half dragged him to the back of the crowd. He raised his voice so that all could hear him, "This is *not* the way!"

Artorius let out a deep breath. It wasn't that he was afraid to fight, he was confident his greater bulk and skill could take down the berserker, but he was concerned about the retributions even though he didn't start it.

To everyone's surprise the boy shouted and charged Artorius, who neatly stepped aside and tripped the youth. Spear and shield flew out of his hands when he hit the ground. Quickly Artorius straddled the boy and closed his hand around the small neck. Not enough to hurt more than bruises, but enough to make it clear that he could snap the boy's neck at will.

"I am a *soldier of Rome*," he hissed. "My battle is not against children, although I will kill them if ordered." The boy's eyes were wide with fear.

A warrior who appeared to be the boy's older brother stepped forward. "Please let him go. He is young and should not be here." Artorius nodded and stood. The boy allowed himself to be led away.

Macro cleared his throat and broke the awkward silence. "Let us consider this matter to be resolved. Understand that any further acts of violence will be perceived as open war against Rome Herself. I am certain you understand full well the consequences of this." He glared at Ietano and the other elders to let the words sink in. The German chief was breathing hard through his nose, but eventually he raised his hand and waved his warriors off. He then stepped forward, face to face with Centurion Macro.

"I agree with your words. But take heed, Roman. There will never be true peace between our nations. We will always be in the background of your thoughts and nightmares, watching, waiting. Maybe not in my lifetime, but one day Rome will fall."

"You will always be a scourge to us I have no doubt," Macro replied, dryly. "Take heed and realize that any such attempts against the might of Rome will end in fire and blood, as you are all too familiar. Good day." With that he turned his back on the chieftain, an insult not lost on Ietano, and ended their meeting. Artorius watched as Ietano started to wave his warriors back towards the village.

"Think they will try anything?" Flaccus asked Macro as the Century marched away.

"I don't know," Macro replied. "I doubt if that chief has any real fight left in him, however the warriors look like they still have plenty. It comes down to how much control he has over them. We will take no chances."

"Understood," Flaccus replied.

✳   ✳   ✳   ✳

The court was crammed with people. The Emperor sat at the head of the chamber, on a raised platform. He appeared nonchalant, but he stewed inside. He made it a point to not talk with Piso in private. Any private discussions between them would be perceived as some kind of negotiation. Senators sat on benches on either side of the Emperor. They came to bear judgment in conjunction with the Emperor, who would pass any necessary sentence.

Piso, his wife, and son sat behind a table surrounded by his defense counsel. The table occupied by the prosecution was crowded to say the least. Four prosecutors, Germanicus' widow, Agrippina, his brother, Claudius, and the Emperor's own son, Drusus, sat together. At length, the prosecutor Vitellius stood to address the Senate and Emperor.

"Caesar, members of the Senate, I come before you today to bear witness against Cnaeus Calpurnius Piso, a man who has sought to further his own interests through sedition, rebellion and even murder. Not only have his acts disrupted already troubled provinces, but the murder of the Emperor's own adopted son, Germanicus Caesar, has deprived Rome of one of her greatest and most competent statesman.

"On the charge of sedition, I give you the following. That while en route to Syria, Piso did needlessly rouse the anger of the citizens of Athens with his volatile and hostile speech. And when ordered by his senior, Germanicus, to send troops to aid him in his Armenia campaign, Piso blatantly refused to do so. Were it not for the competent generalship and diplomacy of Germanicus, the entire province could have been lost. Piso even went so far as to lavish gifts upon the most insolent and unsavory of troops in the province, seeking to gain their favor. Those with distinguished records and superior conduct he either ignored or treated with disdain out of their allegiance to Germanicus, and therefore the Emperor! And when Germanicus fell ill, he accused Piso *by name* of having been attempting to poison him. On his temporary recovery, the people of the east rejoiced. Piso had the audacity to send attendants to disperse them in Antioch!" Vitellius paused briefly. Piso was fidgeting in his chair. He wiped his brow with a handkerchief and swallowed hard. Vitellius continued:

"On the charge of rebellion, of which his son Cneius is also accused," Plancina quietly wept at this. "Germanicus had ordered Piso out of Syria, which he only complied with reluctantly. Upon Germanicus' death, Piso immediately returned to Syria, in spite of the Legate Sentius having been lawfully appointed in his place. Piso then took the town of Celenderis for himself, and even engaged Sentius in open battle. Amongst the charges of rebellion, I recommend that Piso be held liable for the death of every Roman soldier who perished in his pursuit of vain glory!"

There was an eruption of applause from the Senators, many of whom were shaking their fists furiously at Piso. The defendant stared at the Emperor, the slightest smirk crossing his face. He knew what the final charges were, and in that he looked for salvation from the Emperor. Vitellius patiently waited a moment for the disruption to die down.

"And on the final charge of murder, of which his wife, Plancina, is also accused, I offer this. That throughout Germanicus' quarters all sorts of foul and demonic objects were found. Body parts of humans, unholy spells on lead tablets, animal corpses, all the makings of barbaric witchcraft. Again, when his death became imminent, Germanicus accused Piso by name. He also asked that his survivors pursue full justice in his name. Be it known that a notorious poisoner named Martina had been sent to bear witness to the fact that she assisted Plancina and Piso in the gradual poisoning and death of Germanicus. She acted as the executioner to their diabolical plot!"

At this time, the defense counsel for Piso rose and spoke. "It is known that a woman named Martina was in fact bound for Rome. However it would seem that she met with an unfortunate end herself, probably at the hands of one of her own concoctions!" The man spoke lightly, which did not amuse the Emperor and enraged the Senators.

"On the charges of poisoning and murder, it would seem that the prosecution has no case, given that their star witness is unable to testify. It is the final piece of a flimsy attempt at prosecution of a fine and honorable statesman of Rome. One I might add, who was appointed by the Divine Augustus! Therefore we ask that the charges be dismissed."

There was an immediate uproar from Senators that was deafening. It seemed that all order was abandoned as they shouted and jeered at the defense.

"Request denied!" Tiberius boomed. It was the first words he had spoken all day since calling the court to order. There was immediate silence. The face of Piso, as well as his counsel, paled. Outside the crowds screamed for Piso's blood. Plancina grabbed one of the defense councils by the tunic and whispered frantically into his ear. The man looked at her puzzled, and grimaced when she nodded, nudged him hard.

"At this time," he began, "my client has requested that she and her son's defenses be conducted separately from her husband." Piso could not believe what he was hearing. His eyes grew wide in disbelief that his wife was abandoning him. Vitellius glanced over at the Emperor, who bowed his head in consent.

"Very well, Plancina and Cneius Piso will be tried separately and at a different time. For now they will remain in protective custody until their day in the courts." Plancina and Cneius were quickly escorted out of the hall. Piso looked like a broken man. He sat with his head in his hands, the feeling of abandonment overpowering his senses. His defense counsel asked for a recess until the morrow, which Tiberius granted. Piso had to be helped from the chamber as he saw his hope of vindication vanishing.

✳   ✳   ✳   ✳

The night was dark and cloudy. With only a partial moon trying to force its light through the cloud cover, it was nearly impossible to see in front of one's face. Artorius watched intently, all senses heightened. Though he was not required to stand sentry duty, he still took it upon himself to take a shift, lest he get caught unawares by renegade barbarians. He looked around at their tiny camp. It still had the standard palisade and ditch, though the entrance was little more than an overlapping section of the rampart, used to slow down any possible attackers. One soldier from each section was on sentry duty at all times, with two more guarding the entrance. The clearing they occupied was surrounded by forest on all sides, adding an ominous sense of not being completely alone. No light was allowed in hopes of making it more difficult for the Germans to find the camp. The Century was on its own, having failed to catch up with Proculus and the rest of the Cohort. This had visibly frustrated Macro, who did not like the idea of having to camp anywhere on the eastern side of the Rhine. The forests still gave him nightmares of Teutoburger Wald.

Artorius walked over to the entrance and nearly ran into Praxus, who was standing guard with one of his soldiers. Praxus nodded in acknowledgment. Noise discipline was being strictly enforced. It was preferred that if any barbarians were out this night, that they should pass by, unaware of the presence of Roman soldiers. If the barbarians were feeling hostile, which they probably were judging from the way the confrontation progressed earlier, they would have little difficulty in mustering enough forces to overwhelm the tiny camp. Macro knew that any potential attack would be met with shock and surprise. They would have to catch the barbarians off guard and make them forget that the Romans' numbers were few.

One of the sentries grabbed Praxus by the shoulder, pointing into the blackness of the woods not fifty meters in front of them. A cluster of torches could be seen moving their way, though it was hard to tell just how many. Artorius gave his fellow section leader a friendly smack on the shoulder and went to rouse his men. Most were half awake as it was. All had elected to leave their armor on.

In utter silence the Century formed up behind the section of palisade that faced the coming enemy. The plan had been rehearsed a dozen times; everyone knew what to do. Macro, at the head of the formation, peered around the entrance to the camp. In spite of their torches, the Germans were stumbling, practically blind. Many cursed their folly in a language few of the Romans understood. Macro was one of those few. He smiled recognizing a particularly explicit curse as one warrior stumbled and fell into the ditch. It seemed as if the barbarians turned to see their companion's misstep. They were laughing and pointing until a few realized exactly what it was their friend had stumbled into.

"Now!" Macro shouted. With lightening speed the soldiers of the Second Century flew out of the entrance to their camp in two lines. Macro led the first line, Optio Flaccus the second. As soon as the last soldiers cleared the entrance, Macro barked his next set of orders.

"Front rank, action right! Javelins ... throw!" The barbarians were caught completely unawares as javelins cut swaths into their ranks. Artorius found a target in the dim light and let his javelin fly. It caught the barbarian in the throat, which

seemed to explode, his windpipe and esophagus ripped out the back of his neck, a gushing spray of blood in their wake. The barbarian's eyes bulged from their sockets, arms flailing wildly as the weight of the javelin jerked him to the ground, nearly decapitating him in the process. A number of the Germans were skewered and knocked into the trench.

"Second rank … go!" Macro commanded.

"With me!" Optio Flaccus shouted. At a dead run, he ran around the far end of the first rank, took a hard right and moved perpendicular with the rest of the Century, flanking the barbarians. Once in position, they too let loose a torrent of javelins upon the hapless barbarians.

"Gladius … draw!" both Centurion and Optio bellowed. *"Advance!"* Caught between the palisade and two formations of Roman soldiers, the surviving barbarians knew they had been beat and threw down their arms. The legionaries advanced to within a few feet of their adversaries.

"Do we take prisoners?" Flaccus asked. Macro nodded affirmatively.

"Bind their hands and feet and then tie their foot bonds together," he ordered. He then turned to Praxus and Artorius.

"Sergeant Praxus, Sergeant Artorius, take your men and start fetching timber; long pieces that will support the weight of a man. Tesserarius Statorius, set up a security detail to cover them. Optio Flaccus, delegate men to guard the prisoners and then come with me. *Camillus!"* The Centurion walked off with the Signifier as Flaccus delegated men to bind and guard the prisoners. Artorius and Praxus knew exactly why their Centurion had asked for timber, even though he had given no specific instructions. Their gut instincts told them the truth.

"Oh you are so evil!" Camillus said with a cruel smirk after Macro had revealed his plan. Flaccus only frowned and nodded.

"If that doesn't serve as a warning, nothing will," the older Optio observed. Groans could be heard coming from the wounded as they lay broken and bleeding.

"Please … mercy. Our wounded …" one barbarian said in broken Latin. The prisoners were on their knees, their feet and hands bound. One of the guards walked over to the man and kicked him viciously in the back of the head.

"How about that for mercy?" he spat.

"Enough!" Macro barked. He then turned to his Signifier. "Camillus take a couple of men and show some mercy."

"You've got it, Macro," he replied grimly, drawing his gladius. The cries of the wounded were cut short with efficient slashes and stabs. Camillus and a pair of legionaries could be seen walking amongst the fallen barbarians, finishing off any who were still alive. This elicited further cries of anguish from their fellows. One was cursing violently in his native tongue. The words struck a chord with Macro, who abruptly turned and faced the man. He strode quickly to the prisoner and kicked him in the face, speaking to the man in his tongue. None of the legionaries understood the words their Centurion spat, though they knew they must have been brutal, given the barbarian's fearful reaction to them.

"Hey, how many of these prisoners do we need to fix up?" Artorius asked, walking up.

"Optio Flaccus?" Macro asked over his shoulder.

"Eighteen, Sir. We counted another thirty-five among their dead. The rest ran off into the night." Macro nodded and turned to Artorius, who nodded in turn and went back to his task. The Decanus returned to his section to find them standing over the body of a slain barbarian.

"What is it?" he asked, confused by the somber faces of his men.

"Seems we found a friend of yours," Valens replied in a low voice. Artorius looked down and felt his stomach turn at the sight of the young boy who had attacked him in the village; a javelin burrowed into his chest, pinning him to the ground. The soft metal shaft was bent, the weight ripping open the boy's ribcage. The lad was covered in blood; a copious amount of which he had vomited over himself as he had struggled in the throes of death. Artorius closed his eyes and shook his head. Magnus smacked him on the shoulder with the back of his hand and pointed towards one of the prisoners.

"That one looks familiar too, doesn't he?" he asked, an evil glint in his eye.

"That he does," Artorius replied, his anger rising. "I've got something special in mind for him."

As the sun dawned, the barbarian prisoners were horrified by what they saw. Eighteen crudely made crosses lay in a long line; a post hole was dug in front of each. A detail of soldiers stood ready to execute their grizzly task. Macro walked in front of the prisoners who lay prostrate on their stomachs and spoke to them in their own tongue.

"You vile scum deliberately violated the peace that has existed between our peoples for nearly four years. You have made open war on Rome, thereby imperiling your villages and your entire tribe. I do not believe that your actions had the authorization of your chiefs. If they had, surely they would have sent more than such a pathetic lot as you!" He spat on the ground in front of them to emphasize his point.

"Be cheerful that your families and loved ones will be spared from Rome's wrath. You however, shall not." With that, he turned and nodded to Statorius, whose job it was to oversee the executions. The Tesserarius signaled to Artorius, Praxus, and Sergeant Rufio. All three brought their sections forward, each surrounding a prisoner.

"Hello Thrax," Artorius said icily. The barbarian looked up at him in disgust. "Remember me? Of course you do; I am the one who has haunted your dreams, the source of all of your hate. You should have died all those years ago like a man and a warrior. Instead the death of a coward awaits you."

"I piss on you, Roman dog," Thrax replied in broken Latin. Artorius replied with a sinister smile. They cut the cords binding Thrax to his fellow warriors, and dragged him to his fate. Other prisoners continued to wail and beg for mercy. One thrashed about so much, that it provoked a guard into bringing the bottom of his shield down hard on the man's neck.

"Just relax, you're turn will come soon enough," he said casually, as the German cried in sorrow.

Crucifixion was among the most languishing and agonizing means of execution. It involved hanging the condemned from an upright pole planted in the ground; his arms stretched out on a crossbeam. The ankles and wrists were then tied in place. Nails could be used, though this was extremely rare. The condemned would slowly suffocate as their overstretched lungs struggled to take in breath; fatigue would set in, combined with severe dehydration. Death came slowly over a period of many hours, sometimes days.

Artorius' hatred for the barbarians had lain dormant for the last several years. The attack the night before and the sight of the slain child brought it back to the surface. Thrax remained silent, though is breath was coming in rapid gasps. Once they reached the line of crucifixes, Artorius drew his gladius and smashed the prisoner across the face with the pommel.

Magnus held Thrax down as Artorius cut the bonds. Valens and Carbo each grabbed an arm, Gavius and Decimus taking the legs. The barbarian was a big man; however he was helpless in the grip of six legionaries. He cried and moaned as he was tied to the cross and hauled to the hole that would hold it up. The hole had been dug right in the middle of a massive ant hill. Large black ants swarmed the ground in frenzy from having their lair disturbed so violently.

"We thought you could use some new friends," Artorius sneered as soon as the cross was placed in the ground. With his gladius he made several vicious slashes across the warrior's body. The man moaned in pain, his eyes rolling into the back of his head as blood seeped from the wounds. He came alive as he was swarmed by the ants, who sought the exposed wounds with hunger and fury. Unholy screams came from the crucified prisoner as his flesh was bitten into in a thousand different places. Artorius glanced over to see Rufio and Praxus had gotten their prisoners up as well. All three sections went back to fetch their next lot, all the while ignoring the screams of despair and agony coming from the crucified and the soon to be crucified.

Camillus stood to the side looking at the sign he had completed. Though it had seemed like a good idea at the time, writing a sign in blood was no easy task. It had been rather messy and the Signifier was constantly wiping his hands on a cloth that he had stuffed into his belt.

"Think any of those uneducated bastards can even read?" he asked Macro and Flaccus, both of whom were watching the crucifixions.

"I'm sure there's somebody amongst the village elders who can read," Macro replied.

"Well I hope so. You know I hate getting all messy for nothing," Camillus fussed as he carried the sign over to the crucifixion line. In front of the line of wailing and groaning men, he hammered the sign into the ground. In large letters it gave a stern warning to add to the grotesque scene that would greet those who came in search of their missing warriors.

Next time, it will be your women and children

Artorius stood back and gazed at the spectacle as another section took over for his. In all they had crucified five of the prisoners. Each had been an ordeal. All had fought and struggled, even more so after they saw their companion being tortured by the swarm of ants that devoured him. By the time they had finished with their last prisoner all were breathing hard and drenched in sweat.

"Well there is a sight one doesn't forget anytime soon," Decimus observed.

"You got that right," Magnus concurred. "Artorius, you are one cruel bastard. Whatever inspired you to plant that bastard right on top of an ant hill?"

"When I stumbled across them in the dark and they bit the crap out of me," the Sergeant replied, eyes still gazing forward, arms folded.

"Always the practical one," Carbo said; his face even more flushed than usual.

"Fucking beastly task," a legionary said in a low voice. Artorius turned to look at the lad. He was very young and probably new to the legions since Artorius did not recognize him. The soldier's face was pale and clammy. He removed his helmet and started to feverishly wipe the sweat from his brow.

"First action?" Artorius asked over his shoulder, his arms folded across his chest. The legionary could only nod in reply. Taking part in a crucifixion was no easy task, no matter how hardened a veteran was. Though when taken in comparison to some of the more odious deeds he had done, Artorius felt that this was rather tame.

He closed his eyes as the memories of his last campaign flooded into his conscious. The assault on the stronghold at Angrivarii had been particularly brutal. He recalled Magnus being unable to kill a barbarian child. Artorius had murdered the boy himself right after slaying his mother; oh yes, it was *murder*. He had survived battles, covered in blood of slain enemies, and felt nothing. And yet the killing of children sat hard with him. He was simply following orders, and he even knew that if such children had been allowed to live they would only grow into men bent on revenge against Rome. So why did it haunt him so? He rarely spoke of it, though he suspected he was not the only one who suffered from these feelings. Compared to the horrors he had already taken part in during his life in the legions, crucifying a few barbarians paled in comparison.

In relatively short order the crucifixions were completed. The loud cries of anguish had given away to a constant drone of groans, curses and barbaric prayers. Macro then turned to Statorius and gave one final order.

"Break their legs. Let us be certain that no one is able to rescue these pathetic excuses for men."

Statorius nodded and waved several men forward. With pickaxes and stones, they proceeded to break the legs of the prisoners. This in turn elicited fresh cries of agony and pain, which soon died down as the soldiers finished their grim task.

"Alright, let's get the hell out of here," Macro directed. *"Second Century … fall in!"*

As they marched away from the dying prisoners Artorius felt a sense of righteous vengeance as well as feeling sickened by what he had done and witnessed. He would not shirk his duty to Rome, but privately hoped he wouldn't have to partake in another crucifixion soon.

*   *   *   *

The arms manufacturing was on schedule, though finding potential recruits was proving to be difficult. Sacrovir sent recruiting parties throughout the nearby region in order to find the most suitable candidates. Secrecy was a must, of course, and he was confining his efforts to the Gallic hierarchy. His intent was to subvert them, and they in turn would bring their people into the fold of rebellion. A number of desperate men, debtors and thieves mostly, had gotten wind of Sacrovir's intents and had mustered to his calling.

He walked through the ranks of the few hundred who had shown up. They were a sorry lot, most of them, however Sacrovir figured with suitable arms and training, they would prove their worth. Besides, they were nothing more than a means to an end for him. For Sacrovir it was only partially about liberating Gaul from Roman rule; for him it was personal. As he passed by some of the men who would later fight and die for him, he saw one that made him pause.

Sacrovir looked him up and down. The man was better groomed than the others, his face and clothes well kept and clean, his beard cut short. "You're a Greek, aren't you?" he asked the man, who nodded.

"My name is Heracles of Sparta."

"Sparta?" Sacrovir asked, raising an eyebrow. "You claim heritage to a nation that scarcely exists and is but a shadow of its former glory."

"It exists in the hearts of all true lovers of freedom, those who would gladly die to be rid of this yoke of Roman tyranny. You will find that I am a warrior worthy of Sparta." Heracles' face was hard, his eyes cold. He spoke very eloquently, his grammar and speech impeccable. His immaculate clothing and clean appearance took away from his appearance of being a warrior, though his cold, dark eyes told a different story.

"Indebted to the Romans are you?"

"Not anymore," came the reply. "The Romans took my land, my home and everything I loved when I failed to make good on a debt. Unfortunately, it was to the Roman Governor who seized my home as payment. When I tried to resist, I was sold into slavery, as were my wife and children. I was first a gladiator, where I honed my fighting skills. When it was discovered that I could read and write, I was then sold to the house of a wealthy family, to educate their children. I escaped only recently."

"And what special skills are you bringing to our enterprise?" Sacrovir asked.

"I know the Romans, and how they fight," Heracles replied, confidently. "And as a former teacher, I can school your men in how to face the legions. I will teach them in a matter befitting a Spartan!"

"You will indeed serve us well," Sacrovir said warmly. "Walk with me, and we will discuss how you will train these men to become warriors."

While Sacrovir was welcoming his Greek friend into the fold, two rather haggard-looking men were approaching the compound along the narrow dirt road.

"Is that the place?" Radek asked, gazing at the confusing scene in the distance with his good eye; the other covered by a patch. Wagons, horses, and men were milling about, jockeying to try and get through the gates first.

"I think so," his companion Ellard replied. To call Ellard a friend was a bit of a stretch. Both men escaped a prison caravan that was bound for the sulfur mines in Mauretania and were only together because for the time being they seemed to need each other.

Those pathetic slave drivers had been clumsy at best! It had been a simple matter of Ellard distracting one of the guards long enough for Radek to strangle him with a bit of rope that had bound their cage together. Only they had escaped; the others either being recaptured or killed.

As they walked down the path that led to Sacrovir's compound, Ellard contemplated how he had come to this; actually considering fighting in a madman's rebellion against the most fearsome army the world had ever known. He had been a simple gardener for a Roman magistrate most of his life. His master had treated him well, though Ellard had often stolen coin and food from the senile old man. He also had a knack for picking fights with the other servants, whom he used to intimidate into helping him to steal. He was an attractive man; the scruff of his face and devious behavior allowing him to effortlessly work his way into the beds and confidences of many women. His wooing of the women slaves in his master's house had allowed him to carry out his thievery unscathed.

Ellard had expected to be freed upon his master's death; however nothing of this was mentioned in his will. He was returned to the slave market. There his volatile temper would again prove to be his undoing. After a severe flogging for accosting the site overseer, Ellard was sold cheap to a man from Mauretania looking for strong labor. It was on the caravan, in a cage that Ellard met Radek. His recent companion spoke little about himself, though from what Ellard was able to discern the man had a bitter disposition and unhappy past. The only thing he had ever said regarding this was that he had not been born a slave, leading Ellard to assume he was a criminal of some sort who had been sold into slavery.

Ellard was not a bad man; at least not by his own estimation. All he desired was to live free; though what he would do with his freedom he had no idea. He knew that his temper and lack of judgment had caused many of the trials he had faced in life and he wondered if his judgment would fail him again in this venture. His hair had grown long and unkempt following his sale back into slavery, and he no longer shaved his face. His constitution was sound, though lack of food had taken its toll on him over the past week. Since fleeing from the slave caravan they had been on the run. The reward for an escaped slave was more than enough to convince the two men to lay low. It was in a small back alley in Lugdunum that Radek had met one of his 'associates' who informed them of Sacrovir's bloody plans.

"Hard to believe this man is building an army to fight Rome," Ellard remarked.

"Believe it," Radek replied curtly. "And where there's fighting, there's bound to be plenty of coin and plunder."

Ellard could not fault Radek for being driven by want of money. He knew that if he was going to have any chance at a new life, he too would need money and lots of it. Certainly Sacrovir would pay a stipend upfront, with more to follow once the Roman garrisons were destroyed.

*   *   *   *

As the Second Century was making its camp for the night, Centurion Proculus rode up on his horse. The Cohort Commander gave a smirk when he found his subordinate Centurion. Macro had removed his armor and was furiously swinging a pickaxe to break up the thick clay in the surrounding ditch. Several legionaries were working beside him with pickaxes and baskets to scoop away the debris.

"Macro what are you doing?" he asked as soon as he dismounted his horse. Macro looked up and smiled. He posted the pickaxe at the top of the ditch and used it to pull himself out.

"My arms are as good as any," he replied nonchalantly. "Besides, it does the men good to see their officers getting dirty right along with them." As a point of emphasis, he pointed past Proculus to where Camillus and Statorius were planting palisade stakes with a section of legionaries. Proculus shook his head but could not conceal his grin.

"Any news?" Macro asked. The senior Centurion nodded.

"We're to change course and head north," he replied. Macro raised his eyebrows.

"North, eh? So where exactly are we going?"

"Batavia," Proculus replied. Macro blew out a deep breath in a whistle. Marching to Batavia and back would add at least another month to their expedition. Proculus continued, "The Batavi played a crucial role in the campaigns against Arminius. This was quite a gamble for them, given their proximity to Germania and the Cherusci. The tribes of Germania may have been shattered by the war, but that does not stop them from conducting raids of Roman allied lands as a means of retribution. We need to reassure the Batavi that Rome still stands by them and will come to their aid if need be."

Macro nodded. "I understand."

"So what are the women like?" Valens asked. Artorius chuckled. Aside from Magnus none of them had been to Batavia and yet somehow he knew what Valens' initial response would be.

"They're big amazons that kind of look like our friend Magnus," he replied. An incredulous grin spread over Valens' face as he turned towards the Nordic legionary who was hefting his pack over his shoulder as the Century readied itself to march.

"Is that true?" he asked. Magnus shrugged.

"Let's just say it takes a special kind of man to handle one of them," he remarked with a faux reminiscence. "They don't *all* have beards." Valens hooted with laughter and slapped Magnus on the shoulder. "Actually the Batavi are mostly cattle farmers. They love their land and are very particular towards it; hence why they did not attempt to claim any of the Cherusci lands after the war."

"Second Century!" Macro shouted from atop his horse. *"Forward ... march!"* At a slow and methodical pace the century made its way through the forests. At times they were able to utilize trails cut by the barbarians; at others they had to make their way through the dense masses of trees and undergrowth.

"At least the march home will be easier," Decimus observed as he pushed some low-hanging branches out of the way with his shield. These in turn snapped back and caught Carbo on the side of his helmet.

"That's true," Gavius said over the smattering of profanity from Carbo. "I forgot that the main highway parallels the west side of the Rhine and leads straight to Cologne."

"Just how far north does that road go?" Carbo asked picking pine needles out of his helmet.

"All the way to the sea," Magnus answered. "It serves as the border between the Batavi lands and the Roman Empire."

"Okay, I've got a question about that," Gavius interrupted. "Most of us refer to Rome as being an empire, and yet I remember back in Rome hearing a lot of the older folks still referring to it as the Republic. So which is it?"

"Does it really matter?" Artorius asked, stepping over a fallen log. "Rome abolished kings more than five hundred years ago and the very thought of a monarch does not sit well with the average Roman. That was what led to Julius Caesar's downfall; his enemies feared that he wished to crown himself king and they murdered him for it. Octavian was more subtle about his rise to power."

"I wouldn't call it subtle," Decimus conjectured. "I mean after all he did end up fighting two civil wars in his rise to power."

"True," Artorius conceded. "Though the first at least wasn't necessarily about power; it was about revenge. Octavian needed to bring Caesar's murderers to justice. As for the second war … well, Antony and Cleopatra brought that upon themselves." The rest of the section nodded in reply. Marc Antony had been a Roman soldier and statesman, so of course they were bound to feel a bit sympathetic towards him. Cleopatra on the other hand was viewed as a heartless and diabolical woman who brought about the destruction of her own nation in an attempt to satisfy her own selfish desires.

"While I appreciate the history lesson," Gavius said, "that still doesn't answer my question."

Artorius ignored the remark and continued, "After Octavian's final victory over Antony and Cleopatra, he was given the honorary title of *Princeps,* or *First Citizen.* He was quite clever, refusing to be awarded the title of dictator. He was allowed to wear the Civic Crown; for in the eyes of the Roman people he had saved them all. None of his titles or honors gave him any actual power; it was through manipulating the Senate and the constitution of the Republic that he was given absolute power. Four years after Actium Octavian was given the name *Augustus.* The Senate believed that they had their Republic back, while Octavian became Emperor Augustus Caesar."

"Funny how even the most educated of men can be fooled by a façade that the plebeians could see through," Magnus said thoughtfully. "My grandfather served under Octavian during the wars against Antony and Cleopatra. To this day he laughs at the Senate's arrogance and blindness. He could not for the life of him figure out how both Caesar and Antony were so smitten by Cleopatra. He tells me she had a big nose."

"I didn't know 'Mad Olaf' was still alive," Decimus said.

"Alive, and as mad as ever," Magnus grinned as the century made its way onto a dirt road that cut through the forest. "His great hall looks like a Roman Proconsul's palace, and yet he still dresses and looks like a Norseman. I got a letter from him the other day. He said that he's thinking about coming to Rome this fall for the celebration of the fifty-first anniversary of the Battle of Actium; or as he calls it, *the day we gave that Alexandrian twat a damn good spanking!*" Talk of Magnus' deranged grandfather elicited a chuckle from the section. "You know, he's probably one of the only veterans of that battle that's still alive."

"*Anyway,* I think the Senate was just tired after all those years of civil war," Artorius continued, ignoring his friends' sidebar conversation. "Plus they were probably relieved that Octavian never sought to crown himself king and refused the dictatorship."

"His being awarded the Civic Crown was a clever means of getting a crown though," Gavius observed.

As the Century made its way along the forest road they saw an old man and two young children coming their way. The man was leading an oxcart laden with timber. The boy rode on top of the cart and the young girl carried a basket full of berries that she picked while walking beside her grandfather. The old man's eyes grew wide in terror as his gaze fell upon the Signum that Camillus carried. He had seen those standards before, and with them they brought death. The legionaries were not an overly impressive sight; leather covers hid the bright colors of their shields, packs weighed them down like mules, and most had their helmets off and strapped to their packs. Still the old man knew better and the horrors of a thousand memories wracked his conscious. His grandchildren on the other hand, had never seen Roman soldiers before and did not know what they were. The girl ran towards them, curiosity getting the best of her. She reached into her basket and offered a couple of blueberries to Decimus. The legionary smiled, set his shield down, and accepted the berries the girl placed in his hand. He promptly ate them and ruffled her hair before picking up his shield and continuing on his way. He saw Carbo staring at him out of the corner of his eye.

"My daughter is about the same age," Decimus said smiling. Carbo just nodded.

The old man called out to his granddaughter who ran happily back to him, laughing all the while. She did not notice the sheer terror in her grandfather's eyes. He grabbed both of the children and held them close as the century marched past them, hands trembling. As the last of the legionaries moved past his wagon, he still held his grandchildren close.

CHAPTER 5

▼

BATAVIA

The Century did not see any more barbarians after the encounter with the old man and the children. If there were Germans watching them, they did so from a safe distance deep within the forests. En route to the Batavian border they encountered the Ahenobarbi bridges.

As the bridges came into sight, Artorius caught sight of two other Centuries approaching from different directions. One was the Fourth, under command of Centurion Dominus. Artorius smiled when he saw the standard of the other Century. It was Centurion Vitruvius' Third Century. It looked as if they had split off from Proculus as well. All three Cohorts were not due to link up for another day, so the Centuries made camp for the night on the remains of the fort they had erected five years before. That evening, Artorius was taking a walk along the perimeter with Magnus and Decimus.

"Quite a bit different than the last time we were here," Decimus observed.

"Yeah, we're not surrounded by thousands of barbarians looking to eat our guts for breakfast!" Magnus added. Artorius gazed out onto the plains which they had fought the battle.

"This place is a massive graveyard," he said coldly. "Can you not feel it? Thousands died here. On these very ramparts they were cut down." Magnus thought back to that day, the day where they snatched victory and triumph from the very jaws of death and defeat.

"I remember watching those bastards fall in waves as our boys unleashed a torrent of javelins on them." He then pointed to where the gate had once stood.

"Pilate loosed his Scorpions on them as they tried to breach the gate. What a rush it was, charging as we did right out into the open!"

"They didn't see it coming," Decimus added. "They thought they had us beat, that we would lie here cowering, waiting for death to come. What fools they were!"

"I remember we left the bodies to rot," Artorius continued. "Decomposition came quickly in the summer heat. It was but two days before we continued our journey home, and the corpses of the enemy dead created a pestilent stench."

"Ah, but a dead enemy always smells sweet!" Magnus conjectured, giving his friends a morbid laugh. As they walked along the rampart, bantering with the sentries on duty, they came upon Centurion Vitruvius, who was talking with a couple of his soldiers by the camp's gate.

"Good evening men," he said, acknowledging the legionaries.

"Evening Sir," all three replied together.

"So what brings you over to our section of the line?" the Centurion asked.

"We were just reminiscing about our last campaign here," Artorius answered, "and the thrashing we gave those barbarian bastards when they thought they had us cornered." Vitruvius gave a short, mirthless laugh at that.

"Yes, that was quite a day, wasn't it? I remember the hell and frustration leading up to that showdown, to include the loss of Optio Valgus."

"At least Valgus managed to survive his wounds, as horrible as they were," Magnus replied.

"He survived his wounds, yes, however his career and livelihood ended that day," Vitruvius countered.

"Didn't he get a decent pension from the army?" Decimus asked. Vitruvius shrugged.

"He got whatever it is that they give to an Optio. It was not sufficient to get himself the small estate that he had always wanted, however with my sister's dowry it became enough."

"Yes, I had forgotten that they were sweethearts." Artorius said smiling.

"They were more than that," Vitruvius added. "Had anything happened to Valgus, Vitruvia would have skinned me! Now if you men will excuse us, I need to talk with Sergeant Artorius alone."

"Yes Sir," Magnus said as he and Decimus saluted and left. As they left, Vitruvius and Artorius continued to walk along the line.

"I heard about your run in with that rather irate barbarian with the great sword," Vitruvius began.

"I intended to give him the standard *'Vitruvius style'* thrashing, like you taught me," Artorius replied shrugging. "Crucifixion has its own satisfaction though."

"We had a few scuffles ourselves. Nothing like what happened to you guys, though."

"I'm glad none of our men got hurt or killed," Artorius replied, earnestly.

"You've got good men and sound leadership in the Second," Vitruvius remarked. "How is Flaccus working out as Optio?" Artorius shrugged again.

"He does alright. I think he is a little out of his element, especially since he was Tesserarius for so many years and I do not think he ever saw the promotion coming. He's kind of an irritable old bastard, but effective. Honestly, I think Macro did it at least in part to give Flaccus a better pension when he retires in a couple years."

"Of course he did!" Vitruvius said emphatically. "Flaccus is a good man, albeit a bit set in his ways and not very flexible. Still, he has the best interests of the men in mind, and he does what he thinks is right for them."

"He is quite entertaining when dealing with the new recruits," Artorius added. "I think their inexperience frustrates him at times, though he *is* quite affective at correcting their deficiencies! And what about your own Century? I hate to admit it, but even after five years in this Cohort, I rarely ever talk to anyone outside the Second."

"They're a good lot," the Centurion replied. "My Optio, another big brute named Macer, is quite good. He and I made Optio at about the same time. I think with some fine tuning, he will be ready to take his own Century in a couple years."

"What of the rumor that Flavius is retiring soon?" Artorius asked. Word had gotten down to the ranks that the Legion's Centurion Primus Pilus had petitioned the Senate to allow him to retire at last.

"He has been a soldier for nearly thirty-five years," Vitruvius replied, rubbing the back of his bald head. "Though he has come close to being killed in battle many times, I think it fitting that he lives out his days in peace. The gods know he's earned it."

"Any idea as to who his successor will be?"

"Not even a little bit," Vitruvius lied. In truth, he did know who he thought would take over as the Legion's Master Centurion. "Ironically, the rank of Primus Pilus is the only one in the army where a candidate is elected by his peers. The only stipulation is that he must have at least reached the rank of Centurion

Pilus Prior. That makes thirteen possible candidates, what with the nine regular Cohort Commanders, plus the four Primi Ordinones. The rest of us Centurions do get to cast a vote, though we cannot stand for the position."

For the next couple of hours, the former master and pupil walked and talked. Though professionally they no longer fell under the same chain-of-command, Vitruvius would always see himself as a mentor and guide for Artorius. The young Decanus would not have had it any other way.

After several days of using wood cutters' trails as well as moving cross country through the masses of trees, the Romans finally entered the lowlands of the Batavi. Though still vastly populated by trees, Batavia was predominantly cattle country. Improved roads paralleled the eastern side of the Rhine with expanses of farm fields as far as the eye could see.

The people were markedly different in demeanor than the Germans. The Batavi were Roman allies and welcomed the presence of legionaries into their realm. Farmers ceased in their labors to wave and call out greetings to the Romans. Artorius could not understand most of what they said, but figured it could not have been bad things since there were no accompanying rude gestures. Children were awed by the legionaries and soon there was a trail of them following the Century.

A village came into view as the Second Century continued its march. This was more of a town than a village, complete with a fifteen-foot wooden wall surrounding it. The gate was open, and there were a couple of guards standing on either side. These wore mail shirts with legionary-style helmets. Each held an oval, highly ornate shield, and leaned on a metal spear.

"Batavi auxiliaries, allies of Rome," Macro stated, answering the unasked question he knew was on his soldiers' minds.

"I remember hearing of them in action, prior to Idistaviso," Flaccus remarked. "They forded the Weser River, and harried the Cherusci flank. This allowed us to cross the river practically unmolested."

"For which they paid a heavy price," Camillus recalled. "I remember when Centurion Aemilius escorted the survivors back to the fort. All were ravaged by hunger and extreme fatigue after their harrowing ordeal. At least a third of their number had fallen during the sortie, including their chief, Chariovalda."

"You know Germanicus offered to release them to return to their homes after that," Macro replied. "They adamantly refused. Commander Stertinius was so moved by their bravery that he insisted on letting the Batavi fight alongside his cavalry at Idistaviso."

A horn sounded from atop the wall, announcing their presence. Soon a deputation of town elders arrived at the gate. The Batavi had done much to mask their barbaric roots. Almost all were clean shaven, though some did wear their hair long, pulled tight in the back. Those with facial hair kept it trimmed close and well groomed. All were clean and wore well made breaches and tunics of bright colors, mostly red and blue. The man who appeared to be their leader wore an ornate, yet practical-looking tunic, with a cavalry long sword on his belt. He stopped before Centurion Macro and bowed.

"Welcome, Friends, to the land of the Batavi," he said heartily with just a hint of accent in his Latin. "I am called Halmar; Chief of the Batavi." Macro bowed his head.

"It is good to see that we still have friends and allies in this part of the world," he replied, extending his hand which the Batavi Chief readily accepted.

"For what Rome has done for my people, we humbly open our gates to you and your men." With that, he waved them in and started walking towards the center of town.

"For barbarians living beyond the frontier, they seem to do well," Magnus observed.

"I agree. You can see where we influenced them," Artorius pointed to a bathhouse. The architecture of most of the buildings was advanced for the area. Many of the roofs were tiled, with walls made of brick and masonry. The streets were remarkably clean as well. Still, all the structures possessed traits unique to the natives' culture. Soon they came to the town hall. There was an overhang over the entrance, with timber columns on either side. The double doors leading inside were wooden, with ornate shields and spears affixed to them.

"Section leaders with me," Macro directed. "We may be here a while. The rest of you, go ahead and see what you wish, but stay out of trouble." With that he followed the Batavi Chief into the main hall.

The inside was lit with massive torches fixed to the support pillars. Displays of arms could be seen against the walls, going all the way down to a large oaken table that dominated one end of the hall. The Chief waived the Romans to take seats. All did so, removing their helmets as servants came with trays bearing ale. Artorius took a drink of the frothy liquid and nearly choked; it was warm and rather bitter.

"So," Halmar began when everyone was seated and given refreshment, "what brings emissaries of Rome to our lands?"

"We have been conducting an in depth reconnaissance of the lands once occupied by the Cherusci," Macro answered. "Unfortunately, our reception has been less than warm. We had a run in with a band of renegades two days ago. We thought it best to find out from our friends and allies in this area as to what may be happening." Halmar quaffed his ale in one gulp, and immediately called for another before answering.

"Those bastards, the Cherusci, are no more. They are scattered, leaderless, since the death of Arminius. Most have been assimilated by other tribes, though they are little better. The Bructeri are constantly a thorn in our side. That is why you see that we walled up our towns and villages. They will not face us in the open. Our cavalry is superior, plus they know that any blatant violence against us will be construed as an act of war against Rome. Am I right to believe this is still the case?" Macro nodded affirmatively.

"The Batavi have been a loyal ally. Rome values your friendship and will do what is necessary to protect it. If there have been any threats or attacks made against your people, they will be dealt with swiftly and terribly."

Halmar raised his hands in resignation. "I only wish they had been so blatant, since then we could elicit your help in exterminating those vermin. The Bructeri confine themselves to raids in the night, attacks on our livestock and only rarely our people. Since the destruction of Arminius and the Cherusci, life for the most part has been good for us. As you see, we prosper."

Artorius looked around the hall, and was drawn to a raised display towards the far end. Torches were lit on either side, allowing one to view it fully. It looked almost like a grave. Atop was a long cavalry sword and oval shield. Both looked well worn; however they had been placed with much reverence. A brass plaque adorned the center of the display.

"Sir, may I ask what the shrine is at the end of the hall?" he asked. Halmar sighed.

"That is a memorial, erected in honor of my brother, Chariovalda, the late Chief of the Batavi. He was killed during the wars against Arminius."

"We know," Macro nodded. "We are very much aware of his bravery and his sacrifice. His actions allowed our Legions to cross the Weser River and smash Arminius into dust." Unable to control his curiosity, Artorius stood from the table and knelt down in front of the monument, his eyes fixed on the plaque.

"What does it say?" Praxus asked.

"It says, '*In honored memory of Chariovalda, Chief of the Batavi. Never was an ally nobler or more valiant. Erected on order of the Emperor Tiberius Claudius Nero Caesar, by Germanicus Caesar, Commanding General and grieving friend.*'"

"What of my brother's old friend, the great Germanicus?" Halmar asked eagerly. It was Macro's turn to sigh. The mention of their former commander stung his heart.

"He is with your brother," Statorius answered for his Centurion. "They live forever in Elysium, where all heroes spend eternity; their deeds and their valor echoing throughout all time." Halmar's lips pinched together and he smiled sadly.

Darkness was approaching by the time the Century's leadership left the great hall. Outside there were many torches lit, and it looked as if a massive celebration was being held around a large bonfire. The entire Century was gathered around there, mixed with a host of Batavi natives. Upon seeing their Centurion and section leaders return, all immediately fell in awaiting orders.

"Sir, we've abstained from any drink until we know your orders," Magnus stated with a crisp salute. Macro looked around at the darkening sky. He knew it would be pointless, not to mention dangerous, for them to leave that night.

"Please my friends, allow us to act as your hosts this evening," Halmar said earnestly. "You are most welcome here, and I wish for you to make the most of your stay." Macro's brow furrowed in thought for a moment, and then nodded his consent.

"Alright, but hangovers or no, be ready to march at dawn!"

"Um, our celebrations often last until dawn," Halmar replied with a grin. "Surely a meeting like this between allies deserves as much." Macro lowered his head in resignation then chuckled at the anticipation on his men's faces.

"Very well, we will remain your guests through the morrow."

A series of loud cheers erupted from the men. Valens in particular was pleased. He already caught the eye of a rather statuesque Batavi maiden and soon disappeared from the celebration.

"Think she'll break him?" Decimus asked Carbo, his arms folded, sporting a wry grin.

"Without a doubt," the other legionary replied, taking a swallow of bitter ale.

Artorius walked over to where a large boar was being slowly rotated on a spit. A gruff, shirtless Batavi was cutting off strips of cooked meat. Artorius found that he was hungry and so decided to sample some of the local cuisine. The meat was hot and juicy, and nearly burned his hand. Still, once he was able to take a bite he was quite impressed with the flavor; so much so that he found himself going back for more. He found Magnus ravenously tearing into a large hunk of roast boar. Artorius laughed and sat down beside him.

"Hungry old friend?" he asked. Magnus took a minute to chew the huge mouthful that he had taken, and then washed it down with some warm ale.

"Are you kidding? I love this stuff! I grew up on it," he replied. Artorius raised an eyebrow at him. Magnus rolled his eyes and ran his hand through his blonde hair.

"Come on Artorius," he remarked, "you know that my roots are not Latin. My family came from a place even further north than here. It was my grandfather who won us the franchise of Roman citizenship. If you think about it, I'm closer related to these people than I am my own countrymen. I thought you knew."

"I knew that you had less than Latin roots, but then again who doesn't anymore?" Artorius replied. He then thought for a few seconds. "No, in the five years we've been friends, I don't think you have ever told me about your lineage; though Decimus did mention your grandfather, *Mad Olaf.*"

"He *is* quite mad," Magnus replied matter-of-factly. "You see, Olaf came south from the northlands, seeking a better life for his family; though the way he tells it he wanted to fight while getting paid for it! My father had not been born yet. He enlisted as a Roman auxiliary, served out his twenty-five years, and won us citizenship. Campaigned all over the place; this was unusual for an auxiliary. Oddly enough, once he became a Roman, he returned north with my grandmother and two of my uncles, who were still children. My dad was a man by this time, and he elected to remain within the Empire. He moved to Ostia, where me and my siblings were born. He gave us all Nordic names, keeping our link to the old country. Though in my case he spelled my name in the Roman fashion, rather than the Norseman version *Mahgnus.* As for Olaf, he became a minor overlord of a sizeable chunk of land. Seems Roman coin is a valuable commodity even outside the Empire. Most people who meet him think he is completely insane; however if one gets to know him they will find that his mind is sharper than a gladius." As Magnus rattled on his dissertation on his family history, Artorius felt a soft hand touching the back of his neck.

"Uh, hello!" he blurted. The soft hand belonged to a tall, shapely Batavi woman bearing a large tankard of ale.

"Would you like some ale, Sir?" she asked huskily in a thickly accented voice.

"Sure," Artorius replied, "and a few other things," he said under his breath. He did not mean for her to hear, but she winked at him as she handed him the tankard. She then ran her fingers up the back of his hair and walked away.

"She's a foot taller than you," Magnus leered at him. "Aren't you afraid?"

"Maybe a little bit." Artorius almost choked on his ale as his friend roared with laughter and pounded his back. Valens then came running over to the group; he appeared disheveled and out of breath.

"Magnus you were right!" he said as he kneeled down and placed a hand on his shoulder.

"Right about *what?*" Magnus asked. Valens then grinned from ear to ear.

"These women aren't hairy at all. In fact, that rather tall and curvaceous blonde doesn't have hair anywhere except her head!" Artorius looked into the fire, vainly trying to suppress his laughter. Magnus raised an eyebrow at his friend's assessment.

"So you left her all by herself just to come and tell us this?" Valens stared off into space for a second and then nodded enthusiastically.

"Uh huh," he replied. "I don't think I've ever seen such physical beauty."

"Well you'd better get back to it before someone else discovers it!" Artorius blurted out through his constant chuckling. Valens' eyes grew wide; he sprung to his feet and sprinted away, bumping into the Batavian boar cook.

"Sorry," Valens stammered as he held his hands up in resignation. The Batavian just shook his head and went back to checking the boar spit.

On the outskirts of the celebration Marco and Halmar walked slowly along the edge of the darkness. The Centurion noted his trepidation in the Batavi chief's demeanor. Halmar was pacing, his hands clasped behind his back.

"I am indeed glad for the presence of Roman soldiers in our lands," he said at last. "I have a message that I wish to send to the governor in Germania Inferior."

"What message?" Macro asked.

"A warning," Halmar said as he stopped and faced the Centurion. "My people are very much attuned to events outside of our lands. There are stirring south in Gaul." Macro waved his hand dismissively.

"There always are," he replied. "There are many who still pine for the days before Caesar's conquests; such minor subversions are nothing new."

"That may be," Halmar persisted, "however this is something different. Two of my agents have already been killed trying to glean information from certain dark corners of the province, and a third barely escaped with his life. He couldn't locate the leaders of this new threat, but he suspected that they are within the Gallic hierarchy. A rebellion in Gaul would greatly hamper my people's trade, so any potential insurrections must be put down."

"If there is dangerous subversion in Gaul, we will find and crush it," Macro asserted. Halmar gave a half smile and nodded.

"Of that I have no doubt; but be careful with who you ally yourself to. My instincts tell me Rome is about to be betrayed."

CHAPTER 6

▼

TRAITORS AND THIEVES

Heracles quickly proved his worth. He had made it a lifelong study learning how the Roman army operated and acted tactically. He knew their formations and how they would employ their troops against the rebels. With this knowledge he started to train a cadre of the more intelligent gladiators in how to combat the Roman War Machine. They would fight well, though most of the scum of Sacrovir's army would be little more than sheep to be led to the slaughter. That was fine with Heracles. He used his powers of persuasion and motivation to tell them stories of Sparta, and how they would follow in their glorious footsteps. Inside he knew these men were anything but Spartans. They were cowards, mostly. Yet they were also desperate, which made them useful. They would fight the Romans, if only so that they did not have to run in fear anymore.

Sacrovir was equally pleased with the results from his arms makers. Knowledge of Roman tactics would not be enough. He had quite an unorthodox plan to deal with them, a plan that Heracles had helped him devise. His smiths were turning out breast plates and helmets, greaves, arm guards, and gauntlets. He intended to encase his strongest fighters in hardened metal armor; armor that would withstand a Roman javelin storm and render their short stabbing swords useless. Such troops would scatter the massed legionary formations. As he sat contemplating, a lookout called out from the gate.

"Rider approaching; it's General Florus, Sir!" Sacrovir snorted at how Florus had taken to calling himself 'General.' He shrugged it off. Florus was becoming a

pompous ass; however he was one of the keys to the rebellion's potential success. He had money, lots of money, and a profound influence over numerous tribal chiefs and elders within the province. He was of the Treveri, which supplied the Romans with a large number of their cavalry. Apparently he got a hold of the ear of Julius Indus, the regimental commander. An entire regiment of cavalry would compliment his forces nicely.

Sacrovir strode over to where Florus was dismounting his horse near the main gate. He shook his head as he looked at his fellow conspirator. Florus was dressed in Greek military garb from head to foot, complete with a massive plume on his helm and a breastplate that gleamed in the sun.

"Sacrovir, it is good to see you!" Florus spouted, extending his hand with exaggerated enthusiasm. Sacrovir took it and nodded.

"What news?" he asked suppressing a sigh at his friend's sudden ostentatious behavior. Instead of answering, Florus gazed over at Heracles who was standing behind Sacrovir with his arms folded behind his back.

"Who's the Greek?" Florus asked, pointing.

"This is Heracles," Sacrovir answered. "He has been instrumental in training our cadre of gladiators."

"Ah," Florus responded. "Well, let's go inside, shall we? My mouth is quite parched from that ride!" Sacrovir sighed and the three men went inside. The house was rather ornate, decorated in Etruscan fashion. They went into a parlor, where Florus immediately grabbed a goblet of wine from a waiting servant. Once he had downed it completely, he spoke again.

"I have good news. Several dozen tribal chiefs have committed themselves to our cause. I looked for those with the most to gain and the least to lose. All are indebted up to their asses to Rome. Independence means financial freedom. There is a delegation on the way that should be arriving in a few days. In the meantime, I have another little surprise for you." With that he went outside. Sacrovir and Heracles were befuddled by Florus' enthusiasm and boundless energy. Once outside they saw a long line of chained men being escorted in. All one hundred looked bedraggled and haggard, yet with eyes full of hope.

"What in Hades are these?" Sacrovir asked, not bothering to disguise his disgust.

"These," Florus began, "are mostly thieves and petty criminals; bound for the slave galley when I bought them. I offered them a chance at freedom and in exchange take up arms in our cause." Sacrovir did not disguise his disgust, but Heracles smiled.

"So we are building an army of thieves, led by debtors," he mused.

"How do we know they will not desert or worse tip off the Roman authorities?" Sacrovir asked. Florus shrugged, unconcerned.

"All have everything to gain, and little left to lose; desperate men."

"Give me time with them, and their loyalty will be without question," Heracles offered. "I have been working with a number of our men already, and I assure you, these will fight."

"I have several more of these coming as well," Florus remarked. "Combine that with whatever the Gallic chiefs bring us, and we should have quite the army." Sacrovir patted his friend on the shoulder.

"You have done well," he conceded. "Heracles, release their bonds and see to it that they are properly fed and housed in the barracks. Work with them for a few days; gain their trust and their loyalty. There is strength in numbers. Enough debtors and thieves can defeat the finest Legions of Rome!"

"Would you look at that?" Ellard laughed, pointing towards the slaves that were being set free. Radek set down his spear and shield and walked over to see what his companion found so amusing. A smirk crossed his face. Many of the men that Florus purchased were the same men that Radek and Ellard had been imprisoned with.

"I'll be buggered," Radek replied. "Let's go say hello." Both men were full of laughter as they walked down the short slope to where the slaves were gathered. An attendant was walking down the line, unlocking their manacles.

"About time you sorry cocks caught up to us!" Ellard mused. A couple of men looked at them aghast.

"What sight is this," a man named Torin replied as he rubbed his sore wrists. "Sacrovir offer you your freedom as well?"

"He doesn't know we're runaways," Ellard replied proudly. "A hot meal and silver coinage were our compensation." Torin stared at him coldly. Ellard could only grin.

Damn he is ugly, he thought to himself, ever conscious of his own good looks. *The man looks like a ferret!*

"It is a just compensation for the trials we have been through over the past week," Radek added, his arms folded across his chest. Torin spat at him.

"Fuck your compensation," he growled. "You left the rest of us to rot in those accursed mines!"

"You had ample opportunity to join us," Radek said coolly. He glanced at the rest of the men who were now glaring at him. "All of you had the chance to run. Ellard was the only one man enough to take a chance."

"Three others tried to escape just after you did; their crucified corpses were left alongside the road," Torin replied bitterly.

"A better fate than the mines," Ellard sneered.

"Quite," Radek continued. "And now you will have a chance to earn your freedom, not to mention plunder to be had for those who survive this venture."

"Ha!" a man snorted. "You make it sound so bloody easy, Radek. You forget that we were bought to fight the *Romans*! What chance will we have?"

"None," Radek replied quickly. "Most of you sorry bastards will piss yourselves or faint like women at the first sign of trouble. I, on the other hand, have a plan." He then turned and walked back up the slope to where his newly furnished weapons lay.

"What is he talking about?" Torin asked.

"We were once slaves," Ellard clarified. "Now we are mercenaries. But Sacrovir's coin and freedom does no good if we are dead men. We will do whatever is necessary to survive."

✳   ✳   ✳   ✳

Tiberius paced in the atrium as he tried to find the right words to say. Even in death it was hard for him to speak with his predecessor. Finally he entered the small shrine. It was more of an oversized booth than anything. Inside was a raised alter bearing a bust of the late Emperor Augustus. Tiberius had had the monument made specifically for his own use. Though he had never had much use for praying to the Roman gods, he did see something tangible in trying to reach out to the deity that was his step-father. If there was any real divinity to Augustus, then perhaps he could reach out from beyond Elysium and bring guidance and inspiration to the troubled Emperor. Tiberius raised the hood of his cloak over his head and knelt before the stone image. Candles on either side cast a soft glow on the bust, creating an almost lifelike appearance.

"Oh Divine Augustus," he began, his head bowed, "I, your unworthy successor, do ask for your guidance and strength in this hour of my need. I seek justice for my lost son, while his widow seeks petty vengeance. Many within my own family blame me for Germanicus' death. I swear, on all that I honor, that I did not wish that. I ask that you grant me the means to bring justice to the guilty; even if that justice comes at a heavy personal price.

"Have mercy on my soul, help me to quell the fire of rage that burns within me. Give me peace that I may continue to serve in the capacity that you saw fit to leave me." As the Emperor left the shrine, he was greeted with a sight he did not wish to see. Agrippina stood sullen and petulant, still in mourning dress.

"Does my step-father continue to spout off hypocrisies to the dead to cover for his guilty conscience?" There was spite and venom in her voice. Agrippina was chief in implicating Tiberius' guilt in the death of her husband. The Emperor's face grew hard. Unleashing on her would be considered a sign of his guilt. Not to mention would only temporarily satisfy him. However, he had no intention of allowing himself to be a woman's whipping boy.

"Take heed in your tone," Tiberius warned. "You give yourself airs that are not yours, only because you are the daughter of Agrippa and the granddaughter of Augustus."

"And let us not forget, half-sister to your beloved ex-wife," Agrippina's eyes narrowed, her loathing for the Emperor allowed her to tread recklessly into dangerous territory. Tiberius clenched his jaw. It was no secret that he still loved Vipsania deeply, even after all these years apart. It made things awkward from the beginning between him and Agrippina, given that he had been forced to divorce her sister in order to marry her mother. Vipsania's health was failing, and Tiberius loathed the fact that Agrippina would use her own sister in order to hurt him.

"What do you want?" he asked coldly. "Surely you did not come all the way out here to incite further discord between us."

"I want justice, *real* justice. Not some pompous ceremonial garbage that will mean nothing in the end. My husband died serving you. It is only fit that all the conspirators face the penalty for their crimes, whoever they are." Her tone did nothing to disguise her accusation.

"And you think by badgering me, by showing yourself to be a belligerent snake, that you are helping your cause?" Tiberius whipped back, but Agrippina only hardened in her resolve.

"I know about Livia's dealings with Plancina. I know that you will be willing to sacrifice the husband to popular demand, only to allow your mother to save the wife who is the guilty bitch."

"Germanicus' murder is but one of the charges against Piso," Tiberius replied. "Though I doubt very much that the crime of sedition, inciting rebellion, as well as the wrongful deaths of Roman soldiers is of any concern to you. All are being tried, and all will face justice."

"*All?*" Agrippina asked with an eyebrow raised. Tiberius leaned forward; his face to hers until his nose was only inches from hers.

"Take caution, Agrippa's daughter!" he hissed through clenched teeth. "Your grandfather left *me* to run the affairs of this Empire, not Germanicus, and certainly not you! I will take your less than cordial remarks and blame them on your grief. But do not try my patience again!" With that he turned and walked away, fighting to keep his rage under control.

Drusus took a deep breath while standing outside the door to his father's office. It was rare for the Emperor to ask for him with such urgency, though in this circumstance he was almost certain as to why he had. Agrippina had told everyone about her confrontation with Tiberius, and it did not sit well with Drusus. Though he did not condone all of his father's conduct in regards to the trial, he could not believe that he had had a hand in Germanicus' death. It just did not make any sense. Germanicus had been loyal, and Tiberius had viewed him as a worthy successor when he had gone. Though with his death Drusus was now next in line for the Imperial throne, it did not lesson the loss he felt at losing his adopted brother and close friend. In truth, the prospect of becoming Emperor had never really crossed Drusus' mind. He would have gladly served Germanicus in whatever capacity he saw fit. The daunting responsibilities of what now lay before him had not yet sunk in, though he knew it would soon enough. Finally he gritted his teeth and knocked.

"Enter!" his father's voice boomed. Drusus opened the door and stepped inside to see the Emperor pacing back and forth, beads of sweat forming on his brow.

"You wanted to see me, Father?"

"Close the door," Tiberius replied, his calm voice contrasting sharply with his demeanor. He then turned to face Drusus. "I need your help, Son."

"How can I be of service?" Drusus rubbed his hands nervously behind his back. He knew that when his father spoke calmly, yet appeared disheveled, it was because he was not only deeply enraged, but frighteningly focused as well.

"Keep that bitch Agrippina on a short leash. See to it that she causes us no more problems once this trial is over; and afterwards." Tiberius was not one to mince words. He leaned on his hands standing over the table, his eyes piercing into his son. Drusus swallowed hard as the Emperor continued.

"Her words to me today were treasonous. I let them be, seeing that this is not the time for dealing with her. However, I will not have her thinking that she has free reign to do as she pleases, and talk to me like an undisciplined schoolboy." Drusus forced himself to stop rubbing his hands behind his back while waiting for Tiberius to finish.

"By the gods, do they honestly think I had anything to gain with Germanicus' death? *I am not even allowed to mourn my son!*" There was heartbreaking despair and frustration in his voice. Drusus knew all too well what else it was that vexed his father. He gazed over and saw a small medallion sitting on Tiberius' desk. On it was an engraved image of Vipsania. It was old and well worn, and Drusus was saddened at the thoughts of what had happened between his parents.

"Mother was asking about you the other day," he said at last. Tiberius followed his son's stare to the medallion on his desk.

"She gave me that a long time ago, when you were a small boy," he said quietly.

"She still worries about you, even though it is *her* health that is failing. She never stopped caring about you." Tiberius closed his eyes and took a deep breath. He then gazed out the window towards the setting sun.

"She married that bastard Gallus not long after I was forced to divorce her. He continues to use her, and their sons, to cast a perpetual shadow over me. He mocks me from his place in the Senate. Though I have the reins of ultimate power in the Empire, it is he who possesses the one thing I would have given it all up for, and he knows it. You know they haven't lived together for years, and yet he will not grant her the freedom of a divorce. Perhaps this is because he knows I would not hesitate to take her back, back to where she belongs. If there ever was a woman who deserved to be Empress of Rome ..." Drusus suddenly took great pity on his father. For him there was no rest, no peace; only cold duty.

There was another weighty issue that remained unspoken: the unrest in Gaul. Many Senators, particularly Gallus, were clamoring for Tiberius to lead a full-scale invasion of the province and crush any signs of rebellion in an effort to show their loyalty to Rome. Tiberius maintained that if the Emperor was required to quell every bit of unrest within the Empire, then he would never be found in Rome. Gallus' disagreements with the Emperor's foreign policies only served to add fuel to the fire of hate between them.

"I will do what I can to help you," Drusus said after a long silence. "I want you to know that no matter what any of my friends or acquaintances may think, I never once implicated you in Germanicus' death. You have my loyalty, Father. You always have."

*   *   *   *

"I don't care what you say; that woman is an evil sorceress and Livia is doing everything to protect her!" Agrippina snapped. Her face was flushed with anger, eyes swollen with tears of frustration as she paced around the dinning chamber of the house that she had once shared with her husband. Around the table, reclining in typical Roman fashion, were her friends and relatives, all of whom were helping her to seek justice for Germanicus.

Germanicus' brother, Claudius, was sipping wine and snacking on dates, quietly observing everything. Conspicuous by her absence was Germanicus' sister, Livilla. Few cared for the scheming, conniving woman, so her lack of presence was not missed. Most only tolerated her not just because of her relationship to Germanicus, but by her being married to Drusus. Drusus was present and was desperately trying to calm Agrippina.

"Regardless of what we may think of that witch Plancina, we *must* respect whatever verdict the courts render!" he pleaded. "Nothing good can come of your continual vendetta against the Emperor!"

"The Emperor?" Agrippina seethed. "He is the man who caused Germanicus' demise in the first place!"

"What nonsense, woman!" Antonia snapped. Germanicus' mother had been sitting quietly, watching the spat between Agrippina and Drusus. Defaming remarks against Tiberius never sat well with her, given that she was the widow of the Emperor's brother. Tiberius had even named his son Drusus in honor of his brother and Antonia always stood by her brother-in-law.

"Your ridiculous grudge against Tiberius has blinded you!" she continued. "Germanicus was the best soldier and Statesman he had. He would have to be the greatest fool to have ever lived to get rid of him! And what would Livia gain protecting the murderer of her grandson?"

"And if you continue to insult and publicly defame the Emperor, it cannot sit well with you and your children," Drusus added. "Please, Agrippina, allow justice to prevail and let your quarrels with my father lay to rest."

"I will rest my quarrel with Tiberius when I see the entire Piso clan burn," Agrippina replied haughtily with an air of finality.

Drusus stood outside in the garden; head in his hands when Claudius found him. The other guests had long since gone home. Claudius put a hand on his friend's shoulder.

"Th … this is not an easy t-t-time for you, I kno-ow," he stuttered.

"Between this damned trial, Agrippina's goading, Mother's poor health, and now word of unrest in Gaul, nothing is sitting right with either my father or myself." He walked over to a bench by the man-made stream and stared morosely into the water.

"Yes, I was s-sorry to hear about your m-m-m-other," Claudius offered. Being lame with a stutter, the family assumed he was dim-witted and ignored him making it possible to overhear much that occurred within the family. He knew all too well Tiberius' feelings for his long since divorced wife, and the awkward position everything put Drusus in. "Is t-t-there nothing that can be done f-f-for her?"

"I don't think so," Drusus answered, shaking his head. "It's sad. She's not old and she has always been strong in both mind and body. Sadly the body seems to be failing. I know that once she goes, my father will need me more than ever to get him through everything. I'm afraid I cannot be the son I should be."

"W-w-who of us is?" Claudius asked. "All w-w-we can do is make the b-b-b-b-b-best," he struggled pathetically with the word, "of what we ha-have. Your father will n-n-need you to be strong. You are the one hope he has left. I kn-know it cannot be easy, being son of the Emperor. But p-p-perhaps it is time that you learned how to b-b-be one. Know that all of us hope to serve you well one day." Drusus smiled at that as he continued to gaze into the stream. It was the first time anyone had even mentioned what should have been so obvious; that with Germanicus gone, Drusus was now Tiberius' sole heir. He didn't relish the thought.

"I had hoped to serve Germanicus well," he said quietly. "He would have made a fine Caesar."

"Yes," Claudius replied, wiping his eyes. The loss of his brother was still overwhelming. Germanicus had been the world to Claudius; his affection for his brother unmatched.

As they sat quietly, contemplating everything that was happening, Herod walked out into the garden. Herod Agrippa was a close friend of both Drusus and Claudius. He was a Jew, grandson of Herod the Great, and partially named after the legendary Marcus Agrippa. He was dressed in traditional Jewish garb of robes and sandals, though his demeanor was anything but Jewish. He had been raised in Rome since he was a child, and had been a favorite of the Emperor's, at least in part because of his lifelong friendship with Drusus.

"Not interrupting anything am I?" he asked gently.

"No, n-not at all," Claudius replied. Herod sat down on the bench, placing his hand on Drusus' shoulder. There were no words, just the gesture meant to comfort.

"My father said 'keep that bitch Agrippina on a short leash'," Drusus said morosely. "I swear the hatred between those two will never end. Agrippina will always blame my father for Germanicus' demise."

"Then you had better find yourself a good leash!" Herod clapped him on the shoulder heartily with his usual good humor. Drusus couldn't help smiling. This elicited a laugh from all three men. The Jewish nobleman then took a deep breath, his expression becoming sober.

"Seriously," he continued, sobering, "this is a difficult time for us all. My contacts down on the Aventine tell me that most of the plebs will only vindicate the Emperor once Piso hangs from the butcher's hook. As for my own people, well, most Roman Jews are more apt to demand proof of Tiberius' involvement than even the indigenous Romans."

"I've n ... never understood that," Claudius said. "The Jews are among the m-m-most fickle p-p-p-people in the entire Empire. And yet they have a b-b-b-ond with Tiberius."

"That's because my father has always had a soft spot for our friend Herod," Drusus replied.

"It's true," Herod replied with a nod. "I've spent more time in Rome than in my own country. Tiberius became the father figure that I lacked. While most Judeans may view me more as a Roman than as one of their own, they know that it was my influence which guided the Emperor's policies towards them."

"S-s-such as?" Claudius asked.

"Such as we are the only people exempt from Caesar worship. While Tiberius may have refused any such divinities for himself, he did persuade the Senate to deify Augustus. Rome respects an individual's right to express his own religious beliefs provided he acknowledges the divinity of the Roman Pantheon, including Augustus. Strangely enough, it actually did not take much persuasion to convince Tiberius to allow Jews to abstain from such practices. Political his intents may have been, though perhaps he may hold a certain amount of reverence to the one true God."

"That's all well and good that my father blasphemes the entire Pantheon to show respect to the god of the Jews," Drusus replied with a scowl. "But what good will that do us now? Will your god make Agrippina see reason? Will he bring Piso to justice and grant my father peace?"

"One can only hope," Herod replied gently. Drusus sighed. "Agrippina has been my friend for many years. Germanicus was a brother to me, as are you both. I walk a fine line being both Agrippina's friend, as well as loyal son to the Emperor. I hope that once justice is dispensed Agrippina will let her hatred for Tiberius pass."

*   *   *   *

The bathhouse was a gods-send to Artorius. Though their sortie across the Rhine had been anything but a full-scale campaign, his body told him otherwise. The only time they were able to us Roman roads was when they had crossed to the west side of the Rhine at the Batavian border.

"Remind me to start getting out more," he moaned to Praxus, who was getting a massage on a nearby table while a slave worked the soreness out of Artorius' muscles. "Going out on road marches twice a month is not cutting it."

"I agree," his fellow Decanus replied. "I think I'll start going out when Flaccus takes the recruits on their road marches, which should start up soon." The Cohort's recruits had not gone across the Rhine with them, and had instead been folded into the Tenth Cohort's group of recruits and had trained with them. With the Third back, the recruits had rejoined their unit.

"Yeah, I've got to start running them through javelin and Scorpion training soon," Artorius added. "I've got to start training up for the *Legion Champion* tournament as well." Praxus laughed and shook his head at that.

"As long as Vitruvius withdraws from the competition, you should not have any problems."

"I don't know," Artorius said. "I have not sparred in a while, and to be honest I felt a bit rusty against that jackal that I killed on our little sortie."

"Well don't look at me if you are looking for volunteers!" Praxus retorted. "I remember how you and Vitruvius used to pummel the crap out of each other. Okay, so *he* did most of the pummeling, but still ..."

"And speaking of pummeling," Artorius laughed, "what did you make of the Batavian women?"

"That warm, bitter ale did a number on me before I had a chance to find out," Praxus replied sheepishly. Artorius howled afresh with laughter.

"Alright fellas, one at a time please," Artorius stated as he set into his fighting stance. In front of him, in a single-file, were the members of his section. All wore their helmets and carried a practice gladius and shield. Carbo was at the front of the line.

"Let me get this straight; we get a free round of drinks for every time we let you thrash us?" he asked, settling uncertainly into his fighting stance.

"There is no *letting* me do anything," Artorius corrected. "You are all helping your Decanus get ready for the Legion Champion competition. And yes, a free round of drinks for every time you decide to give it a go." Valens raised his hand.

"Artorius, you know I really don't drink much ..." Artorius rolled his eyes.

"Alright Valens, in your case it will be a classy prostitute. But you have to go at *least* three rounds!"

"All right!" Valens shouted, grinning from ear to ear and raising his gladius in triumph.

Carbo came at Artorius punching with his shield. Though each man in his section was skilled in his own right at close combat, they were no match for the Century's Chief Weapons Instructor. Artorius quickly knocked Carbo's shield aside and stabbed him beneath the rib cage. As soon as he went down, Decimus lunged forward, catching the Sergeant across the helm with a blow from his shield. Artorius stumbled back and then settled into his stance once more. Decimus was taking things a little more seriously, and he was not going to let his Decanus have an easy win. After a minute of punching and jabbing with their practice weapons, Artorius charged forward and with brute strength knocked the legionary down. Before Decimus could get to his feet, Artorius had caught him with a jab to the neck. Gavius and Valens were dispatched quickly before Artorius had to face his old friend Magnus.

Magnus rolled his neck from side to side and loosened up his sword arm. He grinned at his Decanus and deliberately advanced on him. Their shields collided several times before Artorius lunged in with an attempted stab to the ribs. Magnus blocked this with his shield, which he then swung and caught Artorius in the midsection. The Sergeant stumbled back, surprised at the ferocity of Magnus' attack. The legionary renewed his attack, nearly catching Artorius in the face with a stab from his weapon. His retraction was too slow and Artorius caught him on the wrist with his shield, knocking the gladius away. Magnus yelped in surprise and raised his shield to block Artorius' attack. Artorius purposely attacked Magnus on his left, pushing him towards where his gladius lay on the ground. In desperation, the young legionary lunged to grab his weapon, only to catch the point of Artorius' gladius in the back of his neck as he attempted to rise.

"Not bad," Artorius remarked, breathing rather heavily. "Since when did you start taking sparring seriously?"

"Since I figured that you shouldn't be the only one in the Century vying for the title of Legion Champion," Magnus replied, rubbing his wrist and the back of his neck. Artorius smiled wide and nodded in respect to his friend.

"Well do us both a favor and give me a better run for it when the actual competition comes!"

CHAPTER 7

▼

THE CENTURIONS' COUNCIL

Gaius Silius sat at the head of the meeting hall, along with the military Tribunes and Master Centurion Flavius. Flavius would have the final say once the counsel of Centurions voted on his successor. At the table directly below the Legate's platform sat all of the Cohort Commanders, along with the Centurions of the First Cohort. Given the importance of selecting a suitable man to hold the highest position in the Legion that a common soldier could hope to achieve, the debates would prove to be long and tedious. Though all Centurions were professionals, and would vote for whomever they felt was most fit, it would be hard for them not to show loyalty to their own Cohort Commanders and vote for them. Such potential impasses had to be avoided as much as possible. Silius had deliberately kept from announcing Flavius' retirement too soon, lest the candidates for the position start focusing all their energies on politicking their fellow Centurions. Word had still gotten out though, and much political effort had already been exerted by those seeking to become the Primus Pilus.

Flavius had been a soldier for so long he knew of little else. His wife, Marcia, had been the ideal military spouse. She had been supportive through every campaign, dressed his wounds from battle upon his return, and held him in the night when the nightmares born of horrors he had suffered to protect her and the Empire came. She bore him two fine sons, one of whom was a scholar, the other a legionary like his father. He had three grandchildren from his eldest son, and thought it not right that a grandfather should still go off to war. He wished to retire and spend more time with his wife and grandchildren while he was still in the prime of his health.

His finances were more than sound. His pension from the army would be impressive, plus he would be elevated to membership within the patrician class. He would be able stand for offices such as Tribune of the Plebes, with even the possibility of becoming a Provisional Governor. He smiled at the thought. He in fact relished the thought of a peaceful tenure in a position where he could still serve Rome. Marcia would be pleased.

"The position of Centurion Primus Pilus is the highest a soldier from the ranks can hope to achieve," Silius spoke. "He is the senior advisor to the Legion Commander, answering only to him. His responsibilities include not only leading the elite First Cohort into battle, but also the development and mentoring of all Centurions and other officers within the legion. It is an epic responsibility, requiring that the man chosen truly be a *Master* Centurion.

"All of you have personal loyalties to friends and fellow Centurions who will be standing for this position. You must put personal loyalties aside, and focus only on which of these men is best suited to be your Master Centurion. Which of these men possesses the greatest skill in battle, the most ingenious tactical savvy, and the soundest leadership? It is up for you to decide." With that, he took his seat.

Deliberations continued for some time. Each candidate stood before the assembly, his merits, awards for valor, and experience laid out. Since it would take a clear majority for a decision to be made, there were numerous votes-off after the initial tally. After each voting, those with the fewest in number were removed from consideration and left the table to join their peers in voting. After three rounds, Centurion Primus Ordo Aemilius, Centurion Primus Ordo Draco, and Centurion Pilus Prior Calvinus were the remaining candidates.

All three were legendary soldiers in their own right. Aemilius was a superior cavalryman who had fought beside the allied Batavi tribesmen during the wars against Arminius. He had been awarded the Civic Crown for saving the lives of numerous Batavi auxiliaries during the fierce fighting along the Weser River. For him the award was bittersweet, seeing as how he had failed to save the Batavi war chief, Chariovalda, who had been a close friend of his.

Draco was a tactical genius and a master of "shock" tactics. He epitomized the Roman ability to adapt to adverse situations in the heat of battle. Often times he was able to manipulate the enemy's strengths against him. Nothing pleased him more than misleading the enemy into thinking he had the Romans outmatched, only to be led into a trap with disastrous consequences. One tactic that he was famous for was keeping half his javelins in reserve during an engagement. As his men closed with the barbarians, he would unleash a second javelin storm just as contact was made. His legionaries would then fall into a hasty wedge and charge full-tilt into the barbarians. His men were so well-drilled at this maneuver that the effects were devastating.

Calvinus, the only Cohort Commander still in the running, was a legend for reasons he wished he wasn't. He had been one of the few to survive the disaster in Teutoburger Wald, something that still haunted him to that day. Only two other soldiers survived from his Century, and while he blamed himself for the deaths of the rest of his men, most gave him credit for saving the ones that he did. Cassius Chaerea, the senior officer who led out most of the survivors, credited Calvinus' sound leadership for keeping himself and his men alive. In fact, Tiberius, at the behest of Cassius, would later award Calvinus the Civic Crown for saving the lives of more than one hundred men during the aftermath of the battle. Calvinus had gone on to lead the Fifth Cohort during the campaigns of retribution against Arminius. His men had been particularly ruthless, looking to avenge their Centurion.

After another voting tally, Silius was smiling; clearly a sign that the assembly had at last come to a decision.

"A majority has been reached," he announced. "The votes cast by the Centurions of the Twentieth Legion in electing the new Centurion Primus Pilus are as follows: Centurion Primus Ordo Draco: ten votes. Centurion Primus Ordo Aemilius: fifteen votes. Centurion Pilus Prior Calvinus: thirty votes." Calvinus beamed when he heard the results. Aemilius closed his eyes, trying to mask his disappointment. Draco grimaced slightly and nodded in acknowledgment.

"Do any here object to the appointment of Centurion Calvinus to this position?" Silius then asked. The room was silent. Silius looked over towards Flavius. "Master Centurion Flavius, do you approve of the assembly's decision?" Flavius rose to his feet and addressed everyone in his ever commanding voice.

"I have served with Centurion Calvinus since he came to the Twentieth Legion over ten years ago," he began. "His service as a Cohort Commander has been distinguished, his valor in battle exemplary. To the Centurions of the First Cohort I say this; Calvinus' appointment is by no means a discredit to any of you. You are still the elite commanders of this Legion. I trust Calvinus will be welcome as a brother into your ranks. He will lead you well." He then turned to his chosen successor.

"Centurion Calvinus, you have been given the greatest responsibility of any Soldier within this Legion. Every man from the lowest Legionary to the Centurions Primus Ordo will be looking to *you* as their example. Do right by them and continue to honor your Legion." With that, Flavius briskly exited the hall. As a whole, the Centurions of the Legion rose to their feet and gave a loud ovation to the man who would soon be their Master Centurion.

Afterwards, Calvinus found he was alone with the four Centurions of the First Cohort. Draco was the first to speak.

"Calvinus, the counsel of Centurions has chosen well." He extended his hand, which Calvinus readily accepted.

"I have to say, I thought the position would be mine," Aemilius added. "However I see that my peers felt differently. Know that we will serve you well," Aemilius added, shaking Calvinus' hand heartily. The rest of the men followed suite, all congratulating Calvinus and promising to work well with him.

"Calvinus, your responsibilities have just been magnified ten-fold," Flavius told him in private. "Leading the First Cohort is one of your many primary tasks. There is much talent in this Cohort, and I advise you to use it well. Your main focus will be training and mentoring the junior Centurions, as well as advising the Legate and Chief Tribune. They will be looking to you for answers. When dealing with them, it is best to guide them so that they can figure things out on their own, however sometimes they need a little nudge of experience to show them the way." He handed Calvinus a goblet of wine, which he readily accepted.

"I am a little nervous about my appointment," Calvinus admitted after taking a long pull off his wine.

Flavius waved him to take a seat. "I've been a Cohort Commander for so long, it is what I am most comfortable with." He continued. "I don't know if I can live up to administering to the machinations of an entire legion." Flavius sat back, his fingers steeple under his chin as he listened.

"Calvinus, none of us ever are," he replied. "I had more than my fair share of pitfalls when I first took the reigns of Primus Pilus. You've got good men to work with. Let the Primi Ordinones run the First Cohort. The First is self-sufficient as it is. Focus your leadership at the Legion level; make yourself available to the Cohort Commanders and junior Centurions. Legates and Chief Tribunes come and go, however *you* will be the mortar which holds this Legion together."

"You leave me with a vast responsibility," Calvinus said. "I hope that I prove to be a worthy successor."

"You will," Flavius reassured. "For it was you whom I wanted to replace me." Calvinus raised his eyebrows.

"Why? You worked with the first rank Centurions for so long, surely you would have wanted one of them to take over!" Flavius grinned and shook his head.

"Calvinus, I see you still have much to learn," Flavius finished his wine and signaled for a servant to refill his cup. "Just because I may be more familiar with the First Cohort's Centurions does not mean I felt one of them was most worthy. Perhaps I should have done more to ensure one of them was most ready for the responsibility. All are fully capable of Legion-level command; however there is something about you that instills the men with respect and admiration for you."

"I'm not sure I'm following you, Flavius," Calvinus replied. "Draco and Aemilius are both my equal, if not my betters, when it comes to tactics and strategy."

"You underestimate yourself then," Flavius said, a slight trace of disappointment in his voice. "Draco can shatter the most disciplined enemy phalanx with his unorthodox tactics; and Aemilius has proven invaluable with his ability to work with our allied cavalry units. They are also two of the bravest men I have ever met. What separates you from them is your ability to work with the Legion as a whole, not just your particular Cohort.

"The First Cohort often-times acts as its own entity, apart from the rest of the Legion. Granted, the veterans of the Cohort have earned the right to be a little bit elitist; however, a Master Centurion is the First Spear of the entire Legion, not just the First Cohort. Your peers know you; they know how to work with you. While none doubts Draco or Aemilius' abilities, they do not know how they would be to work under. They know what falling under your command will mean. I've spoken to all of the Centurions within the First Cohort and made my feelings clear to them. While I encouraged each to make his case before the assembly, they knew that you were the one to beat. They realize that you have the confidence and backing of the entire Valeria Legion."

*   *   *   *

Sacrovir looked over the council of tribal chiefs he assembled. For most, the term "tribal" meant little anymore. Many had long since adopted the dress and manner of the Romans. They lived in lavish estates or in great halls, yet the price of their existence was eternal servitude to Rome, something which these men found to be intolerable. The leaders of the Andecavi and Turani tribes were conspicuously absent. Sacrovir held a separate meeting with them, and their part of the plan was already in the works. Little did they know that theirs was merely a ruse; they would be led by Sacrovir as lambs to the slaughter. Heracles and Florus sat on either side of him. Also with him was Julius Indus, a nobleman of Florus' Treveri tribe. His cavalry regiment was stationed to the east, and Florus looked to subvert them to their cause.

"The Andecavi and Turani are ready to make war on Rome," Florus announced. This caused a stir amongst the various chiefs.

"Then we must rise up and support them!" a chief named Belenus shouted as he rose to his feet, a meaty fist in the air. "Let us join our valiant cousins in the liberation of our lands!" The others started to clamor, voicing their support. Florus looked at Sacrovir, who shook his head.

"If we rise up now, every Roman Legion within a thousand miles of here will be on our doorstep. What we need now is a ruse, a diversion, something that will lull the Romans into thinking that they have our loyalty and support."

"What are you getting at, Sacrovir?" Belenus asked suspiciously. Sacrovir smiled wickedly.

"We will join forces with the Romans, our men fighting as auxiliaries *against* the Andecavi and Turani." The chiefs were appalled. Sacrovir was quick to explain. "These tribes are only a minor political force within the region. Their numbers are few, and the Romans will scarcely unleash the entire Rhine Army on them, *if* they think they have our support. They will send a handful of legionaries, who will bear witness to our loyalty. They will report back that the province is secure, which in turn will cause the Emperor to become complacent in his dealings with us. It will also give our army a chance to test itself in battle, a ramp-up to the real campaign, if you will.

"When the time is right, we will lead our forces in a full-scale revolt, smashing whatever minor legionary forces remain in the region," his voice rose. "This will send a message to Tiberius that he should abandon his plans for keeping Gaul Roman."

There was a hushed silence as the war chiefs contemplated Sacrovir's plan. Only Heracles and the Sequani chief, Taranis, seemed to be amused at the idea.

"Your plan is sound," Taranis conceded. "This battle will provide our men with the confidence and experience they need. Once we make an example of the legionary forces, the Emperor will see that re-conquest of Gaul will be a futile effort."

"Let us not forget the significance of the death of Germanicus," Heracles added. "Rumors abound that Tiberius himself was directly involved in his death.

The Rhine Legions cherish the memory of the son of Drusus, and will be reluctant to conduct a full-scale invasion at the behest of his murderer."

"When will this battle take place?" Belenus asked Sacrovir directly.

"All in good time."

CHAPTER 8

▼

LEGION CHAMPION

With every Century within the Legion supplying a candidate, there was an initial field of fifty-nine soldiers competing for the title of *Legion Champion*. To make it an even bracket, five additional competitors would be allowed to enter. Since there was a plethora of volunteers, a mini-tournament was held the week before the competition. There were twenty legionaries vying for these five spots. A man would have to win two matches in a row in order to earn a placing.

Artorius was assisting Magnus in getting ready for his first match. As Chief Weapons Instructor, Artorius was assured the honor of representing the Second Century. Oddly enough, Magnus was the only other in the Century who wished to compete for one of the remaining vacancies, and even then had done so reluctantly. Artorius had been persistent in his insistence that Magnus compete. The two men had trained together for several weeks in preparation for this event and Artorius was confident that his friend would have little difficulty getting a place in the main bracket.

"You ready for this?" Artorius asked as he checked Magnus' chinstrap and helmet.

"I think so," he replied. "This is the first time I have sparred with someone outside the Century." Artorius shrugged at that.

"Doesn't mean anything. Do like we've been training and you will be alright." With that he gave his friend a slap on the shoulder and walked over to where numerous legionaries were crammed into the stands. This was the first time in many years that they were using the arena.

Magnus walked to the center of the arena and stood face to face with a legionary from the Seventh Cohort. The man was young, looked to be just barely out of recruit training. A Signifier served as the marshal.

"Alright you guys know how this works," he stated. "You fight until one man scores what would be a lethal blow with a service weapon. Listen to my commands, and break off fighting when I tell you to. Any questions?" Both men shook their heads.

The two combatants settled into their fighting stances. The young legionary looked nervous facing the big Norseman. At the sound of a whistle they came together. Magnus braced behind his shield and bore hard into the legionary. The young man held his ground, but was rocked by the force of Magnus' attack. Magnus continued to let their shields collide as he punched and looked for openings. The legionary he was facing had the basic skills, but no real experience. With a quick step to his right, Magnus brought his shield back hard against the young man's, continued to circle to his right, and then reached down and quickly stabbed him in the back of the leg. The young man gave a yelp of surprise as Magnus seized the advantage. He had the legionary's shield tied up and was able to circle far enough to stab him in the back at the kidneys. The legionary gave a yell of pain and frustration as the whistle blew again and he knew he was beaten.

∗   ∗   ∗   ∗

"You are all worthless and weak!" Heracles screamed at the Gauls. "Do you faggots not know what a phalanx *is*?" It had been an exhausting and exasperating ordeal for the Spartan. He knew he was delusional if he thought for a second that the rabble before him could ever come close to replicating a Spartan battle formation. But then, all he needed them to do was learn the rudimentary skills that would allow them to at least attack as one cohesive unit. How many fell when the time came for battle mattered not to him. He thought that by this time they would at least be able to form a phalanx with their shields locked together, spears protruding forward. Instead, they milled about, often crashing into each other, which in turn would lead to brawling amongst themselves. Heracles knew that these troops would be most critical for overwhelming the Roman lines. He took a deep breath.

"If you expect to have a chance at surviving against the Romans, you will learn what it means to fight as one! The phalanx is useful not only for sweeping the legionary ranks, but it is also crucial for repelling cavalry," he instructed.

"The Romans have no bloody cavalry in this region!" a voice spoke up.

"True," Heracles conceded, "however that does not mean they cannot bring cavalry to bear upon us. Remember, the Rhine legions are but a couple weeks march from here. Hence why it is crucial that we prepare for whatever they may throw against us. Now let us try this again."

In the front rank of the makeshift phalanx, Ellard wiped his forearm across his sweat-covered brow.

"How long does that jackal intend to make us play Spartan?" he complained under his breath.

"Until you stupid shits get it right!" Torin retorted from behind him. Ellard snorted. He was disgusted that Torin was actually taking their training seriously. It was as if he actually *believed* in what they were doing.

Radek seemed to already have a grasp of fighting. In his years of thievery, he would inevitably get caught and have to fight his way out. Ellard hoped that when the time came they would not be placed out front.

*   *   *   *

A week later Artorius and Magnus stood outside the arena once more; this time competing for the same prize. Magnus easily won his second elimination match and therefore earned a spot in the main tournament. They stood gazing at the gigantic parchment which had the tournament bracket laid out. With sixty-four men competing, that meant having to win six times in a row in order to become the next Legion Champion. Artorius looked at where he and Magnus fell out in the bracket. He saw that they would not be able to meet in the finals, like they had hoped. They would get as far as the semi-finals before having to face each other. Without a word being said, they entered the arena with the rest of the combatants.

The arena was packed with both soldiers as well as citizens from the city and surrounding areas. The sixty-four combatants stood in the center of the arena facing a raised platform where Silius stood. With him were newly-promoted Master Centurion Calvinus and Centurion Vitruvius. Silius raised his hands, silencing the crowd.

"The greatest honor that can be bestowed upon a soldier for his skill in close-combat is the title of Legion Champion," he stated to the crowd. He looked directly at the men in front of him who would compete for this honor. "You men have been selected to represent your individual Centuries and Cohorts in this competition. You are the best of the best in this Legion. Whoever amongst you walks away victorious will be presented with this." He signaled to Vitruvius, who produced a silver gladius with an engraving on its blade.

"Centurion Vitruvius has held the title of Legion Champion longer than any other," Silius continued. "Therefore he has been given the honor of presenting this ceremonial gladius to the man who proves himself worthy of being his successor to this auspicious title. *Let the tournament commence!*" The roar from the crowd and combatants was deafening.

Artorius left the arena and walked over to a nearby tree, where he laid down. His was the fourteenth match, so he had a bit of time to rest. Magnus, who was fighting even later, joined his friend.

"Not going to watch the early matches?" he asked. Artorius shook his head, eyes closed.

"No. If I watch, I will get all sorts of worked up, when what I need right now is to relax. I have to keep telling myself not to take any of these men lightly, that with one mistake it will all be over. I hope you also do well, Old Friend."

Magnus snorted. "I hope I don't embarrass myself and get eliminated in the first round!"

*   *   *   *

Decimus was a fan of combat sports, and he was anxious for the competition to begin. He watched as two legionaries entered the arena, their friends shouting encouragement and colorful insults to the opposition.

"Think this will be better than that disastrous spectacle we had to witness in Rome?" Decimus asked his friends who were sitting next to him.

"Anything has got to be better than those sorry gladiators," Gavius replied. "Not one of those guys knew how to actually fight!"

Valens laughed. "I think it would be more fun to watch our boys fight with metal weapons!" They watched as the two Legionaries faced each other and commenced fighting. One of the greatest challenges for Roman Soldiers was when they had to face other Roman Soldiers. Each used the same fighting style, with identical weapons. It boiled down to individual ability, rather than style or weaponry that gave a man the advantage. The two combatants rammed their shields together, looking for openings. One took a blow to the wrist, causing him to drop his gladius. His opponent was quick to exploit this, driving into his disabled foe and catching him with a blow beneath the ribs. A whistle blew, ending the match. Friends of the victorious soldier cheered wildly, while he tore off his helmet and ran into his ecstatic companions.

"Not bad," Carbo observed. "Can't wait to see how Artorius and Magnus do, though." He would not have long to wait.

The first round of the tournament had started at sunrise. By the time Artorius entered for his first match, the sun was casting its glow over the eastern edge of the arena. He limbered up his shoulders, arms, and legs as he waited for the signal that it was time. He entered the arena to the cheering from the Second Century. He couldn't help grinning at the smattering of boos and profanity from what he assumed were the friends of his opponent.

He took a deep breath and mentally drowned out all distractions. His adversary was a rather slender Legionary, who looked to be a good sixty to seventy pounds lighter than Artorius. He knew better than to discount the man, though. Everyone fighting in this tournament was a professional Soldier, and he had to treat this match as such. On the whistle, they started moving towards each other. Artorius deliberately stalked his opponent, constantly driving forward. His opponent allowed their shields to collide, but then stumbled, realizing his error. Artorius knew the man would not dare allow himself to get into a test of strength against him, so he waited, stalking forward. Finally, the legionary made a move, trying to rush past Artorius' right. The young Decanus spun hard, swinging his shield for all he was worth. It just managed to impact the Legionary on the shoulder, but it was enough. The man stumbled forward, catching a gladius thrust to the stomach before he could right himself. He fell to the ground, the wind knocked from him, as a loud shout erupted from the men of the Second Century, and indeed most of the Third Cohort. Artorius removed his helmet and raised his gladius in salute. He then walked over and extended his hand to his fallen opponent.

"You really are best there is," the legionary said graciously as Artorius helped him to his feet. "I hope you win it all, Sir."

"I am going to try," Artorius replied. He then left the arena and walked down to his favorite spot by the river. He knew it would be a while before the rest of the matches were completed, and then a mandatory rest period of one hour was taken in between rounds. He had some time to relax. He was still within earshot of the Cornicens' horns that would sound the end of the round and the start of the next.

The larger part of the day was a blur to Artorius. As each round of the tournament commenced, he found his and Magnus' names on the bracket. Magnus was advancing well, and Artorius was pleased when he saw both of them had made it to the quarter-finals. If they both won again, they would have to face each other in the next round. Artorius stepped into the arena, focused and oblivious to the shouts and frenzied activity that was taking place in the stands. The city's populace was completely taken with the tournament, and all had their favorites amongst the legionaries.

Artorius settled into his fighting stance once more. He assumed that as the tournament progressed, his bouts would get progressively harder, but such was not the case. He had literally mauled his first three opponents, and this next one would prove no different. This time he took a chance and bull-rushed the man. He expected his adversary to step aside, but instead he stood his ground and absorbed most of the impact of Artorius' charge. It proved to be his folly as the sheer ferocity of the Sergeant's attack winded him. Artorius swung his shield in a back-handed arc that knocked his opponent to the ground and simply placed the point of his gladius at the man's heart. The Legionary grimaced and nodded his submission.

A little over an hour later, Artorius returned for the semi-finals. He was surprised to see Magnus waiting for him at the entrance to the arena, devoid of weapons and helmet.

"Magnus, what in Hades are you doing here?" he asked, perplexed. Magnus could only lower and shake his head.

"I lost, Artorius," he said sheepishly.

"What do you mean you lost?" Artorius said, disappointment evident in his voice. "We were supposed to fight each other in this round!"

"I know," Magnus replied morosely. "All I could think was *one more match and I get to face Artorius to see who the better of us is.* I lost my focus, and I got careless. I tried to end the match early, and I stumbled." Artorius grabbed his friend by the shoulder.

"That is why I left the arena after each match," Artorius said, "so that I wouldn't lose focus. Not once did I even think about our pending match before this round. That is the only thing that separates us, Magnus. You have more real talent than anyone I know. None of the other alternate fighters even got past the first round, but you did. You have won three fights today against this Legion's best. You have nothing to be ashamed of, Old Friend. I hope you learned to not let your mind wander from the task at hand." He clapped Magnus on the shoulder who pressed his lip together and nodded.

"Do me a favor and thrash that bastard," he replied. "Unsporting son of a jackal spat on me after the match. He said, 'your boy Artorius is next.'"

Artorius laughed. "Well we are each entitled to our own opinions about people. All the same, I shall give him a good thrashing." As he stepped into the arena once more, he took a series of deep breaths, clearing his mind. He would not allow himself to think about this being the man who had defeated his best friend. It was just another opponent, one who would fall like the rest. And fall he did.

Artorius stalked the man, same as before. His adversary tried to thwart his advance, but Artorius was able to deflect every one of his strikes. Finally, he managed to catch the man on the foot with the bottom of his shield. The Legionary yelped and tried to hobble back. Artorius crouched low and blasted into the man like a battering ram. He then fell upon his stricken foe, and with the flat of his gladius gave him a hard rap across the genitals.

"That was for Magnus," he whispered into the man's ear. He then exited the arena as quickly as he had entered.

*   *   *   *

Ellard found Torin leaning over the rampart of the wall that surrounded the compound. As he walked up the steps to replace him on guard duty, he tried to speculate just how old Torin was. The life of a labor slave could be severe and cause one to age well beyond their years. Torin's head was shorn, with a scruffy face and neck. He was of average build, his muscles taught and wiry. The man had done some serious work in his time. Torin looked down at Ellard as he climbed the steps before continuing his gaze into the distance. The sun shone through the distant hills with a light breeze blowing over the rampart.

"I've come to relieve you," Ellard stated. Torin grabbed his spear and shield, and started down the steps without a word.

"You believe that Greek and his rhetoric don't you?" Ellard asked. Torin stopped and turned to faced Ellard.

"That Greek is the one hope we have of survival," he said levelly. "While the rest of you grab ass and fight with each other, *I* try and learn how it is *I* might actually live to enjoy freedom." Ellard raised his hands in resignation.

"Hey I meant no offense, Friend," he replied. "We are here with a common purpose, are we not?"

"No, we are not," Torin retorted. "You come for plunder; you care nothing for Gaul and whether or not it remains enslaved."

"And you do?" There was no doubt of the sneer in his voice. "When a man lives only for his own survival, it is impractical to care about the affairs of an empire. I care not for Sacrovir or the Romans; however, Sacrovir has offered me money, whereas the Romans offer only slavery and death."

"I was not always a slave," Torin said softly. "I once had a family and a life worth living."

"What happened?"

"They were taken from me." There was deep sadness in Torin's face. "Land that I farmed was taken by a Roman overseer. Suddenly I had to pay tribute on land that had belonged to my house for three generations! When I refused to pay, I was accosted by Roman troops, beaten, and taken away in chains. I never heard what happened to my wife and children, though I can only assume they shared a similar fate. When I refused to work for my new masters they did this to me." He removed his tunic and revealed a back covered in scars. "They threatened to have me crucified when the master decided he had better plans for me. Thus how I ended up in that stinking cage with you and Radek." Before Ellard could question him some more, Torin turned and walked briskly down the steps. He bumped into Radek, who was coming up to join his friend; for he had indeed started to form a type of bond with his fellow runaway.

"What's with him?" he asked as he set his weapons against the rampart. Ellard let out a slight chuckle.

"Seems our friend has a noble reason for fighting the Romans."

"Well let him," Radek snorted. "I just wish we would get on with it; though from what I hear Sacrovir has what he thinks is a cunning plan to deal with the Rhine legions." Ellard was taken aback by this last statement.

"Why should he wish to engage the Rhine legions? There are but a few cohorts in the region as it is. Why should he wish to bring more Roman forces against us?"

"Well I can't be certain but I think he wants to make as loud of a statement as he can possibly make," Radek answered. "In order to do that he needs to lure at least some of the legionary forces on the Rhine into battle. Smashing a few cohorts will not send a strong enough message to the Emperor." Ellard let out a loud sigh.

"Well at least in the meantime we get fed and have a few coins in our pockets," he observed. "I would just as soon get this fiasco over with. I would just as soon piss on that pompous Greek than have to endure anymore of his drills or talk of Sparta. Sparta fell long ago to Macedonia, who in turn fell to Rome. That man just needs to let it go already. If he's looking to revive Sparta, he's come to a strange place."

*   *   *   *

It was late afternoon almost evening. While a thief and a former slave in Sacrovir's army went about guarding their little rampart, the final match of the Twentieth Legion's tournament was set to take place. The amphitheater was packed beyond capacity. It seemed as if the entire city had come out for the final match. Artorius noticed that Camillus had brought the Century's Signum, which he planted in front of their section. Artorius took a deep breath and eyed his opponent. This man had also made his way through five battles, though Artorius had no idea as to how hard he had had to fight. He did not recognize the man, though he looked to be a bit older, and was probably from the First Cohort.

The whistle blew and they advanced. Artorius noticed that his adversary was circling, but not backing up. He was not in the least intimidated. Artorius hit him with one of his bull-rushes, yet the Legionary stood his ground and pushed back. The man knew how Artorius fought, and he sought to best him at his own game. Artorius knew he had to change tactics. He immediately increased his rate of attack, trying to work his way quickly around both sides of the legionary's shield. In his fury, he caught a blow to the wrist, which caused him to drop his shield. He then flashed back to a similar match against Vitruvius. As his adversary rushed at him, Artorius grabbed his shield with both hand and rolled over backwards, throwing the Legionary over the top of him, and onto his back. Artorius quickly regained his feet and lunged at the man, his gladius aimed at his heart. The man was knocked almost senseless, having been thrown almost directly onto his head. In an instant, the match was over, and the crowd went into a hysterical frenzy of cheering.

Artorius removed his helmet as members of the Second Century swarmed around him. He extended his hand and helped his fallen foe to his feet. When the man removed his helmet, Artorius recognized him to be Centurion Draco of the First Cohort.

"Well fought, son," Draco said, shaking his hand vigorously.

"And to you, Sir," Artorius replied. He was hoisted onto the shoulders of some of the legionaries and carried over to the reviewing stand, where stood Silius, Calvinus, and Vitruvius. Silius raised his hands, silencing the crowd.

"Sergeant Artorius," he spoke, "you have proven yourself to be not only the most skilled close-combat fighter in this legion, but of the entire Rhine Army! You have indeed earned the honor of being named Valeria's *Legion Champion!*" He then took the ceremonial silver gladius that Vitruvius handed him, and presented it to Artorius. As he turned and faced the crowds of people who had witnessed his triumph, he at last allowed his emotions to break free. He raised the sword high and roared a triumphal battle cry that shook the arena. It was echoed by the men of the Second Century, as well as everyone in the amphitheater. He then let out another howl of victory and held both fists in the air. He lowered his hands and closed his eyes, savoring his hard earned victory.

It proved to be a long night for Artorius, and he was glad he napped between matches throughout the day. His friends were intent on getting him drunk, and each wished to fondle the ceremonial gladius he had been awarded.

"It's not a phallus, Valens!" he jeered as Valens placed the gladius back on the table sheepishly, his face red with embarrassment. Each man that he had fought had bought him a drink, with the exception being the one who defeated Magnus. It mattered not to Artorius. He was feeling the effects of his drinking when Magnus walked over and put his arm around his shoulders.

"We got you something," he said, his face beaming. "Actually it was two 'somethings.' The lads decided that so much masculinity needed a bit of relief and cleansing."

"What, is someone going to scrub my back for me?" Artorius grinned drunkenly.

"Well I suppose they will if you ask them nicely."

"Magnus!" it was a tantalizing female voice behind him, causing the legionary to bolt upright. "I hope your friend isn't planning on keeping us waiting." Artorius squinted his eyes and peered over Magnus' shoulder catching a glimpse at a pair of fetching young ladies standing behind his friend. The brunette who had spoken stood with her hand on her hip. She was well endowed, with full breasts and strong legs and hips. Her friend was blonde, of slimmer build, and was giggling behind the brunette.

"Oh and how I have forgotten my manners!" Magnus replied, throwing his hands up in the air mockingly. "Artorius, meet Meegan and Glenna. Glenna's a bit shy, but a real fireball, I promise!" He leered at the women. "Ladies, meet the pride of the Valeria Legion." Glenna, the brunette, rolled her eyes at Magnus.

"Charmed, I'm sure," she replied, her eyes then falling on Artorius for the first time. She grinned slyly as she looked him up and down, sizing him up. "Well what do we have here? A good thing I brought you along, Meegan!" The blonde's face reddened at the sight of Artorius and giggled afresh. He rose to his feet, swaying slightly.

"Ladies," he said gallantly, taking Glenna's hand, kissing it. She curtsied low, faking her flattery by his gesture. She winked at him boldly.

"Sergeant Artorius!" a voice boomed. All eyes fell on Centurion Draco, who was walking towards him with an oversized goblet in his hand. "Here, you'll need something to help you out a bit." He then offered the cup to the young soldier.

"Sir, I appreciate the gesture, but if I drink anymore, there'll be no helping me," Artorius said, his voice slightly slurred. Draco snorted and shoved the goblet into his hand.

"I *insist*," he commanded, then whispered into Artorius' ear, "this is no ordinary wine. It may taste like rat piss, but trust me; you'll be thanking me tomorrow."

He raised the goblet in salute and almost gagged on the drink, and in fact wondered if he was drinking rodent urine.

"There you are lad," Draco slapped him on the back as Artorius choked down the remainder of the disgusting concoction. He then turned his head towards Meegan and Glenna who were waiting impatiently at the foot of the stairs. "Now go make us proud." The lads raised their goblets to Artorius, cheering.

Artorius was guided into the room at the far end of the hallway by his two female companions. As Glenna opened the door, Artorius gave them a push towards the oversized bed in the center.

"Why don't you two get started while I get comfortable," he said with a sly grin. Both women looked at him in mock surprise and giggled.

"Well aren't you the naughty one!" Glenna teased as she put her arms around Meegan. Artorius face twisted into a deviant smirk as he watched them kiss each other deeply. He then closed his eyes for a second and took a deep breath. His skin was flushed and he felt his body temperature rising. He started clenching and unclenching his fists. Whatever it was that Draco had given him seemed to wash away the effects of the alcohol. He chuckled to himself and took another deep breath as he frantically pulled off his tunic. It felt as if every muscle in his body was tensing and flexing, his manhood engorged with extreme anticipation. The two women, who had also discarded their clothing, looked up at him as he let out a low growl.

"Oh my," Meegan said her eyes widening. "I think someone's ready to join us." Artorius snickered at that as he dove into the fray of flesh and lust.

The legionaries cheered loudly as they heard the unmistakable creaking of the bed. Screams that resonated throughout the inn sounded like a mix of terror and ecstasy. Magnus nearly choked on his wine as he heard a woman's voice cry out indignantly, "don't bite so hard!" This elicited a fresh bout of raucous laughter and cheering from the men still conscious.

"What in bloody hell did Draco give him?" Praxus asked.

"Something I got from an alchemist friend," the Centurion answered as he walked up behind the men. "Let's just say that it was a little *special* something. It was expensive as all hell, too. I was saving it for myself, but the pride of the Legion deserves it more than me."

"That was quite noble of you, Sir," Praxus replied, his face full of sincerity. Magnus pounded the table roaring with laughter before falling out of his chair.

CHAPTER 9

▼

REBELLION AND DECEIT

Gaius Silius was in the middle of getting a rubdown at his personal bathhouse when Calvinus entered.

"Beg your pardon Sir, but an urgent message has just arrived from Gaul," the Master Centurion explained. Silius waved the slaves away and grabbed his robe.

"Have you read the message?" he asked as they walked towards the Legion headquarters, knowing full-well the answer.

"I have," Calvinus answered. "There has been a revolt amongst two of the minor tribes. I say 'minor,' but you know how these things escalate in a hurry."

"Which tribes are they?" Silius pushed open the doors to the meeting hall, and saw that the Tribunes, Primi Ordinones, and Cohort Commanders were already assembled.

"The Andecavi and the Turani. They are among the smaller tribes in the region; however I do feel that we should act quickly and decisively."

"Take your seats," Silius announced to the assembly as he sat down at the head of the table. Calvinus waved the messenger over to him. The man handed the Legate the copy of the scroll bearing full details of the rebellion. Silius was silent as he read the details of the message. Finally he spoke.

"The Aedui, Treveri, and Sequani are all offering to send significant numbers of auxiliary forces to help combat the rebellion. That's awfully nice of them." There was a touch of sarcasm in his voice. "Judging from the size of this rabble, the amount of support being offered, not to mention the sheer logistical nightmare of moving an entire Legion, I do not find it necessary that we should send the entire Legion. However, I do feel that a Roman presence must be maintained in order to stamp out whatever seeds of rebellion may have been planted by this.

"With that in mind, we shall stand up the First, Third, Sixth, and Ninth Cohorts, under the command of Master Centurion Calvinus. You will link up with our allies in Gaul and smash the rebels into capitulation. The rest of the Legion will be placed on alert, should things take a turn for the worse. I will need messages sent to the rest of the Rhine Legions, along with another to Rome."

"Sir is it wise to move against the rebels without first consulting the Emperor?" one of the Tribunes asked. He was a young man, having only been with the Legion for a couple of weeks, and was clearly biding his time before heading back to some type of political appointment in Rome. Silius did not see fit to answer the man, and instead gestured to Calvinus, who answered for him.

"The Emperor does not micromanage his Legion Commanders. He trusts them to do the right thing in a given crisis, and respects initiative. To wait for a reply from Rome can take several weeks, by which time the rebellion could have spread into a province-wide revolt." With that, Silius stood, the rest of the assembly following suit.

"Calvinus, you have two days to ready your men. In addition to your heavy infantry, I want you to take a contingent of thirty archers, as well as two onager catapults, and six scorpion ballistae."

"Consider it done Sir," Calvinus answered as he and the other officers saluted. Silius returned the salute and walked out of the room.

"You know, Gaul is rather pleasant this time of year," Gavius remarked as he tied down one of tarps on a cart. "I used to spend summers at Augustodunum when I was a child."

"I've been there myself a couple of times," Magnus replied. "Father had business dealings with some of the city councilmen. My brother Oleg still travels there in the spring."

"When was the last time you saw him?" Artorius asked.

"Just before we joined the Legions. I had hoped to see him when we were in Rome for the Triumph, but he wasn't able to make it. And the last two times I've been home on furlough, he was away on business. I did get to see my other brother, Hansi. He has been an oarsman in the navy for ten years now. I have to say, working a galley oar all day puts meat on you! He was as thin as a beanstalk when he left, and now I think he is almost as big as you are."

Artorius laughed. His size made him stand out in any crowd, and his years of training with Vitruvius had taught him to make the most of his natural assets. Though he was extremely quick and agile in close combat, he still had a tendency to rely on his strength and voracity. Such had allowed him to win the title of Legion Champion.

Magnus' talk about his brothers suddenly made Artorius sad. Though it had been eleven years since his own brother's passing, he still felt the pain of his loss. His first campaign as a legionary had been to avenge Metellus and every Roman slain during the Teutoburger Wald disaster. Though he had made an uneasy peace with his hatred and lust for vengeance, the dull ache of loss never truly left him, even after the vision of Metellus again … but then such a thing was impossible for a rational man to believe; that he had seen and spoken with his brother long after Metellus was dead! And yet he could still see Metellus vividly, and hear the words he spoke to him, as clearly as if he had still been alive. It had been so surreal that Artorius never spoke of it to anyone, not even his father.

He forced those thoughts from his mind and found himself wondering about the places they were headed to. He had only been through Gaul once, and that was when he was a recruit on his way to their fortress at Cologne. He knew that the region had prospered and advanced socially as well as economically since being assimilated into what was then the Roman Republic. Valens interrupted his thoughts.

"This auxiliary commander that we're linking up with, I heard his name is Sacrovir. Why does that sound familiar to me?" the Legionary asked as Magnus burst out laughing.

"If it's the same guy I am thinking of, he's the one whose gladiator was killed by Vitruvius at the games!" he answered. Artorius thought hard about the briefing he received earlier.

"Macro did mention that the auxiliaries were augmented with gladiators," he replied. "Seems strange that slaves would be willing to fight for Rome."

"Perhaps that is part of the reason for us going," Magnus remarked. "It sounds to me like we are going along just to make sure the auxiliaries and mercenaries hired for this mission don't get out of hand."

"Or worse, turn on us," Gavius added as he joined his section mates. "If this is the same Sacrovir that we met in Rome, I wonder what his motivations might be? You know he had a particular loathing for Vitruvius."

"That I do not know," Artorius replied as he leaned against the wagon, gazing off into the distance. He remembered that slimy, weasel of a man all too well. After Vitruvius killed his gladiator, Sacrovir left the Circus Maximus in a huff screaming profane oaths of vengeance not just towards Vitruvius, but all Soldiers of Rome. So what was he doing fighting along side the Legions? What could he possibly have to gain from this? Artorius hoped that their commanders had the same suspicions and would investigate further.

Later that afternoon, Artorius was strolling over towards the bathhouse when he noticed his old friend Pontius Pilate walking towards him. He smiled and waved to his friend.

"Sir," he said as he saluted the Tribune. Pilate laughed and returned the salute.

"It's been a while, Old Friend," he replied.

"Indeed it has," Artorius agreed. "Where have you been lately? Not getting corrupted by the other Tribunes I hope!" His smile disappeared when he saw the downcast look upon his friend's face. "What is it?"

"I'll not be going with you guys on this one, I'm afraid." Pilate was visibly upset.

"Why not?" Artorius asked. "You're one of the finest officers in this Legion; not to mention our chief of artillery!"

"That's just it," Pilate replied with a sigh, "I've been in this post for too long. It's been decided that it is time for me to move on."

"Where will you go?"

"The Praetorians." Artorius' face lit up, though Pilate still looked grim.

"The *Praetorians?* Are you kidding me? That's *fantastic* news!" He smacked the Tribune on the shoulder enthusiastically.

"It's fantastic if I was interested in pursuing a career in politics and government. Which I'm not," Pilate retorted. "That's the bastard about being part of the Patrician class; one does not always get to choose one's own career path. And when it is the Emperor's closest confidant who selects one, one would be very foolish to decline."

"Did Sejanus choose you?"

Pilate nodded in reply. "The Emperor's right hand no less. I suppose really that I should be excited about my new promotion. It will put me back in the social circle and in the eye of the Senate. Most of the Tribunes that I started out with here have already done time as minor provisional governors." He looked down for a second before continuing. "Listen, I want you to gather up some of the guys and meet me at Lollia's tavern tonight. I at least owe the lads of the Twentieth a good send off!"

＊   ＊   ＊   ＊

It was a sunny day in Augustodunum. Farquhar was conducting his studies outdoors. His father, an influential nobleman named Lennox, had sent him to the city to attend the university. Farquhar was an athletic, bright young man of fifteen winters. He was studying economics and marketing, and hoped to one day expand his family's fortunes beyond their already vast estates. Slaves were always a profitable trade, one which his family had yet to take advantage of. He figured he would speak to his father about this when his term at school ended.

He had heard rumors recently about civil unrest in the province, but that was something he never concerned himself with. Granted, his sense of adventure relished the thought of military glory, however Farquhar was also a realist. The warrior societies of Gaul had ended with the conquest of Caesar. The only Gauls who took up arms now were those whose families were noncitizens seeking Roman citizenship through service in the auxiliaries, or else lower class plebes who enlisted in the Legions. Farquhar was neither a mere Gaul, nor a plebe. He was of Gallic nobility, whose family had been Roman citizens since the conquest. Granted his citizenship meant little to him, for he still bore a Gallic name, and considered himself a Gaul first. He had never been to Rome, much less paid mind to her petty politics. His great-grandfather had fought with Vercingetorix against Caesar, all those years ago. They claimed fealty to Caesar and to Rome as a means of survival. As a boy, his father showed him his great-grandfather's sword and told him great tales of his bravery. Farquhar just laughed and shook his head at the absurdity of it all.

He was sitting on a bench, enjoying the warmth of the sun while he wrote; when he felt a pair of soft hands cover his eyes.

"Guess who?" a girl's voice whispered into his ear. He smiled and lifted her hands off his eyes. He turned to face Kiana, who seemed to radiate in the sunlight. She was a beautiful young girl, a year younger than he. Her father was also a wealthy nobleman, from whom she stood to inherit a considerable fortune in land and treasure. This inheritance would fall to whomever her future husband would be, and Lennox wasted no time in arranging their marriage.

"It's a beautiful day, why are you wasting it studying?" Kiana asked as she pulled him to his feet.

"I have much to get done if I am to enjoy the rest of this day," Farquhar replied. "My father has high expectations of me, and I would hate to let him down."

"Your father has high expectations of both of us," she whispered into his ear. "Oh, I wish we didn't have to wait to be married!"

"Soon, my love. It will happen soon enough. I will be finished with my studies within the next year, I will be able to start my own business, and then we can marry!" Kiana smiled. She truly did love Farquhar and could not imagine her life without him. Being betrothed to him was a matter of course; she was relieved that she had grown to love him as time went by.

"I promise to be a good wife … and a mother." She blushed as she spoke. Just then, Farquhar's friend Alasdair came running up the stairs.

"Farquhar, you are not going to believe this … oh, hi Kiana." He was short of breath and obviously excited. "You are not going to believe what has happened. The Andecavi and Turani have revolted!" Farquhar immediately released Kiana and turned to face his friend.

"*Revolted?*" he asked.

"They threw the Roman magistrates out of their lands and have declared themselves free and independent from Rome! Isn't it marvelous?" Alasdair was of the Andecavi, so the news struck very close to home for him. Farquhar and Kiana were of the Sequani, one of the tribes who had fought Julius Caesar to the last. While Farquhar was proud of his warrior heritage, he knew full-well from the stories of his grandfather the wrath and devastation the Romans were capable of unleashing.

"This is not good," he said as he shook his head. Alasdair looked crestfallen.

"Oh come on!" he retorted as he slapped his friend on the shoulder. "You are of the Sequani, man! You of all people should appreciate those who would look to liberate Gaul from the Roman oppressors."

"The Romans have given our people much in the way of prosperity and wealth," Kiana said as she sat back against the stone railing.

"At the cost of our freedom and heritage!" Alasdair spat. Farquhar grabbed his friend by the shoulders.

"Alasdair, listen to me. I know this strikes close to you, being that you are of the Andecavi. But no good can come from this. You know what the Romans were capable of during the time of that murderer Julius Caesar. They have grown stronger and more fearsome since then. The Rhine army destroyed the forces of Arminius and practically exterminated the Cherusci nation. What makes you think they won't smash right through your two tribes? The Roman army is a juggernaut, it cannot be stopped. Our grandfathers were but children the last time Gauls tried taking arms up against Rome."

"The Rhine army is paralyzed," Alasdair replied, his demeanor now calm. "The death of Germanicus and the implications of the Emperor in his murder will have immobilized the legions due to their grief. Word has it that they are only able to muster four Cohorts with which to put down the rebellion. Can't you see? Once these Legionary forces are wiped out, the Emperor will have to sue for peace! The entire province will follow suit. And then ... and then we will *all* be free."

"The Romans have auxiliary forces in the region as well," Farquhar observed. Alasdair smiled and shook his head.

"The Romans *think* they have auxiliaries in this area. Walk with me, my friend. We have much to talk about." Alasdair put his arm around his friend's shoulders and they walked off, talking in low voices. Kiana stood with her arms folded, unable to hear their words.

"So the auxiliaries have turned against Rome?" Farquhar asked at length. Alasdair nodded affirmatively.

"There has been talk, talk in high places, that the current rebellion is only the beginning. The auxiliaries right now are playing the loyal little lapdogs to Rome, but it is only a ruse."

"How can you be certain?"

"I have friends, who have friends," Alasdair replied with a coy smile on his face. "Trust me, sooner or later the rebellion will find its way here, and when it does, we must be ready."

"Ready for what?" Farquhar was completely lost at this point. The entire concept of a province-wide rebellion seemed a bit too surreal for him. Alasdair rolled his eyes.

"We must be ready to *fight* of course! Farquhar, we are the emerging leaders of this society, and of Gaul. Therefore we must first and foremost set the example, inspire the people to reclaim their warrior heritage." Farquhar looked to the heavens while he allowed everything to sink in.

"Let us see what happens," he replied.

*   *   *   *

The tavern was packed full of soldiers who wished to see off their favorite Tribune. On the small stage where musicians often performed was a table where Pilate and a few of his closest friends sat; the same table where Artorius had been the guest of honor following his win at the Legion Champion tournament. The Tribune was already bleary-eyed from too much wine.

"A bit of a social faux pas, don't you think?" Valens asked. "I mean, how often does a Tribune, or any Patrician for that matter, elect to have food and wine with the likes of us? Most view legionaries as mere insects!"

"Fuck … them," Pilate spoke slowly, working to enunciate his words. "Men are men, regardless of social class. Only slaves should be treated as property, and even they must be cared for."

"You always were one of the good guys, Sir," Praxus spoke as he placed his arm around the Tribune's shoulder. "A bit of an anomaly perhaps, but still one of the good guys."

Pontius Pilate was indeed an anomaly. Years ago, he should have been a magistrate, maybe even a governor. Instead, he had elected to remain with the legions, where he felt most alive. The more he grew attached to the men he served with, the more his peers, and betters looked down on him. He had been promised to wed the lovely—and wealthy—Claudia Procula; though her family was beginning to question the wisdom of marrying off one of their most eligible daughters to a man who would rather live with mud-covered legionaries than advance his career and social status. Only the Emperor appreciated Pilate's sense of devotion. Tiberius had often stated that he would much rather have remained with the legions until his dying days, often calling his time in uniform the best years of his life. In the end, even he had decided that the young knight needed to move on with his career. Sejanus took it upon himself to secure Pilate an appointment within the Praetorian Guard. Such a favor would certainly earn him Pilate's gratitude and loyalty.

"I asked them to allow me one last march with you boys," Pilate spoke, gazing into his wine glass. "Silius told me that there would be no Tribunes going on this one; only four Cohorts would be needed. He then chastised me for trying to stall on my appointment, and that any delays would not bode well with Sejanus. Gods know I am going to get another earful when word gets out that I fraternized with the enlisted men!" He sighed deeply and took a long pull off his wine.

"If it's any consolation," Praxus said in an attempt to lighten the mood, "the lads took up a collection and bought you your choice of one of the most expensive prostitutes in this region. They should be here before too long for you to peruse." Pilate laughed out loud and put his arm around the legionary.

"You men truly are friends," he replied. He glanced over at Artorius. "Care to join me? I'm sure we can get one for you as well."

"Hey, Artorius can get his own tart!" Valens protested. "We paid for him to walk off with a saucy pair the last time!" The Decanus raised his eyebrow.

"No need to worry Valens, I can indeed afford my own physical pleasures," he replied. "If it will make the good Tribune happy, then I can drop a few denarii so he doesn't feel alone and intimidated." This caused a rambunctious cheer from the assembled legionaries.

Pilate struck a sober tone and stood up, his wine glass raised, while Praxus and Valens helped prop him up. "To the Emperor, the Senate, and the people of Rome," he slurred as the legionaries raised their glasses. "And most importantly to *you*, my brothers in the Twentieth Legion. *Valeria!*"

"*Valeria!*" the host of men answered. All quaffed their wine as a procurer and a group of fetching and elaborately dressed young women entered.

"Ah, here we are then!" Magnus said gleefully as he stepped gingerly down the steps and over to the procurer, a pouch of coins in his hand.

"Sir, make us proud!" a legionary shouted to Pilate, who put his arm around Artorius. The young Decanus propped him up.

"If you forget how it's supposed to work, just watch me, and do what I do," he whispered into Pilate's ear.

The next morning Artorius came to the main gate to see his old friend off. There was quite the caravan of baggage carts, slaves, livestock, and various hangers-on. He had forgotten just how large the retinue of a Tribune was. There was a body slave, an auger, two footmen, a cook, steward, and a young woman that Artorius was not certain as to whether or not she served a function or was merely for decoration. Pilate rode up cautiously on his horse. He looked to be severely hung over, something that made Artorius laugh to himself.

"How's your head this morning?" he asked. Pilate simply shrugged.

"Head hurts, but my cock is sufficiently drained, so all is good. Tell me, do you always bite the young ladies on the neck?" It was Artorius' turn to shrug.

"Sometimes," he replied casually.

"Hmm, leaving your mark I suppose." Pilate said lightly, and then became somber. He stared at Artorius before addressing him again. "I'll not forget you. I hope that if I ever need strong leaders at my side, you will not hesitate to heed my call."

"I will always heed your call," Artorius replied. "Just do not hesitate to ask." Pilate smiled and nodded in reply.

"I got a letter today from another old school friend of ours. You remember Justus Longinus?"

"Yes, I remember him," Artorius nodded.

"He's now an Optio with the Sixth Legion, Ferrata; stationed near Caesarea on the Syrian-Judean border. At any rate, he's been doing some type of liaison duty with the Praetorians and the city's urban cohorts, and that he'll be in Rome for about another year. At least now I know that I won't be totally devoid of friends!"

Artorius smiled and then snapped to attention and saluted his childhood friend; a friend who had served with him in battle, through triumph and tragedy. Pilate returned the salute and signaled for the caravan to move out. As he rode out he called out to Artorius over his shoulder.

"I'll be sure to check on your father ... as often as he'll tolerate my company!"

*   *   *   *

Calvinus and the Centurions leading the expedition had been voicing their concerns regarding Sacrovir to each other. Vitruvius found the situation to be rather amusing, given his history with the gladiator trainer. The men were on edge, given the fact that this would be the first real action any of them had seen since the Arminius campaigns. Granted, it was all Centurions leading the expedition; no Legates with worries about political benefits or repercussions, nor would there be any of the inexperienced, and thereby incessantly irritating, Tribunes getting in the way.

"Looking forward to meeting your old friend once again, Vitruvius?" Centurion Dominus asked sarcastically. Vitruvius only snorted at the mock question.

"To tell the truth, I'm wondering whether or not Vitruvius should be taking part in parlay with Sacrovir," commented Cordus, commander of the Ninth Cohort. Draco shook his head.

"Vitruvius' history with Sacrovir is all the more reason for him to be seen," he replied. "Sacrovir's reaction may allow us to gauge his true intentions."

"I agree," Calvinus nodded. "When we link up with Sacrovir and the rest of the auxiliary forces, I want *all* Centurions with me. I have no desire for any type of prolonged meetings with these people; however we may have to play the gracious host if we are to glean any useful information from them."

"What say you, Vitruvius?" Cordus asked. Up to this point, the muscle-bound Centurion had been lounging quietly, sipping on wine, and eating beef cutlets that he found to his liking. He took a long pull of his wine before answering.

"To tell the truth, I'm rather looking forward to this," he replied. He said no more as he waved a servant over to refill his wine and bring him some more beef.

Sacrovir elected to wear Greek military garb for his meeting with the Romans; in a show of support, Florus was dressed the same. He watched as the Romans were ushered in. All were Centurions, judging by their uniforms and helmets, which each carried underneath his arm. One of the men stood out from the others. Though of similar height as his fellows, in addition to be completely bald, carried a copious amount of extra muscle on his chiseled frame. Sacrovir thought hard about where he had seen the man before, and then it dawned on him. He immediately started to sweat, his blood pressure rising. It was *him*, the man who had humiliated him of front of the entire population of Rome! Sacrovir's jaw clenched seething with hatred for a moment. Then he reached a revelation.

How convenient that I should use this rebellion as a means of exacting my revenge against Optio Vitruvius! The lead Centurion interrupted his thoughts.

"Commander Sacrovir, I am Calvinus, Centurion Primus Pilus for the Twentieth Legion," he said, extending his hand. Sacrovir rose and graciously took it, though his palms were already sweating. "Centurions Proculus, Agricola, and Cordus are my other Cohort Commanders." Sacrovir nodded at the other men and took his seat, his eyes never leaving Vitruvius.

"We meet again, *Centurion* Vitruvius?" he asked coolly, but with a respectful air.

"That is correct," the Centurion replied. "It's been a while, Sacrovir."

"Indeed it has." Being in the same room as this man who had cost him so much was insufferable. Still he persevered to remain cordial. Servants brought in trays bearing wine, ale, and various delicacies. "I do apologize that our last meeting was less than cordial. I admit I have lost many nights' sleep agonizing over it."

"I am sure you have," Vitruvius replied politely, taking an apple and biting into it. Both men's gazes remained fixed on each other in a silent test of wills. Florus became uncomfortable and decided to break the silence.

"Centurion Calvinus, it is indeed an honor that you have graced us with your presence, not to mention your reinforcements. However, I feel I must reassure you that your legionaries will not be needed. Our forces will be more than able to handle these upstarts."

"Of that I have no doubt," Calvinus replied. "That is why I only brought four cohorts instead of the entire Legion."

"Quite a responsibility for one of common birth," Florus remarked. "Does this mean then that you intend to fall under our command?" Calvinus smirked at the remark as Cordus choked on his wine. Even though Sacrovir and Florus were Gallic, they were still Roman citizens, and nobles at that. Therefore, they were in a higher social standing than any of the legionaries present. Though Calvinus remained composed, Draco seethed at the remark.

"Leadership of men in battle is a heavy responsibility, regardless of birth!" he snapped.

Sacrovir smiled. Florus was becoming useful after all, getting a rise out of the Romans with his less-than concealed insult. By not sending a single Tribune or Legate with their contingent, the Romans had negated all sense of political superiority and responsibility. He could have taken that as an insult himself, that the only men of rank the Romans had sent were Centurions. Instead, he decided that he would use it to his advantage.

"We have been tasked with providing support to your forces," Calvinus said smoothly. "However, we will still act as an independent force. Our mission is to see to it that this rebellion does not spread further."

Sacrovir listened, though his eyes never left Vitruvius. This meeting was a formality, nothing more. He knew that the Romans were there to spy on him; hence his reasoning for sacrificing the Andecavi and the Turani. Their defeat, in front of Roman eyes, would secure for Sacrovir the impression he needed to make. Just then, Taranis entered the room. He wore traditional Gallic garments, loose-fitting trousers and a tunic. He also wore an ornate cavalry sword on his hip.

"Ah Taranis, my friend!" Sacrovir announced, standing up. "Come, join us! This is Taranis, chief of the Sequani. He will be leading our forces from the front, when the time comes."

Taranis forced himself from sneering at the Romans, and took a seat by Sacrovir and Florus. Taranis passionately hated the Romans, never allowing himself to forget the sufferings they had endured under Caesar. The Romans continued to eat and drink, though all were uncomfortable with the situation. Only Vitruvius seemed to be enjoying himself.

"The Andecavi are by far the lesser threat," Calvinus asserted. "I have sent word to Acilius Aviola, Commander of the Eighth Legion's Eighth Cohort, stationed in Lugdunum. If the Sequani wish, they can link up with him there. The rest of us will mass against the Turani."

"Yes, I had wondered when we were finally going to get some use out of those Roman troops," Taranis said, his voice dripping with disdain. "That Cohort has been leeching off the people of Lugdunum for the last three years. I will be glad to finally get some work out of them!"

"Easy there, old friend," Sacrovir soothed. "Remember, the Romans are our friends and allies."

"Not to mention conquerors," Draco remarked in a low voice. If the Gauls heard him, they wisely kept their retorts to themselves.

*   *   *   *

Artorius watched as the auxiliaries conducted drill and maneuvers. Their weapons and armor varied greatly, though there was some semblance of order. Only a minority were actual auxiliaries, the rest looked to be a mix of gladiators and mercenaries. There was a man dressed in Greek armor, riding a magnificent charger, riding back and forth in front of the formation, shouting orders.

The Roman Cohorts were camped just outside the city walls, with their eastern rampart approximately a quarter mile from the auxiliary camp. Artorius and some of the others had gone over to watch their 'allies' and assess them.

"Looks like they're using a reverse maniple formation," Valens remarked. "Look at how they have got their heavy troops out front." Indeed the Gauls did seem to be in a basic three-line formation, only they kept their heavy troops in front.

"Quite the array of weapons they have," Magnus observed. "They almost look like gladiators."

"That's because a large number of them are," Artorius replied. "Apparently Sacrovir has offered these men their freedom if they fight for him."

"Fight for him, or fight for Rome?" Gavius asked, raising an eyebrow. Artorius smirked knowingly.

"Therein lies the great mystery," he replied. "On the surface one would think that Sacrovir and Florus are perhaps attempting to better their social and political standings by suppressing this revolt. I'm not so certain, though."

"I don't believe it for a second," Magnus snorted. "The cost is too great for this to be a mere display of fidelity and usefulness. The Emperor may dismiss them completely, saying that they were simply doing their duty as citizens. Sacrovir stands to lose a fortune here, whether his gladiators live or die."

"Well, we'll find out soon enough what their intentions are," Artorius replied.

"So those are the legionaries from the Rhine," Radek snorted. "They don't look so intimidating."

Ellard gazed upon their faux-allies with trepidation.

"Those men conquered the known world. I hope Sacrovir knows what he's doing."

"Sacrovir is nothing but a fool, as is that idiot deputy of his, Florus," Radek retorted. "That Spartan of his is completely mental as well. You, my friend, just need to worry about staying alive through all this."

"I intend to," Ellard replied. "I'll give them a good enough showing against the Romans then be done with this affair."

Artorius was walking the perimeter of their camp that evening, when he noticed a young legionary sitting off by himself, gazing at the setting sun. He was going to pay the man no mind, when he recognized him as Legionary Felix Spurius of Praxus' section. The lad had definitely improved his physique since recruit training. His paunch was nearly gone; his arms, chest, and legs filled out with a fair amount of muscle. As Artorius walked over to him Spurius was immediately on his feet.

"Sergeant Artorius," he acknowledged. The Decanus waved him to take his seat.

"Sit down," he replied. "I just noticed that you were off over here by yourself instead of over at the fires with you section mates."

"I needed some time by myself," Spurius replied. "May I speak frankly?" Artorius nodded.

"Tomorrow will be my first action," the legionary continued. "I am ashamed to admit this, but I'm afraid." He closed his eyes, expecting a verbal thrashing from the man who had bludgeoned and chastised him throughout his training. He was perplexed by Artorius' relaxed demeanor.

"What is it you are afraid of?" Artorius asked, gently.

"I am afraid of being shown a coward, of not living up to what I had promised myself I would do."

"And what was it you promised yourself?"

"That I would expunge *Spurius* from my name. My name means 'bastard.' My father is ashamed of me."

"And yet your family name *Felix* is a noble name; it means fidelity, and is a name you should be proud of."

"My father is not proud of me," Felix said bitterly. "Indeed he is a nobleman. His two oldest sons, my brothers, are both patricians with promising careers. He only acknowledges my existence through the persistence of my mother. He signed my letter of introduction to allow me into the legions in order to be rid of me, nothing more." He was now staring at the ground, his breathing coming hard through his nose as his pent up anger grew.

"What of your brothers?" Artorius asked.

Felix shrugged. "They were kind enough to me. There are vast differences in our ages so I rarely saw them." He took a deep breath and let out and audible sigh.

"Are you are afraid of being killed tomorrow?" Artorius asked, changing the subject. The legionary lowered his eyes and nodded.

Artorius nodded in return. "So am I."

Felix looked up at him surprised. At first thought he had not heard the Decanus correctly.

"I am going to let you in on a secret," Artorius said. "*All* of us are afraid. Though we do our best not to show it. We wonder if tomorrow our number will come up, will the gods choose to abandon us to butchery and murder. And you know what? It never changes; it never gets any better. No matter how many times I go into battle, it is the same every time; the same terror that grips a man, *knowing* that tomorrow he may see his last sunrise, that his will be a battle for survival. Though once the first blow is struck, it all becomes instinctive. Your mind and your body become acutely aware of what they are supposed to do. Being afraid does not make you a coward. Not doing your duty does."

"I suppose so," Felix replied. "But how is it someone like you is afraid of going into battle? I watched you destroy the best men this legion has to offer during the tournament, and I hear you are one of the best close-combat fighters Rome has ever borne."

Artorius gave a short, mirthless laugh at the young soldier's remarks. "I will tell you something that someone, my mentor in fact, once told me regarding his own abilities. 'I am not a god. The enemy still has a say in whether or not I live or die tomorrow; but more importantly, so do the men on my left and right.' Protect the men next to you, as they will protect you. For when we fight together, we survive."

"You have much wisdom and experience, Sergeant," Felix replied, "but yet you look so young." Artorius laughed at that.

"That is because I *am* young," he remarked. "I am probably scarcely any older than you are. I joined the legions the day after I reached the age of maturity. I took part in two campaigns in Germania, under Germanicus Caesar. They were brutal, savage, and beyond civilized man's comprehension of barbarism and cruelty. I may appear youthful in both face and body, but my mind and heart are that of an old man."

CHAPTER 10

▼

A BLOODY SKIRMISH

The Turani were mustered on the plains of a low-lying valley. There were perhaps ten to twelve thousand men dressed for battle, most bearing spears, or short swords with small, circular shields. There were about the same number of troops amongst the Romans and Sacrovir's forces. The legionary cohorts were behind the auxiliaries, who were arrayed in three lines of battle, with their heavy troops out front.

"We'll teach these legionaries how to fight!" a gladiator spat. Heracles snorted at the remark. He knew full-well that this army of thieves and gladiators were amateurs compared to the legions. However, it was not through battle that he intended to defeat the Romans.

"We will hold in reserve behind this ridge," Calvinus to Sacrovir. The Gaul seemed taken aback.

"Your men do not wish to take part in the glory of this battle, or the plunder to be had?" he asked.

Calvinus smirked and shook his head. "Let the glory fall upon your men. This will be a good test for them; a chance to allow them to prove their worth. That's what you want, isn't it?"

Sacrovir nodded briskly, drew his sword, and rode towards his restless army. Calvinus turned to face his Cohort Commanders.

"As soon as they move to join battle, we will step off at the double-time, moving around these small hills on our right. Once clear, we'll maneuver the entire task force online and hit those bastards in the rear."

"What of Sacrovir?" Aemilius asked.

"What of him?" Calvinus replied. "We do not work for him. Besides, I foresee Sacrovir only making this a token engagement; whether out of trepidations regarding his army or something darker, I don't know. All I do know is something is just not right. I think he intends to engage just long enough for the enemy forces to retreat. Well I intend to teach these rebels a lesson they will not soon forget!"

Farquhar and Alasdair stood in the shade of a large oak, watching the battle unfold in the valley below. A large hoard of men was massed in the valley floor, the first of many who would look to free Gaul from the oppression of Rome. On the far slope they could see the auxiliary forces and mercenary troops of the noble Sacrovir.

"Where are the Romans?" Farquhar asked aloud. "Supposedly there were at least four cohorts with Sacrovir's men."

"I don't know," Alasdair replied. "Perhaps they have already gone home?" There was an air of levity and giddy excitement in his voice. "If my sources are correct, this will be only a minor skirmish, rather than a real battle. The Turani know they are not supposed to win. They will withdraw, with only minimal losses, and once the Romans are lulled into complacency, they will join with Sacrovir!"

Suddenly, Farquhar's hand was on his shoulder. Alasdair's eyes followed to where his friend was pointing. Both lads' eyes grew wide in horror as they saw coming around the base of the small hills on their left a contingent of Roman soldiers.

"Dear gods, the Turani will be trapped!" Alasdair despaired. "The Romans will chop them to pieces! They must be warned!"

Farquhar's hand restrained him as he sought to run towards the battle below. "It's too late," he replied. "The battle is more than three miles away. You will never get there in time."

Alasdair looked into his friend's face. Farquhar's eyes were wet, fear and emotion overtaking him as he cringed in anticipation of the Turani's pending annihilation. Both lads turned towards the scene below. The Romans were now clear of the hills, maneuvering their way into formation. They blocked the entire width of the small valley, legionaries stacked up six ranks deep. Farquhar closed his tear-stained eyes as the Romans unleashed a storm of javelins upon their unseeing prey.

Sacrovir watched eagerly from atop his mount as his forces clashed with the Turani. Ironically, both sides were in fact working for him, and they all knew it. They looked to this battle as nothing more than a bloodied drill that would prepare them for possible battle with the real enemy—Rome. Sacrovir had even gone so far as to remove his helmet, so as not to be a target for missile weapons.

The Turani knew that they were not supposed to win this battle, and in fact were ordered to begin a mock retreat should they end up pressing the issue too hard. Both sides came together in a clash that resembled more of a sporting match than a life and death struggle. Granted, men were dying, however that was a necessary evil if the Romans were to be fooled. The Turani allowed Sacrovir's men to come down from the high ground and engage them on the level plain.

Sacrovir was pleasantly surprised with the way his gladiators were fighting. His mercenary troops were amateurs at best, a menace to themselves at worst. They would take the brunt of his losses. Several units of these had been outfitted with circular shields and eight-foot spears, which Heracles tried to teach them to use in a phalanx. Their formations were loose and sloppy, however Sacrovir knew this exercise would give them the opportunity to learn their lessons more poignantly, as the price for lack of discipline could be serious injury or death.

Sacrovir gave a sadistic grin as the battle ground its way along. He glanced over his shoulder to see if the Romans were observing or not. Oddly enough, there was no sign of them, not even their standards. His face creased into a frown as he searched for any sign of his so-called allies.

Where could they have gone? he thought to himself.

Sacrovir rode back to where the ridge crested and sloped down into the defilade behind them. He was horrified to see that the Romans were nowhere to be seen. A dark feeling of realization came over him as he wheeled his horse around, back towards the battle. At the end of a small spur that shot off the hillside on his right—well behind the ranks of the Turani—the Romans could be seen moving at a dead run. Within minutes, they were arrayed in battle formation, advancing on the Turani and Andecavi who were completely oblivious to their presence. Sacrovir closed his eyes and raised them to the heavens. He had anticipated only minimal casualties from both sides, and had expected to enlist perhaps another ten thousand Turani and Andecavi into his army as a result. His plan was quickly unraveling as the Romans unleashed a storm of javelins upon their hapless victims.

"Front rank ... throw!" Proculus shouted. At the sound of the order, the Turani turned around and were stricken with abject terror at the sight of Roman Soldiers bearing down on them. A volley of javelins tore into their bodies, an entire wave falling in the torrent. Blood splattered everywhere as javelins punctured and tore bodies asunder.

"Second rank ... throw!" Macro ordered. The Romans had waited until they were very close to the Turani before unleashing their javelins. This increased precision and shock as more of their enemies were skewered from behind.

Artorius was surprised to see that the enemy was only a matter of feet in front of him as he let his javelin fly. It burst through the back of one of the rebels, exiting through his heart and pinning him to one of his companions in front of him. The man in front gave a scream of pain and horror as the javelin struck through the back of his ribcage. He was then wrenched to the ground by the corpse of his friend.

Nearby, Legionary Spurius killed his first human being as his javelin tore through the side of another rebel, puncturing both lungs. The young soldier was breathing heavily, his mind awash in feelings of both triumph and revulsion.

"Third rank ... throw!" Centurion Vitruvius barked. Soon all six ranks of the Cohort had disgorged their javelins. The Turani were caught completely off-guard, not knowing where this threat was coming from. They had been told that this would be a minor skirmish, a simple blood-letting to prepare them to face the legions. In what could only be perceived as an act of betrayal, the Romans had completely outmaneuvered them, and were smashing into the rear of their army. Bodies piled up as the survivors turned about to face this new threat.

"Gladius ... draw!"

The legionaries' audible shout completely panicked the Turani. There was mass confusion, and many started looking for ways to flee the battle. Unfortunately, there was nowhere for them to run. Many still had no idea that the Romans were even behind them, and were caught completely by surprise as a wall of legionaries collided with the rear of their lines. Those engaging Sacrovir's troops in front were readying themselves to withdraw, completely unaware that their escape was now cut off.

Sacrovir's army was just as confused, not knowing if they should disengage or continue to pursue the battle. The Gallic general himself dared not ride down into the fray to try and stop the killing. To do so would be to show his hand and now was not the time. He could only watch through clenched teeth as Roman troops continued to slaughter the Turani. No one appeared to be even attempting to fight back, just survive, and possibly escape.

Alasdair laid his head on his friend's shoulder in despair. The Andecavi and Turani were kin to each other. The young man had many friends and relatives amongst the Andecavi and Turani, who were now being slaughtered by the Romans. Inhuman screams accompanied the din of battle.

"Those bastards!" he cursed through his tears. "They fight with treachery and deceit! My friends, my kinfolk, I should have died with them."

Farquhar grabbed Alasdair by the shoulders and shook his head. "No," he replied, "not this way. There will come a time for us to take out our retribution against Rome, but not today."

"Does this mean you intend to join us?" Alasdair asked.

Farquhar nodded and said passionately: "I renounce my family's Roman citizenship! I am a noble of Gaul, and we shall lead our people by our example and all will rise with us against those barbaric bastards that dare to call themselves the heart of civilization!"

Alasdair embraced his friend. As long as he had Farquhar with him, he would be alright. Together they would rid their homeland of the Romans.

Artorius stood ready as the Third Cohort pushed deep into the Turani lines. They were giving way quickly, and it was turning into little more than a killing frenzy. Indeed, he felt the battle would be over before he had a chance to engage the enemy. Then Proculus gave the order, *"Set for passage of lines!"*

Proculus' Signifier raised his standard as a signal to the rest of the Cohort. Soldiers in the front rank ceased in their advance and stood defensively. The Turani, who had been getting steadily pushed back, did not know what to do. None had ever seen the Romans execute precision maneuvers before, and they were unaware as to what was coming. Artorius rocked onto the balls of his feet, ready to spring as the next command was sounded.

"Execute passage of lines!"

With a unified shout of rage the Second Century stepped off and passed through the rank in front of them. By this point, many of the rebels had already thrown down their weapons in an attempt to surrender, aware as they were of the hopelessness of their situation. But, no order had been given to cease the attack.

Artorius tilted his shield and smashed the bottom edge into the face of a rebel who had just thrown down his spear and shield. The blow knocked the man down, rendering him unconscious. Artorius elected not to finish him, instead focusing on another Turani who wielded a short sword, and small, circular shield. The man attempted a punch with his shield, but before he could pull his arm back, Artorius brought his gladius down hard upon his forearm.

The rebel screamed in pain as the gladius cut a deep gash into his arm, smashing the bones in the process. Artorius followed up by punching with his own shield and stabbing the man beneath the ribcage. Before he could engage his next adversary, Cornicens sounded the halt.

"Cohort stand fast!" Proculus shouted. As soon as the legionaries ceased in their attack, the Turani started throwing down their weapons en mass. Many were weeping, their heads bowed in shame.

"We've been betrayed," Artorius heard a Turani say quietly to the rebel next to him. The Decanus cocked his head to one side, curious as to what the man had said.

"Who betrayed you?" he demanded. The Turani stared at him, eyes filled with hate and spat at him.

"Go fuck your mother, *Roman*," the man growled. This earned him a blow from Artorius' shield flush on his jaw. The rebel's eyes rolled back in his head as he crashed to the ground. His face emotionless, Artorius stepped forward and rammed the bottom of his shield into the man's stomach. The rebels surrounding the man stood wide-eyed, faces full of fear. The soldier's expression remained stoic.

"Artorius stand down, damn it!" Statorius shouted at him.

"Don't insult my mother again," Artorius said calmly before returning to his place on the line.

On the extreme right of the line, Calvinus stood breathing heavily. The adrenaline rush that followed close combat was still strong, even after twenty-five years in the legions. As he readied to give orders regarding the taking of prisoners, Sacrovir rode up on his horse.

"What the hell do you think you are doing?" the Gaul screamed at him. "You were supposed to hold in reserve, not go off on your own without even consulting me!"

"Don't you *ever* give me orders!" Calvinus snapped. "Instead of allowing the rebels to escape with their noses bloodied, we have routed and captured practically all of them. Now I suggest you round up these prisoners and get them into the stockades! Trust me; you don't want my men to do it." Calvinus' defiant smirk told Sacrovir that he had planned his little maneuver from the very beginning.

Sacrovir regained his composure, lest he show his hand to the Centurion. He turned his horse around and rode back towards his army. Across the plain, many of the Turani were unaware that they had been taken from behind and could not understand why instead of retreating, they were being forced to surrender.

Calvinus then turned to his Cornicen. "Sound recall," he told the man. He then addressed the Centurions of the First Cohort. "We will recover any dead and wounded we may have and retire to our barracks. Then we will wait and see what moves the rebels ... *and* Sacrovir make."

Ellard did not know what to make of the chaos that erupted in front of him. Their part in the skirmish had been going well enough-he had even succeeded in skewering an unsuspecting Turani through the guts with his spear-when suddenly he had spotted Roman standards behind their adversaries. Panic had engulfed the Turani as they were cut down in numbers by the legionaries. After the Romans stopped the attack, Ellard glanced at his companions. Radek seemed unconcerned, while Torin hung his head. Ellard decided to make use of the lull. He set his weapons down and started searching the dead in front of him.

Most of the men bore little except their weapons; however, he did find a small amulet around one man's neck. He could not tell if the red stone or silver-like metal were valuable or not, but there was only one way to find out. He pulled out his dagger and started to cut the leather cord that bound the amulet to the slain man's neck when a pair of hands shoved him hard from behind. He fell to the ground, the cord snapping in his hand. Ellard sprung to his feet, coming face to face with Torin, whose face was red with rage.

"How dare you plunder from these men!" he growled.

Ellard spat at him. "How dare I? *Fuck* you and your piety! If this is the only way for me to get anything out of this accursed affair, so be it!"

"You will not desecrate our people!" Torin shouted, leveling his spear at Ellard.

Radek stepped around behind him, his own spear coming between the two men. "Stand down, Torin," he hissed. Torin swallowed hard, yet he continued to glare at Ellard. Ellard started laughing.

"Look around you, Torin," he exclaimed, waiving his dagger in a sweeping motion behind him. "Our men are already plundering the dead. Are you going to stop all of them? The Romans strip the prisoners of their valuables; are you going to tell them they cannot?"

He walked up to Torin so that their faces were but inches from each other. "Or how about you go and tell them the entire plan? Shall we cut your throat in order to keep you quiet? The dead get plundered after a battle … get used to it! You want nothing to do with it, fine. Go and pretend that this is all for some noble purpose, but don't piss on the rest of us!" Torin lowered his spear, a tear starting to well up in his eye. He turned and walked away as Ellard continued to heckle him. Radek placed a hand on his friend's shoulder.

"Leave him be," he said. "We have enough enemies as it is. Do not go and make any more needlessly. Besides, if he doesn't wish to take part in the plunder, it just means more for the rest of us." With that, both men continued their search of the dead.

Felix stood trembling slightly, gazing down at the gladius in his hand. The blade was bloodied from where he had thrust it into the back of an unsuspecting rebel. He was awash with a mixture of feelings. He was partly shamed for having stabbed the man in the back like a coward. Yet he also felt a feeling almost of exhilaration brought on by the sheer power he felt himself in control of; it was as if he had the power to play gods, to decide who should live and who should die.

"But you're not a god, are you?" Artorius asked, startling the young legionary. He knew exactly how Spurius felt. He had felt the same way when he had killed his first human being, though there had been no remorse given the circumstances. Artorius' first blood-letting had taken place during the campaigns against the Cherusci in Germania, a campaign of vengeance brought on by the disastrous battle of Teutoburger Wald; a disaster in which his beloved brother had perished.

"It is a strange feeling," Felix answered. "I know not whether I should feel ecstatic or ashamed."

"I suppose it is natural for one to feel both," Artorius replied. "You have taken life, and it is instinctive to feel like we have done wrong. By the same token we feel ecstatic because we have survived; the enemy has fallen and not us. By killing those men, you may very well have saved the life of one of your companions. Unfortunately, those troubled feelings you get will always be there. I feel them myself after every battle. I also wonder how it is that I am still standing while others fell."

"My fear is that I may grow to like it," the legionary stated as he began cleaning the blood off his blade. "I find this to be both exhilarating and repugnant at the same time. Will it always be like this?" Artorius nodded in reply, to which Felix let out a sigh. "Well as long as the repugnance overwhelms the ecstasy, I'll be alright."

*   *   *   *

Night had long since fallen by the time Sacrovir made his way over to the makeshift holding pen that housed the prisoners. The moon shone through the wicker bars that prevented the defeated Gauls from escaping. As the guards opened the gate to allow Sacrovir in, Broehain, a leader of the Turani, looked upon him in disgust.

"I should have known that you would betray us to the Romans!" he spat. Nearly half his men had been slain in what was supposed to be a minor skirmish to fool the Romans; the rest were imprisoned with him, caged like animals.

"Please, you misunderstand," Sacrovir pleaded. Broehain was immediately on his feet.

"What is there to misunderstand? You allowed them to get behind and slaughter my men! More than four thousand now lay dead, the rest of us damned to rot in these cages! Shall I tell the Romans of your real intents? That you only wished to use us as sheep to be slaughtered in order to mask your own rebellion?"

"Gods damn you, man, listen to me! The Romans acted on their own! They assured me that they would not leave the ridgeline. It is I who has been betrayed." Sacrovir hissed at the man, incensed at how his plan was disastrously thwarted. "But we're going to change that."

"You had better be right about this, Sacrovir," Broehain warned. "Play us false again, and I will have your head myself!"

"The Romans have retired to their barracks," Sacrovir explained. "It is my men who have you imprisoned, not theirs. Therefore, it is my men who will free you."

Broehain was loath to trust the man after the horrific slaughter of his men, but it seemed the only way to free himself and his men. "You take quite the risk by freeing nearly six thousand prisoners of war. What is your price?"

"I will be sending you and some of your men with Florus to the east. Proceed to Augustodunum and link up with him. You will first rally the remnants of the Turani, and from there you will carry on to where an entire regiment of Treveri cavalry is stationed. Florus will undermine their loyalty to Rome and subvert them to our cause. When all of you have returned, we will exterminate any Legionary forces that remain in the province."

Broehain took a deep breath through his nose and stood erect. "It will be done," he replied. Sacrovir's blunder had cost many of his men their lives; however, he was still the only means any of them had of attaining their freedom from Rome. As Sacrovir left the stockades, he saw Julius Indus waiting for him.

"I think you have gone completely mad," Indus remarked as they walked back to where Sacrovir's mount stood waiting to take him back to Augustodunum. "Centurion Calvinus will not like it, and he will be suspicious what with you freeing all those men like that."

"Centurion Calvinus is no longer of any concern to me," Sacrovir replied, coolly. "My men have already fallen upon Augustodunum; the revolution has started in full. We have taken the sons of the province's nobles as hostages, in assurance of their continued loyalty. I further intend to subvert those young men to our cause."

"But surely the Rhine Legions will not let this go on unchecked," Indus retorted. "Yes, they only sent four Cohorts, but that was before this rebellion turned into a full-scale revolution." Sacrovir turned and faced him.

"You knew this day would come, Indus," he said, his eyes boring into him. "If you really wish to prove your worth in this enterprise, you will accompany Florus to Augusta Raurica and help him to subvert your cavalry regiment that has conspicuously remained out of this conflict thus far. In fact, you will take Broehain with you tonight, and link up with Florus." Indus nodded in reply.

"It will be done," he replied. Indus waited until Sacrovir had ridden off before returning to find his own mount. He then rode off in all haste, alone, and not in the direction of Julius Florus.

CHAPTER 11

▼

BETRAYAL

Valens was the first to see the rider approaching. The section was posted on picket duty; with the purpose of providing early warning against enemy fugitives attempting to use the forest road paralleling the small fort. They took turns with two men awake, the rest asleep, in full armor. Valens smacked Decimus on the shoulder and pointed down the trail, where the moonlight shown through the trees. The man was armed with a cavalry sword and wore a brass breastplate underneath his purple cloak. He rode at a slow canter, eyes searching desperately. Decimus nodded and silently went to rouse the rest of the section. Artorius was immediately alert, and raced to Valens' side without taking time to don his helmet. He signaled for Gavius and Magnus to hide behind the small barricade on the opposite side of the road, javelins at the ready. Carbo and Decimus ignited their torches and followed Artorius out onto the road. The rider was at first taken aback, but then gave an audible sigh of relief.

"Thank the gods that I have found you," he said.

"What business brings you out this way? Travel along this road is forbidden after sunset," Artorius replied.

"My name is Julius Indus, and I bring an urgent message for your commander," the rider replied. "Please, my time is short, and it won't be long before they notice that I am gone." There was no mistaking the nervousness in his voice.

"Indus … you're one of Sacrovir's men, aren't you?" Artorius asked. Indus nodded affirmatively.

"That is correct. Please, I beg you. Take me to Master Centurion Calvinus without delay. My message is urgent and cannot wait." Artorius nodded and motioned for the rest of the section to rise to their feet.

"Leave your weapon with my men, and come with me," he said. Indus nodded and dismounted his horse. He immediately unbuckled his sword, which was taken by Valens. Artorius signaled for Indus to follow him. As they entered the small building that Calvinus was using for the detachment's headquarters, an orderly inside rose up from behind the desk in the center of the room.

"I need you to fetch the Master Centurion. Tell him it's urgent," Artorius told the legionary, who nodded and went into one of the rooms in back. Moments later Calvinus walked into the room, having hastily thrown on his tunic, and was wiping his eyes of sleep. Artorius stepped off to a corner by the front door and stood with his hands clasped behind his back.

"Indus, what the hell are you doing here at this hour?" Calvinus asked. He knew that the Gallic nobleman would not have come all the way to their outpost without reason. Indus did not hesitate to explain.

"I only regret that it has taken me this long to get my message to you," he replied. "I ask that you forgive my delays, however it is only this night that I have been able to get away without rousing suspicion. Honorable Centurion Calvinus, I regret to inform you that you have been betrayed." Calvinus' face hardened at the remark, his face twitching slightly as he cinched up his sword belt. His instincts had told him this would happen, hence why he had already sent dispatches to Silius, urging him to place the rest of the Legion on alert.

"The entire uprising that you have helped to quell was nothing more than a ruse," Indus continued. "Sacrovir and Florus planned the entire rebellion as a diversion to draw attention away from them and to lull Rome into thinking of them as allies. As we speak, there are six thousand prisoners of war who are being freed under Sacrovir's orders. He intends to explain to you that it is simply an act of mercy, to show compassion to the people. In truth, he is sending these men to join his army at Augustodunum. They have been rallying their forces for many months. He intends to soon make himself master of Augustodunum and to declare the province free of Roman rule."

"And he plans to do this right underneath the noses of Roman Soldiers?" Calvinus asked.

"With the freed prisoners, Sacrovir now has an army numbering well over thirty thousand men. He has made himself popular amongst the youth of our nobles in Augustodunum, and intends to arm them as well. This will add perhaps another five to ten thousand men to his ranks. Florus has been sent to rally the remnants of the Turani, as well as subverting my own cavalry at Augusta Raurica.

"Sacrovir thinks that given the overwhelming odds, your men will simply go home or else face annihilation. He is also counting on the Emperor's unpopularity in the accusations of conspiracy concerning the death of Germanicus to paralyze your forces from being able to move against him." Calvinus' face was hard, his anger rising at these last remarks.

"Sacrovir has underestimated the Emperor, as well as the resolve of the Legions! I take it all auxiliary forces have sided with him?" Indus nodded affirmatively.

"They have, with the exception being my own cavalry. But I must tell you; this uprising does not have the popular support of the people. Sacrovir had hoped by this point to have an army numbering around one hundred thousand. Instead, he has only a third of that. His army is that of debtors and thieves mostly, led by impoverished nobles with outstanding financial debts to Rome. However, we must strike at him fast, before he is able to swell his numbers further. As I said, Florus is looking to rally both the remnants of the Turani, as well as our own Treveri."

"His 'army' is nothing more than an unorganized rabble," Calvinus said, disgusted. "I saw how his gladiators fought. They do not intimidate me. All the same, if the only forces I have in this area amounts to my four Cohorts, then Sacrovir potentially has me outnumbered forty to one, even without the Turani and Treveri. I need you to give me written details of Sacrovir's plans. I will send them with you on to Legate Gaius Silius, who is only about a week's march from here with the remaining six Cohorts of the Legion. I'll send riders out to other Legionary forces within the region as well. Their numbers add up to three additional Cohorts. If Silius is able to bring the First Legion, Germanica with him as well, that will improve the situation dramatically."

"I agree your men should be able to break Sacrovir's ranks quickly, though be advised. His men are not well disciplined, however they are well equipped. He is arming the young nobles of Augustodunum with suits of metal armor that will completely encase them, making them impervious to javelin attacks. They will not be very mobile; however, they will create an obstacle that he will use to break up the formations of your Legions. We also have an opportunity to take out Florus before we even engage Sacrovir." Calvinus held up his hand, silencing him for the moment.

"You and Florus are both of the Treveri, are you not?" he asked. Indus nodded affirmatively.

"We both share similar ancestry; however I am a Roman first. Florus is nothing but a traitor to the Empire, and to our people."

"Alright," Calvinus replied. "I'm going to send Aemilius and some of our cavalry to escort you to Silius. What of your own troops?"

"They are encamped at a forest pass not too far from Augusta Raurica."

"That's right at the base of the Alpes," Calvinus observed. "Augusta Raurica is a prosperous trade center, as well as a place of leisure for our troops."

"That is where Florus intends to meet with them. The survivors of the Turani have already started rallying there. I admit that I do worry that Florus may be able to sway some of my men into betraying us. No doubt he intends to wipe out the traders there as a message to the rest of us." Calvinus closed his eyes and exhaled audibly at the thought. The massacre of loyal Roman citizens would be a disaster that they could ill afford.

"I've ordered my men to delay Florus as long as possible," Indus continued. "My deputy is to meet us here in five days. I can be back from delivering my message to Silius before then. From him we will know for certain if our forces have remained steadfast in their loyalty."

"You seem to have doubts about the fidelity of your own men," Calvinus remarked. Indus shook his head.

"My men are fiercely loyal to me; however I do know that Florus will promise them much in gold and valuables if they should turncoat. I do not doubt that as a whole they will remain true to their oaths; however we must prepare for the worst."

"Alright," Calvinus nodded. "I'll get a letter to send to Silius myself. Can you ride tonight?"

"I can," Indus replied. "If we are to keep the initiative, we will have to move fast. Can your men be ready to move tonight as well?"

"I will have them ready to ride in an hour," Calvinus said dryly. He then snapped his fingers, summoning his aide. "Fetch Centurion Aemilius. Tell him to gather up thirty of his best riders and be ready to move in an hour."

"Yes, Sir," the young legionary saluted as he headed out the door. Indus left with him, heading back to his mount. As Artorius moved to follow him, Calvinus noticed him for the first time.

"Sergeant Artorius," he said, "I didn't even notice you there."

"Sir." Artorius didn't know what to say. He felt awkward in the Master Centurion's presence. Artorius' brother, Metellus had served under Calvinus in the Seventeenth Legion years before. At Teutoburger Wald Metellus had died saving the lives of Calvinus and a pair of legionaries. Calvinus gave the impression that he felt like he owed Metellus a debt that could never be repaid, yet he wished to atone for that debt through Metellus' brother.

As the Master Centurion, Calvinus' power within the legion was immense. While technically subordinate to the Senatorial Legate and Chief Tribune, the Centurion Primus Pilus was by far the most influential man in any legion, with the power to make or break those under his command. Artorius vehemently resented the idea of using the Primus Pilus to gain favor or promotion. Such politics ran rampant in the Roman army, and it always turned his stomach. He would stand on his own merits, or not at all.

"You've gained quite the reputation as of late," Calvinus observed. Artorius allowed himself a small smile, knowing that Calvinus was referring to the recent Legion Champion tournament.

"All I did was bludgeon a few oafs who were out seeking personal glory," he said lightly.

"One of those *oafs* was Centurion Draco," he replied coldly. Artorius grimaced, realizing his blunder.

"My apologies, Sir," he replied. "I meant no disrespect."

Calvinus snorted. "Draco was indeed an oaf in thinking that he could best you in close combat. He is one of the most feared tacticians I have ever witnessed, and his skills in individual battle are indeed impressive. However, he was outmatched by you before the fight even began." Artorius looked perplexed.

"Let me put it to you this way; the Legion Champion of the First Germanica was given an invite to challenge you," Calvinus continued. "He refused. So did the Champion of the Second Augusta. Fact is Artorius; you've gathered a bit of a reputation for being the most feared close-combat fighter in the entire Rhine army."

"There is still one who is better," Artorius countered, looking away. Calvinus shook his head.

"He disagrees with you," the Master Centurion remarked, knowing that Artorius was speaking of Vitruvius. "He told me at the tournament that he could never have mauled those men the same way you did. He said that you have grown far beyond what he taught you." Artorius sensed that Calvinus did not merely wish to exchange pleasantries regarding the tournament. He looked him hard in the eye before replying.

"Sir, does anyone besides Centurion Macro know of our connection through my brother?"

"No, why do you ask?" Calvinus was taken aback by Artorius' sudden change in conversation.

"Because it is better that no one ever knows. I know you feel you owe my family a debt. But fact is Sir, I am not my brother, and you are not in debt to me. I will make my own way in the Legion, not have someone make it for me."

Calvinus gave an audible sigh. "It is true that I feel a certain amount of debt for what Metellus did. I watched him die, knowing that it could just as easily have been me. I appreciate what you have said. However I will do this still, I am going to keep an eye out for you.

"Artorius, your reputation has the potential to cause animosity. Many have noticed that your star is on the rise, or at least it will be in a couple of years. Without political support, or worse if you should garner political dissension, your potential may never come to fruition. Be that as it may, I will respect your wishes. None will ever know of the connection we have through your brother, nor will that ever grant you any favor or special treatment from me.

"I was going to ask if you would be interested in transferring over to become my aid de camp. I know that the strength of your intellect rivals your sheer physical power, and I could use a man of your talents. However, I see that you belong on the line, leading Legionaries into battle. Dismissed, Sergeant."

Artorius saluted and then left. He felt foolish for having so blatantly turned down the Master Centurion's implied offer to act as his patron. Such sponsorship would almost guarantee his rise to Optio and then to Centurion in short order. But he knew that his conscience would never have allowed it. He suspected that Calvinus knew this as well. He sensed the Master Centurion was testing him. If so, then Artorius knew he had passed.

*   *   *   *

Piso was dead. Tiberius' heart was heavy when he received the news. Rather than allow the trial to run its course, he had elected to take his own life. Tiberius read the letter that Piso had left, addressed to him.

Crushed by a conspiracy of my foes and the odium excited by a lying charge, since my truth and innocence find no place here, I call the immortal gods to witness that towards you Caesar, I have lived loyally, and with like dutiful respect towards your mother. And I implore you to think of my children, one of whom, Cneius is in way implicated in my career, whatever it may have been, seeing that all this time he has been at Rome, while the other, Marcus Piso, dissuaded me from returning to Syria. Would that I had yielded to my young son rather than he to his aged father! And therefore, I pray the more earnestly that the innocent may not pay the penalty of my

wickedness. By forty-five years of obedience, by my association with you in the consu-
late, as one who formerly won the esteem of the Divine Augustus, your father, as one
who is your friend and will never hereafter ask a favor, I implore you to save my
unhappy son.[2]

"And yet not a word about his wife," Sejanus noted. Tiberius snorted at that.

"She abandoned him, in spite of saying that she would follow him to whatever end," the Emperor replied. "Now she goes to trial separately. Livia has asked me to see to it that she is spared." Sejanus raised an eyebrow at that.

"Sparing the murderess of her own grandson? That will induce the mob's ravings even more so." Tiberius shot an angry glare at his Praetorian Prefect.

"If Livia has asked for Plancina's life to be spared, then she has a reason for it. Perhaps the wife and the sons were innocent after all," he snapped.

"Forgive me Caesar if I have my doubts." Sejanus candor was a relief to Tiberius, even when it offended him. If only the Senate were made up of men who had the courage to tell their minds to the Emperor!

"The people are convinced of her guilt, I know this. I have had my informants scribing notes on what the people are actually saying. The following speech was given in the forum just yesterday. Quite an eloquent speech, I must say. Shall I read it to you?"

Tiberius grimaced and nodded. Sejanus then proceeded to read:

"So it was the duty of a grandmother to look a grandson's murderess in the face, to converse with her and rescue her from the Senate. What the laws secure on behalf of every citizen had to Germanicus alone been denied. The voices of a Vitellius and Veranius had bewailed a Caesar, while the emperor and Augusta had defended Plancina. She might as well now turn her poisonings, and her devices which had proved so successful, against Agrippina and her children, and thus sate this exemplary grandmother and uncle with the blood of a most unhappy house."[3]

He rolled up the scroll when he was done and looked at the Emperor expectantly. A half smirk crossed the Emperor's face.

"If Plancina were to turn her poisonings on Agrippina," Tiberius stated coldly, "she may very well do the Empire a service."

There would be no pacifying Agrippina. Though Piso was dead, she was incensed that Plancina and her son were to be spared. It further enraged her that all of Germanicus' family and friends seemed pacified by this turn of events. Claudius' attempts to soothe her only made it worse.

"You are a weak-minded fool!" she spat at him. Claudius hung his head at the insult.

"You c-c-cannot know how much I loved my b-b-brother," he replied in a soft voice. "The m-man who murdered him is dead, as is the woman who executed the vile d-d-deed. It may not be t-t-total justice, but it is something."

"All of us loved Germanicus, and we still grieve for him," Herod added. "But that grief has not allowed us to be blinded by hate."

"Oh I *see*," Agrippina mocked. "So it is I who am blinded, not my stepfather's Judean puppet!" She immediately regretted her rude words and Claudius looked shocked, though Herod seemed unaffected by them.

"I'm sorry Herod," she continued, her voice suddenly tired. "Please understand that I still do not hold the Emperor as completely blameless in this affair. I *worry* about my children. Tiberius swears that he will look upon them as family, but does he? What will happen to them: Nero, Drusus, dear little Gaius Caligula? Will he view them now as a threat to his own son Drusus?"

"The children of Germanicus are no threat to me," the elder Drusus stated as he walked into the room. "Nor would my father have you think of them as such."

"Your words are of some comfort," Agrippina replied, trying to force a smile. "But I know that Tiberius is constantly falling under the spell of the vile Praetorian, Sejanus. What will he have done with the sons of Germanicus?"

"I will handle Sejanus," Drusus replied, his eyes cold.

*　　　*　　　*　　　*

Silius was seething as he read Indus' and Calvinus' dispatches. The situation in Gaul had just become complicated. With Sacrovir's betrayal, he could easily overwhelm the small number of Roman troops in the region. Silius was certain that Calvinus would rally the local Cohorts under him, but still that put his total strength well under that of a single legion. He was suddenly thankful that the Legate of the First Legion had insisted on his troops accompanying him. The pompous old fool was looking to gain glory for himself; however, he was infirm and would not be able to make the journey. Silius had convinced him to stay in Cologne and to transfer authority to his Master Centurion.

"We are still a week's march out," Silius announced to Indus and Aemilius. "Can you hold until we get there?"

"If Sacrovir moves against us in force, I don't think so," Aemilius replied. "Calvinus has sent word to the legionary cohorts in the local garrisons. They will take a few days to arrive, and there are only three of them. More than just additional infantry, what we need is cavalry."

"Which is where I come in," Indus interjected. "I have an entire regiment, which we will snatch out from under Sacrovir's nose. If we can send a contingent to link up with them, they can also smash Florus and the remnants of the Turani."

"That is quite the gamble," Silius replied. "I do not think that Calvinus will be able to spare more than a single Cohort. Tell him to send troops to aid the cavalry in routing the Turani; if they can kill or capture Florus, so much the better. But tell him to use his best judgment. I do not want to be losing men in needless folly."

CHAPTER 12

▼

A RECKLESS GAMBLE

"The rest of the Legion is on its way to us, as is the First Germanica," Aemilius reported. "Silius has affirmed that he wants us to send a contingent to assist Indus' cavalry in trapping Florus and preventing him from linking up with Sacrovir."

Calvinus frowned in contemplation. While he was relieved that Silius had succeeded in rallying the First Legion to reinforce the Twentieth, he was reluctant to split the forces he had on hand. The Cohort from Lugdunum was still at least a day and half's march away, and it would be at least another three to four days after that before the Legionaries from Axima and Augustonemetum arrived.

"We cannot afford to spare more than a Cohort," Agricola remarked. "Any more than that and we will have no chance of holding should Sacrovir decide to attack us."

"My only question is will a Cohort be enough?" Cordus asked. "We have not only the Turani to deal with, but they may have been augmented by defectors from the Treveri. We risk losing an entire Cohort and still have those bastards to deal with."

"I assure you, most of my men have remained loyal," Indus replied. "However, your point is valid. I have ordered my cavalry to demonstrate against the Turani and try to fix them in place. That will slow down their movement."

"I will go," Proculus stated before the issue could be debated further. "If we move now, we can entrap the enemy while they are still confined to the mountain passes. They will have Indus' cavalry on one side, and us on the other."

"The old 'hammer-and-anvil' approach," Calvinus observed. "I like it. Ready your men to move at first light. Indus, you will accompany them. Just remember, time is not your ally on this mission. We will need every man we can muster once we do face Sacrovir's army. Even with the First Germanica and the legionary garrisons, we will still be badly outnumbered, at least four to one."

"My regiment has roughly a thousand men to augment our ranks," Indus added. Calvinus nodded in reply.

"We'll need them," he said. "The local garrisons have no cavalry to speak of, besides couriers, and the combined cavalry forces of both legions amount to only about six hundred men.

"Agricola, you will dispatch one century towards Augustodunum to act as an early warning in case Sacrovir decides to move against us. They will also be tasked with scouting out the best place for us to encamp, once the rest of the army arrives."

"We'll make it happen," Agricola replied. "I'll go myself with my First Century and report back on any movements of the enemy." With that, he turned and left. Proculus was right behind him.

"Calvinus, with your permission I am going to have the Third ready to move tonight," he said over his shoulder as he stood in the doorway. The Master Centurion nodded.

"Use your best judgment, Proculus. I need you back here as soon as possible, but do not get careless. We cannot afford to lose you."

"A nighttime road march; isn't this fun?" Carbo said sarcastically under his breath.

"Quit complaining," Magnus retorted before Artorius could chastise the legionary. "You've had the whole last week to catch up on your beauty sleep! Besides, we need to make sure we are back in time for the real battle."

Artorius noticed that Magnus seemed to handle most of the minor discipline problems within the section. He was glad for it. Though he held no command authority, Magnus had the respect of his fellow legionaries. They listened to him without question, something which eased the workload on Artorius immensely.

The Third Cohort was moving at the quick step. Every legionary traveled light, carrying only a week's worth of iron rations, and a single javelin instead of the usual pair, along with their entrenching tools. The lighter loads allowed for them to increase their pace on the march, as did the absence of baggage carts. While sleeping on the ground without a tent was not preferred, the nights were pleasant enough that the legionaries did not seem to mind. Besides, all understood full-well the urgency of their mission.

*   *   *   *

Only a pair of Praetorian Guardsmen accompanied the Emperor and his son to Vipsania's home. Her time was growing short, and Tiberius knew that if he did not see her now, he may never get another chance. So many things did he already regret, that he only hoped he could try and make it right at the very last.

A servant opened the door, and the men walked into the foyer. As they did, Senator Gallus was seen coming out of one of the rooms. He smirked when he saw the Emperor.

"I should have known you would come," he sneered.

"Where is she?" Tiberius asked, his expression stony. The last thing he wanted was to have his final moments with his beloved ruined by conflict with this man.

"You giving me orders in my own house, Caesar?" Gallus asked curtly, walking over until his face was mere inches from the Emperor's. "I may not live here, but this is still my house, and Vipsania is still my wife."

"Why did you never grant her a divorce?" Tiberius asked, his voice calm, though his face noticeably hardened. "You never loved her. You have not lived together for years, so why did you not let her go?"

"So that she could be taken back by you?" Gallus snorted. "Oh you would have liked that, wouldn't you, to have her once again as your own, as Empress of Rome no less? How big a fool do you take me for, Tiberius? I would be lying if I said I didn't take *distinct* pleasure in watching you suffer all these years, pining after her, and yet keeping her out of your reach. I know that she was the only thing saving me from your spiteful vengeance, and that is why I kept her around. If I had divorced her, what would have stopped you from destroying me and my family?" Tiberius could not deny it. Though he had never intentionally used his power as a means of settling a personal score, he had certainly felt the temptation to do so against Gallus.

"Get out of my way," he replied, his voice extremely calm. Drusus took a step back, recognizing the danger that Gallus was in. The Senator stood fast in defiance.

"Or what? You going to have your Praetorians here throw me out of my own house? That would not be so clever, Caesar." The Emperor's eyes narrowed slightly, a smirk crossing his own face.

"Oh no, I do not need them to take care of my dirty work for me." In a flash he grabbed Gallus by the throat and by his toga, slamming him against a pillar. Then with terrifying strength, he lifted the man off the floor. Servants looked on, horrified. They wished to protect their master, but not daring to come near the Emperor. Gallus was petrified as Tiberius slowly crushed his throat. As he started to black out, he was thrown to the floor, where he lay coughing and wheezing. The Praetorians looked on amused. Both men were veterans who had served under Tiberius in Pannonia and had witnessed his maddening feats of strength when in a rage.

"I am going to *ask* you again to leave, Senator Gallus," Tiberius remarked, his voice still calm. "And you may want to think things through before you go running to your cuckold in the Senate. It may not reflect well upon your masculinity to have it known that an old man was able to manhandle you like a wolf would a hare." Gallus struggled to his feet, coughing and clutching his throat. As he started to stagger away, he fell into Drusus, who calmly guided him to the door.

"I will escort the good Senator out while you have a moment to yourself," the young man remarked over his shoulder. Tiberius allowed himself a half smile, but was sullen once more as he remembered why he was there. Tiberius wanted to race down the corridor to her, but kept himself at a very brisk walk.

The Praetorians posted themselves on either side of the door to the Green Room. Tiberius stopped and glanced at the elder of the two. The man grimaced slightly and nodded. The younger looked at the Emperor with sympathy. The men were truly devoted and they felt their Emperor's pain, as much as if it were one of their wives or lovers who were dying. Tiberius knew this and he was grateful to them; nameless men in armor to most, but to the Emperor they were friends, companions from a different and happier age in his life.

As he slowly opened the door to Vipsania's bedchamber, the sight of her broke his heart. In the soft light of a brassier, he saw his beloved—the woman who had been life itself to him. Her once slender body had been ravaged by the disease and was painfully thin and withered. Though her face had aged tremendously by sickness, it still held the elegant beauty that captivated him in his youth.

Vipsania's eye lit up when she saw Tiberius. "I knew you would come," she said smiling weakly. Her voice was raspy and feeble. Tiberius could see that it hurt her to speak. Kneeling by her bed, he ran his fingers through her hair and kissed her on the forehead.

"All I ever wanted was to take you back," he said, his voice breaking. So much he wanted to tell her, and yet he was uncertain if he would be able to find the right words. "If ever there was a woman who should have been Empress of Rome ..."

Vipsania raised a finger to his lips, quieting him. "Do not live in regret, my Love," she replied. "It was a terrible thing they made you do, forcing you to divorce me. I never faulted you for it; I pitied you, I wept for you." Her voice trailed off to a whisper on the last few words, so fragile had she become.

Tiberius wanted nothing more than to lay his head on her shoulder. He wanted to hear her speak soothing words while her soft hands stoked his hair as she did when they were first married and he was grumpy or melancholy. He quickly regained his composure. *She is sick and dying,* he told himself savagely. You *need to be comforting* her.

"I never ceased loving you," Tiberius said softly forcing down his tears and smiling gently.

But Vipsania knew him all too well. Wordlessly, she reached out and drew his head to her shoulder. Her hands stroked his hair, almost absentmindedly. For the briefest of time, they were young again, like when they were newly married. Only when he was readying to take his leave did she speak again, her voice as soft as the rustling of leaves.

"Do not be so quick to follow me into the next life, Tiberius. You know I will wait for you." Tiberius tenderly kissed her lips and held her close for what he knew to be the last time.

The Emperor felt completely numb as he left the house, oblivious to the presence of his guards, or of his son. The only thing he could comprehend was her final words to him. They echoed in his mind, like he knew they would for the rest of his days. *I will wait for you.*

*   *   *   *

In just over a day and a half's march, the Roman contingent reached the base of the hills where they knew beyond the Turani was encamped. Thankfully, the enemy had yet to reach the open plains, where they would have a decided advantage and could easily encircle the legionary troops. As the Cohort came to a halt, a man on a charger, wearing the uniform of an auxiliary cavalryman rode up. Indus, Proculus, and the other Centurions rode out to meet him.

"What news?" Indus asked.

"The Turani are about a half day's march from here," the trooper replied. "They are encamped on high ground, though their maneuverability is severely restricted by the forests and rough terrain."

"Aside from directly on the road, are there any practical avenues of approach?" Proculus asked. The cavalryman shook his head.

"None," he answered. "The rocks and trees will break apart our formations and slow any advance to a crawl." Proculus let out a sigh of frustration. With his forces already outnumbered, attacking an enemy entrenched on high ground would be supreme suicide. He was severely pressed for time, yet he would not do Calvinus any good if his Cohort was rendered ineffective by excessive casualties.

"And with clear skies and a full moon, our chances of a surprise attack, even at night, are nonexistent," Centurion Dominus observed. Indus and Proculus both nodded their heads in acknowledgment. Macro sat with his chin resting in his hand, deep in thought. At length he spoke.

"Do the Turani even know we are coming?" he asked.

"I wouldn't think so," the trooper replied, "though they definitely know our cavalry our close by. We have not risked any kind of sortie against them because of their numbers and advantage of terrain."

"How many do they have?" Indus asked.

"About five thousand," was the reply. "Our defections were low, and we still have around twelve hundred men ready to fight."

"That still leaves us in a sticky predicament, especially if they have the high ground," Proculus remarked.

"And since time is not our ally here, we cannot afford to wait them out," Macro added. "What about a diversionary attack, one that would draw them down from their position?"

"It's possible," Indus answered. "As long as they don't know about your troops and think their only threat is my cavalry."

"What do you have in mind, Macro?" Proculus asked.

"I think we should scout ahead and see just how close we can get to their position before we risk being spotted. If we get close enough, we can have Indus' cavalry strike against the Turani. Have them engage just long enough to bait them into pursuit. With no other threats in the area known to them, they will see it as an opportunity to smash the Treveri cavalry and eliminate any chance of being pursued further. Once we have the terrain advantage, we can sweep them. If we strike hard and quickly enough, we may be able to induce them to panic; they are not professional soldiers. And," Macro cracked his knuckles. "They do not know our true numbers."

"Such a brazen attack may make them think we actually have *them* outnumbered," Proculus nodded approval. "Alright, a couple of us need to conduct a leaders' reconnaissance of the enemy positions. Who is coming with me?"

"I'll go," Vitruvius immediately answered.

"So will I," Macro added. "Though I think you should stay, Proculus. If something goes wrong, we cannot very well afford to lose our Cohort Commander. We will take a couple of men with us."

"Very well," Proculus replied. "It is almost midday. I want you back before nightfall. Don't take any unnecessary risks. Just scout out their positions and find out where we need to stage our forces." He then turned to the cavalry trooper. "Can you make it back to your regiment without being seen?"

"It took me all night in the dark to navigate my way around, but in the daylight I'll be alright."

"Whatever you do, do *not* allow yourself to be spotted," Indus emphasized. "The enemy needs to think that all Roman forces are confined to the northeast of their position. Have our men advance towards the Turani. At midday tomorrow we will sortie against them and lure them into the low-lying areas."

"And once we have taken over their positions, a Cornicen will sound the order for them to come about and attack," Proculus added. The trooper nodded in reply and rode off towards the thick forests that covered the hills to their right.

"Artorius!" Macro waved the Decanus over to him. "You can ride well enough, can't you?"

"Yes, Sir," Artorius replied.

"Good. You're coming with us." At that, Artorius removed his helmet and started unlacing the straps of his armor.

"What are you doing?" Vitruvius asked.

"We won't get within five miles of the enemy wearing armor and helmets that reflect the sunlight," he explained. Vitruvius frowned and nodded. He and Macro removed their armor and helmets as well. Sergeant Rufio was also selected to accompany them, as were two legionaries from Vitruvius' Century.

The six men kept their eyes and ears open as they rode up the mountain road. It was steep on both sides, with the right-hand side going up the mountain, and the left into the valley below. Both sides were also covered in trees and tall grass. At length, Rufio noticed smoke from cooking fires in the distance. He grabbed Macro by the shoulder and pointed towards them. Macro nodded and signaled for his contingent to move off the road to their right, into the trees. They moved up the steep slope until it leveled off, allowing their mounts to traverse more easily. Through the mass of trees, they were still able to make out the smoke from the fires. When they were almost parallel to what they surmised was the enemy camp, they dismounted. Rufio and one of Vitruvius' legionaries stayed with their horses while the rest of the men moved slowly towards the enemy positions.

About fifty meters before where the tree line opened up, the ground rose sharply. The legionaries got down on their hands and knees and crawled up the embankment. At the top they found they had a perfect vantage point with which to observe the Turani camp. The forest road rose up sharply, before leveling off for about three hundred meters. It then dropped back down, continuing on its winding way through the base of the Alpes. Off to their right they could just barely make out the camp of Indus' cavalry, at the base of the next ridgeline. They were keeping their distance, but staying close enough to let the Turani know they were there. With no horsemen of their own, the Turani knew that any attempts at smashing the Roman cavalry would be futile.

Directly to their front, on the opposite side of the forest road, was a large meadow that the rebels were encamped in. It was filled with tall grass and flowering plants, but devoid of the masses of trees. Though the conditions looked cramped, it was indeed large enough for all five thousand of the Turani to camp. Macro noticed a figure wearing a gleaming bronze cuirass and Greek helmet with a magnificent purple plume walking across the meadow. He immediately recognized the man as Julius Florus, given that he had worn the same audacious attire during their skirmish against the Andecavi.

The Centurion felt a hand on his shoulder. He looked to his left to see Artorius pointing towards a bend in the forest road. It was about four hundred meters short of where the ground rose up sharply. Six men could be seen milling about; pickets tasked with keeping an eye out for any potential threats. Macro nodded and pointed this out to Vitruvius. Macro then produced a wax tablet and stylus and began making diagrams of the enemy positions. Once he was satisfied, he signaled for them to leave. After linking up with Rufio and their mounts, they made their way slowly back towards their positions. Just out of the enemy pickets' field of vision, Macro led them back onto the forest road. He then took a piece of red cloth and tied it to one of the trees.

"Here will be the staging point," he explained in a low voice. "This is about as close as we can get without running the risk of being spotted." At about a mile down the road, he stopped and tied off another piece of cloth to a tree. This particular marker would show where the Cohort would ground all of its gear and the men would ready for battle.

Proculus had had the Cohort on the march and it did not take Macro and the others long to reach them. The Cohort Commander came out to meet them.

"How far?" he asked as the contingent dismounted and gathered around.

"Not five miles," Macro replied. "I have sketched out their location and positions. Everything tomorrow hinges on Indus' cavalry being able to draw them down from their camp."

"They are not expecting us, however they have posted a small group of pickets to warn against any pending attack," Artorius added. Proculus looked over Macro's scribing in contemplation.

"We will be ready to march at two hours after sunrise," he said at last. "We will get into position with plenty of time for the cavalry to execute their diversion."

"Where is Indus?" Vitruvius asked looking around.

"I sent him back to his regiment. His task with us was done, and his troopers need him. Alright, go ahead and brief your men on tomorrow's engagement. Have them start the rotating sentry watch and then get some sleep."

Artorius lay his head down on his pack. It was a cloudless night, and the moon shone brightly. He placed his hands behind his head and took a deep breath. He was nervous about the pending engagement with the Turani.

Magnus, who had just returned from sentry duty, picked up on his Sergeant's mood.

"Talk to me," he said as he removed his helmet and sat down. "You've got something on your mind; I can see it in your face."

Artorius continued to stare at the stars, lost as he was in thought.

"Oh come off it," Magnus persisted. "Artorius, we have been friends for too many years for you to be able to hide stuff from me. We are all nervous about tomorrow, and it is not just the normal anxiety that comes before combat."

"I know," Artorius answered. "The entire outcome of this engagement hinges on the ability of Indus' cavalry to goad the Turani off the high ground. Some of the cavalry have already defected, and I wonder about the loyalty of the rest. They take a great risk by allowing themselves to be used as bait like that."

"I think they will do what they can," Magnus replied. "Proculus seems to have faith in Indus; otherwise he would not have allowed him to return to his regiment before the battle. My worry is whether or not the Turani will take the bait.

"I will be honest with you, Artorius. This is kind of a weird feeling that I have. It is not the sense of dread like what I had before we stormed the Angrivarii stronghold at the end of the Germanic wars. I cannot explain it. Something tells me that things are going to go really well tomorrow and we will rout the rebels without difficulty, or else it will be a complete disaster."

"Not many probabilities in between," Artorius replied. He then sighed and rolled onto his side. "Whatever happens next, the die has been cast. Tomorrow we will know if it rolled *Venus* or not." With that he closed his eyes and started to drift off to sleep. He could faintly hear Magnus removing his armor and giving a grunt as he removed each of his sandals. His friend then gave a loud sigh as laid down and stretched his legs. Artorius took another deep breath and let him be taken by sleep.

The die has been cast.

CHAPTER 13

▼

THE DIE IS CAST

"General Florus, the Roman cavalry appear to be moving to sortie against us." Florus sat up from his nap and waved the warrior off.

About time, he thought to himself. Having the Treveri at his heels was slowing his progress, and he needed to get to Augustodunum as soon as possible. He was angered that so few, less than twenty, had defected in spite of his lavish offers of gold. He was still licking his wounded pride from having had his horse snatched away by the indignant troopers. He relished the idea of thrashing Indus' horsemen once and for all, for they were not Treveri warriors, as he was. Their blind loyalty to Rome deprived them of their heritage and status in Florus' mind. They were no longer kin to him.

He donned his helmet and walked over to the edge of the camp, where a large number of his warriors were rallying. He gazed down the hill and saw that indeed the Treveri were on the move towards them. All were adorned in mail shirts and Legionary helmets, each carrying an oblong shield and seven-foot lance. Florus scowled in disgust when he saw Indus himself at the head of the formation.

"So the mighty Julius Indus has betrayed us," he muttered. *"Form up the rest of the army!"* Aides immediately went about rallying the rest of the Turani force. As they started to mass along the ridgeline, one of Indus' equestrians blew a loud note on a Cornicen's horn.

The legionaries of the Third Cohort heard the sound of the horn. All were immediately on their feet, shields and javelins at the ready. Centurions and Optios signaled for their men to stand easy.

"Easy lads," Macro said in a low voice. "We do not move until the second trumpet sounds."

As he leaned against his shield, Artorius reviewed in his head once more how it all was supposed to work. The forest road allowed for no more than a dozen men abreast, and the entire Cohort found itself stretched out in a very long column. Artorius' section happened to be at the very front of it all, and their job would be to take out the pickets and breach the entrance to the camp. Once inside, the Cohort would form up into battle formation and sweep through. Once the camp was cleared, they would launch the brunt of their attack on the Turani, who would hopefully be off the high ground and engaged with the cavalry.

"Indus, you are a traitor and a coward!" Florus bellowed. "You have sold your very soul to the Roman occupiers!"

"I have come to finish this, Florus!" Indus' shouted back. "I will not sit back and let a rabble such as yours sow the seeds of rebellion! Gaul has been at peace for more than seventy years, and you look to unravel it all! Let us settle this and be done! *Archers!"*

At his command, approximately thirty men carrying short bows rode briskly to the front of the formation. As soon as they halted, they started firing towards the Turani formation. Though the rebels were at the furthest range of the short bows, as well as being uphill, some of the arrows managed to find their mark. A man standing next to Florus gave a high-pitched scream as his upper arm was punctured. Another took an arrow straight through the side of his neck. He fell to the ground in a thrashing heap, clawing at the flights of the arrow as blood gushed from his jugular and spewed from his mouth. Florus seethed in rage at Indus' audacity.

"General Florus, we must attack!" one of the sub chiefs shouted. Florus drew his sword and pointed towards the Roman cavalry.

"Destroy the traitors!" he roared. "Leave none alive!" With a battle cry that had not been sounded since their ancestors had stood against Julius Caesar, the Turani charged.

Indus gave a grim smile as he braced himself for the pending onslaught. His archers continued to pick off small numbers of rebels as the distance between the two forces rapidly closed.

"Lances ready!" Besides Indus, only his senior officers carried swords. Their men lowered their lances and braced themselves. The trumpeter had just enough time to sound the second order before the Turani smashed into their ranks.

Proculus and the rest of the Cohort stood up as they heard the second trumpet call. Artorius closed his eyes briefly and breathed a sigh of relief. Without a word, they started to quick step towards the battle. As they rounded the bend in the road, the Cohort increased its pace and stared to move at a jog. Artorius was surprised to see that all of the pickets had their backs to them, intent as they were on trying to listen to the battle between their forces and Indus' cavalry. By the time they were aware of the sound of Roman soldiers rushing towards them, it was too late.

Decimus loosed his javelin just as one turned around. It impacted the man square in the chest, penetrating through his heart. The man was dead, his eyes hollow and lifeless, yet he stood there still, his hand clutching the shaft of the javelin, which had stuck itself into the ground.

Carbo threw his just as one of the pickets started to turn and run. It struck the rebel in the back of the leg, knocking him to the ground, where he lay screaming in pain and terror. Carbo drew his gladius, and without missing a step swung his weapon hard in an underhand slash. His blow cleaved through the man's jugular, as well as his esophagus. The remaining pickets fled at a dead run, quickly outdistancing the advancing legionaries, who continued to move together at a fast jog.

Indus swung his sword in desperation and rage. His men were better trained and equipped than their adversaries; however they were getting overwhelmed. He brought his sword down and crushed the exposed head of one of the Turani; bone and brain matter spraying everywhere. He felt his shield arm quiver under the blow of another enemy before one of his men ran the rebel through with his lance. Indus knew they had to pull back soon, as his men were starting to fall under the force of the wave of Turani warriors. He brought his sword around in an underhand swing. He felt the sickening crunch as it cleaved through the neck of a Turani rebel. His horse reared up in the face of enemy spears, nearly throwing him.

"Fall back!" he shouted. His cavalrymen started to turn their mounts around and ride away from the battle. He prayed that the Roman infantry had timed their attack well and would be right behind them.

Broehain ran his sword through one of the Treveri cavalrymen that had fallen from his horse. His pent up rage and aggravation was boiling over as they fought the traitors of Indus' cavalry. His last battle had been a complete disaster and he wished to atone for it. His warriors had been ambushed and slaughtered by the Romans in what was supposed to be a ruse; those who survived goaded into continuing to fight for Sacrovir and Florus.

They had rallied even more of their men, along with numerous Treveri, and had hoped to subvert Indus' cavalry. The gall of those bastards not only refusing to return in fealty to their heritage, but also attempting to hunt them like animals was insufferable. They should have been in Augustodunum a week ago! Now at least they were able to take their revenge on the traitors. The Treveri started to retreat, their losses mounting.

"*Come on!*" he shouted, waving his men towards their fleeing enemy. He did not care that his foe was mounted; they would catch many of them before they could escape.

The guards at the far entrance to the Turani camp were completely surprised when their own pickets rushed past them in a panic. They too had been listening to the sounds of the battle and were oblivious to the threat fast approaching them.

"*The Romans are coming!*" one of the frightened pickets shouted as he ran for his life. The guards turned around and gasped in horror as they saw a host of Roman legionaries bearing down on them. The lead guard opened his mouth to sound the alarm when a Roman javelin slammed into his chest, knocking him to the ground. It had been a perfect hit, directly through the heart. His makeshift breast plate had done little to stop the force of the blow, his punctured heart convulsing in death as it shot spurts of blood through the gaping wound.

Artorius threw his javelin as hard as he could and watched as it slammed into the chest of one of the Turani guards. The force of his throw knocked the man completely off his feet. As he drew his gladius, he watched Gavius throw his javelin with even greater force, skewering one of the rebels through the neck and pinning the twitching corpse to a nearby wagon.

"Nice!" he said in genuine admiration. The rest of the men out front unleashed their javelins on the hapless rebels as a skirmish ensued over by the cluster of wagons staged near the camp entrance.

"Macro, secure this area!" Proculus ordered. "I'll take the rest of the Cohort and push through."

"Sir!" the junior Centurion acknowledged. As the remainder of the Cohort started to push through the camp, killing whatever stragglers they found, the Second Century proceeded to finish off those poor souls who had been tasked with defending Florus' precious cargo in his wagons.

"The Romans have breached the camp!" one of the terrified pickets shouted to Florus as he ran up to him, out of breath and at his wit's end.

"Impossible," Florus replied, casually. "We have the Roman cavalry on … the … run …" His words died off as he looked in horror at the sight of Roman legionaries sweeping through his camp. What drove him to madness was the handful of soldiers who could be seen milling about his wagons.

"My money!" he despaired. He then started to grab whoever was nearest and pointed them towards this newest threat. "Save the wagons!" Any rebels not directly engaged with Indus' cavalry turned about to face this new threat.

"There aren't supposed to be any bloody legionaries in this region!" one despaired.

"I don't care about the money," another stammered. "It does me no good if I am dead." Florus grabbed the man by his shock of unkempt hair and cuffed him on the ear.

"Well I care about the money, you fucking coward!" he shouted at the man. "You sorry cocks wanted to fight the legions, well now is your chance!"

He shoved the Turani towards the wagons where several dozen of his companions were attacking; a sense of desperation overcoming them. Florus was fixated on his precious treasure that he scarcely acknowledged the legionaries that were ransacking his camp.

Artorius stopped and caught his breath as he surveyed the action going on around them. The Cohort had almost finished clearing the main camp and was starting to sweep towards the road and the main battle. As he looked down the road itself, he saw a number of Turani rushing towards them. His eyes grew wide as he turned around and butted Valens with his shield.

"Form it up!" he ordered.

"Oh shit!" Valens swore as he caught sight of the enemy coming towards them. He immediately started rallying the rest of the section. "On-line!" Artorius gave a shout towards two of the other sections that were close by.

"*Rufio, Ostorius, on me!*" As Artorius set into his fighting stance, the rest of his section fell in on his left. "*Section set!*" he heard Magnus shout. In his peripheral vision, he could just make out Rufio's and Ostorius' sections forming up to the left of his. He took a deep breath, knowing that by placing himself on the extreme right he was in a precarious position.

"Advance!" he shouted. As the three sections moved towards their enemy, those with javelins disgorged them as soon as the Turani were in range. Their impact made the rest of the rebels halt in their tracks, their uncertainty apparent. Already they were rattled by the mere presence of legionaries; the sights and screams of their dying companions causing fear to overtake them. Artorius smiled sinisterly as he issued his next order.

"Charge!" The Romans hit the Turani at a run, their shields linked together, smashing into the rebels like a human battering ram. As waves of Turani were felled by the force of their onslaught, legionaries quickly slew them.

Artorius plunged his gladius into the throat of a stricken rebel. This was a favorite target for him; it ensured a quick death and was usually not as well protected as the heart. The sight of gushing blood reassured him subconsciously that his foe was dying and no longer a threat. The mass of rebels scrambled away, reforming in time to watch their less fortunate friends butchered and disemboweled by legionary blades. Tears of anguish filled many an eye. For the majority this was not the first time they had been lulled into a massacre by the legions of Rome. Most had fought in Sacrovir's mock battle and taken prisoner after the Romans attacked them from behind. And now, seemingly out of thin air, more legionaries had descended upon them; inflicting suffering and death. One particularly young man lost all control of his fear and sobbed loudly in despair.

"I cannot fight anymore!" he wailed as he dropped his weapons and fell to his knees. Carbo snarled at the pathetic wretch and stepped towards him; both sides ceasing in their attack to watch the legionary.

"Then die a coward's death," he hissed as he buried his gladius into the man's side. The Turani's mouth was agape, yet he was unable to make a sound. Carbo growled and sliced his weapon across his enemy's stomach; blood and entrails spilling from the slash.

"Carbo, formation!" Artorius shouted as the legionary stepped back into the ranks. The rest of the rebels stood appalled at what had transpired.

"You will not have me so easily!" an older Turani shouted. His companions renewed their war cries and charged into the legionaries.

Macro felt at ease for the first time in many days. The camp was cleared; the rest of the Cohort acting as the hammer to Indus' anvil. The plan had worked, and at last he felt like he could release the tension that had been causing him many a sleepless night. His fears were renewed when Camillus grabbed him by the shoulder and pointed to the fray behind him.

"Dear gods," he whispered. Nearly a third of his men were fighting off a hoard of Turani rebels, by themselves and in a single rank. The Centurion looked to his right to find the nearest Decanus. Praxus had noticed the commotion himself and was running up to investigate; the same look of horror crossing his face when he realized what Artorius and the others were up against.

"Praxus!" Macro shouted, "Take your men and flank those bastards!"

"Sir!" The Decanus acknowledged. With a wave of his arm, he and his section rushed in a file towards the right flank of the skirmish.

"*Second Century, on me!*" the Centurion ordered as he started forward at a slow jog. Camillus planted the Century's Signum and was at Macro's side, his gladius drawn. In three ranks, the remnants of the Century advanced. Macro hoped that he wasn't too late to avert disaster for his men.

Indus' cavalry had completely broken off contact with the Turani and were gradually falling back. As he started to despair that perhaps the plan had failed, Indus saw Roman soldiers cresting the ridge of the Turani camp. A Cornicen sounded his horn, drawing the attention of both the Turani, as well as the cavalry.

"*Come about!*" Indus shouted. With drilled precision, the Roman cavalry wheeled their mounts back towards the Turani, who had stalled in their pursuit, aware as they were that they were being threatened from both sides. What they did not know was that the force of Roman legionaries only amounted to a single Cohort, not nearly enough men to overwhelm their ranks. All they could comprehend was that somehow the Romans had managed to send legionary troops to cut off their chance of reaching Augustodunum. And these troops were now raining javelins down upon their heads as they rapidly advanced down the hill.

Vitruvius found himself in the lead as his men stormed down the hill. He had deliberately taken up position in the very center of his men, his plan of attack dependant on it.

"*Wedge formation ... on me!*" he shouted. While still moving at a jog downhill, legionaries guided themselves into a massive wedge, linking their shields together. At the apex of the wedge was the powerful Centurion. He braced hard against his shield as he felt soldiers on either side of him linking their shields with his. He could also feel the legionaries to his back pushing against them.

Once he sensed all were set, Vitruvius gave a howl of rage, one which was echoed by all legionaries in the wedge, and increased his speed to an all-out sprint. Turani rebels looked back in terror as the formation slammed into them. The Centurion knew that for the wedge to have full effect, he had to push as far as he could into the enemy ranks before engaging. Men were knocked down in the wake of their onslaught, trampled underneath by the legionaries behind Vitruvius and his men. Eventually their momentum slowed, and he knew the force of their charge was expended.

"Online!" he ordered as his soldiers unlinked their shields and started to hammer the rebels in close combat. Many Turani were knocked down or into their companions, their ranks compressed together. Vitruvius started to stab rapidly with his gladius, his weapon finding the vitals of a rebel with every strike. Five men had fallen to his ferocious assault before he even had to start engaging opponents in single combat. Legionaries on either side of him attacked the rebels with equal brutality. Vitruvius knew that in the close confines of this battle passages-of-lines would be impossible; therefore, everything pended on how well they carried their charged and shocked the enemy into panic.

Panic was indeed gripping the Turani. Broehain looked back to see Roman troops pouring down the road, hammering into the rear of their army. He grimaced hard, knowing that the cavalry's sortie against them had been a hoax. He turned his eyes front and watched as Indus' horsemen wheeled their mounts around and came at them.

"Eyes front!" he shouted to those who could hear him.

The Turani were horrified to see Indus and his troopers bearing down on them. *"Brace for impact!"*

Having managed to get some distance between themselves and the rebels, Indus' cavalry was now able to build up momentum as they charged at the full gallop. His men lowered their lances and gave a shout of fury as they smashed over and through the Turani ranks.

At the far end of the mass of rebels, javelins were continuing to rain down, killing or crippling all who fell in their path. The Turani had become so clustered together by the force of Vitruvius' charge that it was impossible for the legionaries throwing the javelins to miss. Their advance gained momentum once again, the force driving them deeper into enemy ranks. Vitruvius in particular was a machine of terror. That a man of his size and brutal power could strike so quickly cowed the rebels unfortunate enough to find themselves in his path. One after another they fell to his fury; a wake of death left in his path.

A sense of shock and surprise gripped the whole mass of rebels, inducing them to panic. Most fled straight into the woods on their left, leading downhill and away from the battle. As they ran, they threw down their weapons, stumbling and falling over rocks and fallen trees. Those in the immediate vicinity of the Romans started to surrender.

Proculus saw the mass of Turani fleeing into the woods. He pointed to Vitruvius and then towards the woods. Vitruvius nodded and signaled to his men.

"Third Century, follow me!" Proculus signaled for the Fifth Century to do the same, both Centuries forming up in a long line, carefully but quickly making their way down the hill.

As the skirmish continued in the Turani camp, Artorius brought his shield about in a hard left hook, the boss connecting squarely on the side of a rebel's face. He felt the facial bones crush under the force of his blow as the man collapsed to the ground unconscious. Instinctively, Artorius brought his gladius down in a hard thrust, ramming it into the base of his throat. He then saw two more coming at him. As he was on the extreme right, his flank was completely exposed. One of the Turani saw this and elected to exploit it. Artorius sought to fend the man off with his gladius as the rebel's companion brought the full bear of his weight onto Artorius' shield. Sensing this threat to his Sergeant, Valens sidestepped and stabbed the rebel in the side. Artorius felt the weight of the man against his shield go limp as he deflected another blow from his adversary's sword. He then shoved the dead man off him and swung his shield around hard, catching the Turani on the shoulder. This spun him partially around, allowing Artorius to stab him beneath the ribs. He kicked the dying man away, blood dripping from his sword as several more adversaries came at him. He caught sight of legionaries running past his right shoulder towards the rebels. As he braced himself against the onslaught of one attacker, a legionary collided with the man, his shield and body knocking him down with the force of a demon possessed. The soldier fell on top of the rebel, violently slicing his throat open with his gladius. Artorius recognized him to be Legionary Felix as the young man struggled back to his feet. He then noticed Praxus leading the rest of his men straight into the enemy flank.

As he turned back towards the remainder of their foe, Artorius saw that those who had not been killed or maimed had thrown their weapons down and placed their hands behind their heads.

"Are we taking prisoners?" Rufio asked. Artorius nodded affirmatively.

"Yes. Bind their hands and start setting up a prisoner collection point." He turned around to see that most of the Century had just come up to assist. Though it felt longer, their entire ordeal could not have lasted longer than a minute or so. As he stood catching his breath again, Artorius was mildly surprised that Rufio had deferred to him as to what should be done with the Turani who surrendered. Rufio had four years seniority over him and Ostorius probably more than that. He shook his head, not wishing to make more of the situation than what it was.

"Everyone alright?" Macro asked as he walked up to Artorius.

The Decanus nodded. "I think so; surprised the bloody hell out of us, though."

Macro turned and saw a glint of metal in the trees on their right, leading uphill. As he focused his eyes on the sight, he was able to make out the figure of a man in a brass breastplate and helmet. Macro's eyes narrowed as he grabbed Artorius by the shoulder.

"I see him," he acknowledged, grimacing as his anger rose.

"Get that bastard!" Macro growled. Artorius took a deep breath and waved towards the man with his gladius.

"Let's go!" he shouted to his section as they ran after the man they knew to be Julius Florus. Shields were grounded and gladii sheathed, as they knew they would need both hands and feet to climb the steep slope.

Florus watched from the woods in despair as his men were crushed by the Romans. He spat in disgust as he watched a number of them surrender without as much as a fight. He trembled in anxiety as he saw legionaries gathered around his wagons. His precious money was lost. *Lost!* He was almost sobbing in frustration when he looked to his left and saw several Roman soldiers running his way. He then looked down and saw that the sun had cast its light through the trees and was gleaming off his breastplate. He cursed himself for his vanity as he turned and started to flee up the hill. His army was routed, his fortune gone, and if he failed to get away, his life would become forfeit as well. He grabbed at tree branches and roots as he pulled himself up the side of the hill. Roman soldiers were phenomenally conditioned, however Florus hoped that the head start he had would be enough to save his life.

A glare caught Indus on the side of his face. He turned to see where it came from and saw a glimpse of a man in brass armor fleeing up the side of the mountain. He could also just make out a small group of legionaries pursuing the rebel leader. Indus scowled as he realized just who the Roman soldiers were pursuing. He turned back towards his men, who were helping legionaries round up prisoners. Florus could not be allowed any chance at escape!

"Stay here and help with the prisoners," he told his deputy. He then signaled for two of his men to follow him.

There was a small path that led up the hill, arching off to their left. He hoped that it would allow them to get far enough ahead of Florus to cut off his escape.

Florus' chances of outrunning his pursuers were quickly vanishing as his lungs burned, unable to suck in enough air. His legs were cramping up in knots, his feet numb from the climb. He had become so accustomed to riding that even walking great distances had become arduous, let alone running. He threw off his helmet and struggled to work out of his cuirass. As his armor dropped, he found himself using his gilded sword as a crutch to help pull him up the steep hill. Florus could hear the sounds of the Romans struggling up the hill behind him. He was even able to make out their heavy breathing and the curses they muttered. They were getting closer. As he struggled to pull himself over a massive fallen tree, he could make out a trio of horsemen moving across his front. He then watched horrified as they wheeled around and came at him. He lowered his eyes when he saw that Indus was one of them. With a sigh of resignation, Florus drew his sword and leaned back against a tree.

Artorius and the rest of the section slowed their pursuit when they saw Florus back against a tree with his sword out. He too was able to make out the riders approaching from higher up on the hill. Though the shadows of the trees prevented him from making out their faces, he was able to recognize Indus' voice as he spoke.

"It's over, Florus," he stated as he rode up. Florus could only nod his head. Indus slowed his horse and moved ever so slowly towards him. Florus gulped hard, his mind working desperately to find a way out of the situation. In the end, there was only one way out.

"Stay where you are, Indus!" he barked as he turned his sword on himself, resting the point against his abdomen. Indus halted his horse and signaled his men to stay where they were.

"I am *not* carrying him back if he offs himself!" Magnus whispered into Artorius' ear. The Decanus raised his hand for him to be silent. He then pointed for

Valens and Gavius to start moving around the far side of the tree. With Magnus, Decimus, and Carbo he started to slowly advance towards Florus.

"*I said stay away!*" Florus cried out in desperation.

"Don't do it, Florus. Don't let it end this way." There was genuine concern in Indus' voice. Though they had been political rivals, and were now enemies in a war of rebellion, Indus could not help but feel sorry for him. If he could perhaps convince his fellow tribesman to see reason, perhaps he could help end this disgusting rebellion.

"What do you care how this ends?" Florus despaired.

"We are both of the Treveri," Indus replied, "fellow countrymen, kinfolk through our tribe ..."

"*You are no kin of mine!*" Florus snapped, suddenly angry. "You betrayed your people so that they could remain slaves of Rome!" Artorius quietly drew his gladius as he continued to slowly advance. Indus raised a hand, ordering him to stop. He wished to take Florus alive, if possible. He had already spoken with Silius about sparing Florus' life, should he surrender peacefully. The Roman Legate had been noncommittal, but had at least not rejected his request outright.

"You can help us end this thing, if you just surrender peacefully," he pleaded. "Countless lives have been needlessly lost already. Do not let more die in vain. Put down your sword."

"I will do no such thing! Surrender will only mean delaying the inevitable. The Romans will have me publicly strangled like a common criminal! No Indus, it ends now." With final resolve, Florus fumbled with his sword and fell upon it. In his despair he had neglected to angle his sword upwards, so that it would penetrate his heart and kill him quickly. Instead, he ran himself through the stomach, the blade exiting out his back as he collapsed onto the ground. A horrifying realization came over him as quickly as the insurmountable pain. He tried to cry out, but found he was unable. He clawed at the sword as his body started to tremble uncontrollably; his skin became clammy with sweat. Blood and intestinal fluid seeped from his self-inflicted wound as he lost all control over his bowels.

Indus lowered and shook his head, removing his helmet. Artorius let out a sigh and signaled for his men to finish advancing to Florus. Valens and Gavius came walking around the far side of the tree.

"Hey, this bastard is still alive!" Valens shouted. "Bloody fool couldn't even kill himself properly!" With that he kicked Florus hard in the head.

"Take it easy, Valens!" Magnus remarked as he walked over to where Florus lay dying. He then turned to Artorius.

"Finish him," Artorius nodded affirmatively. He looked at Indus who nodded the same.

Florus was awash in feelings of desperation, overwhelming fear, deepening sorrow, and horrifying pain. He no longer had any control over his bodily functions; his spasms continued to worsen, and his bowels unloosed themselves again. He could just make out a burly legionary kneeling over him, his gladius drawn. The young soldier removed his helmet and lifted up on Florus' head, exposing his neck. His terror increased as he felt the cold blade push against the side of his throat.

Florus was aware of nothing but the agonizing mortal wound in his belly. When Magnus knelt beside him, he looked at him with mute anguish and despair. Another person would have felt pity for the wretch, but there was none to be had from the young legionary. His passage to death was quickened by the cold steel of Magnus' gladius.

The six legionaries stood over the corpse of Julius Florus. Indus signaled for his men to take the body and throw it over his horse.

"Sergeant Artorius, we meet again," he said. His tone was pleasant, though his face bore no emotion. He knew that Indus had borne a much greater share of the responsibility regarding the outcome of this battle than any. The stressful and harrowing ordeal left him tired and worn. Artorius wondered how many days it had been since the cavalry commander had had any sleep.

"Commander Indus," he acknowledged. He and Decimus then helped the two cavalrymen carry the body over to Indus' horse.

"You and your men have brought us one step closer to ending this sickening rebellion," Indus said. "If not for you, Florus may well have escaped to sow the seeds of dissent elsewhere. I will personally make note of your actions to Legate Silius."

"We did our duty," Artorius replied. He was beat, and his legs ached from the climb up the rugged hillside. He dreaded the walk back down to the camp. With his adrenaline surge wearing off, the pain in his muscles and joints would become that much more acute.

Indus pressed his lips together in a tight line and nodded. He understood the legionaries' sense of duty, and that they felt they had only accomplished what they had to. All the same, the removal of Florus not only crushed one aspect of the rebellion, it solidified his personal standing both amongst the Treveri and the Romans. The least he could do was make note of the men who helped him dispatch Florus to their Commanding Legate.

"I will want to get the names of all your men for my report," he said politely as he and his troopers rode back down the hill.

"Yes Sir," Artorius said under his breath. He then started down the hill with his section. Though he said little, he was very proud of them. Something inside told him that they had personally taken part in a historically significant event. He wondered if posterity would even remember their names.

"Hey, look at what I found!" Decimus exclaimed. He reached down and picked up a magnificent helmet, complete with purple plume on top.

"Well there is a nice trophy for you," Gavius said with a laugh. The rest of the legionaries stopped to admire Decimus' new prize as another figure quietly slinked off with Florus' breastplate in tow.

"Think Macro will let me keep it?" Decimus asked. Artorius shrugged his shoulders.

"I don't see why not," he replied. "After all, you found it."

Camillus had planted the Century's Signum over by Florus' wagons. While most of the men were busying themselves taking care of the prisoners, he decided to see for himself what was in these precious crates. There were two large ones, each bearing a hasp and heavy lock.

"Hey Praxus!" he called to the nearest section leader. "Find something that will bust open these locks."

"An entrenching pickaxe should do the trick," the Decanus replied. "Hold on a minute, I'll go grab one." With that, he raced back down the hill to where the Cohort had grounded its gear. He grabbed a pickaxe from one of his legionary's packs and headed back to where Camillus was hammering away on one of the locks with the butt of an enemy sword.

"Here, let me at that," Praxus said, hefting the pickaxe. He then proceeded to smash away at the lock, until finally it broke. He and Camillus then opened the heavy lid on the crate. Both men stood in complete awe.

"Well there is something you don't find every day," Camillus remarked.

As Artorius and the rest of the section came stumbling down the last stretch of the hill, they could hear excited shouts coming from the direction of the main entrance to the camp. Men from the Second Century could be seen gathered around the wagons by the entrance, shouting and dancing about excitedly. Macro was beating some of the men back.

"That's enough already!" he shouted. "We are legionaries, not a fucking barbarian rabble! *At ease, all of you!*" Artorius walked over to see what the excitement was about. His heart felt like it skipped a beat when he saw the gleam of gold and silver coins in one of the crates. Camillus was sitting on a crate, his face beaming. Just then, Centurion Proculus walked over to Macro.

"Macro, what the bloody hell has gotten into you guys ... oh my," he came to a quick halt when he saw the treasure. "Well fancy that. I guess that's what Florus intended to use to bribe Indus' cavalry with. Speaking of Florus, does anyone know what happened to him?"

"He's dead, by his own hand," Indus answered, riding up on his horse. He gestured towards Artorius and his section. "If not for these men, he may very well have escaped."

"Well done," Proculus nodded towards Artorius. "You men have brought about the end of one half of this rebellion." He then turned back towards Indus. "I need to know how bad our losses were, and how many wounded we need to transport."

"Proculus, we have no real facilities with which to treat the wounded," Macro conjectured. "Not only that, but we need to get back as quickly as possible; and these wagons will slow our pace to a crawl."

"Augusta Raurica is close, and it has good hospital facilities," Camillus interjected. "If we can detach a handful of escorts to take the wounded, then the rest of us can head back to link up with Calvinus."

"What about the gold?" Statorius asked. "These crates are taking up a lot of space."

"Camillus grab the other Signifiers and get a total count on everything here," Macro ordered. Camillus nodded and hurried off to find the Signifiers of the other Centuries. "I suggest we divvy it up now. I also recommend that the cavalry get a slightly larger portion as a token to their discipline and valor; that they remained loyal in spite of such a lavish offer." Indus gave small smile in appreciation of Macro's gesture.

"Very well," Proculus replied. "Indus, I need you to detach about a hundred men to escort the wounded and prisoners to Augusta Raurica. How bad were your losses?"

"We lost sixty-five dead, and about twice that many wounded." Proculus grimaced at the numbers.

"Our legionary losses were twelve dead, with another thirty-five wounded." He then gave an audible sigh. "While regrettable, we have to accept the losses we have borne, and be thankful that it was not worse. We all know just how bad it could have been. I'll get word on how many prisoners and enemy wounded we have, once my pursuit centuries return."

About a half hour later, legionaries from the Third and Fifth Centuries were seen making their way back through the tree lines. They had only a handful of prisoners with them.

"Any losses?" Proculus asked.

"None," Vitruvius replied, shaking his head. "Those bastards got a good head start on us, and we were only able to capture a few. Still, we did see weapons and shields strewn all over the ground. My guess is we won't be seeing those traitors again."

Centurion Dominus walked over at that moment, scribbling on a wax tablet. "Best we can tell we have a total of approximately six hundred prisoners to move; about half of whom are wounded to one degree or another. We also counted over five hundred rebel corpses." Proculus was pleased when he heard that. What should have been a suicide mission had turned into a complete triumph.

"So how are we looking?" Macro asked. Camillus and the other Signifiers had divided the gold and silver into piles, and each had been taking notes as to the complete count.

"Given the total number of men we have, divided into the total haul … it looks like we should have about seventy-five denarii per man; eighty for the cavalry."

"That's a third of a year's legionary pay," one of the Signifier's remarked. "I bet they won't mind carrying the extra weight back!"

"Alright," Macro acknowledged, "once we have all of the wounded and prisoners on the move, we will line up by Centuries and divide out the treasure before we start moving back."

"We are ready anytime," Camillus replied. "And just so you know, we have already separated out the shares for the wounded, as well as the escort cavalry. We left it in one of the crates."

Seventy-five denarii in gold and silver added some weight to their packs, but Artorius did not mind. They had started their march back about two hours before the sun set. He laughed when he looked back and could clearly see the plume of Florus' helmet protruding from Decimus' pack. Macro had allowed the legionary to keep the helmet, provided he agreed not to sell it. It would remain as a trophy of the Second Century, until a time came that Decimus was either transferred or retired. Artorius then considered the other trophies that his section had collected over the years. There were a few weapons, mostly daggers; their previous enemies being short on swords. Magnus had purchased a Batavi shield from one of their allies. Artorius' only contributions were a copper chalice and a rather ornate dagger that he had acquired while plundering a Marsi village at the end of the Germanic wars. Florus' helmet would make a fine addition to their collection!

At around midnight, Proculus gave the order to halt. They were still deep in the woods, and there was no room for them to set up a proper marching camp. Most of the legionaries elected to either sleep on the road, or just off to the side on the grass. Sentries paced up and down the lines, making certain that no one intruded upon them. Indus' cavalry had stayed with the Third Cohort to provide extra security, though Indus himself had ridden back with a handful of men to report back to Calvinus. Artorius had just sat down on a patch of trampled grass when he noticed Centurion Macro standing over him. Immediately he came to his feet.

"Sir," he said, standing rigid.

"At ease, Sergeant. Let's take a walk." Without waiting for a reply, Macro started walking down the road. Artorius was quickly at his side. When they were out of earshot of the sentries, Macro stopped and turned to face the young Decanus.

"You did well today," he said. Artorius saw the consternation on his face; almost as if Macro were uncomfortable talking with him.

"We all did well today, Sir," he said. The Centurion shook his head.

"Not all of us," he said. "Instead of reforming the Century after we secured the wagons, I became fixated on them. Thoughts of plunder became my focus; so relieved I was that we had succeeded in driving the rebels out of their encampment. Had it not been for your actions and ability to make decisions in the heat of the moment, those rebels could have caught our entire Century off guard and inflicted many needless casualties. You saved many lives today; to say nothing of you and your men putting an end to that vile bastard Florus."

"Well actually he put an end to himself," Artorius corrected, a wry smile on his face. He became sober when he saw Macro's expression unchanged. "Sir, I reacted the way any soldier of Rome would have. The enemy was coming at us, I grabbed whoever was available and held them long enough for you to bring up the rest of the Century."

"It should never have come to that," Macro remarked. "The battle was not yet decided, and I knew better than to allow the men to fall into complacency."

"No," Artorius replied, shaking his head. "All of us knew better. But we recovered and routed the enemy."

"That you did," Macro replied, allowing a half smile. "I've already spoken with Proculus and he agrees that your section deserves to be recognized for what you did today. He concurred with my assessment that had you not reacted so quickly to the threat, many of our men would have fallen before we had a chance to reform. You have done well."

Broehain skulked through the shadows of the trees. The moon shone brightly, as if the gods themselves were trying to help the Romans find him. The light glinted off the breastplate he carried. Florus may have been a pompous fool, yet Broehain still felt a certain kinship to the slain nobleman. His instincts told him that he would be the only one returning to Sacrovir; the rest having fled into the hills, where they would stay until they felt it was safe to return home.

Slowly he made his way up the hill. The slope was steep and the breastplate a burden, but still he persevered. He knew he had to stay off the roads; no doubt they were swarming with Roman soldiers. In reality he had no idea where the legionaries had come from or how many there had been. He had been in the midst of the battle with Indus' cavalry when their army started fleeing around him. He was fortunate enough to have made it away from the fray as the Romans routed the Turani once again. Broehain was shamed by what had transpired. Twice now his people had been surprised and decimated by the Romans. Even if none of his men continued to fight, he knew he had to. He would avenge his people; alone if need be.

Artorius unlaced the straps on his armor and felt a surge of relief as the weight came off him. As he lay down with his head against his pack, he could not help but think what he would do with his portion of the captured gold. At the same time he was worried that he may not get a chance to spend it. After all, once they returned they would have Sacrovir's main force to deal with. And when that time came, there would be no surprises. They would have to face Sacrovir in the open, badly outnumbered.

The die rolled 'Venus,' he thought to himself as he drifted off to sleep. *I only hope we can cast it again.*

CHAPTER 14

▼

THE NOBLE YOUTH OF GAUL

The great hall of the Augustodunum University was crowded with nobles, as well as Sacrovir's top men. When word reached the various nobles that their sons had been taken by Sacrovir, they swarmed angrily on Augustodunum. Sacrovir lounged on a raised dais, his bodyguards in a line to his front. He was resting his head in his hand as he listened to the mob of noblemen, his peers, as they cursed his name.

"This is an outrage!" a nobleman named Lennox shouted. "You dare to come here and take our sons as hostages!"

"Your sons are not hostages, but rather my guests," Sacrovir said in a slow and steady voice. "Many of them have flocked to my banner of freedom."

"Your *freedom* is a death sentence to our sons!" another noble named Kavan stated.

"Legionary forces are heading this way, even as we speak," Lennox continued. "Do you really think you have a chance against the Rhine army?"

"Two legions are all the Romans are sending against us," Sacrovir answered. "I already know who they are and who they have brought with them. With your sons fighting for me, I have the Romans outnumbered nearly four to one. We will roll right over them and take this province as our own!"

"Vercingetorix had the Romans outnumbered as well," Kavan remarked, "you should remember what they did to him!"

"Vercingetorix became overzealous and blundered at the last," Sacrovir retorted sharply. "My men, and your sons in particular, are much better equipped to fight the Romans than he was. You speak of the past, of Gaul's *defeats* by Rome; I speak of the future and of victory! Your sons are the *Noble Youth of Gaul*, an iron force that will break the oppression of Rome!"

There were a few cheers at this from the young "guests."

"My son is but a boy," Lennox pleaded. "You have filled his head with tales of a glory that does not exist …"

"Wrong!" Sacrovir boomed as he slammed his fist down on the arm of the chair and stood up. "I have filled your son's head with that which you have denied him! You, the noblemen of Gaul, have forgotten your heritage and the virtues of the Gallic people." He began pacing across the dais. "Instead you look to Rome to give you the scraps off their tables; for that is all they give us. We are of the same social standing as those within the Senatorial class, and yet they deny us the most basic rights. I have cast off my Roman citizenship, as have your sons. If the fathers will not reclaim what is theirs by right, then I look for strength in their sons!" With that, he turned and stormed out the back of the hall. Guards prevented any from pursuing him further.

As Lennox and scores of nobles walked out into the daylight, he clutched at his pounding head; his heart filled with anxiety. He was surprised to see his son waiting for him. Farquhar was leaning against a pillar, his arms folded across his chest. Lennox found his breath coming rapidly as he grabbed his son by the shoulders. Farquhar did not return the embrace.

"Son, please … do not give in to this madness," Lennox said sternly, their gazes locked. "Do not throw away your future for what can only bring suffering and death."

"If by my suffering and death I can bring freedom to Gaul, that is a price I am willing to pay," Farquhar replied coldly. "If you are to honor me, and honor our family, you will not try and stop me from doing what I must do. I have seen what the Romans can do; they fight with deceit and trickery. I watched them murder the Turani like cowards, even after they had surrendered. I will not submit myself and my family to such a race." Lennox shook his head slightly.

"I cannot believe what Sacrovir has done to you," Lennox said. "I do not doubt your bravery, but listen to me. I do not care what training Sacrovir has tried to give you—boys are not soldiers. Outnumbered or not, the Romans will roll right over you. This army of his is made up of the dregs of society. His gladiators and thugs will run once they face the wrath of the legions."

"What is this blind fear you have of the Romans? Sacrovir was right, there is no bravery left in the noble fathers of Gaul." Farquhar stormed down the stairs. Lennox was on his heels.

"The Romans nearly exterminated our people at one time. Since the time of Caesar, we have become part of their society. Our people have prospered! Surely, you cannot forget how well our own family has done over the past few generations. We have acquired much in the way of land and status. You throw that all away, and for what? There is virtue in bravery, when it serves a higher purpose. But this … this is foolhardy, a foolish expedition to sate one man's lust for glory!" Farquhar immediately turned to face his father.

"I fight to restore some dignity to our family!" he spat. "The so-*called Fathers of Gaul* have allowed us to become the Romans' lapdogs; they sell their souls for scraps of land that were already theirs by ancestral right! Well I am no lapdog, Father. I will not stand idle and let our people suffer this humiliation and servitude any longer." He turned and briskly walked away. Lennox's heart was in anguish; a deepening sense of sorrow at his son's determination. He knew Farquhar's mind was made up, but he could not allow things to end between them this way.

"Farquhar wait!" he shouted.

Farquhar stopped and stooped his shoulders slightly, waiting for yet another chastising from his father but wouldn't turn around. Instead Lennox walked around to face him and spoke softly, "you have chosen your path. I have done all I can, and now you feel you must accelerate your ascension into manhood. I *pray* that the gods spare you. But if not, do it with this on you."

From beneath his cloak, he produced a fine sword, with a long, thin blade, and an ornate scabbard covered in etchings depicting men and horses. "At least die with your ancestors' weapon in your hand."

Farquhar took the sword and embraced his father hard. "I will make you proud, Father. You will see. It will all be over soon, I promise you." As he watched Farquhar walk away, Lennox almost felt something prophetic in his son's words.

Indeed it will all be over soon, my son.

＊   ＊   ＊   ＊

Calvinus could not help but feel a sense of relief as he strolled out into the night air. Florus had failed to undermine the loyalty of the Treveri cavalry, his forces of Turani rebels had been dispersed, and Florus himself was dead. Two Cohorts from city garrisons had arrived, with another expected within the next two days. The Third Cohort, along with Indus' cavalry, was expected on the morrow, as was Silius. He had with him the rest of the Twentieth Legion, along with the entire First Germanica.

The Master Centurion took a deep breath as he gazed over the fort rampart and into the hills. For over those hills, about fifteen miles away, lay the city of Augustodunum, where Sacrovir was marshalling all of his forces together.

Calvinus started calculating numbers in his head. The losses amongst the Third Cohort and Indus' cavalry had been less severe than expected, though a full hundred of the cavalry were escorting prisoners and wounded to Augusta Raurica. With the entire First and Twentieth Legions, the garrison Cohorts, and Indus' cavalry, their combined force still numbered less than thirteen thousand men. Sacrovir was said to have more than three times as many under arms, maybe more. His thoughts were disturbed as he saw a rider coming through the gate. It was Agricola, coming to report back to him. Calvinus dismounted the rampart and went to greet the Centurion.

"It's pretty quiet out there, but definitely tense," Agricola reported as he removed his helmet.

"Do explain."Agricola pulled out a rough sketch that he had made of the area his men were observing.

"We managed to get within about three miles of the town, but no closer. The ground opens up there, and we could not get any closer without the risk of being spotted. As it is, I think Sacrovir probably knows we are there anyway.

"Traffic coming in and out of the town has come to almost a complete standstill. The enemy knows that he cannot disrupt the lives of the entire city for long, so I think he may be finalizing his preparations to face us."

"Where do you think they intend to muster their forces?" Calvinus asked.

"There is a wide open plain, not too far from here. It's large enough for him to encamp his entire army, plus it is far enough away from the city. I think they will probably stage there and wait for us to attack. Or, if we don't have the rest of the army on site, he may decide to sortie against our positions here."

"He *has* to know that we've got reinforcements coming," Calvinus remarked, his brow furrowed in thought. "I don't see why he has not attacked us already. That way he could wipe out a portion of our army before the main force even arrives."

"He has the men, but they may not be completely armed yet," Agricola replied. "I said traffic was at a standstill, but that was not entirely correct. There have been wagons going *in* to the city, but nothing coming out. Those going in were all under armed escort as well. I think they are loaded with arms and armor for his men. Once fully equipped, they will be on the move."

"Well, there's no way they can reach us in less than a day, and hopefully Silius will have arrived well before then."

"Any word from Proculus and the Third?" Agricola asked. Calvinus nodded in reply.

"Yes. Florus, happily, is dead, the Turani routed, and the Third is on their way back, along with Indus' cavalry." Agricola closed his eyes and breathed a sigh of relief.

"Thank the gods for that," he muttered. "And now, with your permission, I will leave these diagrams with you and head back to my men." Calvinus nodded and waved for him to go.

As the Third Cohort drew closer to their outpost, they saw that Silius had arrived. A massive camp had been erected, the Eagles of both the Twentieth Valeria and First Germanica posted in the center. Calvinus rode up to meet them.

"Good to have you guys back," he said as he clasped Proculus' hand.

"It's good to be back," Proculus replied heartily. The men of the Third Cohort still marched with energy and purpose, though it was clear that their ordeal of the last few days had taken its toll on them.

"I want you to put your men down once they get back to their barracks and cleaned up. They look like hell," Calvinus observed.

Indeed the men of the Third Cohort were a haggard sight. Even though they had only been gone a total of four days, much had happened to them. They had gotten little, if any sleep, none had shaved or bathed, and all were worn from the endless marching, to say nothing of the battle they had waged against a vastly superior force. The men of the Third were elated by their victory and spoils, though all were too exhausted to show it.

Artorius dropped his pack on the floor, removed his helmet, and sat down on his bunk. Most of his men fell right on their bunks once they dropped their packs.

"You guys can sleep once you take care of stowing your equipment and servicing your weapons and armor," he stated. He heard a groan from some of them, but they knew there was nothing for it. They had maybe a day or two before they would march against Sacrovir and priority was making certain their equipment was fully serviceable.

"Come on guys, let's get it done," Magnus added as he started kicking at bunks. There were no further complaints as the men went about checking their armor and weapons. Though they were exhausted, they were as fully aware of the gravity of the situation as Artorius was.

Once he was satisfied with his own equipment, Artorius headed to the small bathhouse on the post. It was much smaller than the ones that graced legionary fortresses, but it still had all the facilities needed to thoroughly clean and rejuvenate one's self. He made sure that he took the time to shave as well, even though this was an almost unnecessary routine. Even after four days, his face bore few facial hairs. In truth, Artorius was glad for it. Roman soldiers kept themselves clean-shaven, for facial hair was seen as a sign of barbarism. The fact that he could not even grow a beard made it easier for him.

It was mid afternoon when he walked back towards his billet, cleaned and wearing a fresh tunic. Though there was much activity going on at most of the barracks, the Third Cohort's was dead as a tomb. As he walked by he could hear the audible snores coming from most of the section bays. He quietly opened the door to where his section was bunked, and could hear the sounds of slumber coming from his men. Only Magnus had opted to go to the bathhouse right away as well, and he had not yet returned. Artorius knew he would sleep better, now that he was cleaned and his muscles relaxed by the heated water. It was not until he lay down that the ordeal of the last four days hit him fully. He closed his eyes and did not open them again until well into the next morning.

✷   ✷   ✷   ✷

Whilst Artorius and his legionaries slumbered, a tense silence gathered over Augustodunum as the rebels occupying the city awaited their leaders' orders.

"Our men are fully equipped and ready to move against the Romans," Taranis reported. Sacrovir stood on the balcony and gazed over the city. People were cautiously milling about, though many were fearful of Sacrovir and his army. Even more so, they feared that the Romans would lay siege to their town and destroy it.

"Still no word from Florus?" he asked after a long pause. Taranis shook his head.

"None. We should have heard from him by now. I wonder if his efforts to succor the Treveri were in vain; or worse if he fell afoul of the Roman army."

"We will have to move without him," Heracles remarked, walking out onto the balcony. "We should have attacked the Romans much sooner. Their four Cohorts have now expanded into two full legions, plus several Cohorts from surrounding garrisons. Had we done so, we could have wiped out their little force before these arrived." Sacrovir turned to face him.

"Heracles, I appreciate your candor as always. However, I have made it a point of defeating the Romans when they had mustered their forces. It will have a much deeper impact than for us to have simply routed a few Cohorts holed up in a tiny fort."

"Well I do agree with our Greek friend that we should attack soon," Taranis replied. "Our forces are not nearly as large as we had hoped, though they are still significant enough to smash two legions."

"We *must* move now, before they bring up any more troops," Heracles continued. "We have trained our men on how to fight against the Roman legions, but our army still lacks that unnerving discipline that the Romans possess." Sacrovir looked thoughtful for a moment then nodded.

"I agree with your assessment, Heracles. Two legions will have to suffice for the slaughter. Our forces outnumber theirs nearly four to one. We will shatter their pathetic formations and feed them to the wolves!"

Secretly Heracles wondered whether or not they had waited too long. Two legions of Roman soldiers was a formidable force, no matter how badly outnumbered.

"They are on the move!" a legionary shouted as he ran up to Agricola. The Centurion rushed to the edge of the wood line to see for himself. Augustodunum's gates were open with thousands of armed men pouring out. Agricola swallowed hard when he saw how well many of them were equipped.

Though there were many light troops amongst their ranks, a significant number were completely encased in armor. These particular troops wore gladiator helmets, and each carried a small buckler and gladius. Agricola surmised that these would make up the van of Sacrovir's army. Thankfully they had no cavalry to speak of, only their senior leaders riding on horses. Agricola signaled to his Tesserarius.

"Take my horse and ride like hell back to the rest of the army. Tell Legate Silius that the enemy is on the move. Ask him to send a dispatch rider to me. I will update him as to the enemy's progress at that time."

"I'll come back myself," the Tesserarius replied. Agricola nodded in reply and waved for him to go.

"Optio Castor!" the Centurion called. His second came running over from the line.

"Sir?"

"Get the men on their feet and ready to move. Leave six of our best runners with me. We will keep a visual on the enemy while you take the rest to link up with the Cohort."

"Right away," the Optio acknowledged. *"First Century, on your feet!"*

"I'll see you in a couple hours," Agricola said to his Tesserarius as the man saluted and then turned his mount and rode away at a gallop. The Centurion then turned to see his six runners awaiting orders.

"Alright lads," he said, "let's get back up to the tree line and see what those bastards are up to. I want you to take notes on everything you see; get as accurate of a count as you can regarding their overall strength, as well as light and heavily troops. Any questions?" All The men shook their heads. "Let's get this done."

Artorius was lounging next to the open gate of their tiny fort when he saw the rider approaching. He recognized the man as Agricola's Tesserarius, and he was riding for all he was worth. He rode into the camp of the main force, and looked to be headed right for the Principia, where Silius' headquarters was posted.

"Anything good happening?" Magnus asked with a yawn. Artorius had not even noticed his friend walking up to him. He could only nod in reply.

"Make sure the lads are up. If they haven't had breakfast, have them do so now. I sense that we may be moving soon."

There was a flurry of excitement going on in the main camp. Artorius knew it would not be long before the order to move was given. He was suddenly thankful that he had gotten a full night's sleep, for his body had sorely needed it. He was still a little stiff, but his muscles would loosen up once they were on the march. It would not be long before the issue was decided, and Artorius was tired of waiting.

"I agree with Agricola's assessment that the enemy intends to face us here," Calvinus remarked as he pointed to a section on Agricola's map that showed an open plain just a few miles away.

"We can get there well before Sacrovir does and deny the terrain to him," Decius, the Chief Tribune replied. Silius sat with his chin resting in his hand.

"What do you guys think?" he asked his First Centurions, who always were part of the Legion's tactical planning.

"I say let Sacrovir have it," Draco offered. "That terrain will work more to our advantage than his. It will be a confusing mess if we try and fight him in the woods."

"I'm with Draco on this," Aemilius added. "Though I do feel that as soon as we are ready, we strike quickly." Silius nodded affirmatively.

"I agree," he said after giving the matter some thought. "The plain is only about three miles from here. I don't see Sacrovir getting there until late in the day, maybe not until nightfall. We will scope out the terrain and see how we can work it to our advantage. I want the men to focus on building a solid defensive palisade. Should things take a turn for the worse, we need to be able to fall back to a strong defensive position."

"We'll make it happen, though I assure you we will not need it," Calvinus asserted.

Once he was satisfied that they had a thorough assessment of the enemy's strength, Agricola had his small force move rapidly back through the woods, along the road. Anytime they could find some high ground, he would order a halt and look back to keep an eye on Sacrovir's movements. It would be close to nightfall by the time they made their way back to the main army. At no time was Sacrovir's army more than a mile or so behind them.

"Think they'll try and catch us Sir?" one of his men asked as they caught their breath from atop a small knoll.

"I don't think so," Agricola replied, shaking his head. "They have but a hand-ful of horses, and those are bearing their leaders. I doubt that any of them would have the stomach to fight us themselves." The legionaries smirked at the assess-ment of their enemy. "Come on, the open plain is not far from here. Once there, we will make a break for it and head back to camp. If Silius is following my advice, the legion will be encamped just beyond the plain."

Running for miles in armor took its toll on the Centurion and his men. Agri-cola smiled weakly as he saw the newly erected camp come into sight; thankful that Silius had indeed heeded his recommendation. It would have been a much further trek back to friendly lines, otherwise. He was hungry and thoroughly exhausted as they moved at a slow jog through the gate.

"You men are exempt from sentry duty tonight," he told his companions, all of whom stood panting with their hands on their knees. "Go find your section mates and get some supper in you." With that he slapped each one on the shoulder, told them how well each had done, and sent them off. Silius came walking up to him, a goblet of wine in his hand.

"Here, it looks like you could use this," he said with a grin.

"Actually if I could get some water first, my mouth is about dried out," the Centurion replied. Calvinus walked over and threw his water bladder at him, which Agricola proceeded to drain in one long pull. After a few deep breaths, he accepted Silius' offer of wine.

"The enemy is already arrayed in battle formation," he said as all three men walked over to the Legate's tent. "They've got quite the unique formation that they plan on using. I have to give them credit; it is a rather creative way of trying to disperse our ranks."

✳   ✳   ✳   ✳

Vipsania was dead. Tiberius rested his hand against a pillar and lowered his head. From his balcony he could just make out the smoke of her funeral pyre. He had elected not to attend, feeling the entire spectacle was an insulting charade. That bastard of a husband of hers would be giving the eulogy; the professional mourners would wail and chant and shed tears as if they indeed bemoaned the loss of Vipsania Agrippina. Tiberius bit the inside of his cheek at the thought of such hypocrisy. He had already said his goodbyes to his beloved, and besides he did not need to provide more fodder for the gossips. He could not win, of course; for the very people who would cry "shame" at his being present at the funeral of a woman who was no longer his wife, would be the same who would now call him two-faced and hypocritical for having professed his love of Vipsania in life, and yet he failed to even say farewell to her in death. It was these types of people who had used his not having attended the funeral procession for Germanicus as a means of implicating him in his death. Would they now be so crass as to suggest that he had murdered his beloved Vipsania as well? As he stood tormented by that foul combination of anger and grief, his son Drusus walked out onto the balcony. His head was hung low, and he held a medallion by the chain. It was the same one that Vipsania had given Tiberius so many years before.

"The answer is yes," Tiberius spoke without taking his eyes off the slight wisps of smoke. "You may take that medallion that your mother gave me and use its image to issue a series of currency in her memory." Drusus gave a sad smile and looked down at the medallion.

"Thank you, Father," he replied hollowly. When he did not leave immediately, Tiberius turned and faced him. Drusus' face was filled with misery. There was something added to his burden of the loss of his mother. "Gallus pulled me to the side not two minutes after the funeral was over."

"Did he now?" Tiberius' face darkened. Gallus wishing to have words with Drusus would not come from any sense of mutual mourning. Indeed Tiberius ventured that the Senator was glad to be rid of her finally. Drusus swallowed hard, sweat forming on his brow.

"He told me that with Mother gone it was time for the truth to be told," he continued.

"And what truth would that be?" Tiberius asked, folding his arms across his chest.

"He said that I am not the son of the Emperor of Rome. The cad said he had had a brief 'fling' with my mother many years ago—yes he even put it so crassly—and that I was the issue of that affair." The Emperor's face hardened. Such a story was impossible to believe. Gallus scarcely even knew who Vipsania was when Drusus was conceived and would have paid little heed to the wife of a man who at the time was merely the less-favored stepson of the Emperor Augustus. Drusus also shared many of Tiberius' physical traits, traits that a father would pass down to his son. Tiberius knew that Gallus was not looking to stake any legitimate claims into the parentage of Drusus Caesar; he knew that Gallus' sole purpose was to cause him further harm and grief. He realized that with Vipsania's passing the Emperor was weakened. He was also smarting from the humiliation Tiberius rendered him at his own house just a couple of weeks previously.

"You know I don't believe it; I swear that bastard will say and do anything to harm us," Drusus continued, reinforcing what his father already knew. Tiberius remained silent and in thought. At that moment, Sejanus walked out onto the balcony. He stopped when he noticed Drusus and stood with his hands behind his back. Drusus glared at him, eyes filled with hate.

"What the fuck are you doing here, Sejanus?" he asked with venom.

"I only came to extend my condolences to your grieving father ..."

"Like bloody hell you did!" Drusus interrupted. "Come to play upon his sympathies so that you can further your own endeavors, more like. I have no time for you." As he stormed through the doorway, Drusus made it a point to ram his shoulder hard into the Praetorian Prefect.

Tiberius gave an audible sigh. It troubled him much to witness the sheer animosity that his son displayed towards Sejanus, a man who had come into his own of late. Tiberius had come to depend on both men equally, and he could not favor one at the expense of the other.

"Forgive my son for his ill manners," he said once he was certain Drusus was well out of earshot. "He mourns for his mother."

"As a son should," Sejanus replied with a short smile. "I apologize for interrupting you, Caesar. It is only that there were some rather disparaging things said towards your person at the funeral of Vipsania Agrippina."

"So I've heard," Tiberius replied curtly, turning back towards the city and the now dissipating smoke of the funeral pyre.

"I do not speak of Senator Gallus," Sejanus remarked. "His disdain for you is of no secret to anyone. No, I speak of others, others who have besmirched the name of the Emperor of Rome under the mantle of mourning. Most are simply malicious; however others could be construed as treasonous." Tiberius gave a loud sigh at the last remark.

"Sejanus, I have told you how I feel about treason trials. Roman citizens are free to speak as they see fit, even at the expense of the Emperor's character."

"I think you will want to look at these," Sejanus persisted, holding up a small bundle of scrolls. "Many of the worst utterances came from friends of Agrippina."

Tiberius turned abruptly and he snatched a scroll, his temper finally getting the best of him. Sejanus smiled internally. He had struck the final nerve, the one that would bring the Emperor to do that which he despised.

Once word reached Tiberius that Agrippina, or at least her associates, were using her sister's death to strike at him, Sejanus would be able to use the Emperor to bring them down, one by one. The only thing that would be left standing between Sejanus and the Emperor would be Tiberius' own son. He would handle Drusus another day.

CHAPTER 15

▼

THE WRATH OF GERMANICA AND VALERIA

"That is one hell of an odd plan," Flaccus replied when Macro had finished briefing the section leaders and senior officers.

"We are Romans, we adapt," Camillus replied. "I kind of like it."

"Calvinus said it was actually Centurion Draco's idea," Macro added. "Have to give him credit for his creativity. Alright let's go over this again."

"Seems simple enough," Statorius remarked. "The first two Centuries each form up in two ranks, with these men grounding their javelins. The remaining four ranks will be in standard battle formation, about twenty meters back."

"Correct," Macro replied. "And we make certain that all of our men in the second rank pair off with someone in the front rank. I'd prefer it if they can do so by section, if at all possible. With a plan like this, they will feel more comfortable having their best friends protecting them."

"I've already ordered the lads in the second rank start sharpening their pick axes," Statorius added.

"Good," Macro nodded. "So we all know what we need to do then."

"Once the cavalry sets to engage the wings, we charge the van," Ostorius replied.

"Soldiers in the front will provide protection with their shields, while those in the second will use their pickaxes to chop down the heavily armored troops,"

Artorius observed. "Second rank will have to ground their shields in order to use both hands on their pickaxes. It's going to be tricky, because every blow that lands will likely cause the pickaxe to get stuck once that armor crumples."

"That means each pairing needs to work together ever more diligently," Rufio added.

"Just remember that we are not the main effort," Macro continued. "The purpose of this is to prevent the enemy from disrupting our remaining formations. Working together on this will be crucial, for we *have* to shock the enemy quickly. They have us sorely outnumbered, and once deployed online, we're *it*. We have no reserves for this battle.

"Once the remaining ranks push through us, we will have to fall back quickly and gather up our shields and javelins. Though if this works right, hopefully the enemy will be in disarray and we will not have to engage them again."

Magnus sat leaning against a tree, running a sharpening stone over his pickaxe, when he noticed Artorius returning from his meeting. The sun had set and legionaries were gathered around their cooking fires talking in low voices. Magnus rose to his feet and greeted his Decanus.

"So do you want to carry this, or shall I?" he asked, hefting the pickaxe.

"We're both carrying them," Artorius replied. "You and I hit harder than the rest of the men. I want you pairing up with Gavius; I will pair up with Valens. Carbo, you'll be the other axe trooper for the section. Decimus, you protect him."

"Why do I have to protect Carbo's fat ass? There's no way both of us can fit behind my shield!" Decimus said in mock protest, only to take a cuff behind the ear from Carbo. This in turn got a chuckle out of everyone, including Artorius.

"Alright, let's gather up our equipment and go over this," he directed as he, Magnus, and Carbo grabbed their pickaxes. The rest of the section picked up their shields and gladii. "Okay, we are going to have to be in a slightly looser formation than we're used to. Those of us with the axes will have to be able to come off either side to strike their targets. I figure if we leave two meters between each soldier in the front rank, we should be good. Let's practice then."

As they lined up, Artorius, Magnus, and Carbo hefted their pickaxes in one hand, and grabbed the collar of the legionary in front of him. They then started to walk, acting as if their foe were in front of them.

"*Go!*" Artorius shouted. He pulled with his left hand to help propel him around Valens' right flank. Magnus and Carbo executed similar maneuvers, swinging their pickaxes to simulate an engagement. Decimus and the others stepped in quickly to cover their exposed companions.

"That works, let's try it again," Artorius directed. The next attack would have worked just as well, had not Magnus slipped around Gavius' right side, while Carbo attacked around Decimus' left. The two legionaries collided, knocking each other down. A smattering of applause and catcalls arose from the fires where other sections were watching.

"Okay, that one could have been done better," Artorius remarked while suppressing his own laughter. Even in such dire circumstances, with their very lives dependent upon their ability to execute on the morrow, they still found it in themselves to allow a little levity. He offered a hand to help Magnus up; Valens offered his hand to Carbo, while uttering *"nice one, dumb ass"* under his breath. Carbo kicked him in the shin in response.

"How about we agree to only maneuver around the right side?" Praxus asked, his section walking over with their equipment. "Mind if we join you?"

Macro and Camillus watched as Artorius' and Praxus' sections started rehearsing the plan for the morrow. As they did so, other sections joined them, all the legionaries talking with each other, and making certain that their actions were smooth and precise. The mood lightened, Artorius' sound orchestration of the rehearsal relieving their anxiety. They were further surprised to see legionaries from Vitruvius' Century join them. Artorius had the men working in small groups, everyone paired up for the battle. Macro folded his arms and cracked a half smile.

"That man is a true leader," he said in a low voice.

"The rest of the men follow him," Camillus agreed, "and I don't just mean those in his section. Hell, he's got both Centuries on their feet and rehearsing the plan for tomorrow. Moreover you can see the lads relaxing, their confidence rising. He makes them believe in themselves."

"That he does. I wish the rest of the Decanii had his initiative. Most seemed content to simply brief their men on the plan and leave it at that. Artorius knew better; he knew that it would take coordination and rehearsal to execute a battle plan the men had never done before. I'm just glad to see the rest of the lads followed his lead."

Artorius dropped his pickaxe and lay down with his back against his pack. The exertion felt good; his anxiety about the morrow was nowhere to be found. This would be the second time in a few days that they were going into battle greatly outnumbered, yet he was not worried. He closed his eyes and stretched his arms out, yawning deeply.

"You seem pretty content, like you don't have a care in the world," he heard Magnus say as his friend sat down and unlaced his caligae. Artorius grinned slightly, his eyes shut and his hands folded on his lap.

"We've done all we can," he replied. "Whether or not it goes well for us tomorrow, there is no sense losing any sleep over it."

∗   ∗   ∗   ∗

"You men are the iron youth of Gaul!" Sacrovir proclaimed. He stood on a makeshift pulpit, Heracles and Taranis standing behind him. Most of the men he addressed were not men at all; they were very young, more like overgrown boys; the sons of Gallic nobles from all over the province.

The majority had been attending school in Augustodunum and had subsequently become hostages of Sacrovir in order to assure their fathers' allegiance. He had held spectacular rallies, decrying their status as second class citizens of Rome, and expounding upon the virtues of "old Gaul."

The impressionable young men were swept up on a tide of patriotism and hunger for military glory. These lads were the ones who would form the van of the army; first to engage the Romans, encased in plate armor so as to make them impervious to the javelin and gladius.

"I look into your faces," Sacrovir continued, "and I see not young boys. Rather I see men of Gaul, valiant youth who will rid our land of the Roman scourge once and for all!" This elicited a series of cheers and battle cries from the assembled host. Sacrovir was indeed proud of his men. While his initial motives for rebellion had seemed selfish and petty in nature, he too had become caught up in the spirit of liberation. His cause was no longer just one of vengeance and personal independence. No, it was bringing liberty and a sense of nationalism to all of Gaul. Once the Roman army that faced him was destroyed, surely the rest of the province would follow.

He dismounted the dais as a messenger came running up to him. It was Broehain, carrying a brass breastplate in his hands.

"I bring word of General Florus," the man spoke, his normally stoic face was shaken. "He is dead, his forces routed by a single Roman Cohort along with Indus' cavalry."

"Impossible!" Taranis spat. "Even if he were unable to enlist the Treveri, his forces still numbered over five thousand men. Surely you have are mistaken."

Broehain presented the breastplate to them. Sacrovir closed his eyes at the sight. Florus' ornate armor was unmistakable.

"He was a good man," Broehain said quietly. Sacrovir could only nod in reply.

"What is worse is not only did we lose his force, but we still have no cavalry!" Taranis observed. He then turned to Broehain. "Did you see any cavalry amongst the Roman ranks?"

"We did," the man replied. "In addition to their standard compliment, we saw the standards of a cavalry regiment. Not only that, but we fought against them in the mountains. Indus has in fact sided with the Romans, as have his men."

"I gave that man my friendship and my trust," Sacrovir growled, "and this is how he repays me? We will crush the Romans on the morrow, and I will feast on Indus' heart before this is over!"

*   *   *   *

As day broke, Silius sat on his horse gazing at the massive army the enemy had arrayed before him. As predicted, their heavily armored troops were in two ranks, forming the van of their force. The rest were formed up in a mass on the gentle slope that rose just a few meters above the plain. Thankfully, they had no cavalry to speak of. Only a few of their senior leaders could be seen riding on horses. A man that Silius assumed could only be Sacrovir was riding a splendid charger back and forth in front of the formation. His gestures were wild, and his men were answering audibly with battle cries not heard in a generation. Silius spat in contempt at the sight and turned to face his men.

"What a pity it is," he stated, "that the very forces who not four years ago vanquished the Cherusci and the hordes of Germania, only to have to face such a pathetic rabble that the enemy has marshaled against us! Why, only recently the Turani and rebellious Treveri were smashed by a single Cohort of this very army. Teach these rebels what it means to violate the peace of Rome. Show them no mercy in battle, but spare them when they flee.[4] *Into battle Germanica and Valeria!*"

"*Cohort!*" Proculus shouted.

"*Century!*" came the reply from his Centurions.

"*Advance!*"

Without another sound the Germanica and Valeria Legions advanced towards their foe. The first two ranks advanced about twenty meters ahead of the rest, legionaries bearing pickaxes keeping close behind their companions who would provide them with protection while they chopped down Sacrovir's armored troops.

On the far slope, Heracles watched, puzzled at this strange formation.

"Something is not right," he said to Belenus. "Look at how their first two ranks are clustered together, well ahead of the main force."

"I see it," Belenus answered. "Their files are spaced apart, almost like a skirmishing formation as well. What could it mean?"

"I don't know," Heracles replied. "These Romans have a plan of some sort. Look, the men in the front ranks are not carrying javelins either. What *are* they up to?"

In the van of the rebel force, Farquhar noticed as well that something was not right about the Roman formation. Though he could not see the forces behind the front rank, he could clearly make out that these men were devoid of javelins, and that the second rank was very close to the first.

"They are not carrying javelins," he said to Alasdair. The other lad just snorted.

"Perhaps they know that we are impervious to them!"

"I wonder." The young man felt safe encased in the armor that Sacrovir had provided for them, yet at the same time he knew he was severely constricted, his mobility greatly hindered. All around him his companions were chanting ancient Gallic battle cries, beating their weapons against their armor, exhorting their own valor and the impetuousness of the Romans. He then started in with cries of his own and beat his sword against the small buckler attached to his left wrist.

The legions were advancing slowly and deliberately, the cadence of their steps drowned out by the battle cries of the Gauls. Farquhar beat his weapon harder against his buckler, his chants growing ever louder as he tried to work himself into frenzy. He was fast becoming a man, a man of Gaul, fighting for that noble thing called *freedom*. The Romans were getting closer, and Farquhar knew it would not be long. He could almost make out the faces of individual legionaries. He eyed the sword that he carried. It was a fine weapon, the best on the line no doubt. It had served his ancestors for generations; would it serve him as well?

Suddenly, and without a sound, the Romans broke into a fast jog. The young nobles noticed that their front rank was in a looser formation than they were told the Romans were used to fighting. Their shields were not linked together, and there was a noticeable gap between their files, as the soldiers in the second rank stood directly behind them. The young man became fearful as the gap closed.

Such discipline, he thought to himself. He was suddenly afraid as the foolish-ness of this venture became clear to him. Vercingetorix and his warriors had failed to break the Romans; what chance did a handful of youths who had never even seen combat? These men they faced were professionals; battle-hardened vet-erans who were bred to kill. Farquhar braced himself as his father's words echoed in his mind. This was indeed madness, and there was no escape, for when the Romans were within a few paces, they came alive audibly. Legionaries in the sec-ond rank rushed around their companions; each carrying an entrenching pickaxe.

Farquhar became terrifyingly aware of the Romans' battle plan as he saw a well-muscled legionary rushing straight for him, eyes filled with rage, pickaxe ready to swing. The young man tried to block the coming blow with his buckler, but his armor made him too slow and unwieldy. He gave a cry of pain and the pickaxe smashed through his armor. The sharpened point punctured the side of his breastplate, as well as the bottom flank of his ribcage. He felt his ribs break as his lung was ruptured by the blow. A howl of shock and pain took his breath from him. As he fell to the ground, the pickaxe became embedded in his ribs and armor. He cried out again as he hyperventilated in sheer panic. Blood seeped from his mouth as he felt the pickaxe wrenched from his side. The pain blinded him, and overwhelmed his senses. He lay on his side, his sword lying useless in his twitching fingers.

"Mother," he whispered as he longed for the maternal comforts that only she could provide. "Father ... Kiana, my love." As he lay dying, his father's warning rang hollow in his ears. His life was coming to an end before it had even begun. He sobbed in pain and sorrow for the few seconds it took the Roman to swing his pickaxe again. He was not even aware of the subsequent blow that smashed through his helm.

Artorius stepped on the helmeted head as he wrenched his pickaxe free. His titanic strength made punching through the enemies' armor an easy task. What threw him off was the awkwardness of having to retrieve his weapon, which became stuck with every blow. As he stumbled back, Valens rushed in and rammed his shield into another armored rebel, who impeded by the weight of his armor stumbled to the ground.

"Go for the throat!" Artorius yelled. "There's a gap just beneath the helm and the chest!" Valens saw this as well and ran his gladius across the man's neck.

Artorius watched briefly as the rebel thrashed in the throes of death, blood gushing through the gap in his armor. As he did so, another rebel came at him, screaming wildly, sword raised high. Artorius rushed forward, raised his pickaxe over his head and brought it down with a crushing blow that punctured the man's heart. As his adversary fell dead, Artorius found his pickaxe wrenched from his hand. Before he could move to retrieve it, he had yet another armored enemy bearing down on him.

In a move that surprised the rebel, Artorius rushed him, quickly getting between the man's buckler and sword. With his left hand he grabbed his opponent's wrist, and wrapped his right arm around his waist. With maddening strength he threw the rebel over his hip and hard onto the ground. Rapidly he drew his gladius and fell on top the man. He wrenched the rebel's face mask up as he raised his weapon to strike. The face that looked up at him in terror was not that of a man, but of a boy. The lad looked to be in his mid teens at the most; not even old enough to require a shave. Artorius was shocked; he flashed back briefly to the young German boy who had tried to fight him. He then grimaced hard and rammed his gladius into the lad's neck. The rebel's eyes grew wide as blood gushed from his neck and mouth. Artorius wrenched his weapon free as the boy's eyes glazed over, devoid of life.

He looked to his left and right and saw what had become a disorganized brawl. The legionaries were working well in pairs, but they were starting to scatter amongst the mass of armored rebels. He watched as Magnus smashed his pickaxe into the back of a foe. Gavius then rammed his shield into their stricken enemy as Magnus wrenched his weapon free. Artorius then sheathed his gladius as he scrambled over to retrieve his own pickaxe from his slain adversary's chest.

"You alright?" Valens asked as they paired up once again.

"I am. You?" The legionary nodded in reply. Without another word they sought out other foes to slay. Valens would tie up a rebel by hammering him with his shield, while Artorius swung around either side and slew them with his pickaxe. Macro and Camillus could be seen paired up together, the Centurion electing to carry a pickaxe while the Signifier protected him. As he was not carrying the Century's Signum into battle, Camillus had elected to go without the bear's skin over his helmet and shoulders. He also wielded a standard legionary scutum shield, as opposed to the much smaller circular one that he normally carried.

"Keep it up, lads!" Macro shouted. *"They're breaking!"*

Proculus grasped the pommel of his gladius roughly. He watched the frenzied melee taking place to their direct front and was anxious to get the rest of the Cohort into the fray. Macro and Vitruvius were doing a spectacular job of mauling the enemy's armored troops, and Proculus knew he had to time his advance well. The main force of Sacrovir's army was arrayed behind these men, and he needed to make certain that he was able to push his remaining Centuries past the Second and Third in order to keep their formations intact once they engaged. Sacrovir's men in the van were falling rapidly, and he knew it would not be long.

"Our armored troops are being mauled by the Romans!" Taranis growled. From their vantage it looked as if the legionaries were chopping down small trees with their pickaxes.

"The majority of their forces are holding fast," Belenus observed. "Their front ranks are dispatching our armored men so as to keep their formations intact."

"Taranis," Sacrovir replied, "ready the main force to attack." Just then they were able to make out the dust coming from the hooves of the Roman cavalry. They formed up on either side of the legions and were moving at a slow gallop. Sacrovir was able to make out the form of Julius Indus on the right, being as he was bearing a sword instead of a lance. He scowled at the sight.

"And so the traitor Indus has returned."

"Wedge formation ... lances ready!" Indus shouted as his force closed with the left wing of Sacrovir's army. The legions were heavily engaged with the armored men in the center; all Indus and his cavalry faced were light-armed skirmishers and infantry. They grew closer; he raised his sword and nodded to the horn blower who rode next to him. As the charge was sounded, Indus gave a great cry and spurred his horse to a full sprint.

The rebel forces on the wings were in no way prepared for the ferocity of Indus' assault. Panic swept their ranks as the wall of men on chargers raced towards them, lances pointed at their hearts.

"Set your spears, keep together!" Torin shouted. The gallop of the Roman chargers was growing louder. Ellard swallowed hard at the sight.

"Fuck this!" he retorted. "I'm not going to stand here and get trampled by one of those beasts!"

"Nor am I," Radek said in a low voice. He scowled and watched as Indus' cavalry rapidly drew closer. Many were stirring amongst the rebel ranks. All seemed to understand that in order to stop the horsemen, they would have to chance being trampled and ran through. Yet no one wished to be that man who died so that the others might live.

"Gods damn it, stay together!" Torin was in a rage. "It is our only chance of survival!"

"Like bloody hell it is!" Ellard shouted. He turned and started shoving his way back through the mob behind him. "Get out of my way!"

Ellard and Radek both threw down their weapons as they sought to escape. Their panic proved infectious. Those bearing spears and shields immediately forgot their discipline, as well as the tactics that Heracles had taught them for repelling cavalry. Instead of forming a wall of spears in the way the legions were famous for, they started to break and run; too late for most of them. The Cornicen's trumpet could be heard clearly; the pulsing sound of horses galloping and men yelling became deafening. His escape clogged by the disorganized mob that could not decide whether to fight or flee, Ellard turned back in time to see the Roman chargers bearing down upon him. He let out a resigned sigh as a lance was run through his side. He collapsed to the ground as his guts were torn from his body. His intestines were mutilated; parts of them left hanging from the Roman's lance. He clenched his teeth as the unbearable pain engulfed him.

As the cavalry continued to smash into their ranks, men were skewered by lances, while others were trampled underneath. The Roman cavalry penetrated deep into their mass before engaging in a frenzied melee. Radek caught a lance in the back as he tried to flee. He screamed in pain as he stumbled into the dirt. As he sought to regain his feet, a Roman brought his lance straight down, catching him in the back of the leg. Another cry of pain erupted from his mouth as he slowly crawled away, seeking an escape from amongst the carnage. The body of a mortally wounded rebel fell on top of him, pinning him to the ground. The injuries to his leg and back prevented him from rolling over and removing the man. The stricken rebel thrashed about, his fist slamming into the gash on Radek's back. The pain became too much and he blacked out.

Torin stood his ground as best he could. He brought his spear about and managed to bring down one of the Roman horsemen, stabbing him through the sternum, rending the man from his horse. His spear became stuck, and he let it go as panic got the best of him. A charger crashed into his shield, sending him reeling to the ground. As he rolled onto his stomach, another horse trampled his shield arm. He wrenched his arm free, holding it into his chest. Remarkably, it was not broken.

He scrambled amongst the scene of death which surrounded him. He saw a number of men rushing up a small hill on their flank, which led away from the battle. He made his way towards them, keeping his injured arm close to his side. Men and horses charged past him, lances missing him by inches. At last he reached the base of the hill, where he used his good arm to help pull him up the steep slope. He could hear the sounds of men and horses behind him; the cry of one poor fellow who was brought down by a Roman lance before he could make his way up the hill. Torin was ecstatic to be alive, yet shamed by his actions. He consoled himself in that he had tried his best, and had slain a Roman cavalryman. Still the tears came freely as feelings of loss and persistent fear threatened to incapacitate him. He then steeled himself and renewed his surge up the slope with renewed passion. Whatever became of Sacrovir and his rebellion, he knew that he had earned his freedom.

Torin's attempt at valor was a rare sight. The rebels were mostly thieves and cowards. Their concern was their own survival, and they did not wish to face death at the end of a Roman lance. Those who could flee did so, whilst the less fortunate were forced to fight for their lives. The reach of the Roman lances proved too great for most, as they could not get close enough to engage man or horse. Some did manage to drag horsemen from their mounts before viciously slaying them, though this was done out of desperation rather than any kind of organized battle plan. Little did they realize that had their companions not panicked, their numbers alone would have been enough to overwhelm Indus and his cavalry. This observation was not lost on Sacrovir.

The number of armored adversaries was dwindling rapidly. Artorius and Valens had run out of men to fight, as had many of their companions. Macro wrenched his pickaxe from the chest of a rebel and quickly assessed the situation. Sacrovir's main force could be seen advancing.

"Second Century, disengage!" he shouted. *"Reform behind the Cohort!"* Decanii echoed their Centurion's command down the line.

After making certain that his men had heard the order, Artorius started down the slope, pickaxe over his shoulder. The rest of the Third Cohort was advancing towards them, shields parting at intervals to allow the Second and Third Centuries through. Artorius stopped just shy of the formation and waved his men through the gap. He slapped each man on the shoulder as he passed through, quickly getting accountability for his section before allowing himself to withdraw from the fray.

"Our wings are collapsing!" Belenus shouted, terror rising in his voice.

"The Roman front ranks appear to be disengaging as well," Heracles added his voice much calmer. "It would seem they are bringing the bulk of their legionaries forward."

Indeed, the soldiers in the front ranks had pulled back once they saw the hordes of Sacrovir's army rushing towards them. With precision timing, the remaining four ranks rushed past the wreckage that was the *Noble Youth*, forming up in time to disgorge their javelins.

"Front rank … throw!" Proculus shouted.

"Second rank … throw!" came the order from Centurion Dominus. The rebel force was within a few yards when the javelin storm was unleashed. To miss was impossible at such close range; some rebels managed to catch a javelin with their shields, only to be punctured by several more. One poor man had taken a javelin through each eye socket, his head literally torn apart by the shock of the blows. Others had their shields pinned to their bodies, or at best stripped from their hands. Aside from the commands of the Centurions, and the occasional grunt from heaving their javelins, the Romans had been unnervingly quiet up to this point. That changed with the next order from Proculus.

"Gladius … draw!"

"Rah!" The Gallic army by this time was in complete disarray, and like their companions on the wings, they too forgot that they still had the Romans badly outnumbered. The dying screamed in pain, those now devoid of shields panicked. Survival became their one concern as the legions charged into their ranks. Those who stumbled caught legionary shields and gladii in their backs.

Proculus caught a rebel in the back of the leg with his gladius, bringing him down. He then stabbed the man through the base of the neck before he could rise. His men battled their way uphill, slaying all in their path. The slope became slippery as bodies piled up; blood and intestinal fluids saturating the ground.

"Fucking cowards!" Taranis growled. "I thought you said your gladiators were warriors, Sacrovir!"

"If you will notice, it is my gladiators who continue to fight," Sacrovir replied coldly. "It is your Sequani who are running."

"Then I shall rein them back in myself!" Taranis drew his sword and spurred his horse towards the battle. *"Turn and fight, if you honor yourselves as Sequani!"* A few of his men did heed their chief's call, though most were too panic stricken to fight any more. Taranis' mount crashed hard into the Roman lines, knocking soldiers down and creating a gap which Sacrovir's gladiators quickly tried to exploit. He ran his sword through the throat of a surprised legionary, only to have it wrenched from his hands. His weapon gone, he swung his shield about, catching a Roman on top the helm. Just then, another soldier leapt up and stabbed Taranis through the groin. He gave a cry of pain as he was pulled from his mount. He was surrounded by legionaries, who started smashing his face and body with their shields. His arm snapped, his nose shattered, and his esophagus was crushed underneath the force of their blows. Blood and urine flowed freely from the wound to his groin; a wound that itself would have proven fatal, though his spine snapped underneath the Romans' onslaught. The chief of the Sequani was dead long before the enraged legionaries quit bludgeoning his broken body.

Sacrovir's gladiators were indeed brave, but they were no match for well-disciplined legionaries. Roman soldiers found their strength in working together, each man protecting his companions on his left and right. The gladiators, on the other hand, were used to fighting as individuals in an arena, and were in no way prepared for close combat with such a disciplined force. The gladiators held the high ground, but they were slowly giving way; the rest of Sacrovir's army having broken and ran.

Proculus struggled up the gradual slope that was now littered with corpses. Legionaries were fighting their way through the mass confusion; the remaining gladiators not knowing whether to fight or flee. The Centurion rammed his gladius into the belly of one assailant. He then shoved the stricken man down the hill behind him. One rebel threw down his weapons in the face of the Roman onslaught and raised his hands in the air. Proculus paused for a second as the confused rebel knew not what to do. He then went to reach for his weapons again. Proculus turned his shield up a rammed the bottom edge into the man's face, just above the bridge of the nose. The rebel gave a short cry as he was knocked to the ground, the Centurion ripping out his jugular with his gladius. The severed artery sprayed Proculus with blood as the dying man lay convulsing. In an act of bravado, a gladiator leapt high into the air, body tackling one of the legionaries. Though he had succeeded in knocking the Roman down, as well as several men around him, the gladiator took a blade to the heart for his efforts. The battle was turning into a rout and there was no one left to exploit any such breaches in the Roman lines.

Belenus seethed as watched their army collapsing underneath the Roman assault. As their casualties mounted, the gladiators had turned and fled with the rest of Sacrovir's force. They had held the longest, but their numbers were too few.

"It is over," he heard Sacrovir say, his voice surprisingly calm. "I guess they win this one."

"Our entire army is routed!" Belenus protested. "What are we to do?"

"What *can* we do?" Heracles asked, his own voice matching Sacrovir's sense of calm. Belenus was exasperated with the situation.

"Surely we had more than enough men to overwhelm the Romans," he said, his voice chalked full of emotion. Their dreams of liberation from Rome were disappearing as they watched groups of their men stumble in their flight, only to be slaughtered by the oncoming legions.

"That we did," Sacrovir replied. "And we still do, if we could get some order restored. Come, let us leave this place. We will reform our army and not make the mistake of facing the Romans in the open again."

The Second and Third Centuries raced back to where they had grounded their shields and gear. Quickly they dropped their pickaxes, hefted their shields.

"Form it up! Second Century on me!" Macro shouted. With drilled precision, legionaries fell into line to the left of their Centurion. Camillus sheathed his gladius and retrieved the Century's standard. Macro pointed towards Flaccus at the end of the line with his gladius. The Optio mimicked his gesture, signaling that the Century was set.

"Let's go!" Macro ordered, waving his gladius forward. The Century started at a run back to where the battle still raged. They merged with the Third Century; Vitruvius and his men falling in behind them. Other units could be seen doing the same up and down the line. Silius was riding up on his horse, signaling for them to cease their attack.

"The rebels are routing," Artorius heard him say to Macro and Vitruvius. "Have your men start rounding up prisoners, as well as our wounded."

"Yes Sir," Macro and Vitruvius said together. Shields were once again grounded, gladii sheathed, and rapidly they jogged back to the site of their battle with Sacrovir's armored minions. There were many dead amongst the rebel ranks, along with a significant number of wounded that were trying to crawl away from the battle. Their injuries, as well as their armor, prevented this. Still others were alive and unscathed, and were simply knocked senseless by the Roman onslaught.

Artorius and his section was tasked with checking the defeated rebels for survivors while others rounded up wounded and dead legionaries. The battle had been decisive, but no side ever survives unscathed. Solemn were the legionaries who carried their fallen brothers from the battlefield. Wounded soldiers made every effort to mask their pain as their friends tended to them. Artorius was glad that he only had to deal with enemy casualties; it hurt too much when he had to deal with one of his brothers suffering or dying.

"What do we do if we find a live one?" Valens asked.

"We disarm them and take them prisoner," Artorius replied. "We will also check them for wounds and send them to the surgeons as needed."

"Just be careful. Some may be lying in wait to try and kill one of us," Magnus added.

"Any treachery and I'll cut their balls off," Carbo replied icily. As they started stripping the enemy dead of their armor, they came to a morbid understanding.

"These are bloody *kids*," Decimus said horrified as he removed the helmet of a slain rebel. "These aren't men at all!"

"They were the sons of Gallic nobles," Artorius observed. "Sacrovir sent them to fight in order to keep their fathers in line."

"The true sign of a brave and noble man!" Decimus spat with macabre sarcasm. "I guess the barbarians east of the Rhine are not the only ones who use children to fight their wars for them!"

"Here is a live one!" Valens called out.

It was Alasdair, who was gripped with terror as the legionary removed his helmet. He had been knocked over during the battle and struck his head on a rock, rending him senseless. He had awoken to find himself surrounded by Roman soldiers. He was panting and unaware that he had soiled himself.

"Oh gods please don't kill me! Please don't kill me! *Please don't kill me!*" his voiced was a constant heaving sob. Valens slapped him hard across the face.

"Knock it off!" he barked. "If we were going to kill you we would have done so already."

"Easy there," Magnus said calmly as he helped the lad to sit upright. Valens knelt behind him and started to unbuckle his armor. Alasdair was paralyzed with fear and shock. He could not believe that he was still alive. He was certain that the Romans would slay any that survived the battle and was therefore baffled by their behavior. His mind raced out of control, unable to focus on anything … except one thing.

When he was struck down by a legionary's shield he caught a glimpse of another soldier swing his pickaxe at Farquhar. An icy chill went up his spine.

"What's your name, son?" Magnus asked his voice surprisingly calm. Alasdair jolted, suddenly brought back to the present. The Roman kneeling in front of him was a big, intimidating man; and yet his manner was, surprisingly, soothing.

"Alasdair, son of Kavan," the lad replied as he caught his breath. "Oh gods, what have we done?" He shook his head, trying to release the shame and sorrow within. His thoughts then turned to his friend. "Please, I need to know, where is Farquhar?"

"Who?" Magnus asked.

"He is my friend," Alasdair replied. "We stood next to each other during the battle. Please, he is like my brother; I *must* know that he is alright."

"Is this him?" Carbo asked, removing the helm of a slain rebel. Alasdair's eyes filled with tears. The side of Farquhar's head had been rendered by a pickaxe, brain matter and bits of bone were splattered on his face. His eyes were open and lifeless, a trickle of congealed blood running from his mouth down his cheek. Alasdair placed his head in his hands, his emotions overtaking him.

"No, it cannot be … oh Farquhar, I am so sorry I led you to this. *I have become your death!*" His speech became inaudible as he sobbed.

"Get him out of here," Artorius said in a low voice as Magnus and Valens helped the lad to his feet. The legionaries then bound his hands behind his back and guided him away from the scene of carnage and death. To their rear Statorius was marshalling prisoners into a holding area that other soldiers were hastily building barricades around.

"Noble lads, sacrificed like sheep at the slaughter," Decimus said in a low voice.

"Sheep at the slaughter die with more dignity," Gavius scoffed. "At least their heads are not filled with foolish notions of glory and victory."

Artorius scowled at the thought and was about to turn away when something caught his eye. He noticed the sword that lay in Farquhar's outstretched fingers. It was longer than the blades carried by the other young men they had fought. He leaned down and examined the weapon. It was old; not something hastily crafted in mass numbers. Someone had put a lot of work into this weapon. The blade was well-worn from countless blows; the leather straps of the handle faded. He then saw the scabbard on the slain lad's hip. It was leather and wood, adorned with embossed metal engravings. Small images of men hunting a stag and of wild horses abounded. Artorius unbuckled the scabbard and sheathed the sword. The weapon was a fine prize; born of the Gallic nobility during a different age. Gaul had at one time been a land of valiant warriors, but those days were long since gone; Julius Caesar having broken their fighting spirit. Now the only warriors that Gaul produced wore the uniform of either the Roman legions or auxilia. The young boys they had massacred were no warriors; Artorius considered them victims of Sacrovir's brain-washing. He let out a sigh of resignation as he strapped the sword to his belt.

"That's a fine prize," Gavius observed. "At least you are getting something from this nightmare."

"Am I?" Artorius asked; his eyes still fixed on the slain Farquhar.

"Well if you don't want the sword, I'd be more than happy to take it off your hands," Gavius remarked, causing Artorius to allow a slight smirk. "But you did kill the little piss ant, so it is really yours by right."

"It is a fine weapon," Artorius conceded, his eyes wandering down to the ornate scabbard. "Gaul was at one time a land of warriors. Now they send children to fight their battles."

The rebels had been routed before the Romans had executed their first passage-of-lines. Sacrovir's gladiators had made a brief surge forward, but they were outclassed by the discipline and cohesion of the legions. As he wrenched his gladius from underneath the ribcage of a slain enemy, Proculus watched as the remaining rebels turned and fled en mass.

"*Cohort stand fast!*" he ordered as he men ceased any attempts at a pursuit. "Gather up any prisoners, as well as our dead and wounded." He then stopped and rested, leaning on his shield with his free hand on his knee.

"I'm getting too old for this," he said in a low voice.

"Oh come now, you are only too old if you allow yourself to be," he heard reply in front of him. He looked up to see Calvinus standing over him. The Master Centurion's face and armor were saturated with blood and gore. His own breathing was heavy, though he still stood erect and strong.

"Calvinus," Proculus replied with a slight nod. The Master Centurion gave him a friendly smack on the shoulder.

"Your lads did well," he remarked, "particularly those who routed the van. Silius has ordered us to start laying out the rebel dead. He wants the families of the slain to be able to identify them."

"What of the live ones?" Proculus asked. Calvinus gave a wicked smirk at that.

"We have plans for them. Suffice it to say, the dead have paid the price for their warmongering. On the other hand, the living still have a debt to settle with Rome."

CHAPTER 16

▼

A GENERATION LOST

Kiana clutched Lennox's hand as they walked past the rows of Gallic dead. A search of the prisoner stockades had left them with no sign of Farquhar. The Roman General Silius had posted a decree directing all citizens of Augustodunum to come and claim their dead. Many were paralyzed with fear; fear of being implicated in the rebellion, and the even greater fear of finding out the worst had happened to their loved ones. Still many came in hope of finding the lost husband or son; that they might be alive and able to return home.

"Perhaps he has escaped," the young lass said in a near whisper. Lennox could only shake his head. He feared the worst for his son, and his heart was near breaking with the sense and dread of the unknown. They gazed in horror and sadness at the sight of thousands of slain Gauls, all laid out in long rows. Roman soldiers were pacing back and forth around the outside of the mass, driving off dogs and other wild animals as grieving families carried away the bodies. The air was filled with the sounds of weeping and mourning. Kiana watched a mother overcome with grief, wailing loudly as she clutched the body of her son. The woman violently resisted any efforts by her husband to pry her away. The father soon broke down and joined his wife in heart-wrenching sorrow.

Kiana put her hand over her mouth at the sight of the corpses. In all her life she had never witnessed such carnage. She felt herself getting sick, but quickly composed herself. She could not let Lennox face the possibility of Farquhar's death alone. She shuddered as she gazed upon each of the bodies in turn. All bore

fearful wounds, begotten by the pickaxe, javelin, or gladius. Others were completely mangled from where they had been trampled by Roman chargers. Every
last body was saturated in blood. Flies were already gathering around the corpses,
adding to the pestilent nature of the spectacle. Kiana winced as she passed a
young woman, scarcely older than she, arguing vehemently with the mother of
her slain lover; the girl insisting that the body could not belong to the boy she
loved. Kiana gagged as she caught sight of the corpse they argued over; the face
completely crushed like gourd smashed with a sledge.

She stopped; a startling realization came over as she felt Lennox release her
hand. At a slow and almost limping gait, with tears flowing freely, he staggered
over to the body of his son. Farquhar's eyes were still open; the Romans had done
nothing more than move the bodies to a central location once they had been
stripped of their weapons and armor. Lennox fell to his knees, placed his hands
over his face and quietly wept.

Kiana kneeled beside him, placed one arm around the grieving father, and
clutched the son's cold hand. She laid her head on Lennox's shoulder as he
reached down and closed his son's eyes. Kiana's grief was mind-numbing. She
struggled to cry, and felt guilty when the tears did not flow as freely as they
should have. She wondered if she was in denial, or if her beloved's death had broken her ability to emit feelings of any kind. They stayed like that for some time,
the Romans respectfully keeping their distance.

Kiana marveled at how none of the legionaries came to gloat over their fallen
enemies. She had heard stories of the atrocities committed by victorious legions
after battle. Instead, there was a certain air of sadness about them. These were not
foreign barbarians they had slain. Gaul or no, the majority of the dead were
Roman citizens, many from the nobler classes; most of the slaves, beggars, and
thieves having fled once the battle was fully engaged. Kiana surmised that with
Gaul having been a Roman province for so many years, many of these legionaries
were probably of Gallic ancestry themselves. How many of them had slain a
cousin, a friend, a brother?

As Lennox and Kiana sat mourning the brutal death of Farquhar, they were
approached by a pair of legionaries. Each had removed his helmet and grounded
his shield. It was the first time Kiana had been able to look upon the faces of the
Romans who had killed so many of her friends, and the boy she had known in
her heart she would spend her life with. Of course she had seen Roman soldiers
before, but had never paid them any mind. Oddly enough, she did not feel anger
towards these men, nor was she intimidated. In a way she pitied them, though
she could not fully understand why.

Both men were of average height, though noticeably bigger and more muscular than their companions. The larger of the two looked to be of Latin origin, though the other had blonde hair and fair skin. Kiana guessed by his facial features that he was a Norseman; of a people yet to be eclipsed by the Roman Empire. Lennox had noticed the legionaries approach as well. His voice was chalked full of emotion as he tried to speak.

"He fought for what he believed in," he stammered, his hand clutching his son's shoulder. At length the bigger of the two legionaries spoke.

"He fought because Sacrovir filled his head with vain dreams of martial glory. It is a shadow that does not exist. What a pity that the price of that lesson was his life." Artorius gazed at the body of the young man. The wounds to his side and head were deep, rendered by someone of considerable power. Artorius swallowed hard as he recognized the face of the young man.

Lennox's eyes fell on the sword strapped to Artorius' hip; the sword of his ancestors that his father and grandfather had carried in battle before him. Artorius folded his arms and followed Lennox's gaze.

"You know this weapon," he stated, eyes now on the Gaul. Lennox nodded his head slightly.

"I do," he answered, his voice weak and cracking. "It was my father's sword, and his father's before him. I gave it to my son just yesterday, in hopes that it would protect him."

"Arming rebels, I see," Magnus muttered.

"Consider the loss of such a sentimental heirloom to be the price paid for your arming of a rebel against Rome; be content that we do not demand *full* retribution." Lennox lowered his head, eyes closed tightly. Kiana simply stared in wonder. Artorius' face broke into a scowl, his eyes darkening. Did this Gaul really think he would return the very weapon that his son had used against him? He should have considered himself lucky that Artorius did not run him through with his sword, or better yet crucify him for his crimes! Lennox continued to clutch at his son's shoulder. He was a broken man; even crucifixion would be better than the torment of seeing his dead son.

"Death would come as a relief," he said softly. Artorius then understood that Lennox cared little for the sword, now that his son was gone. And yet he found that he was unmoved by pity. He did feel for the sons who had perished in a war they did not understand, but he blamed and despised their fathers for allowing it to happen.

"And that is why you will live," he said slowly. "For the loss of your son is the price you have paid for your failure as a father."

Such a waste, he thought to himself as he and Magnus turned and walked away.

Kavan was desperately searching the prisoner stockades for any sign of his son. He refused to believe that his son was dead. As he walked the perimeter, he searched the faces of the young men who stood forlorn on the other side. Many he recognized, friends of Alasdair. All were visibly shaken, some were openly weeping at their plight, and for their friends that they had watched die. It saddened Kavan deeply, for these were not men at all, but overgrown boys. They should have been continuing in their studies, playing sport, flirting with the young girls, and above all being *boys.*

Instead, they had been brainwashed into fighting for an ignoble cause. It was a cause that had destroyed an entire generation of Gaul's nobility. As he continued to walk the perimeter of the stockade he saw a sight that gave him joy. Alasdair stood with his head resting against the bars, his eyes closed and his face vacant.

"My son!" Kavan cried out as he rushed to him. Alasdair hardly noticed as his father grabbed him through the bars of his makeshift prison. "My son lives!"

"Father?" Alasdair replied weakly. His mind was in shock from the torment and devastation he had witnessed. Farquhar's brutal slaying sat fresh in his mind. The bitter shame of his having been knocked out of the fight without so much as scratching a single Roman soldier; that his friend had perished while he still lingered shattered his very soul. Suddenly his mind raced back to reality. He saw Kavan's face beaming at him, his hands clutching his tunic.

"Alasdair, my boy," Kavan swallowed hard before continuing. "You have suffered much."

"Farquhar's dead," the boy said flatly. Kavan bit his lip and nodded.

"I am sorry, my son; he was a good lad. Come; let us leave this place of death and suffering."

"I am afraid that's not possible," a voice behind him answered. Kavan turned to see a Roman Centurion standing with his arms crossed; a concerned yet foreboding expression on his face. "Your son is a prisoner of war. Legate Silius will decide his fate."

"My son is but a boy ..." Kavan began.

"A boy who fought in open rebellion against Rome!" the Centurion interrupted. While Vitruvius felt nothing but loathing and spite towards Sacrovir and his band of beggars and thieves, he could not help but pity the young nobles who had had their impressionable minds warped and corrupted by Sacrovir. He felt a sense of injustice that they had collectively paid the gravest price of any in the rebellion. And that price would only continue to grow, for Silius would demand a heavy ransom to atone for the treachery of those who survived.

*   *   *   *

The Senate rose to its collective feet as the Emperor entered the hallowed halls. Deliberately, Tiberius took his seat at the head of the Senate. In his lap sat a series of scrolls, whose contents he would unveil soon enough in detail. But the time for that would have to wait. He had a few words of his own to speak to the Senate.

"Senators of Rome," his voiced boomed in the hall, "I come before you with word of both the beginning, as well as the ending, of the revolts in Gaul. It is with great disdain that I consider how you dared to question my judgment on not sending either myself, or my son to the front to take command personally. Your accusations are like those of frightened women, not men fit to lead the most powerful Empire the world has ever witnessed." A few grumblings could be heard from within.

"This is an outrage, Caesar ..." Gallus started to speak, only to be cut off by Tiberius slamming his hand down on the arm of his chair, his anger rising.

"Do not interrupt me again, Senator Gallus," he said with ice in his voice. "If an Emperor's presence is required at the front of every potential trouble, then he would never remain in his capital. But then, perhaps that is what this body wants." He glared at the Senators coldly; many of them fidgeting in their seats.

"*I* will decide when it is fitting for me to take command in the field. You forget, noble fathers of Rome, that aside from our good friend Caecina Severus, I have fought in more wars and endured greater battles than most of you put together. Now, here are the official reports from Gaul. Sacrovir and Florus are dead, the rebellion crushed."

With that he unfurled the first scroll that covered the campaigns against the Belgae. One by one he read through each official report, listing in detail the exploits of individual units who distinguished themselves. Finally, he handed the scrolls to the scribe at his side.

"The honor for this victory belongs with the men who led and fought in this campaign. I recommend that they be formally recognized for their actions. I am leaving the details of such recognition in your care. Deal strictly with the facts when handing out honors and awards; do not allow such honors to become cheap and meaningless. That is all." He rose and walked past the assembled host of Senators and out of the main hall.

"Do you think it wise leaving the awarding of honors to the Senate?" Drusus asked once they had left the senate chamber.

"They will do the right thing," Tiberius replied, allowing a slight grin. "Otherwise they will gain my displeasure, something they now look to avoid at all cost. They will deal strictly with the dispensation of awards. When a senator has to dole out honors for anyone other than himself, he is apt to hold the honoree to a higher standard than he would for his own actions. I would rather they erred on the side of frugality, rather than see the awards and decorations of Rome's legions cheapened like the favors of a common street whore." Drusus smiled and nodded. His father know how to deal with the senate; to put them in their place, yet allowing them to persist in their façade of authority by leaving the awarding of honors in their hands.

*   *   *   *

It was well after dusk by the time Kiana and Lennox made it back to Augustodunum. Kiana sat in the back of the wagon, her hand never releasing Farquhar's. His eyes closed and head turned to one side; one might almost believe that he was merely sleeping. It was only when the cart hit a bump and his head rolled to the other side that the terrible wound where his skull had been ruptured glared hideously at her. As they passed through the gates, she noticed Lennox's wife waiting for them. He stopped the cart and nodded to her. Her subsequent sobs echoed throughout the entire city, mingled with the sounds of other mothers and wives who had been given the sorrowful news of their loved ones' demise. It angered Kiana that most of the rebel army had survived, yet the noble youths had been unable to run, the armor Sacrovir had encased them in had served as their coffins.

The city was flooded with Roman soldiers, searching for Sacrovir and the rest of the rebel leaders. Ransom and pardon for the majority of the survivors could be negotiated; however, Sacrovir himself would pay with his life.

Kiana hoped that the Romans would make him suffer unspeakable torments, so enraged as she was at the suffering he had wrought. He had at first taken the noble youths as his hostages, and then brainwashed them into becoming his minions. As a result, an entire generation of Gallic nobility had been annihilated by the Roman onslaught.

The inn's great hall was crammed with patrons and Torin sought to be anonymous in its midst. He sat back in the far corner, seeking to hide himself from the world. His injured arm in a makeshift sling, he ate and drank in silence.

He had a fair amount of coin, but no idea of how he would spend it; or for that matter what to do with his newfound freedom. He thought that perhaps he could go and search for his wife and children. But then he knew that such a search was futile at best. He didn't know if they were even in the province anymore. He prayed to his gods that fate had been merciful to them.

There were a great many people in the hall, more than one would normally expect to see. People were afraid to be out on the streets this evening, what with the town now occupied by Roman soldiers. Torin wondered how many in the inn were rebels like him just looking to disappear. He took a sip of his mead as the door was forcibly opened. At least a dozen legionaries strode into the hall, flanking a Centurion.

"Gaius Silius, commanding Legate of the Twentieth Legion, has ordered all patrons to leave this establishment immediately!" the officer boomed. "This building is now the headquarters of the Rhine legions while we search for Julius Sacrovir and his accomplices." The Gauls shifted in their seats, uncertain as to what they should do.

"Move!" the Centurion barked. Immediately patrons started filing out of the tavern. The man behind the bar started to protest, only to have a Roman spear leveled in his direction. His hands raised to his shoulders, the man backed away slowly. Torin found that he was trembling in fear as he made his way towards the door. He was utterly terrified that one of the soldiers would recognize him. He started to cover his face, but realized that to do so would only arouse suspicion. He swallowed hard, beads of sweat forming on his brow as he walked between the files of Romans.

"What did you do to your arm?" a legionary asked him. He stopped and quickly tried to suppress his fear. Was the Roman merely inquisitive, or was he suspicious of something?

"Um … horse riding accident," he stammered. The legionary frowned slightly and raised his eyebrows.

"Hmm, you might want to be more careful next time," the soldier remarked. Torin forced a nonchalant smile and hurried out into the street. He broke into a cold sweat when he saw the street lined with Roman legionaries. He swallowed hard and walked away as quickly as he could without causing alarm. He clutched at his injured arm, the pain making him feel sick.

"Why couldn't they just leave me alone?" he asked himself in a low voice. He knew he had to leave Augustodunum at once; sooner or later a Roman would become suspicious and Torin knew his fate if he were discovered. An entire section of legionaries guarded the main gate, which was partially shut. Only small groups of people could get in or out at any one time, and the Romans were keeping a close eye on everyone who passed through. Sweat formed on Torin's forehead once more and he clutched his injured arm close to him. He averted his eyes down, not wishing to look at the soldiers. He hoped that if he did not look at them, perhaps they would not notice him. A hand against his injured shoulder stopped him. Torin bit the inside of his cheek, trying to suppress a cry of pain. He looked up to see the Decanus in charge of the gate blocking his path.

"Where are you heading this late?" the Roman asked, his eyes fixed on Torin's mournful gaze.

"Home," the Gaul replied in almost a whisper. That at least was not a lie. He then stepped around the Decanus and walked out the gate. A puzzled legionary walked over to his leader.

"You want us to go after that one?" he asked. The Decanus shook his head.

"No. Even if he is a rebel, he's too short and too young to be Sacrovir. Just let him go." Torin just made out the words of the Roman as he slipped out into the night. He closed his eyes and breathed a sigh of relief, a lone tear running down his cheek.

Once Silius had established his headquarters the great hall was crammed with officers from his legionary forces. Several tables had been pushed together in order to make for a decent area to lay out maps and reports.

"This city is too large for us to conduct a thorough search," asserted Caeso, the Master Centurion of the First Germanica. In the absence of a Legate, Caeso was acting as the Legion Commander. "Still, we've got every known exit manned by legionaries. It is the unknown exits I worry about."

"I concur," added Master Centurion Calvinus. "If we try and search this entire city house-to-house, Sacrovir is just going to slip out from under our noses."

"If he hasn't already," Silius remarked. "I would be very surprised if he was still in the city. My perception is that the locals blame him rather than us for their suffering and loss. If he is still in Augustodunum, it will only be a matter of time before they turn him over to us ... alive or dead."

"In the meantime, we need to decide how we are going to find him if he has fled," Caeso replied. Centurion Aemilius then spoke up.

"We've got men seeking out information from the populace, trying to see if anyone knows of Sacrovir's whereabouts. Surely someone had to have seen him flee."

"Still going to be difficult to know who's telling the truth and who isn't," Calvinus remarked. "This was not a popular uprising, so we must use care when it comes to torturing suspects for information."

"I've got a detachment that I can have start torturing slaves," Caeso added. "Most slaves will sell out their most loving masters after a few lashes; though I must admit that it would be pretty haphazard at best." Silius shook his head.

"Save your torture detachments for when we actually need them," he directed. "If Sacrovir has slipped through our grasp, there is little to gain by torturing random slaves. However, you can start questioning the prisoners and see if any know where he might have fled."

"Already being done, Sir," Caeso said with a self-appreciating grin. As if on cue, a pair of legionaries entered the hall, a bound prisoner in tow.

"This is a rebel who says he knows where we can find Sacrovir," one of the soldiers said.

"Bring him here," Silius waved the men over. The Gaul was dirty and reeked of sweat; his hair was unkempt and matted with blood. Bruises could be seen on his body through his ripped tunic and his left eye was closed shut with a deep gash running from his cheek to his eyebrow.

"What did you do to him?" Calvinus asked, scowling at the wretch of a man. "Caeso, your men need to work on their torture techniques; this is sloppy work at best!"

"We didn't do this, Sir," one of the soldiers stated. "We found him like this. I think he got trampled by one of Indus' horsemen. No sooner than we discover he's alive that he's swearing to us that he knows where to find Sacrovir. We told him he'd better; otherwise we'll crucify his sorry ass."

"And in that you are correct," Silius asserted. He then addressed the Gaul directly. "Play us for fools and you will be nailed to the walls of this very building and I will personally chop off your cock and make you suck on it!"

"I assure you, I know where to find Sacrovir," the rebel replied through slurred speech, a line of slobber and blood falling off his swollen lip.

"What is your name?" Silius asked.

"My name is Broehain," the man replied. "I am of the Turani. I have fought your armies thrice now in the last few weeks."

"Indeed," Silius replied coolly. "So tell me, why is it that you are now looking to hand Sacrovir over to us?"

"My people have suffered inexplicably because of that man," Broehain replied. "Nearly half our fighting men were slaughtered in what was to be no more than a ruse. Sacrovir then compelled us to fight for him again. So we did; only to be outflanked again by a single Cohort of your men. Romans truly are the masters of warfare."

"You can spare us the flattery," Calvinus admonished.

"It is no flattery, I assure you," Broehain asserted. "I have witnessed too much suffering and death to be concerned with such petty things." There was a bitter note to his voice. Broehain knew that of all those from his village who had joined Sacrovir's cause, less than a third would ever return home.

"I do not care about my own welfare," he continued. "I know that as a leader of this rebellion, my life is forfeit. I only ask that you spare the lives of my men, and that you make that bastard Sacrovir pay for what he has done to our peoples."

"You are of the Turani?" Calvinus asked. Broehain nodded in reply. "Then you were not a part of Sacrovir's inner circle."

"That is correct. He used us as sheep to be slaughtered; a ruse to fool you into thinking him loyal to Rome."

"The leaders of this rebellion have indeed forfeited their lives," Silius replied. "You however were not part of that circle. You may yet have a small chance at redemption. Lead us to Sacrovir and your life will be spared.

"Your lands however, will still be confiscated. You will be left with a small farmhouse and a plot of land." Broehain closed his eyes as they welled up with tears of disbelief. He was only going to request that the Romans kill him quickly, and yet he was being offered his life. A life devoid of his lands, prestige, and wealth; however a life where he would be able to see his sons grow up to become men, where he would be able to hold his wife in his arms again. He was a broken man, but he would still be able to live for his family.

"Sacrovir has an estate, well hidden in the hills," he said in a low voice. "That is where they have fled. I will take you to them."

"Of course you will," Silius replied. He then directed the soldiers, "Clean him up and see to his wounds."

"Yes Sir."

Lennox sat at the table and placed his head in his hands. He had taken up residence in a small apartment in Augustodunum, awaiting the end of the rebellion. His body shook as he silently wept for his son. Kiana sat across from him; his wife stood sullenly off in the corner.

"You could have done more to help him," she said, her voice hoarse from crying. Lennox looked up at her, his eyes red and swollen.

"What else could I have done? His heart was set on seeing this through. I could not stop him."

"You should have fought beside him." Her voice was quiet.

Kiana's eyes grew wide in disbelief, not believing what she had heard. She hated Sacrovir and the rebels; and she blamed them for Farquhar's death rather than the Romans. The lad's mother felt differently.

"You heard me," she continued, in a louder, accusing voice. "You and all the other nobles should have fought beside your sons! Better to have died honorably as our ancestors did!" She was almost shouting.

"Will you be quiet, woman!" Lennox snapped. "These walls have ears, and we are not in a friendly house."

"So what if the Romans do hear more seditious talk!" his wife continued to rant. "I have lost my son, and my husband is nothing but a coward! I would rather be taken by the Romans ..." Lennox lunged to his feet and struck her hard across the face before she could continue.

"I will *not* be named a coward by my own wife!" he spat. "I did not choose to throw my life away foolishly. I gave Farquhar our ancestral sword, the most sacred artifact this family possesses, and now it is lost as well. It was all I could do ... it was all I could do." At that, Lennox started to break again, and he put his hands over his face while his wife started to wail and sob as she curled up in the corner of the room.

Kiana stood and backed towards the door. "I should go," she said quietly. Lennox took her in his arms and held her close.

"I am sorry you have seen us like this," he said through his tears. "Please forgive me."

"There is nothing to forgive," Kiana whispered as she returned his embrace. He released her and she stepped out into the night. She tilted her head back and closed her eyes once she was outside.

"An abominable predicament to be in," a voice spoke. Kiana leapt up, startled. It took her a second to recognize the voice. She quickly looked to her left and saw her father walk into the torchlight. He was dressed in a Roman-style toga; his face worn and tired. With him were two of his body slaves, as well as a group of four Roman soldiers. Kiana rushed into her father's arms, finally letting her own tears go.

"It's alright, Daughter," he said soothingly. "Everything is going to be alright now."

"You have found your daughter, sir. Now it is time for you to leave," the legionary Decanus spoke.

"Come," the elder Gaul remarked with a motion of his head, "let us leave this place, Kiana. There is a carriage waiting for us outside the main gates. These men escorted me here to ascertain that it is my daughter I seek, rather than a wayward son."

"Let's go," the Decanus spoke again, pointing down the road. He waited for Kiana and her father to start walking before following close behind with his men. Not another word was spoken between father and daughter until they were in their carriage and away from the city.

"It was a noble thing you did," the father spoke at length. "I feel for Lennox, I really do. He is an old friend, and Farquhar was a fine young man."

"I feel sick," Kiana said. "I saw the bodies of many of my friends today ... mutilated ... ripped apart by such savagery."

"Yes and a young girl should not have to see such things. I saw the carnage the Romans had wrought. War demonstrates humankind at its absolute worst, and the Romans have become masters of it. And yet, in the end we got off pretty fortunate."

"How so?" Kiana asked. She failed to see how the loss of her lover and friends could have been anything resembling fortune.

"I have no sons," her father replied. "I have land, slaves, a wealth of coin, and two beautiful daughters, but no sons. The Romans know this. Therefore there is no chance of us falling victim to their purge."

"What purge?" Kiana felt a sinking feeling in the pit of her stomach. She then realized that her people's suffering had only begun with the defeat of Sacrovir's army.

"Reparation and retribution, my dear. The noble youths who were not killed in the battle were captured to a man. Legate Silius will ransom them, and demand a fearful toll for their safe return. And yet they should count their blessings in that the Romans are not enslaving the lot of them, to include the fathers and immediate families. Had this rebellion garnered more popular support, I do not doubt that Tiberius would have unleashed the entire Rhine army on us and burned the entire province to the ground." Kiana folded her arms across her chest, the sound of the carriage moving through the night playing an ominous tone as her father continued.

"The ransoms demanded will destroy the families who choose to pay them. Lands will be confiscated, slaves taken, and the nobles will be stripped practically down to their last denarii. Already I have heard that Silius is planning a massive auction for the lands they take."

"And what if a family is unable to pay the ransom?" Her question caused her stomach to seize up, for she feared the worst in her father's reply. Instead, he was evasive in his answer.

"That is something we need not worry about," he answered with finality. "I mourn for my friends, as well as my daughter, in their loss. But I still count my own family's blessings. At least I know that I can still provide you with sufficient dowry to attract a suitable husband. I will have to search the province now in order to find a suitable man, but it will be done." Kiana smiled weakly and averted her eyes downward. Her father leaned forward and placed his hand in hers.

"Farquhar was a good lad," he remarked, "and he would have made you a fine husband. The union between our families would have been great indeed. But he is gone now, and there is no bringing him back. He chose his path and paid the ultimate price for his foolishness. There will be few young men left in this region with any kind of status or position worthy of my daughter. But let us not think of these things now. You are safe, and we will be home soon." He kept a watchful eye on his daughter as she lay back in the carriage and drifted off to sleep; exhaustion having overcome her at last. The drone of the carriage rumbling caused him to nod off eventually as well.

"Lost! All is lost!" Belenus wailed. Sacrovir fought to maintain his composure even as the rest of his entourage seemed to be falling apart.

"What happened to this mighty army you supposedly trained to fight like Spartans?" one commander fumed at Heracles. Sacrovir stepped between the men as Heracles looked to be going for his sword.

"Enough," he said in a calm voice. "We have suffered a setback, nothing more. Our army fled, yes. But the majority survived to fight another day."

"You forget something," Belenus retorted. "The *Noble Youth*, the sons of our noblemen. *They* fought to the last, because they had nowhere to run to. With so many of their sons slain, their fathers will hardly forgive us for leading them to annihilation."

Sacrovir spat on the ground. "I do not need the bloody nobles," he cursed. "They are little more than lapdogs to Rome! I used their sons to keep them in line, that's all. What I need is for my army to pull itself together and regroup! We still have the Romans badly outnumbered. They think we are beaten, but I tell you we can still overwhelm them if we can reform our minions!"

*   *   *   *

Indus rode alongside Broehain. The former rebel leader took them deep into the hills. They were only sparsely populated with trees, mostly shrubs and tall grass. There were also no trails to speak of. Centurions Calvinus and Aemilius accompanied them, along with elements of the Legion's cavalry. As they came around the right-hand side of a hill, they saw the land open up to a flat plain, surrounded by the hills. There was a grove of trees to the left, and a large manor house on the right, surrounded by a short wall. Behind the manor was what looked to be at least a score of blacksmith shops.

"Well there's something you don't see every day," Aemilius observed.

"Looks like he's had every available blacksmith in the entire region working for him!" Calvinus said, pointing to the structures behind the manor. Broehain nodded in agreement.

"That is where Sacrovir has manufactured all of his arms and armor," he replied. "It is also where those of us closest to him would meet."

"Let's go say hello then, shall we?" Aemilius remarked.

"The Romans are coming!" a servant shouted as he burst into the hall where Sacrovir and his men were meeting.

"What?" he asked alarmed. "That's impossible!" As Sacrovir ran out of the hall, Heracles slinked slowly towards the back. The door had been left half open, and he silently disappeared.

Sacrovir stood on top of the wall surrounding his estate as a contingent of Roman horsemen started to encircle the complex. He bit his lip as he recognized both Indus and Broehain riding with a pair of Centurions. He lowered his eyes to the ground in contemplation before raising them to the sky. He took a deep breath as he made up his mind.

His rebellion was over; thwarted by betrayal and the lack of true support from the masses. Very well, if it was truly over, then it would end on his terms, not the Romans'!

"Summon all the household staff," he ordered the servant as he returned to the great hall.

"What is happening?" Belenus asked as Sacrovir returned.

"It is over," he replied. Sacrovir then faced all of his companions. "The Romans have indeed found us. I am sorry to have led you to this end, gentlemen. But let the Romans know that we died fighting for what we believe in; for the rights they have denied us from birth, for our heritage that they stripped from us; for the freedom from oppression and fiscal servitude." He then turned to his servants who had gathered behind him.

"All of you are now free," he said. "Let the Romans bear witness to your freedom, and do not allow yourselves to be denied. My last order is for you to set fire to this mansion, that it may not be used by the Romans for profit!"

Calvinus was puzzled to see a plume of smoke rising from inside the estate. He was further perplexed when he saw a large group of men and women in servants' clothing walking out the main gate and walking towards them. He then rode forward with Indus and Aemilius, stopping in front of the group of slaves.

"What has happened?" he asked. An older man at the front of the group addressed him.

"It is over, honorable Centurion," he replied. "Sacrovir lies dead, slain by his own hand. His closest companions died with him, and per his last request, the mansion now burns over their heads. Our freedom was granted, and we ask that you honor this."

"You are in no position to ask us anything!" Aemilius snapped. "Your master was a traitor to his people, and as such I piss on any final requests of his!"

"You will not be returned to slavery," Calvinus replied, a cold look in his eyes. The former slaves looked troubled and frightened by his demeanor. After Aemilius' rebuke, they feared the Centurions. Calvinus saw their anxiety and explained.

"Each of you will be interrogated to validate your story of Sacrovir's demise. You will provide any and all details of his rebellion and any accomplices who might still be alive. Prove yourselves useful, and I will honor your freedom. Play us false, and I will not sell you back into slavery; rather I will break every last one of you myself and have what's left fed to wild dogs!"

CHAPTER 17

▼

REPARATION AND RETRIBUTION

The prisoners were arranged by class and social status. Each was then brought before a group of Roman officers. With the sheer number of prisoners needing to be tallied and ransomed, Silius had granted all officers of the rank of Centurion and above authority to pass sentence on his behalf. He and the Tribunes would deal with the leaders of the rebellion. Most of these men would either be executed or at best enslaved, and Silius knew that he could not delegate the authority to pass capital sentencing.

Centurions sat behind rickety desks with their Optios, as well as any other officers that they saw fit to include in the interrogation. Macro had designated Flaccus and Camillus to sit on the sentencing board, with Camillus acting as his scribe.

He had wanted to include Statorius as well; however the Tesserarius had been tasked with supervising the stockade, as well as the marshalling of prisoners to their designated interrogators. In a surprise move, Macro had tasked Artorius with filling in for Statorius.

Praxus was on hand as well, helping to root through the piles of paperwork that needed to be sorted. As each man came forward, he was required to state his full name and birthplace. Praxus and Artorius would then sift through the census rolls, which in addition to tracking the population of the province, also logged each family's wealth and social status.

The Roman bureaucracy was thorough in its tracking of subjects within the Empire. From this information Macro would determine the ransom of each prisoner. Most of the 'common' prisoners were accompanied by their spouses, siblings, or other relatives. The nobles, being as most had not yet reached the age of maturity, were accompanied by their fathers or patriarchs. If a man could not provide a viable family name that appeared on the census roles, he was presumed to be an escaped slave or criminal, and was condemned to slavery.

At close to midday, Artorius saw a prisoner escorted to them that he immediately recognized. It was Alasdair, the young man whose friend Artorius had slain. His father, Kavan, was with him, his hand never leaving his son's shoulder. Though he pitied the boy, it did not deter Artorius from his sense of justice. Alasdair was the first noble prisoner they had had to deal with, and he knew the price of his ransom would be severe.

"Name and place of birth," Macro demanded.

"Alasdair, son of Kavan," the lad replied quietly. "I am from the city of Avaricum." Artorius and Praxus systematically started through the census roles for Avaricum. Praxus whistled quietly when he saw the amount of lands and wealth Alasdair's family possessed.

"Can you believe this?" Praxus asked in a low voice. "The price for this one will be extreme."

"Quite," Artorius replied as he handed the documents to Macro, who then quietly read through them. He scribbled some notes, which he then showed to Flaccus and Camillus. The Optio and Signifier nodded in agreement with their Centurion's assessment. Macro bore into both father and son with his piercing gaze.

"Your son has been found guilty of supporting rebellion against the Emperor, Senate, and people of Rome," he said to Kavan. "In his mercy; the Emperor Tiberius Caesar has decreed that all prisoners of war be eligible for ransom, based on their family's status and ability to pay." It was the same spiel he had been giving all day, and yet there was no sense of monotony in his voice. "Your family holds Roman citizenship, and is of the noble class of Gaul. Your status gives you a responsibility to the people. By allowing your son to be taken in by Sacrovir's serpent tongue, you have failed in this responsibility. You have failed your people, and have disgraced your family and social class. By authority of Gaius Silius, Commanding Legate, your son's ransom is set at one hundred talents. He is further prohibited from ever leaving the state around Avaricum without permission of the Roman censor, who he must appear before annually."

Kavan closed his eyes and lowered his head as he heard the sentence. One hundred talents was a considerable sum, one that would cost him the vast majority of his lands, and require him to decimate his household staff, as well as his other servants.

"Such a ransom will cripple my family ..." he began. Macro slammed his hand down on the desk.

"This is *not* a negotiation!" he barked. "Your son has committed treason, and as such should be executed like a common criminal! Be glad that we have allowed him to live! Either pay the ransom, or else your son can join the slaves and thieves that are bound for the sulfur mines in Mauretania. Those are your only options."

"Alright then," Kavan replied, nodding slightly. "I will pay the ransom."

As they were escorted away by a pair of legionaries, a horrifying scream came from two tables down, where Centurion Dominus sat. He held a particular loathing for the rebels and as such Artorius knew that the ransom he demanded would be even more brutal. Silius had given little specifics as to how the sentencing should be conducted. All he had said was that he would rather they err on the side of severity rather than leniency, though he had stated that the ransoms demanded had to be within the ability of the prisoners and their families to pay. Artorius correctly deduced that the screams came from a young nobleman whose family had refused to pay his ransom.

"No! No! No!" the lad screamed in terror. *"Father ... please do not abandon me!"* The lad's father exited the hall as the boy struggled against the legionaries who held him. As he was thrown to the floor, one of the soldiers drew his gladius and smashed him in the mouth with the pommel. The other legionary grabbed the boy roughly by the hair and proceeded to punch him repeatedly in the face.

"Hey!" Proculus shouted as he strode across the hall to where the boy now lay limp. "Don't break him! He needs to be able to make the journey to Mauretania." Other young prisoners started to tremble in terror, realizing their fate if their fathers refused their ransoms. One urinated in his tunic, which brought a sharp cuff across the ear from one of his legionary handlers. Another passed out completely.

"Hey Macro, tell me we don't have to escort those bastards to Mauretania," Camillus remarked. Macro allowed himself a half grin and shook his head.

"No, there are auxiliary troops coming up from Massila," he answered. "They will escort the slave traders to the sulfur mines in Africa."

"Pretty harsh sentence," Artorius observed.

"Tell me about it," Flaccus added. "I had to do an escort mission like that one time. If you lads ever plan on traveling to North Africa, don't bother. It is inhospitable, and the climate insufferable. I got to take a tour of one of the mines when we got there. The foreman seemed to get some macabre sense of satisfaction from his job. It is brutal down there. You live, work, eat, and sleep underground. Most slaves don't realize when they arrive that they have taken their last glimpse of the sun. Day and night become as one, and you lose all sense of time. I would imagine that many don't survive even a year."

"Tiberius wants to be able to balance mercy with justice and retribution," Macro added. "He gives these people a chance at reparation, and if refused, we impose the harshest sentence we can on them."

"This is much worse than being sent off to be a gladiator," Camillus noted. "At least there you get to see the sun. Not to mention death probably comes quickly."

"That and you are able to live with the hope of winning your freedom," Artorius remarked. "These men are dead the moment they walk out of here."

For two more days they continued in their hateful task of ransoming prisoners. Artorius could not even count how many they had processed. Two prisoners had been denied their ransoms and suffered the same fate as the lad they had watched taken away screaming on the first day.

One man they had discovered was a criminal, wanted for a variety of offenses that ranged from horse thievery to arson. This one had tried to attack Macro with his bare hands, bound as they were. Artorius and Flaccus had been quick enough to intercept the man, Artorius throwing him over the desk, knocking papers everywhere. The man had then tried to bite into Artorius' forearm as Flaccus repeatedly smashed him across the head with the pommel of his gladius. He then turned his weapon and went to stab the man, when Artorius stayed his hand.

"Don't grant this bastard a quick release by death," he remarked. Flaccus nodded and sheathed his weapon. After that incident, Macro made certain that all prisoners were bound at the feet, as well as the hands.

That evening Artorius walked down to where Magnus and some of the others were dismantling the stockade. They were just going to tear it down, but then some of the legionaries had decided to use the timber to start a series of bonfires. Soldiers could be seen lounging in the glow of the flames, glad to be done with prisoners and rebellion. Artorius found Magnus roasting some type of meat on a long stick that he had stuck into the fire.

"What *are* you cooking?" he asked as Magnus smiled at him.

"Goat; I got it real cheap from a local herdsman on his way to the market. You want some?" He pointed to a mess tin that was piled high with cooked meat. Artorius realized that he had not eaten most of the day and he was very hungry. He also shared many of the same tastes as Magnus.

"Thanks, it smells good." He sat down on a fallen tree they had made a bench out of and proceeded to eat some cooked goat, something he had never had before. It was actually quite good. His Nordic friend had a knack for cooking fresh meat.

"Bloody hateful task," he remarked as Magnus pulled his stick from the fire.

"I don't know about that," Magnus remarked. "I rather enjoy this type of cooking."

"I meant the task I had to do, sitting on the sentencing boards!" Artorius replied, exasperated.

"Oh that," Magnus said with a dismissive wave. "I'm just glad this bloody rebellion is at an end. I heard Sacrovir killed himself and burned his estate over his head. Quite dramatic, don't you think?"

"Quite," Artorius replied. "I found it rather disturbing the number of nobles who refused to ransom their sons. Their lands and treasure meant more to them than their own flesh and blood."

"Such men are driven blind by greed," Magnus remarked as he turned his makeshift spit over and stepped away from the fire. "In their minds, sons can be replaced. By the way, I saw that sword you got off that dead kid. A fine weapon, that!"

"Indeed," Artorius acknowledged. "I didn't want some jackal in the rear taking it for his own collection, or that of the Legion for that matter. It is too fine of a weapon to remain so discarded, collecting dust."

"So you took it for your own collection?" Magnus interjected. He raised his hands in resignation as Artorius stared at him. "Hey, I'm not judging you. Just making a small jest is all. I mean, you killed the lad; the spoils of war are yours. I just wish I had found something nice and shiny to take back with me. You got that sword, and Decimus got Florus' helmet." He gave a short laugh. "Now *that* was a prize!"

"Would your father have ransomed you?" Artorius asked abruptly, bringing them back to the original subject.

"Sure," Magnus replied with a casual shrug. "Of course he would have beaten me to death as soon as he got me home! I think I would rather deal with the sulfur mines in Mauretania rather than face my father like that!" Artorius had to laugh at his friend's dark humor. He then thought about what Flaccus had said about the mines. Such a place would break any man, no matter how strong he was in mind and body. One could only go on for so long once all hope was lost.

*   *   *   *

The forum of Augustodunum was a swarm of activity. Proculus knew the auctions would bring every Roman citizen with a talent to his name within a hundred miles. He recognized a few Centurions and Tribunes who were looking to increase their wealth and lands on the cheap. Silius himself was overseeing the auctioning of Gallic estates, having already procured a prime piece of real estate for himself. The Legate stood behind a podium, a gavel in his hand. There were other auctions going on as well. Proculus noticed Vitruvius standing with his arms folded, deep in thought.

"Vitruvius, old boy!" he stated with a friendly smack on the shoulder. His lesser Centurion nodded in reply.

"Here to take part in the raping of the Gallic nobility?" Proculus asked. He could not help but contain his excitement. His wife Vorena would love nothing more than to have a country estate to escape from the confines of the cities. "So what are you in the market for?"

"Slaves," Vitruvius replied. "I figured I can buy some decent stock really cheap and turn them over for a profit when we get home. I may even pick out one or two to keep for myself. It seems the fashion for a Centurion to have his own personal attendants."

"So will you be looking for something practical, or maybe a little more seductive?" Proculus asked with a wry grin. Vitruvius smirked at the question.

"A manservant will be practical, of course. And if I were to find something that could bring some relief to my loins—not very likely, judging from this lot-she'd still better be a damn good cook!" Proculus laughed and shook his head.

"Yes, and I see that some of the men from the ranks have pooled their resources together to try and acquire themselves a slave or two. Well if they want someone to clean out the section bays and cook their meals for them, so be it."

"Quite," Vitruvius said. "So what about you, you're not in the market for more slaves are you?"

"I'm good on slaves," Proculus replied with a shake of his head. "I'm after land. I still have quite a bit of my winnings left that I got from your little gladiatorial exhibition."

Vitruvius snorted. He found it odd that everyone but him had made a fortune off his killing Sacrovir's prize gladiator. At the time he thought it would be tempting the fates too much if he were to have bet on himself.

Proculus left his friend to his business and walked over to where Silius was getting ready to start to land auction. He was determined to get Vorena that country estate. He thought that perhaps he would pick up a pair of horses as an extra. He also knew they would need someone to run the estate while Vorena was in Rome. He then remembered Diana.

Diana Procula was a distant relative of his; his father and her grandfather being second cousins. Whereas her grandfather was a very influential Roman magistrate, Proculus' father had been a simple stone mason; and he himself was a mere soldier who had risen from the ranks. Still he and Diana had shared a close bond over the years. He was nearly old enough to be her father, and as such had become a type of paternal figure to both her and her sister.

Diana's sister, Claudia, was in a long-term engagement with the Tribune Pontius Pilate; a good match for both families. Not that Proculus had faired too poorly in the marriage game. After all, his wife was the granddaughter of the famous Centurion Lucius Vorenus, who had distinguished himself during Julius Caesar's Gallic campaigns. As a boy Proculus had lived to hear stories about the man that Caesar himself had made famous in his Commentaries. Even after more than seventy years since the end of the Gallic conquest, the exploits of Lucius Vorenus and Titus Pullo still set the standard for valor expected of a Roman soldier, particularly those of the Centurionate. Centurion Pullo had had the misfortune of siding with Pompey Magnus during the civil war; and though he was later pardoned, he slipped into obscurity. On the other hand, his friend and rival Vorenus had retired as Centurion Primus Pilus of Legio XI. Vorenus' son, Lucius the Younger, had been able to channel his father's fame into boosting his own career which helped him to later become *Tribune of the Plebs*.

"The auction will now begin!" Silius' bellow and the bang of the gavel brought Proculus back to the present. He took a deep breath and listened to the details of the first estate being auctioned. He was determined to find a country home befitting the granddaughter of Vorenus!

*   *   *   *

Artorius was surprised that he had been singled out for being decorated. He had rallied enough troops to repel a horde of Turani rebels; however he did not feel as if he had done anything extraordinary. Lives may have been saved, but they were not by his actions alone.

"*Sergeant Artorius,*" Macro's shouting interrupted his thoughts, "*Legionaries Magnus, Praxus, Decimus, Valens, and Carbo ... post!*" The Century was in parade formation in the otherwise empty square at the Augustodunum University. The section stepped out of formation and marched up to their Centurion. Next to Macro Optio Flaccus stood bearing several ornate embossed discs bearing the profile image of a man wearing a Greek helmet. They were about palm size, the same as a campaign medal.

"The elimination of an enemy of Rome brings distinct honor to the men responsible," Macro said. "Julius Florus was a traitor to the Gauls, and to the Senate and People of Rome. His death saved countless lives and stifled further rebellion. Therefore, by order of Gaius Silius, Legate and Governor General of Germania Inferior, you men are awarded the *Florian Crest*. The Florian Crest is a special award given to those responsible for Julius Florus' demise. Let all bear witness to your initiative, determination, and valor." Macro then nodded to Optio Flaccus who handed him the medals. Macro handed one to Artorius with his left hand, clasping his right with the other.

"You and your men are a tribute to the Valeria Legion," he said to Artorius in a low voice. As soon as the last medal was awarded, Macro stepped back and rendered a salute to the legionaries, who returned the courtesy to their Centurion. The Second Century erupted in a serious of voracious cheers and accolades. Besides Artorius and his section, Julius Indus and his two cavalrymen were also awarded the Florian Crest. It was indeed a distinct honor that only nine men would ever receive.

＊　　　＊　　　＊　　　＊

Kiana had agreed to ride with Alasdair on his journey home. His father had had to stay in Augustodunum in order to see to the formalities of paying the ransom. As they rode in silence down the road, they saw a slave caravan moving down the perpendicular road heading south.

"Dear gods," Alasdair said quietly.

"What is it?" Kiana asked. She was not aware of the sentence passed on those who failed to pay their ransoms, or were found to be former slaves or criminals.

Alasdair spurred his horse and rode towards the caravan. Roman auxiliaries, mounted on horses, flanked the long train of prisoners; their menacing presence preventing Alasdair from getting any closer. Kiana rode up beside him, her eyes widening as she saw some of the faces that peered out from behind the bars of their wheeled cages. Though most were the ragged countenances of thieves and slaves, she recognized one or two who were friends of Farquhar's.

"Alasdair, what is happening to them?" she asked. The young man swallowed hard.

"They are the ones whose families refused to ransom them. They are being sent to the mines in Mauretania."

"They are slaves?" Kiana was in shock. After the suffering and horror she had witnessed, this just added salt to the wounds. It was the final and by far most brutal retribution to come from the Romans.

"Once nobles with a future full of hope, promise, and prosperity," he replied. "Now they are but slaves, to be sold and disposed of at the will of their new masters. The sulfur mines will break them. It would have been better had they died in battle." Kiana turned her gaze towards Alasdair. His face was set hard, and she could not help but notice that he somehow seemed much older; as though he had suddenly aged from a young boy into an old man.

"Come," she said, "let us leave this despair behind. You still have a future, Alasdair. You may not have the life of privilege and wealth that you had before, but at least you are alive, and *free*. Farquhar would have wanted you to live life once again." Alasdair turned towards her and smiled weakly.

"Farquhar was indeed a lucky man, to have had you in his life. He loved you so much." He then took a deep breath and exhaled hard through his nose. "Go home, Kiana. Know that I will always cherish our friendship; however this journey I must finish alone." With that he turned and slowly rode away. Kiana did not protest as she watched him.

Once he was out of sight, she turned and rode back towards her home. She had stayed with and comforted Alasdair as much as possible. It had been done out of the love she still bore Farquhar. The two had been like brothers. She then made a vow to herself that she would visit his grave on the anniversary of his death, placing one flower on the small monument his father had erected. Though she was still but a young girl, Kiana could not help but feel as if she too had been aged considerably by the Sacrovir Revolt.

CHAPTER 18

▼

THE NEW ASSIGNMENT
AND INDUS' HORSE

Silius sat with his hands behind his head, eyes closed. The ransoming of the prisoners was finally complete, those that remained on their way to enslavement in the mines of Mauretania, and the execution of the captured leaders of the rebellion had also been accomplished. Broehain had been allowed to be ransomed along with the prisoners; however the rest of the rebel leaders had been crucified in full view of Augustodunum. He was physically and mentally exhausted, the rush of the full effects of the rebellion and its aftermath coming down on him. Suddenly there was a knock at his door and Calvinus walked in. Silius did not bother to open his eyes.

"Sorry to bother you, but I had to bring this to your attention," the Master Centurion stated, a rolled parchment in his hand.

"What is it?" Silius asked with his eyes still closed.

"The Cohort from Lugdunum is being recalled to their garrison station, their three-year tour in the region being complete. I took the liberty of looking at the rotation schedule for the Lugdunum garrison, and we happen to be next."

"Damn it, I had forgotten about that," the Legate replied as he leaned forward and rested his forehead on his hand. He figured a spell at the bathhouse and brothel would do him good, except he was too exhausted to even leave his quarters. "I remember looking at that before we were distracted by the rebellion. We are fairly close to Lugdunum as it is, so whichever Cohort we dispatch may as well head straight there from here. No sense in them even going all the way back to Cologne."

"I agree," Calvinus asserted. "Lugdunum is a rather posh assignment. I think it should fall upon whichever Cohort distinguished itself the most on this campaign."

"You are not taking the First," Silius remarked wryly. Calvinus only laughed at that.

"No, I did not mean my own Cohort. Rather I was thinking we should send the Third. They are the ones who took out Florus and brought Indus' cavalry back with them. They also distinguished themselves during the main battle at Augustodunum as well." Silius nodded his consent.

"Very well, inform Proculus to get his men ready to move to Lugdunum that is if you haven't done so already!" Calvinus could only grin at that. Silius knew full-well that his Master Centurion had already given Proculus his orders, and he wouldn't have been surprised at all if the Third was already on the march. His trust in Calvinus' judgment was absolute, and if he had said the Third Cohort needed to go to Lugdunum, then the Third Cohort needed to go to Lugdunum.

Indeed the Third had been on the march for several hours by the time Calvinus had informed Silius of their new assignment. Lugdunum was approximately four or five days march away, and the Soldiers of the Third Cohort were looking forward to new horizons.

"Lugdunum, now that is the place for us!" Carbo asserted. "Warmer weather, prettier ladies ..." Valens eyes lit up at Carbo's last statement.

"Come again?" he asked.

"What he means is you won't have to dip your wick into the vaginal wart holes of trashy frontier whores anymore," Decimus answered.

"Decimus, you are as eloquent as always," Artorius rolled his eyes. "I have not heard what kind of billets they have for us, though."

"I already checked into that," Decimus answered proudly. As the section's resident gossip, he took pride in rooting out information, and had an alarmingly vast circle of sources. "It would seem that there are blocks of flats at one end of town that the state purchased for our use. It seemed more practical than having to build us an entire fort. The only things they had to build were the drill halls, as well as an extra bathhouse."

On the fourth day of the march, the Third Cohort chanced upon the same slave traders that Kiana and Alasdair had had the misfortune of coming across. Two young lads were being thrown to the ground by their merciless captors. One was sobbing incessantly while the other just lay limp. This fellow was being whipped by a burley slaver who wore nothing but a pair of breaches and a rag on his head.

"Get up you worthless little shit!" the man spat. He thrashed the lad thrice more with his barbed whip before kicking him hard in the ribs, which gave a sickening crunch. He then stood looking dumbfounded.

"Bugger it, I think this one's dead," he said to his companion, who was struggling with the other boy. The rest of their caravan kept creeping along, both slavers and their quarry paying no heed to what was going on behind them.

"Just leave him to rot," the other slaver retorted. "Meanwhile I'm going to use this one for a bit of sport!" A deviant sneer crossed his face. The lad, his own eyes full of terror, bit the man hard on the forearm. As the slaver screamed in pain, the young prisoner used the last of his strength to attempt to run from the scene. He was delirious with fear, and had no idea that he was heading straight for the column of Roman soldiers.

"Hey, you!" the slaver screamed as his companion laughed at his plight. *"Somebody stop him!"*

Proculus called the column to a halt as the newly liberated slave stumbled towards them. A nearby legionary dropped his pack and javelins, turned and belted the young man hard across the face with the boss of his shield. The lad fell to the ground, stunned and unable to regain his bearing. Proculus rode over to where the lad lay as the slaver came running up to him. The Centurion's senses were assailed by the sight and stench of the man. He was overweight and scraggly in appearance; his body odor was strong, and Proculus wondered if the man had ever had a bath.

"Nice one," the slaver remarked as he stooped with his hands on his knees, his breath coming in heaving gasps. "Thought this one was going to get away before I could have my way with him." Proculus dismounted his horse and walked over to the man. As the slaver started to rise up, Proculus punched him hard in the mouth, sending him sprawling.

"Idiot!" the Centurion shouted. "You almost let a prisoner of war escape just so you could satisfy your sick carnal lust!" The slaver started to push himself up to his feet when Proculus stomped him on the side of the face with his hobnailed sandals. The flesh on his face split and started bleeding profusely. The slaver wailed loudly, his voice at a gratingly high pitch. Proculus stomped him again.

"Another word out of you and you can join your quarry in the mines!" he growled.

The young prisoner was now lying on his stomach, his face filled with joy and hope. The scowl on the Centurion's face diminished any hopes he may have had.

Just then a pair of auxiliary cavalrymen galloped up to them, one of whom saluted Proculus.

"And where in the *hell* were you when this piss-ant lost his prisoners?" the Centurion barked, the scowl never leaving his face.

"Beg your pardon Sir," one of the troopers replied. "We've been chasing down the others that this jackal let out. He and his partner up there decide they wanted to play with a couple of the young nobles. So they go and open the cage, and sure enough three more manage to escape into the woods! We've spent the last hour hunting them down."

"Any get away from you?" Vitruvius asked as he rode up on his horse.

"No Sir," the cavalryman replied with a shake of his head. "Unfortunately, we had to slay the lot of them. A mercy, really; these are all headed for the sulfur mines."

"Yes we know," Proculus replied with a dismissive wave. He then glared at the slaver, who was now cowering with his hands over his face. The Centurion smashed his foot into the man's face once again, eliciting a chuckle from both Vitruvius as well as the auxiliary troopers.

"I want this scum and his companion lashed for their gross incompetence," Proculus continued. "Take the prisoner back with you and see to it that he makes it to the mines alive and unspoiled."

"Right away Sir," the trooper acknowledged as the prisoner let out a series of despairing cries.

"No! Please do not make me go back! I am a nobleman; I can pay whatever you want! Please, I beg you!" He came at Proculus, his arms outstretched piteously. Proculus swallowed hard and remembered why the young man had been sentenced to the mines of Mauretania. The Centurion punched him in the nose, sending him tumbling over the slaver. The lad lay their weeping in sorrow.

"Lost, I am lost," he sobbed, his face buried in the grass.

"Yes you are," Proculus replied as he stood over him. "Perhaps you will make sounder decisions in the next life." With that he gruffly pulled the young man up by the hair and threw him towards the cavalrymen, one of whom prodded the lad with his lance back towards the caravan. Proculus then kicked the slaver in the small of his back, forcing him to scamper to his feet. The other auxiliary trooper saluted once again before following his quarry back to the slave caravan.

"Well that was something I could have done without seeing," Magnus muttered under his breath as the column continued its march.

"Those sick fucks must be desperate for some really good sport," Valens observed.

"And to think, we thought *you* had low standards!" Carbo snorted.

"At least my standards never involved young boys," Valens retorted. "I prefer the ass of a woman to that of a boy."

"A few days in the mines and he will wish he was back to being that slaver's little play thing," Artorius observed, watching as the prisoner limped along, the lance of the cavalryman never far from his back.

"Are the mines really that bad?" Gavius asked. Most of the section grunted in reply.

"From what Flaccus said, they are far worse," Artorius said. "The sulfur burns your eyes until you go blind from it. Not that it matters because once you're down there you've seen the last of the sun. The very air you breathe is a poisonous fume; you are given just enough food and water to be kept alive. Three months is about the longest most survive, although I'm sure there are exceptions."

"Such as?" Gavius persisted. The other legionaries were gazing intently on their Decanus, curious as to what else he may have heard.

"There are a few cases where a slave will show the intestinal fortitude to survive for years down there. Sometimes their masters will take pity and retire them to lesser duties on a farm; though more often than not they are blind and completely mad by then."

The Gallic countryside continued to roll past them as the column made its way towards Lugdunum. The scenes of activity from the villages they marched through would have made one forget that the province had recently been in the grips of rebellion. The peoples encountered were mostly indifferent to the legionaries; neither fearful like the barbarians across the Rhine, nor openly friendly like the Batavians. Few of the Gauls were old enough to remember the conquest of Caesar; indeed most regarded being a Roman province as beneficial. Roman architecture influenced even the smallest of Gallic villages. Artorius found it odd to see a bathhouse or rudimentary aqueduct amongst the thatched huts. There were even shrines dedicated to the Roman gods dispersed throughout the region.

As the Cohort marched into Lugdunum, they noticed a number of tents erected just on the outskirts. The outgoing Cohort had already vacated their billets and living in tents for the few days it would take for them to relinquish control. They found a sign posted outside of a renovated tavern that read:

Cohort VIII, Legio VIII Augusta
Acilius Aviola, Centurion Pilus Prior

"Here we are then," Proculus announced as he dismounted his horse. He and the Centurions entered the tavern to find that it had been modified into a type of Principia. Stairs led to rooms upstairs, and the entire bottom floor had been partitioned off into a series of offices and other rooms. There was a flurry of activity going on, seeing as the Cohort was getting ready to leave and return to their fortress at Poetovio in Pannonia.

"Ah, good you have arrived!" a boisterous voice said behind them. They turned to see an older Centurion walk in the main door. He had just removed his helmet, revealing a head that was sparse in hair, and that which he had was completely gray.

"I am Centurion Aviola, commander of the Eighth Cohort, Eighth Augusta," he said as he stuck out his hand.

"Valerius Proculus, Third Cohort, Twentieth Valeria," Proculus replied, accepting the man's hand. "This is quite the setup you fellas have here." Aviola shrugged at the observation.

"We've had a pretty good run here," he replied. "Things got a little anxious when we had to rush north to help you guys put down Sacrovir's rebellion, though. That was the first action any of us had seen in years."

"We were damn glad to have your boys with us," Vitruvius observed. "Helped to even the odds a bit." Aviola waived his hand dismissively.

"It helped us bang off some the battle rust. Come, I'll show you around. All Principal Officers stay over here in the rooms upstairs, legionaries staying over at the flats. It's a pretty good setup all around."

After much confusion, Artorius and the section found their flat. It was actually a pair of flats, with an interior door added. Similar to the setup in a legionary barracks, one room had four pairs of bunks, a table, cooking stove, and other personal effects; the other room was for storing armor, weapons, and equipment.

"Well this doesn't look bad," Magnus remarked as he gazed at the interior.

"No, not bad at all," Valens replied, setting down his carrying pack next to one of the bunks. Artorius set his gear down next to a bunk at the back of the room, where there was a desk and chair for his use.

"I think we will make do just fine," he said with a smile as he lay down on his bunk. Lugdunum was a rather luxurious town, and Artorius knew he would enjoy this assignment immensely. Indeed, the men of the Eighth Legion seemed heartbroken to be leaving.

*   *   *   *

Indus and Silius both stood before the Emperor, members of the First and Twentieth Legions on hand, along with Indus' entire regiment. Vast numbers of civilians had arrived as well, many of whom had never even seen their Emperor, aside from his image on coins and statues. Tiberius took a deep breath as he gazed at the sight. Being around such men invigorated him; such manliness had defined his life for so many years. In truth there had been no need for him to even come. The rebellion had been crushed almost as soon as Rome had been made aware of it. Yet Tiberius had used the opportunity to visit the Legions. The First and Twentieth had both been under his command at one time, and he felt a certain bond with these men. While he was in Rome he had to live with Senators and Nobles who amounted to little more than old women; but these, these were *men*.

"Commander Julius Indus, come forward," the Emperor commanded, his voice carrying across the parade field outside Augustodunum. Indus stepped onto the raised dais where the Emperor and Drusus stood. Drusus then handed Tiberius a simple crown made of oak leaves, which the Emperor placed upon Indus' head.

"For your loyalty, courage, and impeccable savvy in battle," Tiberius began, "you are awarded the Civic Crown. Your actions have saved the lives of countless Roman citizens." He then turned to Drusus, who handed him an ornate scroll, which Tiberius started to read off of. "In recognition of your superior leadership, fidelity, and service to the Empire, the Treveri cavalry regiment shall from this day forth be forever known as *Indus' Horse*. As this name brings with it no small amount of honor, Indus' Horse will always be a regiment made up of only the finest cavalrymen." He then handed the scroll to Indus, who took it and bowed low before the Emperor. Silius then came forward with a magnificent standard. It bore a red cloth banner, emblazed with the image of a black horse with the words *Indus Equus, Fidelis Victrix*; or *Indus' Horse, Fidelity and Victory*.

"I am deeply honored, Caesar," he said. Tiberius shook his head.

"No," he replied, "the honor is mine to be able to bestow this upon you." With that, he stepped back and saluted Indus. His face beaming, Indus returned the salute before turning to face the crowds. His men immediately broke into a frenzy of howls and cheers for their commander, chanting his name over and over. Even the Legionaries gave a loud series of ovations for their friend and ally, as did the crowd of civilians. No title, award for valor, or accolade from the Senate could ever compare with the honor the Emperor had just bestowed upon him. In a sense he had been given immortality; for in the years to come, even long after he had crossed over to the afterlife, there would always be *Indus' Horse*.

*   *   *   *

Life had been hectic for Pontius Pilate now that he was back in Rome. His future father-in-law had wanted to see him before he even had a chance to get settled. Apparently he had been planning a special "welcome home" banquet for the Tribune for some time. Though his betrothed Claudia was in Gaul with her sister, this did not stop the elder Proculus from following through on a massive celebration to welcome Pilate home. This was immediately followed by another banquet held by the Praetorians as a means of acknowledging him into their ranks. The Emperor himself had attended, and it was the first time Pilate had ever met Tiberius in person.

Their meeting had been cordial enough, though Pilate found he was rather intimidated in the presence of the Emperor. Even when Tiberius took the time to congratulate Pilate on his posting and express his utmost confidence in him, he could not help but feel as if he was being tested; that Tiberius was scrutinizing him, trying to find fault in him. Perhaps that was just his way.

Pilate found the Praetorians to be a different lot. Most viewed themselves as being of a better class than those serving in the legions. This was true in some ways; the Praetorians were the Emperor's personal bodyguards and as such were paid significantly better than their brother legionaries. The premise was that the Praetorians were the elite of the Roman army, selected for their ability as fighting men. While Pilate did not doubt that the men in the Praetorians were talented, he wondered just how many were hardened veterans and not merely from influential families.

*   *   *   *

The mines came into view as the caravan made its way into the dusty outcropping of rock formations. Radek gave a wicked sneer over towards a young boy who was whimpering in the corner of their cage. The lad was sick with a fever and trembling badly. Radek cursed his luck that his injuries had prevented him from escaping during their slave drivers' botched attempts to relieve their carnal lust on some of the young nobles. His wounds had somewhat healed, though he would never walk correctly again. His eye patch was gone, revealing a puss-filled hole where his eye used to be. Not that it mattered; with a little luck he would be dead within a month. He then leaned over and grabbed the sickly youth by the thigh.

"Welcome to your new home," he said mockingly. The lad just looked up at him, eyes distant. "Don't worry my poppet; you and I will have enough time to grow close before this place consumes us ... *really* close." The boy's eyes grew wide in terror, though he was too weak to even protest. Radek let out a loud guffaw, only to succumb to a harsh coughing fit. The butt of a spear rapped him on the back of the head through the cage.

"Quiet in there!" an auxiliary shouted at him. Radek then leaned back and stared at the bright sun that shone through the bars.

"Take a good look at the sun, lads," he said in a hoarse voice, "for it is the last time any of us will ever see her."

CHAPTER 19

▼

INTO THE SHADOWS

Artorius opened the window of their barracks flat and stretched his arms overhead as the morning breeze caressed him. After a deep breath he rested his hands on the sill. He gazed upon the city, which was just starting to come awake. His flat looked over the city's lower aqueduct, which led into the forum. He watched as an ornate litter made its way into the slowly filling markets. Over his shoulder he heard Magnus let out a rather loud and obnoxious yawn.

"So where to today?" the Norseman asked, wiping the sleep from his eyes. The section was tasked with 'city patrol' that day; a term that was vague at best. Proculus' only stipulation was that sections on patrol duty make their presence known throughout the city, thereby making the populace feel secure. Lugdunum had its own urban police who were little more than hired men armed with clubs tasked with keeping the peace. The sight of legionaries within the cities gave the citizens confidence and a sense of ease.

"I think we'll hit the forum this morning," Artorius replied, his gaze still fixed on the litter. "Looks like we've got some patrician guests; we'd better make them feel at home."

"Hmm," Magnus replied, his thoughts elsewhere. Artorius had moved his bunk and desk into the rear room of the flat where the section stored its weapons and kit. The rooms were significantly larger than those of a legionary barracks; with a little rearranging Artorius was able to have his own room with a relative sense of privacy. His soldiers lived in the other room and were able to spread their bunks out so as not to have to stack them on top of each other.

He opened the door to the section bay and walked over to the shuttered windows. He pulled these open as Magnus proceeded to kick the bunks of the legionaries.

"Another beautiful morning fellas!" Artorius shouted.

"Piss off," he heard Carbo mutter as he pulled his blanket over his head. Artorius raised an eyebrow at the remark, grabbed Carbo's gladius—still in the scabbard—from the end of his bunk and brought the flat of the weapon down in a brutal smash across the legionary's buttocks.

"Ouch!" Carbo bellowed as he pitched out of his bunk, head-first into the wall.

"You dumbass," Decimus snickered as his fellow legionary stumbled over his bunk, one hand covering his forehead, the other on his buttocks. Decimus elbowed him in the ribs "Know who you're talking to before you get castrated for insubordination!"

"Alright, let's get moving," Artorius ordered. "You all know what your duties are this morning. Gavius get started on breakfast. I want everyone cleaned up, shaved, and ready to patrol in one hour. And Carbo, you've got latrines for the next week and are banned from the taverns during that time." The legionary hung his head sheepishly and nodded. Carbo knew he had been spending too much time at the ale houses a figured that a week sober, along with some correctional details, would do him good.

The forum was started to fill with patrons by the time Artorius arrived with his section. Imperial cities were an odd mix of peoples from the very corners of the Empire and beyond. There was one particular merchant who proclaimed that he was from the very end of the world. Given the man's appearance, it was believable. He was shorter than average, with a face that bore a slight resemblance to the barbarians from the far-east Steppes; however he had stated that he was from a region to the south of, and even further east. His trade involved mostly spices and medicinal herbs which he said took a full year to reach him from the ends of the earth. It was here that Artorius found the patrons he was looking for.

A litter, along with several attendants, sat next to the oriental spice shop. Artorius was a bit surprised to see Centurion Proculus talking with the two ladies who had been riding in the litter.

"Looks like Proculus beat us to it," Magnus observed. Artorius looked back at his legionaries. All were kitted in full armor; however, he felt that shields and javelins would have been too cumbersome to carry through the crowded city and had his men armed with gladii only.

"Looks that way," he replied with a touch or resignation. "Alright, let's head over to the docks; there's usually something of interest going on down there."

"I heard that the Scriptorium has a copy of Horace's *Odes IV*," Decimus said. "Can we stop by there; I've wanted to read that for some time."

"I don't see why not," Artorius replied as he turned back around, ignoring Carbo's remarks regarding Decimus' literacy. As they started to march away, his eyes glanced back towards the pair of ladies with Centurion Proculus. One was very young, still a few years away from womanhood. It was the elder one that caught the Decanus' eye.

She was almost as tall as Artorius, with shoulder-length hair that, as was the latest fashion, was dyed a dark blonde. Her stola could not hide the athletic curves of her body and Artorius found no way to describe the beauty that seemed to radiate from her face. Her smile was warm and inviting; her eyes dark and piercing. So enraptured was Artorius that he did not notice the pillar until he walked into it with a crash of his helm. His vision blurred for a second as his head jarred to the side. He stepped back and looked around, though no one seemed to have noticed his mishap aside from his legionaries, who were trying to suppress their sniggering.

"Well I'll be buggered," he said, his face turning red. "How long has that pillar been there?" From across the street he saw Proculus raise his eyebrows and give a short laugh of amusement. His lady companion turned and looked Artorius' way. Her eyes snared his gaze, and he found that he could not look away. She gave him a friendly smile and he winked at her in reply. Proculus then took her by the arm and escorted the two women away, all the while suppressing his amusement.

*   *   *   *

Daily drill and training complete, Pilate was relieved to finally be able to take his friend Justus up on getting together for a spot of wine and storytelling. He invited the Optio to his residence; a rather plush and ostentatious house near the Praetorian barracks.

"Justus, old boy!" he said boisterously as his friend walked onto the covered balcony where Pilate had directed servants to bring the wine and appetizers.

"It's been too long," Justus replied as the two embraced and smacked each other hard on the back. Each then stepped back to appraise the other, for it had been ten years since last they saw each other.

Justus Longinus was a big man; slightly shorter than Pilate, but with a broad, powerful frame. His red hair was already starting to thin, something Pilate made note of immediately.

"And you're already starting to turn a bit grey!" Justus replied with friendly sarcasm. Pilate laughed and waved him to a seat.

"So tell me, what brought you all the way back here from the east?" Pilate asked. Justus gave a shrug.

"Seems like the governor wanted a representative to act as a liaison between the eastern provinces and Rome. He wanted it kept low-key, so they decided to send a ranker under the premise of working with the Praetorians. The very day I was promoted to Optio that I get my assignment orders."

"Well it has to have been a nice change of pace for you," Pilate conjectured as Justus took a long pull of his wine.

"I admit that it's been pretty decent," he replied. "Though Flavia was probably more excited about it than I was."

"That doesn't surprise me." Pilate had momentarily forgotten about Justus' young wife, given that for the most part soldiers below the rank of Centurion were forbidden from marrying. "I never understood how you were able to stay married once you joined the legions."

"It wasn't too hard," Justus said. "Flavia's father you remember is a rather wealthy grain merchant. Well let's just say that a spot of coin in the right hands and all of the sudden I had a special dispensation that allowed me to remain married." Pilate smirked at that.

"It's ironic how a little gold can buy an exception to almost any rule. Still, I am happy for you; Flavia is a good woman. And how is little Gaius?"

"Not so little anymore," Justus sighed, "Though he's still a royal pain in my ass!"

"Well that's how sons are," Pilate laughed. "How old is he now?"

"Almost eleven," the Optio replied, "and little Gaia will be two in a month. So do tell, when are you going to start having children?"

"You forget, Claudia is still a young girl, scarcely older than your Gaius," Pilate answered.

"A beautiful prize that one, if she blossoms into anything resembling her sister," Justus added as he took another pull off his wine. His remark caused Pilate to wince. "Did I say something to offend, Old Friend?" Pilate shook his head.

"No, it's not that," he said. "I do not deny that Diana is a strikingly gorgeous woman. However you must remember that she was married and subsequently divorced at a young age once it was discovered that she could not bear children."

"Yes, I forgot about that," Justus replied, a look of concern crossing his face. "You don't think Claudia suffers from the same affliction, do you?"

"I hope not. It would be a shame to be betrothed for all these years, only to have to divorce right away because she cannot have children. What a shame it would be if the Pontius line ended with me." Pilate drained his goblet and reminisced in silence for a minute. He then cheerfully acknowledged his friend. "At least we know the Longinus line will continue after you!"

"True," Justus remarked. "Gaius is a good lad. He's strong, intelligent, and eager. It's this last trait that gets him in trouble. He tries so hard to please me, but in doing so he becomes reckless. I do hope that when he gets older he'll be able to temper his aggression with prudence."

"Think he'll follow you into the legions?" Justus nodded immediately at Pilate's question.

"Without a doubt. He's incredibly smart, and his potential is unlimited no matter what career path he chooses. However, I know that in his heart he wants to be a soldier. I can't say I'm disappointed, although I do make certain he studies his academic lessons well. If my son is going to be a legionary, then he will be an educated one!"

Pilate smiled at his friend's enthusiasm. Justus was not known for showing emotions of any sort to his children, and yet he could not stop from beaming when talking about them to his friends. Inside Pilate wondered if Gaius would ever know how his father felt about him.

"So do tell," Justus said, changing topics, "what do you think of the Praetorians so far?"

"They're not bad," Pilate replied with a shrug. "Rather pompous, most of them. But then I guess they have earned that right."

"Yeah, most of them just avoid me if they can help it," Justus observed. "They see me as nothing more than a minor irritant; not only because I am but a soldier from the legions, but also because they know my purpose here is not simply to build goodwill between the rankers and the Praetorians. They know that the eastern governors do not trust all that comes through the Imperial post, but they did not want to cause a stir by having to dispatch a diplomat."

"And is there reason for them to feel that they are being left in the dark?" Pilate's voice was lined with concern. Justus sought to dispel it.

"It's not that bad," he replied. "I mean everyone knows your boss Sejanus screens everything going in and out through the Imperial post. However I think the eastern legates are given all the information that is relevant to their duties. If anything, Sejanus censors the bits of unsubstantiated gossip that would only serve to tarnish the Emperor's good name and act as a distraction to the governors. A private courier comes about once every six weeks to see what information I may have. I give them just enough to keep them intrigued, and therefore keep me here in Rome."

Pilate laughed and slapped his friend on the shoulder. Justus was a good soldier; one who had seen his fair share of battle in the east. He despised being used as a political pawn; however, with no wars to fight he figured he would make the best of his situation. Pilate could only do the same.

*   *   *   *

"So who in the bloody hell was that?" Artorius asked later when the section was sitting at a table outside a café by the docks.

"Lady Diana Procula," Decimus replied without missing a beat. All eyes turned towards the legionary who was busily devouring his lunch of strip steak and freshly baked bread. He looked up and stopped chewing when he saw his companions staring at him.

"What?" he asked with a shrug. "She's Proculus' cousin, or at least some type of relative; comes from a much higher social class, though. She came here to see him before going off to run his new country estate."

"What of the young girl?" Magnus asked.

"That's her sister, Claudia," Decimus replied through a mouthful of bread. Gavius nearly choked on his wine.

"That's not our Pilate's Claudia is it?" he asked. Decimus nodded in reply. "I knew she was young, I just did not realize she was still a little girl."

"Well that works for Pilate," Magnus conjectured. "From what I remember he loves the bachelor life and he won't have to marry her for some years yet. Getting the betrothal out of the way just secures his alliance with her family, which I must say is quite influential."

"That they are," Decimus concurred.

Artorius remained quiet; he had hardly spoken a word since they left the forum. He knew that Diana Procula was of the equestrian class and therefore off limits to a lowly legionary; and yet he could not help but still feel enraptured by her gaze. In the moment that he had been able to lay his eyes on her, he knew that she exuded everything he found most noble; a strong mind, a physically fit body, a strong yet kind demeanor, and to say nothing of her sheer physical beauty.

"Artorius, you haven't said much," Carbo remarked as everyone turned their attention from Decimus to their Decanus.

"Huh?" Artorius shook his head quickly, clearing his mind. "Sorry, I was miles away."

"No you weren't," Carbo retorted. "You were still back in the forum, admit it!" Artorius' blushing caused his friends to start laughing and heckling him in their amusement.

"Alright, so maybe I was still back there," he replied. "You can't tell me none of you were stunned by her beauty."

"To be honest, we were all too busy watching you run into the pillar," Magnus said, causing Artorius to turn an even deeper shade of red.

"I caught sight of her," Carbo remarked, eyes looking distant. "She really is beautiful; clearly out of any of our league, though. I wouldn't even know what to do with someone like that." Valens put his arm around Carbo's shoulder and started to speak in a consolatory tone.

"Well you see it's like this; when a man and a woman who love each other very much ... actually they don't necessarily have to *love* each other ... in fact, as a man even *liking* them is really optional ... anyway, they get these certain urges ..." a quick rap from the back of Carbo's hand interrupted the rest of his dissertation.

"Alright, finish up and let's get ready to move out," Artorius ordered. "There's a new slaver in town that set up shop by Four Corners road, and I want to make certain he's keeping a watchful eye on his wares." As the section donned their helmets and started away from the docks, Magnus gave him a smack on the shoulder.

"If it helps," he stated, "I know the town brothel got in some new stock yesterday. You might be able to get something fresh and unspoiled, if you know what I mean."

"Those girls are expensive!" Valens complained.

"You get what you pay for," Gavius observed. Valens could only shrug and nod in reply.

Artorius took a deep breath and stepped out ahead of his men. They were right, of course. Someone like Lady Diana would view the likes of him as little more than a serf, even if her cousin had come from similarly humble beginnings. He would have to settle for spending a few coins on some new and exotic entertainment to satisfy what he figured was nothing more than overborne lust.

He was still adjusting to their new assignment, but after the Sacrovir Revolt, he knew he owed it to himself to enjoy his good fortune. Policing a rapidly growing city was far different than securing the frontier against rampaging barbarians, or suppressing rebellions when outnumbered and uncertain as to who one's allies were. Still, it was part of his duties as a soldier of Rome.

∗   ∗   ∗   ∗

Heracles strode through the rubble and ash that still smoldered; the charred remains of Sacrovir's mansion house. The Romans had taken anything of value that they had been able to find; corpses were left where they lay. He climbed over mounds of fallen roof tiles and collapsed walls; searching for … well he was not sure exactly what.

He came to the remains of the great hall they had been meeting in. The roof, as well as the entire second story, had collapsed on this area. The charred ruins of furniture still smoked, even though the rains had long since put out the fires. And then he saw it, a glint in the gloom of the destroyed building. He crawled over until he could see it plainly; a gilded sword handle, sticking out of the pile of rubble. It was Sacrovir's weapon, the one he had had made by the best smiths in all of Gaul.

Heracles pulled hard and the handle, the rubble giving way as the weapon came free. The blade was covered in dark crimson, Sacrovir's blood. Heracles knew the man lay charred and buried beneath the rubble. As he gazed upon the sword, a fierce sense of determination welled up inside him. The Gauls were not his native people, yet it was Sacrovir who had liberated him. In that a debt was owed to the man. Into the shadows would Heracles go; from thence he would rise again. He would see Sacrovir's dream to fruition; he would raise another rebellion, stronger than before; and he would liberate Gaul!

"All in due time," he said to himself in a sinister voice, his eyes burning with hate.

978-0-595-48331-0
0-595-48331-3